Sea Glass Cottage

by
VICKIE McKEEHAN

beachdevils
PRESS

Sea Glass Cottage
A Pelican Pointe Novel

Published by Beachdevils Press
Copyright © 2014 Vickie McKeehan
All rights reserved.

Sea Glass Cottage
A Pelican Pointe Novel
Copyright © 2014 Vickie McKeehan

beachdevils
PRESS

ISBN-10: 0692330348
ISBN-13: 978-0692330340

Published by
Beachdevils Press
Printed in the USA
All Titles Available at Amazon

Cover design by Vanessa Mendozzi
Pelican Pointe map by artist, Jess Johnson

You can visit the author at:
www.vickiemckeehan.com
www.facebook.com/VickieMcKeehan
http://vickiemckeehan.wordpress.com/
www.twitter.com/VickieMcKeehan

Don't miss these other exciting titles by bestselling author

Vickie McKeehan

The Pelican Pointe Series
PROMISE COVE
HIDDEN MOON BAY
DANCING TIDES
LIGHTHOUSE REEF
STARLIGHT DUNES
LAST CHANCE HARBOR
SEA GLASS COTTAGE
LAVENDER BEACH
SANDCASTLES UNDER THE CHRISTMAS MOON
BENEATH WINTER SAND
KEEPING CAPE SUMMER (2018)

The Evil Secrets Trilogy
JUST EVIL Book One
DEEPER EVIL Book Two
ENDING EVIL Book Three
EVIL SECRETS TRILOGY BOXED SET

The Skye Cree Novels
THE BONES OF OTHERS
THE BONES WILL TELL
THE BOX OF BONES
HIS GARDEN OF BONES
TRUTH IN THE BONES
SEA OF BONES (2018)

The Indigo Brothers Trilogy
INDIGO FIRE
INDIGO HEAT
INDIGO JUSTICE
INDIGO BROTHERS TRILOGY BOXED SET

Coyote Wells Mysteries
MYSTIC FALLS
SHADOW CANYON
SPIRIT LAKE (2018)

For those survivors who went through the hell
of domestic abuse and got out.
And for all those who weren't as lucky.

Hope is the thing with feathers
That perches in the soul
And sings the tune without the words
And never stops at all.
Emily Dickinson

Sea Glass Cottage

Sea Glass Cottage
by
VICKIE McKEEHAN

Welcome to Pelican Pointe

To see the complete **Cast of Characters** list go to my website:
www.vickiemckeehan.com
under the **Pelican Pointe Series** tab.

Prologue

The morning broke gray and dreary with the sky spitting down at her in disapproval. After spending the night in the middle of nowhere, miserable and cold, Marisa Lattimer had to admit her plan had come completely undone. She wasn't sure how it had fallen off the rails so quickly.

A short twenty-four hours earlier she'd set in motion what she'd thought was a brilliant escape plan. But this wasn't like the movies. In *Sleeping with the Enemy*, Julia Roberts's character's blueprint to fake her own death to get away from her controlling husband had gone off without a hitch. Marisa was learning the hard way that reality was a lot different.

She hadn't counted on slick roads last night or wrecking the car. Sliding off into the ditch and breaking an axle hadn't been part of the grand plan. Maybe she should've waited until spring. The only problem with that strategy was that she was fed up with waiting for her chance to escape, fed up with taking the verbal battery and humiliation dished out on a daily basis. That's why she wasn't about to give up now.

Instead of panicking, Marisa realized the car accident might actually work in her favor. If she could ever find her way back to the highway, she could maintain the course of action, maybe hitch a ride. That way, she'd still be able to cross the Canadian border. She'd be on foot in rugged terrain but it could be done. Once she reached Alberta she'd make contact with Shelby Bullock. Shelby had promised to help her lose herself in the new country, start life over again with a new identity, and provide a safe shelter until everything settled down.

On that air of hope, Marisa raised her head and peeked over the ridge where she'd spent the night, taking note of her surroundings. It seemed the prairie grass went on for miles in either direction, broken up only by thickets of juneberry along the ravine. A wind whipped up causing the branches to crackle and dance with raindrops. The swath of tall beargrass bent in the chilly breeze. Even the songbirds seemed too cold to sing this morning. She knew Montana just before Thanksgiving could be an unforgiving place. It had to be at least twenty degrees, colder when she stuck her head up out of the gulley to look around.

Though she was decked out in winter garb, a coat, a ski cap, a pair of gloves and a scarf, the clothing didn't keep her from shivering in her tracks.

Glancing up at the ominous clouds overhead, she huddled from the frosty bite of the wind. Plunked down between two banks of a narrow riverbed, she fought the urge to cry. Any other time, she might have. On any other given day, the circumstances might've broken her spirit. But not today. Today, she had to be strong. She had to get moving. It wasn't a good idea to stay in one place for too long. The way her luck had gone, by this time, someone probably had found the car.

Forced to regroup, she had to think fast. The last road sign she remembered on the highway—before she'd smashed Garth's BMW—had indicated she was near Lewis and Clark National Forest. She recalled passing through a heavily wooded area before the car had careened into the ditch, which meant she most likely still had a good two hundred miles left to go before crossing into Canada.

Of course, that was a rough estimate on her part. It felt like she'd walked a good five miles after the wreck. But in the dark she hadn't been sure of the direction. Only when she'd spotted an oncoming car's headlights barreling straight toward her had she taken off into the desolate stretch of landscape. She remembered falling in some kind of hole and having to crawl out. During it all, she'd somehow gotten turned around.

And this morning, without any sunlight, she had a difficult time getting her bearings. The fact that she'd hit her head in the crash didn't help matters any.

She looked at her watch. It was a little after eight. By this time Garth would've contacted the cops back in Denver and reported her missing.

Let Garth go crazy on them for a change, she decided as she set off toward the next ridgeline that she hoped like hell led northward. If only she'd thought to pack a compass with her. Sad to say, after all her careful planning, she'd left with nothing but the clothes on her back and a knapsack filled with a few essentials. It was the only thing she'd been able to squirrel away over the past six months without Garth missing specific items and catching on.

Because the lonely grassland beckoned to her right and the rolling hills to her left, she decided to head away from the safety of the ravine and look for a road, maybe circle back to a service station or quick mart so she could pick up some supplies.

As she maneuvered through creeping juniper and sedge, past Douglas fir and cedar, the cold raindrops turned to icy flakes. But she refused to allow a little sleet to dampen her resolve and give up. She'd reach the border or die trying. It was just that simple. She'd never go back to her abusive way of life with Garth. Never. Not even if she had to hide for weeks in the wild, live off the land, and wait for the right opportunity to cross over into Canada. She wouldn't go back.

After several hours of trudging, though, she'd ambled farther into bushes and scrub without seeing any sign of life. Hungry, she sat down on a rock, rested her head back on a fragrant pine. Shrugging off her rucksack, she dug into its contents and came up with the only food she'd brought with her—several fruit grain bars. She'd have to eat sparingly and make them last. She pulled out the bottle of water she'd been hoarding since last night, half gone now, and took a few precious sips.

As she munched on the dry oats and blueberry combo, the snow came down harder, bigger, faster. Chilled, she closed her eyes, leaned back against the lace bark and soon fell fast asleep.

She woke trembling and covered in a layer of fresh snow. Blinking awake, she puffed out a heavy breath, not wanting to move but knowing she couldn't stay where she was for too long. She swung her pack to her shoulder and stood up.

It was then she thought she heard a noise. A thwack, thwack, thwack echoed off the heavy air. Perhaps that sound was what had caused her to stir in the first place.

Doing her best to determine where the sound had originated, she turned in a circle, decided it was coming from beyond the patch of woods on the other side. She started walking in that direction.

As soon as she came out of the trees and reached the meadow, a dog began to bark and set up a din. Her eyes landed on the tail-wagging golden retriever about the same time she spotted its owner.

Not knowing what else to do, she waved at the forty-something man dressed to chop wood. Standing in front of a rustic cabin, he wore a gray puffer jacket over a dark brown sweater and blue jeans. She tried to ignore the ax he held mid-air in his fist in such a protective manner, and the menacing scowl on his face.

"What are you doing out here?" the man asked, surprise written in his brown eyes.

"I got lost. I'd appreciate it if you could point me the way north from here."

His brow furrowed. "Now? But it's almost dark. Besides, there's a storm brewing. Forecast says we'll likely get five inches by morning, temp hovering around single digits."

"I just need to find my way back to a road so I keep heading north. Is one nearby?"

He finally dropped the ax with a whack and left it wedged in the chopping block. "Did you have car trouble?"

"No." Determined not to give anything away, she kept her face blank, tried to keep her hands from shaking.

"So you just appear out of the blue in my front yard headed for Canada, eh?"

"I'm just trying to get home, mister." She stared at the doubt on his face, knew he wasn't buying a word of her story.

The dog sauntered over, flopped on his back hoping she'd rub his belly. She took her eyes off the man long enough to oblige.

"Looks like you've captured Rusty's heart."

She looked up, saw him studying her. In the waning light, she weighed her options. Could she really rough it in a snowstorm? Deep in those misgivings, her own self-confidence beginning to falter, she wasn't prepared at his offer.

"Okay, I'll go get my truck keys. How about if I drive you across the border?"

"Just like that, no questions asked? You'd do that for a complete stranger?"

She saw him staring at the bruises on her face, some fresh from the accident, some yellowish ones left over from two nights before when Garth had put them there. She held her breath waiting, wondering if there was any kindness left for people like her who had taken off to start life over.

She noted he answered her question in a determined, matter-of-fact voice. "Like I said, I'll get you across the border during what will surely be an epic storm bearing down on both of us."

"I don't know what to say or how to thank you."

"Survive. Live. Make a new life for yourself. Next time, try to remember the devil sometimes comes in pretty packages offering everything under the sun except the most important things of all, kindness and honesty. Try to keep in mind that old saying, if it sounds too good to be true, it usually is."

Marisa swallowed hard and nodded. "Should I remember that about you? This sounds too good to be true."

"I have no desire to hit a woman. In fact, a bully, male or female, makes me sick to my stomach. Do you want something to eat before we go? I could throw a couple of sandwiches together for the trip."

Her stomach rumbled. "That would be great, but the sooner I get this over with, the better it will be before I lose my nerve."

"You don't want to do that. You can wait in the truck if you want while I go throw together some food for the road and grab my keys."

"Thank you."

He nodded. But as he turned to go, she caught the wave of embarrassment on his face. Even with that, she was taken aback by his next bold statement. "My mother took it from my father for years, never did anything about it, stayed when she should have left. We're going to do something about that today, tonight."

"Thank you," Marisa stated again. "I'll never forget what you're doing for me."

"Then one day return the favor. Be there for someone else. My mother could've used a friend when she needed it the most. But there was no one for her to turn to, no one who would help her leave."

"Okay. Sure. Will we make Alberta by tonight?"

"Count on it."

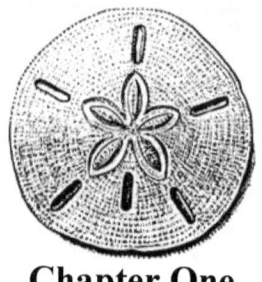

Chapter One

Present Day
Pelican Pointe, California

Isabella Rialto felt like a bird in flight, wings spread, soaring high over ocean and beach. To her, freedom meant she would never take anything in life for granted again. She could make up her own mind about things, even if those things meant simple decisions. If she wanted to, she could stay up late at night and watch a movie of her own choosing, or watch re-runs of *Friends* until the wee hours of the morning if that struck her fancy. Or she could curl up with a good book or her Kindle in front of the fire and read until her eyes were blurry. She could do any of it without a hassle or an argument. She no longer had anyone standing over her, telling her what to do or when to do it.

It was true she'd once been beaten down—which made her newfound independence seem like a bud sprouting and then slowly opening so that the world might fully appreciate its beauty. Each day she blossomed fuller and stronger. That was Isabella. Somewhere during the last few months, spending time inside Sea Glass Cottage, she'd rediscovered her soul, its independent streaks, something she'd forgotten she possessed. Sad to say, it had been chomping at the bit to unleash itself after getting stymied for so long.

She knew a few of the more curious in town were still wondering about her, whispering, talking. But it was only a matter of time before they came around. At least that's what her friends, Logan Donnelly and his wife, Kinsey, had said. She wanted to believe them. Since her arrival in town the closest thing she had to a job was babysitting the couple's twins, Liam and Leah. Not only did the job give her something to do, it also gave her a glimpse into what she'd missed married to a bully. Children. And after spending a few hours with other people's babies she'd determined that kids were a lot of work. It took patience and devotion and most of all a generous amount of love. All vital things the bully had lacked.

But Henry was in her past. The divorced Isabella Rialto could look forward to the future again, to waking up in the mornings to possibilities. She'd take that any day over being told what to do and when to do it.

From the front door of the keeper's cottage, she had a view to die for. The address where she got her mail officially read 14 Lighthouse Lane.

Standing in the doorway, she looked out over the glistening water and the plush carpet of velvety grass that led to the cliff. Logan, her landlord, had added a porch that ran the length of the house. She liked to sit outside in the evenings and stare out over the bay and the ocean beyond.

To her right she gazed at the step-stone pathway Logan had carved out that led to the massive lighthouse, the lighthouse that kept her feeling safe and secure, especially during the long nights she spent here with herself for company.

The cottage she rented from Logan had been around since 1935. It had undergone major renovations—from a one-thousand-square-foot WPA work project under President Roosevelt had doubled in size with a modern design throughout. It had brand-new electrical wiring, new windows, new doors, and a new roof. Cherry hardwood floors had replaced the old, worn-out planks.

Despite all the improvements, she knew from the rumors floating among the townspeople that during the remodeling the workers had found a body in a walled-up space in what used to be the kitchen. When she'd asked

Logan about it, he'd admitted that at one time a serial killer had used the grounds and the surrounding woods to conceal victims. Even though Logan had downplayed the dangerous element, Isabella had known for years about the disappearance of his sister, Megan. She'd been sad to learn the young girl's fate.

Besides her father, Javier Rialto, Isabella had been one of the few close friends Logan had confided in about Megan's disappearance. The fact that Isabella now lived in close proximity to where the remains had turned up was cause for alarm. She'd be lying to herself if she deny it didn't bother her at times, especially during a bad Pacific storm when the wind swirled and whistled between the keeper's cottage and the lighthouse.

On those spooky nights she tried to focus on why she'd made the journey here. Logan's loyalty to her father had been one reason. But once she'd made the decision to leave Henry, Logan had supported every step she'd taken to cut ties with the man. Logan's friendship went a long way to making her feel like she could accomplish that goal.

With Javier's passing, Logan had stepped up to fill her father's shoes, to encourage, to support, to be there. For the last three years the two friends had become more like family, not by blood, but because they'd shared mutual heartache. Logan had lost his sister. Isabella had lost her father. They had a history that brought them closer, like a bond between siblings that couldn't be broken.

Logan had been the one to suggest that moving to the West Coast might be the very thing she needed for a new beginning. That's one reason she'd picked up the threads of her life to try out the place Logan couldn't seem to shut up about. After all, she no longer had ties to keep her back east in New York. Without her father there, she had no reason to keep up the estate in Oyster Bay or keep ties to any other business dealings.

So if there was a problem living in Sea Glass Cottage, if it made her feel uneasy at times at three in the morning,

Isabella knew Logan and Kinsey were a simple phone call away if she needed them.

Not only that; there was something comforting in knowing Logan had finally found the love of his life, someone kind and wonderful, someone like Kinsey who seemed to be the missing piece he needed in his life. It made her feel better knowing other people had a chance at happiness, at finding a soul mate.

Even if she did feel somewhat isolated living in the keeper's cottage, she also felt at home here, more so than any other place she'd ever lived. No doubt the cottage had a past with spirits that roamed through the grounds day or night.

If only the spook factor ended at the edge of the woods. She'd seen a man she knew wasn't real. The town had named Phillips Park after him. Scott Phillips had a habit of walking the land, broad daylight or dark of night, it made no difference. Scott was like a sentry guarding his domain. She didn't resent the intrusion. In fact, she'd accepted his presence with a knowledge that few could understand. There was nothing to fear in a ghost that seemed more protective than menacing. It was others—those who were flesh and blood—she needed to be on guard against.

Which is why after months of living here, Isabella was still settling in. She'd made the move without a car. She hadn't yet decided to buy one. Even without four wheels she managed to get around town just fine. So far she'd been able to get where she wanted to go by riding the bicycle she'd bought used from Paul Bonner. Paul had tacked up a note on the bulletin board at Murphy's Market. She'd been the first one, or maybe the only one, who'd been willing to plunk down seventy-five bucks for it.

Whenever she headed into town, like today, she could walk the bright red bike down the steep, paved hill before jumping onto level ground. It was a lot easier that way, especially since she'd been out of practice for so long. Not since she'd been ten had she gone everywhere she wanted to go on two wheels.

As she pedaled her cruiser down Ocean Street to the grocery store, she looked around the little town. Lately she'd noticed there were days it seemed like she'd gone back in time. The old shops along Main Street looked ancient. But there was new life on the horizon. Like herself, she could see the town rising, coming out of years of despair.

Since her arrival the town had already made significant changes. The old elementary school had reopened and was now a state-of-the-art educational center for kindergarten through sixth grade. Brent Cody, the town cop, had a new police station. A little hobby shop had opened its doors, along with a boatyard. This summer the town had turned a wasted, weeded lot into a park where families could picnic and kids could run wild for a couple of hours.

On top of all that, businesses had changed hands. Tucker Ferguson had taken over the reins of the hardware store from his father. There were rumblings that someone had bought the building at the corner of Main and Pacific. Plans were in the works for a pizza joint. Isabella hoped it would come to pass. There were nights she craved the taste of a New York-style Italian pie.

Which is one reason it hadn't taken long for her to realize the little town had a rhythm to it. After spending years catering to her abusive ex-husband's every whim, after moving from one coast to the other, she desperately wanted to fit in here, to become a part of the town's ebb and flow.

Deep in those thoughts and distracted, she'd just turned the corner from Ocean Street onto Crescent when she looked up to see a 1982 tan Range Rover barreling its way into her path. She didn't have time to react other than to dive for the curb to get out of its way. Avoiding the careless driver, she tumbled off her bike and into the street in a heap.

Harrison Thane Delacourt turned the steering wheel just in time to miss the idiot woman riding a bicycle without a care in the world down the middle of the damned road. But just barely. He almost nicked the fender on the front of her strawberry-red bicycle.

Slamming on the brakes, he pulled to a stop, nearly skidding up on the curb. Rattled, he threw open the door and darted over to see if the woman was injured.

He glanced at the female sprawled on the pavement. Irresponsible woman wasn't even wearing a safety helmet on her stupid head. But his mood tempered somewhat the minute he looked into her soulful green eyes. Her full, pouty mouth caught his attention and had him settling on the striking face and its olive complexion. He resisted the urge to run his fingers through all that silky golden-brown hair of hers that had tumbled out of its clip in the fall. Instead he barked, "Are you okay? What the hell were you doing riding down the middle of the street?"

Any other time, Isabella might have retreated at the tone. But not today. If not now, when? Today was for showing the world she'd regained her moxie, her spunk, her courage. She'd start with this overgrown jerk who sported a mass of blond hair tied back in a thick ponytail along with a pair of sharp, indigo-blue eyes.

Adjusting her anger so she could get out the words the way she once had in the past, she sucked in a breath. "If you hadn't been such an idiot *and* if you'd been paying more attention in the first place, you'd know the speed limit in town isn't anywhere near the fifty miles an hour you were doing. For God's sakes, this is a neighborhood with kids not the damn freeway. Watch where you're going next time, will you?"

"Me? I wasn't the one pedaling down the middle of Crescent with my head in the clouds without a mind to vehicles that weigh several thousand pounds."

When she started to get up he reached out to help her to her feet. "Are you sure you're okay? Did you hit your head?" He automatically took her chin, checked her eyes for glassiness. "Concussions can be tricky and hard to detect."

A little unsteady on her feet, she slapped away his hand, challenged his assessment, even though he towered over her by at least a foot. "I didn't hit my head. I'm fine. Just so you know, around here we aren't in the habit of running over people, especially those we consider neighbors, which is pretty much everyone."

"And I wouldn't have come anywhere near you if you'd been riding closer to the curb with traffic instead of what you were doing—coming right at me. Have you ever heard of staying as far to the right as possible, unless you're making a turn, which in this case you clearly were not doing." He glanced up and down the street. "In case you haven't noticed, you're in the middle of the block here. Need I remind you, bicyclists are subject to the same rules of the road as vehicles?"

Fed up with his self-righteous attitude and refusing to admit she'd been daydreaming, she snapped out, "Oh, pipe down. I'm not going to sue you or anything like that if that's what you're so worried about, although I should."

"Sue me? Of all the brazen…"

"I said I wouldn't, didn't I?"

He ran a hand over the stubble on his chin, blew out a pent-up breath. "As long as you have no injuries, I'll let you get on with whatever it is you were doing." He turned to go and then stopped, faced her again. "A little advice though. Stay out from in front of cars. In the future, try to pay closer attention to your surroundings. And for chrissakes, if you plan on riding that thing, buy a helmet for your hard head."

Before he could get back into his SUV, she blurted out, "There's not one reason for you to be so snotty and rude to me. Not one!"

When that didn't get a reaction she threw out the only bit of detail she had left in her arsenal. "From where I live on the cliff, I've seen you surfing south of town, off Turtle

Point with your little boy. Surprisingly, you don't suck at it."

She noted the glower on his face and took pride that she'd put it there. Pleased with herself, she went on, "But then Logan says your name is Thane Delacourt and you used to play in the NFL. If that's true I guess you'd have a modicum of athletic ability in you."

He bristled at the reminder and the insult. "The optimum phrase there is 'used to.' I've moved on. I wish everyone else would as well. And you are? Ah, wait. You'd be the mystery ballerina in the keeper's cottage everyone's been wondering about." He cracked up laughing and looked her up and down in a seductive perusal and then added, "Ballerina my ass, more like exotic dancer."

"I'm sure you'd know a lot more about exotic dancers than I would know," she huffed out. She wasn't certain how the ballerina rumor had taken flight in the first place. All she knew for sure was that some people believed it. But when the accusation she'd been a stripper began to fully sink in, her blood did a slow rolling boil. "The name is Isabella Rialto. People I consider my friends call me Izzy. You, however, can stick to Isabella. It's always awkward when you learn firsthand that one of your neighbors is a real asshole, which you definitely are. I'll take your advice and head to the market now and leave you to infect others with your special 'misery and woe' persona."

That hit a little too close to the mark to suit Thane. He puffed out another sigh, left the driver's side door long enough to go over and reach out his hand in friendly introduction.

On his approach, she refused to take it and took a step back instead. She watched as he recovered from the slight and gathered up her bicycle from the roadway. Why should she be nice to this ass? "Don't do me any favors. I've got this."

"Yeah?" At the realization they'd gotten off to a really bad start, Thane simply added, "Look, I apologize for yelling at you. But you scared the crap out of me. I thought you'd fallen and hit your head. I thought you were seriously hurt. It shook me up."

"Such concern is touching and appropriate since you were driving like a crazy person."

"That is so not true."

"Oh really? I'm the one on the pavement and you're the one shouting at me. You have a booming voice. It must unnerve a lot of people."

"Sorry," he said again as he inspected the bike for damage. "My mother used to say the same thing."

"One reason I'm sure you were so successful playing sports—you're used to bullying people."

"Men. I bullied men on the field wearing an opposing jersey, which they paid me to do. Not women, never women. Huge difference." Finding the bike frame intact, he held it out to her and tagged on, "You're a piece of work, aren't you, Isabella Rialto? Looks like you're good to go now."

She took hold of the handlebars to hop back on. "Out of curiosity what position did you play exactly?"

"Linebacker."

"Figures, I bet you were the head bully of the team. Logan says you gave it up because you suffered an injury."

"Then maybe it would be easier if you had this discussion with Logan and asked him all these stupid questions and left out the middleman."

She snickered. "But then I wouldn't get to irritate you so much up close and personal. It's so much more appealing this way."

That got a grin out of him; the smile spread wide across his face, showing off a set of deep dimples.

"You should do that more often."

"What?"

"Show those dimples to the world. It makes you look almost human." As she climbed on and took off, over her shoulder she tossed out, "See you around town, Thane Delacourt. In the meantime, try to keep your road rage in check. You don't want a rep in a small town like this when you know how people tend to talk."

Thane shook his head as he watched her pedal down the block. Once he settled behind the wheel, he reminded himself that he no longer cared what some stubborn female thought of him. Come to think of it, he didn't much care what the entire town thought of him either. Nor did he care what the tabloids wrote about him anymore. Those days were long gone when he got upset reading about himself online. Thane knew when you were no longer playing, no longer making headlines for some stupid stunt you'd pulled the night before, the public rarely gave you two thoughts.

That was fine by him.

For all he cared, every last journalist could go take a flying jump into Smuggler's Bay. It was true when he'd lived his life in the fast lane he'd often made an ass out of himself, sometimes to the point of exhaustion, most times with a measure of embarrassment. Eventually after burning himself out, he'd found the limelight greatly overrated. He was no longer that person who blitzed quarterbacks for a living. Did he sometimes miss making those QBs pay for bad decisions? Sure he did. Did he miss closing up gaps with his body and taking down speedy running backs? He did. While he might miss the game itself—those glorious hours he'd spent on Sunday afternoons knocking heads with other people—he definitely relished his time spent calling plays for the defense and putting an end to offensive drives. There was a time he'd lived for fourth downs.

What he didn't miss though were the reporters and cameramen taking note of his every move on the field and off. He hadn't bargained for living out his life with people following him around all the time waiting for him to screw up. Most days, he'd done his best not to disappoint them. He'd made headlines, giving the reporters the stories they craved to fill up their news blogs. His antics had taken up airtime. Anchors had spent their time questioning his latest falls from grace or discussing the path he'd chosen for his messy life. At one time he'd been incredibly hard on each nemesis who'd written ugly things about him.

Even in high school he'd possessed an undefinable spirit, never quite fitting squarely into anyone's pigeonhole. He took that quirky attitude to UCLA where it morphed into bold and daring. Like most young people on their own for the first time, once at college, he'd discovered his distinctive individual style made him the quintessential leader. In his sophomore year, his teammates responded and elected him team captain.

A rebel at heart, he always wore his hair longer than any other player and resisted coaches who suggested that he conform to other people's standards. That original thinking often got him in trouble. But more than that, it was his talent on the field that made him a standout to other players, other schools, other coaches. The attention magnified an outspoken nature that no one could muzzle, not even when he reached the NFL.

Maybe that's one reason he'd thrived.

At six-four and two-forty, it hadn't taken long to catch the attention of football coaches from Florida State to Washington. They'd discovered Thane's willingness to put in the hours necessary to improve. He lifted weights, was never late to practice, and worked on his form and timing. If he could develop his raw gift and turn it into major league talent at a school like UCLA, his size alone might afford him notice on the college level. At the time, getting that full ride to a four-year university had meant everything to him, his one and only goal. By his junior year that had changed when NFL scouts came knocking. Despite the buzz to turn pro, he'd stayed around for his senior year to graduate because his working-class parents wanted one member of the family to have a college degree.

Above all else, once he reached the pros, Thane had wanted nothing more than to make his parents proud. He had no way of knowing that those first few years he'd end up getting attention for all the wrong reasons. Initially his success had come with plenty of attitude, a willingness to work hard, and a stubborn persistence that even his competitors marveled at. It was only later that he'd had to reevaluate a chunk of it.

Thane liked to think that when it had counted, he'd done the right thing. No doubt he'd gotten sidetracked along the way. But he'd finally come back to his roots and brought his little boy with him. Too bad his mother and father were no longer alive so they could see the one-eighty he'd pulled.

Even now he was in the process of rehabbing a storefront to open his own pizza place two blocks from the house his mother had left him on Landings Bay. Home was just down the street from the school where Jonah started first grade.

So far Jonah's days there had proved uneventful. No major disasters. Yet. But he knew that would probably change. With a boisterous six-year-old it was only a matter of time before all that energy bubbled to the surface and spelled trouble. If his boy was anything like he'd been at that age, it was inevitable. He'd just have to deal with it when it happened.

Overnight it seemed as though Thane's life had changed—from the days of living in a self-absorbed fishbowl to becoming a full-time father. Those nights spent carousing at every club in Manhattan, doing all kinds of stupid stuff, were behind him. He was a responsible dad now who wanted nothing more than to do the right thing by his kid.

The days of spending hours boning up on defensive strategies were over, too. Now, he was an ordinary stay-at-home dad, who packed Jonah's lunch every morning, picked him up after school every afternoon. He dusted the furniture, did laundry, and even changed the bedding on a regular basis.

So far he'd resisted the advice from his neighbors, Logan and Kinsey, to hire a nanny to look after Jonah when the restaurant opened up.

He'd have to find a way to do it all himself, he decided. A hands-on dad didn't hire a nanny. Having someone else in the house would be a distraction and a pain in the ass, especially since Jonah was still grieving the loss of his grandmother. He missed his "Mimi" every single day, still mentioned her when he went to bed every night. Truth be told, Thane was still having a problem dealing with his mother's death, as well. That's why lately it had been just the two of them—father and son—making their way on their own. And for that, Thane would forever be indebted to Alyson Benning. She'd given him his son. Maybe it hadn't been his initial reaction to the situation at the time, but nonetheless, it was how he felt now. That had to count for something.

While Jonah's birth might not have been part of his original master plan, he could be proud of how he'd stepped up when he found out. However it had happened, he'd ended up a father, for Jonah's sake, or maybe his own it was now his full-time job. The amount of work it took was unbelievable. Some days he had to remind himself that he'd made it through the diaper stage, learned that the terrible twos didn't come to an end on the third birthday, and weathered a four-year-old testing independence with a full-blown temper tantrum thrown in a five-star restaurant in the middle of dinner rush.

No, when the pizza place opened its doors next month, his life would surely get more complicated. But somehow he would find a way to keep up the pace and continue taking care of his son—the same way he'd been doing it for six years. Granted, without his mom around, it would be a tougher challenge. But Thane Delacourt had never run from a difficult task.

So, for now, he intended to enjoy the ride as much as he could and do it all himself. With that resolve, he shoved the car into gear to go about his errands.

Chapter Two

Isabella made her way into Murphy's Market still fuming about the encounter with Thane Delacourt. Whenever she'd had conversations with Logan about Pelican Pointe—both before and after her decision to move here—he'd failed to mention the major asshole tendencies of some of its residents. Oh well, didn't every town have a curmudgeon, someone who seemed to take pleasure in bringing misery to neighbors? That was Mr. Delacourt.

She thought back over the last several months when she'd met practically the entire town at various events— the opening of Phillips Park, the outdoor movie nights held throughout the summer, the concerts over the bay, parties she'd ducked. Now she knew why she hadn't crossed paths with him before today. He probably didn't get many social invitations and didn't yearn to make new friends.

But then she realized she'd done her fair share of shunning social engagements over the past several months. It wasn't that she was aloof or unfriendly. It wasn't because she wanted to remain a mystery to people. But how could she explain that she hadn't wanted to answer the inescapable questions about her past, those that came with settling into a new place. It meant her absence at get-togethers had led a few around town to believe she was standoffish and distant.

That included the good-looking Zach Dennison. Zach was a nice guy. Ever since meeting at Julianne Dickinson's Memorial Day barbeque last spring they'd crossed paths a couple of times around town. After one of the concerts, the two had even shared a meal, sort of, when Kinsey had insisted on inviting everyone back to her place to celebrate the opening of Tradewinds Boatyard, Zach's new enterprise he'd started with pals, Ryder McLachlan and Troy Dayton.

Now that she thought about it, there were nice guys all over town. NFL career or not, Mr. Delacourt definitely wasn't one of them. In fact, his moniker from now on should be something similar to "Oscar the Grouch."

Maybe she'd stop by Tradewinds Boatyard and say hello, in a neighborly sort of way, to Zach. Maybe she'd take the initiative and do the asking out.

After grabbing a shopping cart from the row, she began to feel the aftereffects of falling on her bike. Soreness began to settle in, especially around her right knee. Realizing she was fortunate to have nothing but a few bumps and bruises and not a broken bone or two, she entered the produce aisle, perused the selection of grapes. She stopped to add a few vine-ripe tomatoes to her basket but as she turned to toss in a bunch of kale, her head started to ache. Determined to forge on, she moved past a table piled high with Tuscan melons. She reminded herself that she was on her bike and was therefore limited to how many items she could carry home at one time. But as the pain in her head increased she decided that maybe she needed to get back home. But first she had to troop through frozen food to pick up a carton of chocolate caramel gelato. That would make any ailment feel better. If it melted on the trip back, so be it. She'd lap it up soup-style and be in ice cream heaven.

With enough supplies to hold her for a couple of days, she headed to the front of the store to check out. But as she stood in line behind Prissie Gates, her head began to pound even worse. Her vision blurred before everything went black. Slowly she crumpled to the concrete floor. The last face she remembered belonged to Thane Delacourt.

On his way back from the hardware store past the pizza place he had yet to name, Thane spotted the ambulance parked outside Murphy's Market, its lights still flashing. Knowing Isabella had been headed that way, his first thought was of her. Turning the wheel, he pulled into the lot, and rushed through the double doors only to see her laid out on the linoleum.

"What happened?" he asked Murphy.

"Damned if I know. She was standing in line and the next thing I knew she hit the floor. I guess she must've passed out."

Thane shook his head. "She was in an accident earlier while riding her bike. I almost hit her with my car. It's possible she hit her head when she tumbled off her bicycle."

"We need to tell that to the EMTs." Murphy turned to the paramedics. "Hey, Deacon, Brian. The girl may have blacked out from an earlier accident."

"Okay," Brian replied as he slapped a blood pressure cuff around Isabella's arm. "We'll roll her over to Doc's then for a look-see, have him evaluate her head."

"I'll follow you over there," Thane offered, catching the other EMT staring at him.

"I know you," Deacon said in recognition. "You used to play for the Giants, right? Linebacker, all-American at UCLA, you grew up here."

Irritation flickered in Thane's eyes and had him frowning at the paramedic. He didn't want these guys focusing on him when what they should be doing was to get Isabella over to Doc's. "That was me, a few seasons back though," he finally grumbled. "Look, is she gonna be okay?"

"When did she hit her head? Do you know?"

"Yeah. About forty-five minutes ago on Crescent Street." Thane watched as the two men got Isabella onto a stretcher. One of them took out a cell phone, hit speed dial and began detailing Isabella's vitals to Doc Prescott, the town doctor.

Grateful for something to do, Thane followed them out the double doors.

Once he got to the clinic, a renovated Mission-style house off Tradewinds Drive, Thane paced in the outside waiting room while Doc worked on Isabella in one of the three exam rooms. Despite the slapdash looks of the place, he already knew Doc ran a state-of-the-art facility.

With a kid, Thane had tested the waters two weeks after moving back when Jonah had jumped out of the pecan tree in the backyard and landed on a spike sticking up out of the dirt. It had taken four stitches to close the gap in his hand. During that visit Thane had discovered Jack Prescott knew his stuff. You didn't spend twenty years as chief resident of emergency medicine in one of San Francisco's busiest ERs without learning a thing or two.

And recently the rock star physician had talked his wife, Belle, a former pediatric nurse, into becoming his receptionist. The job was a temporary fix because Belle hadn't been keen on resuming her duties. Both husband and wife were simply biding their time until Sydney Reed, an ER nurse out of St. Louis, and sister to Hayden Cody, could move to town and take over as Doc's assistant.

Hayden had already announced to everyone that Sydney had bought a house on Cape May. She claimed her sister was chomping at the bit to get here and settle in. Thane knew Doc and his wife felt the same way since Belle didn't exactly want to spend her days at the clinic.

When Thane finally took a seat in one of the uncomfortable chairs, he tried skimming a magazine article but couldn't focus on the words. Maybe he shouldn't have even followed her over here. Isabella Rialto wasn't his responsibility. Of course, he realized he was the reason she was injured. But that didn't mean she would like to have him sitting here…waiting for her.

He wondered if he should call Logan and Kinsey, who both seemed to treat her like close family. As he pondered what he should do, Thane had no way of knowing that inside exam room number three, Doc was in the middle of his own conundrum.

Jack Prescott eyed the film he'd taken of Isabella's knee and decided to move on to the brain scan. He picked it up, studied the MRI. Glancing over at his pretty patient as she began to come around again for the second time, he waited for several moments while she gained a more cognizant awareness. When he could see her look around and clearly take in her surroundings, he said, "Do you know where you are?"

"Doctor's office," she muttered.

"That's right. I need to make certain you understand what I'm about to say." In a no-nonsense voice, Doc went on, "Ms. Rialto, your knee is swollen and hyperextended. If you stay off it for a few days, it should be fine. Your head, however, is another matter. You suffered a small contusion at the back. I'm guessing you're lucky you turned your head when you did, otherwise you would have hit your temple, a very tender part of the brain where the middle meningeal artery is located. You hit that, and it can easily cause an epidural hemorrhage. That's why it's so important bikers always wear a helmet. Soft tissue hitting concrete rarely goes well for the rider. A concussion, young lady, is serious stuff. I'll need to keep an eye on you for the next twenty-four to forty-eight hours. Do you still feel nauseated?"

"No. Not anymore."

"Still experiencing blurry vision?" he asked, shining his light into her pupils.

"No."

"Good." He switched x-rays, held up the one he'd taken of her knee. "It might be none of my business, but I see by the images you've suffered several broken bones before. The break at your ankle, for example, is old and has healed. There are other breaks, some hairline fractures, still showing up from thigh to heel. Were you recently in a car accident?"

"No."

"I see. Then did you ever play contact sports where you suffered several broken bones?"

"I ran a little track in high school and college."

"Hardly contact sports that would yield such repeated damage." He thought he already knew the answer but asked the question anyway. "Would you like to tell me how you came by so many fractures over the course of your young life?"

Isabella closed her eyes. "That's... It doesn't matter now. He's in the past."

"No chance of him showing up out of the blue and doing the same thing to you all over again?"

"No."

"Okay. Then I'll release you to go home. I want you to spend the rest of the evening taking it easy. It isn't necessary to be in bed but I want you off that knee and taking better care of yourself. Thane Delacourt is waiting outside to take you home."

That news brought her to a sudden sitting position on her elbows. "What? Why is he here?"

"You'll have to take that up with him. He followed the EMTs to my door and insisted on waiting to see how you were." Doc picked up a chart, began making notations. "I'm prescribing a long, restful weekend. I want you to avoid stress and excitement. That's a real prescription by the way. Do you think you can manage that?"

"I live alone. I'll manage just fine."

"Then get dressed. If you need help, I'll send my wife in."

"I'll manage," Isabella repeated.

Doc left her alone and wandered out into the outer room where Thane was. As soon as the two men made eye contact, Doc held up a hand before the man could leap to his feet.

"She's fine. A three-day rest with someone making sure she doesn't have a repeat of what happened in the store and she'll be even better."

"How were her x-rays? Did you do an MRI?"

"Even if I did, since you aren't family or related, I can't share those kinds of details with you."

"Can I see her?"

"She's getting dressed. She'll be out in a minute. You can take her home though and make sure she gets settled. Keep an eye on her. You don't have to sit by her bedside or anything like that but I'd like to know that she doesn't lose consciousness again."

"I will. I can do that. I do feel responsible."

"That's nonsense," Isabella said from the doorway. "I took a tumble off my bike when I saw your car heading straight for me. That's all there was to it." She looked over at the physician who'd treated her. "He's worried I'm going to sue him, which I'm not."

Thane rolled his eyes. "I'm not worried. Maybe my Rover did get closer to you than I thought it did, maybe grazed the fender of your bicycle. It's possible the car inched you over to the curb."

"Don't be absurd. I fell off my bike," Isabella stated again. "I was daydreaming just as you said earlier and not paying one bit of attention to where I was going. I didn't even realize I was pedaling down the middle of the street until you pointed it out."

While Doc and Belle took note of the couple's squabbling, it was Belle who reminded them both, "This is exactly what Isabella does *not* need right now. She needs quiet for the next several days without stressing out or arguing."

"See, we should avoid discussing the entire incident while I drive you home," Thane pointed out.

"Just call Logan or Kinsey. They'll pick me up."

"I did. They'll be over later to check on you *after* I get you home. But right this minute Logan is dealing with an issue with his agent and Kinsey—"

"Has the babies," Isabella finished through gritted teeth. "I get it. Fine. But I have to settle my account first and go back to Murphy's to get my bike." She reached in her jeans pocket for her debit card which she'd planned to use at the market.

But Belle waved her off and pointed to Thane. "He's already taken care of your copay."

"And I threw your bike in the back of my Rover."

Isabella's head began to throb again. She stared at the ex-football jock. "I'll write you a check as soon as I get home. I'm no one's charity case."

"Who said you were? I just thought you might not feel like dealing with the bill once you were ready to leave."

That had her feeling like an ill-tempered shrew. "Just tell me how much it is and—"

"You'll write me a check as soon as you get home," Thane mimicked her voice. "Yeah, I may have hit my head a time or two in football, but I get it."

As the two headed out the door to the car still engaged in verbal battle, Doc shook his head. "Do they even realize they're attracted to each other?"

"It's probably too soon. What's it been? A couple of hours since he almost hit her with the car. You have to admit it's a distinctive way to start out but it's not unheard of."

"I suppose so. From what I've seen of Thane Delacourt, would you consider him to be a decent sort of guy?"

"Sure, I guess. I read he did have some issues in the NFL, dating a different woman every month and all that. Playboy bunnies one week, actresses and models the next. All the stories made me wonder why he came back here to settle down, here of all places when he could live anywhere in the world. Why do you ask such a question?"

Doc shook his head. "But no domestic violence issues during all that hype, right? I mean Thane was a helluva competitor on the field, but all those stories about him dating women had nothing to do with domestic violence issues, correct?"

Belle shook her head. "No, not one. They were geared more about the hunky bachelor who refused to settle on one woman. It was only when that model, Alyson Benning, I think it was, got pregnant with his child that he seemed to change his attitude."

"Having a child gets your attention."

"But even then there was no scandal about violence, just a few stories about his off-the-field antics. Want me to look it up on the Internet?"

Doc nodded. "Okay, that's a start. As I recall he never failed a drug test either." He looked around the empty waiting room, a rarity on a Friday afternoon. "It seems like we both have a chance to do a little research."

"Is that code for fishing or maybe a quickie in the empty exam room if we lock the doors?"

Doc grinned. "I always did like the way you think. But no, this time, I really am turning on my computer to see what I can find out about him. You do the same and we'll compare notes."

Inside Thane's Range Rover, there was a round of awkward silence until he finally wanted to know, "Mind if I ask why you don't drive a car?"

"Who says I don't drive? I drive."

"But you don't *own* a vehicle? That's the buzz."

"Maybe I have a Benz stored away somewhere gathering dust."

He wasn't quite used to her sense of humor yet. But he was getting there. "Right. It's probably sitting at the same place mine is."

Glancing around the interior of the older model Rover, she lifted a shoulder. "I'd ask you about your choice of vehicles but I figure that's your business."

"I prefer old cars." He tapped the dash with a loving hand. "My dad bought this Rover used from a guy over in Santa Cruz in 1994. I remember making the drive over there with him to pick it up. We had to tow it because it didn't even run. But together we fixed it up and look at it now."

"So this has sentimental value? I get that. I don't own a car because I haven't gotten around to buying one yet. Look around you. It's a small town. Getting from point A to B is fairly quick and simple."

"Unless you're riding down the middle of the road..."

"And encounter a crazy person. Don't start with me again."

"When you get ready to buy one, I know a guy who'll give you a great deal."

"Really? Sure." She changed the subject back to him. "So you grew up here? In Pelican Pointe?"

Thane bobbed his head in answer. "Lived over on Landings Bay in the house I now share with Jonah. Graduated from San Sebastian High School—where I hope to send him one day. When my mom died last year, I inherited the house. She'd been battling breast cancer for almost three years. Her death happened just about the same time in the off-season I found out that the narrowing in my vertebrae was a career ender. One more hit and I could suffer paralysis."

He shook his head. "With a kid, it just wasn't worth the risks. What with my mom's death and that cheery news, both pretty much coincided with the need to get my son away from the spotlight. So I packed up everything and came back here."

"And just like that decided to open up a pizza place? Do you know anything about making pizza, the good kind, not that cardboard crap?"

"I wouldn't put my name out there to serve cardboard crap."

"Do you even cook?"

"Are you kidding? With a kid, believe me I fix my fair share of meals. Just because I own a pizza parlor though doesn't mean I'll be the one making the crust. I'll hire people to do that."

"Have you already filled that position?"

He turned his eyes from the road long enough to look at her. "You want to make pizza? For the asshole neighbor who almost ran you down? That's a one-eighty from this morning."

"We both know it was a close call for both of us. Besides, I could use a job and something to do with my time."

"I thought you worked for Logan and Kinsey as their nanny."

She filled the car with a loud sigh. "I'm not officially the nanny. People spot you pushing a stroller a couple of times along the sidewalk and automatically figure you're the nanny. Hasn't anyone noticed Kinsey works out of her house every day?" She waited a beat. "I guess not. I go over there to help her out with the kids, give her a break from diaper duty and feeding. Anyway, sometimes I watch the twins to give her and Logan a chance to have a little alone time. Having two babies is a handful. That's all there is to it. You didn't answer my question."

"About the job? I have the position filled. A friend I know from New York wants to make a new start somewhere else. He was here in August to check the place out. He'll be back in a couple weeks to set things up."

"So he knows how to make pizza?"

"Fischer Robbins knows how to make just about anything from pan-seared Ahi to a perfect grilled steak. He worked as the sous chef at the bar I used to hang out at, makes the best New York pizza you'll ever put in your mouth. That's how I got the idea."

"I still can't get over it. Thane Delacourt moves here and opens a pizza parlor. That's a mighty big drop in limelight. Although I suppose people will probably come from miles around just to get a chance to eat at your place and get an autograph. The legend of Thane Delacourt will always be a force around these parts."

He grinned. "Every town needs a good legend, don't you think? What's your story?"

She stiffened. "I don't have one."

"Sure you do. Everyone has a story. You just don't want to share it with me while mine, mine's an open book for anyone who goes online to judge or enjoy as they see fit."

"I wouldn't like that at all."

"Not many do."

"When did you lose your father?"

"A couple months after Jonah was born. By that time my dad had discovered he had pancreatic cancer at a routine doctor's visit. He died within the year."

"So your mother took over caring for your son before she died?"

He nodded. "That is, until she got too sick to do it. She and my dad were living with me in New York during the season. That way when I would go out of town on road games, my parents could watch Jonah, get to spend some time with their grandson. I'm glad they got that time with him even if Jonah doesn't remember my dad. There are pictures though so I'll be able to tell him about the grandfather he never knew. Now Jonah has no living grandparents. But he does remember my mom reading to him and playing certain board games with him, which is good."

"I'm so sorry. It sounds like you've had several rough years back to back. I know what that's like. I lost my dad three years ago."

"I'm sorry. What about your mother?"

"She died in a car accident when I was in my teens. You never quite get over the traumatic loss of your parents."

He pursed his mouth. "Very true. But you don't know the half of it. If losing them wasn't bad enough, I had to come to the realization that my string of less-than-stellar life choices had to come to an end. During the time I played football I wasn't exactly known for my restraint. I did a lot of stupid things with a lot of stupid people. I'm willing to admit I made some bad decisions, bad choices. Alyson was one of those. Of course, if I hadn't met her, I wouldn't have Jonah. So, in a way, my recklessness had an upside. When I found out about Jonah, that's when I straightened my life out. Once he entered the picture I knew I had to become both mommy and daddy."

"You know, you can't say something that profound and not get the ultimate question. Where is Jonah's mother?"

Thane felt himself flinch at the question. "You don't know? For real? You might be the only person on the planet or at least in town who doesn't know. Alyson's gone. She was heavily addicted to drugs even before I met her. One night she called me up at two in the morning after a road game, dropped the bombshell that she'd had my baby. Of course, I didn't believe her. I thought she was running a con and just wanted money. But she persisted until I had my lawyer ask for a DNA test. One day I got a call after practice. The test confirmed Jonah's paternity and a few other things I didn't want to hear."

"Like what?"

"Like the fact that Jonah had major health problems."

Isabella sat back as if deep in thought. Then it hit her. "Oh my God. She was on crack before the baby was born?"

"Yeah. I found out later the crack made Alyson psychotic. Jonah was born addicted to the damn stuff. He had a rough go of it for the first year of his life. But he's like his old man. He's a fighter."

"Poor little guy."

"After learning about the drug use, I fought for full custody. When he was a little over four months old the judge made it official. He was mine. About a month later I got the call that Alyson had overdosed." He took his eyes off the road long enough to send Isabella a lethal stare. "Don't look at me like that. My winning custody had nothing to do with what Alyson eventually did to herself. I'm convinced she didn't give a shit about Jonah. And before you ask, I didn't know when I got together with her that she was that heavy into cocaine. She didn't have a sign on her forehead that read, 'danger, danger, I'm a crack addict.' All I knew was that she had made the cover of a couple magazines, hung out with famous people, did the name-dropping thing. So if you're thinking of judging me, it won't do you any good because I've judged myself about seven hundred and fifty times already. It'd be a little hard for anyone else to catch up."

"I wasn't going to judge you. We all make mistakes we regret."

He narrowed his focus on those lovely green eyes. "Which makes me ask, what were yours?"

The sigh she let out filled the interior of the car. "Let's just say, they've been doozies and leave it at that."

"Fair enough. I know the desire for privacy. Unfortunately, there's very little I've been able to keep from public scrutiny about my own life."

"The price of NFL fame?"

"That's one way of looking at it. I like to think since I got all that out of my system early, I've reached a point where I deserve a little solitude, somewhere I can raise my son away from the spotlight."

"I don't think I could handle the fishbowl."

"I don't want that for Jonah," he said as he pulled up next to the keeper's cottage and cut the engine. "It's pretty up here. You have a great view of the entire bay."

For the first time since getting in the car, her lips curved. "It is. Peaceful. Talk about solitude. I love it here. Even though it has a bit of a spooky history." She told him about the serial killer and the bodies they'd found in the woods last year.

"Yeah. Carl Knudsen. Weird guy. I remember when I was a kid going into his drugstore to pick up Band-Aids or whatever for my mom and he'd watch me like a hawk afraid I'd steal something. My mom used to say he gave her the willies."

Isabella tossed out the name Scott Phillips, determined to include him among the area's colorful past.

Thane nodded. "Yeah, I've heard those stories too about the soldier. I remember him a little bit. I'd expect that kind of thing from Professor Hawkins because he's a little out there to believe that stuff. But I'm surprised you buy into it, too."

"Because I've seen him walking up here on the cliff. Scott, not Wade. And believe it or not, his presence makes me feel secure like he's watching over me." That admission made her sound like a nutcase. She met Thane's doubting eyes. "I know how it sounds. But I also know what I've seen."

"I reserve the right to be a skeptic," Thane said, checking his watch. "Okay, here's the deal. I have to pick Jonah up from school. Will you be all right here for forty-five minutes or so until I can make it back?"

"Don't worry about me."

"Sorry. That ship sailed. I'm picking up Jonah and coming back here. You have to be starving. I know I am. We both missed lunch. I'll stop and pick something up from the Diner. Any preferences? Now's the time to make them known."

"You don't have to—"

Her protest was interrupted. "Don't even start with me. My mind's made up. If your stomach can stand waiting, I'll be back with food. Give me the prescription Doc wrote for you."

"I'd planned to take a couple of ibuprofen instead."

"Come on, hand it over, no need to be stubborn about it. I'll drop it off at the pharmacy while I pick up the food. Where's your phone?"

"Why?"

"I need your number so I can tell you when I'm headed back. You need mine if you should think of anything else you need while I'm at the pharmacy or the Diner. Also it'll come in handy if you need to go back to the doctor."

How could she argue with an offer that nice and neighborly? She dug the folded piece of paper out of her pocket and handed it off.

"Now was that so hard?"

"I guess not."

"I'll be back soon."

"And with a little boy, right?"

"And a little boy," he answered, his brow turning into a deep furrow. "Does that bother you, me bringing Jonah by?"

"Not at all. I'm looking forward to meeting your son."

Chapter Three

After months of planning, Tradewinds Boatyard had become a reality.

As the week drew to a close, business partners Ryder McLachlan, Zach Dennison, and Troy Dayton, had seen to it. They'd lived and breathed and practically slept with each other for the past two months to make sure they were ready to begin building boats as soon as the first order came in.

The trio had spent long grueling days cleaning out the rat-infested hole—a hole the three of them jointly owned—getting the table saws in place, ordering supplies and getting down to business. The day they got their first order via fax, they'd looked at each other in stunning realization knowing this was the real deal.

"It's official. Nick says the wire transfer cleared from somewhere in the Cayman Islands—a viable deposit—the balance will be paid on completion and delivery of the sailboat we designed." Zach held up a six-pack of beer. "Today we celebrate."

Ryder turned from the plans he'd drawn up with the help of a software program and said, "So do we know yet who this mysterious client is? So far all we've seen are faxes, a few emails and the cash."

"Maybe we're building this gorgeous 22-footer for some gangster on the other side of the world," Troy speculated as only a guy of twenty-two could.

"Maybe," Ryder noted. "Do we know for a fact this isn't for your friend, Jacob Hettinger?"

"It isn't Jacob," Zach said with a shake of his head. "He's still going back and forth with what he wants. And frankly, I'm glad it isn't him. Until Jacob figures out exactly what it is he wants, I'd just as soon not start building anything at all."

"Good thinking. So, whoever it is, all we know is their deposit cleared and they'll pick this baby up here in three months in Pelican Pointe," Troy pointed out.

"You got it. You know as much about the buyer as I do. But as long as their money is good, do we really care who it is? They didn't ask us to design any secret compartments for smuggling so that's always a good sign," Zach cracked, twisting the top off a brew.

"All I'm saying is our design kicks ass," Ryder went on with pride. "Kyle said this was the best design he'd seen in five years. And we're just starting out. Imagine what we'll be creating ten years down the road."

"That's why we hired Kyle Graham as consultant," Zach touted with a grin. "He knows talent when he sees it."

"Our first boat design and just look at all that beautiful teak we plan to use on the deck," Troy said in awe at the lumber stacked high on one side of the room.

"According to his latest Hotmail account, the client wants a little more flare across the hull and for us to put in a slightly wider cockpit to curve right about here," Ryder said tapping the computer screen. "We do both those things and I guarantee this little baby will fly through the water. You watch and see."

Zach nodded. "Put the storage lockers under the full seat here, add a separate battery locker about here, add in the racing package our client ordered and we're talking Tradewinds Boatyard's first real beauty right off our very own assembly line."

"In ninety days," Troy said. "Not only will we deliver this boat on time but when we do, it will be the perfect craft for either a day sail or a weekender. Whoever it is will get a helluva boat. Wish we knew who it was."

"Do you plan to let the fact we haven't seen our client's face bother you?"

"I'd just like to know who it is. That's all."

"I wouldn't mind knowing that myself," Ryder admitted.

About that time, Zach looked up to see Drea Jennings standing in the open doorway. The pretty brunette held a beautiful fall bouquet of mums and daisies. "Sorry to interrupt but I have a delivery."

"For us?" Troy said in wonder. "Are those for Bree? I know she's working with you to do our wedding flowers but I didn't order these."

Drea laughed. "No, I'm sure these are for you, all three of you in fact. Here's an idea. Someone read the card and find out who ordered them."

"Good idea," Zach said, taking the vase from the lovely florist and handing it off to Ryder.

While Zach snatched the card attached from its plastic holder and opened the envelope, Ryder stood there stuck with the bowl of flowers. "The card says, 'From one business owner to another, congratulations on Tradewinds Boatyard, Nick and Jordan.' Wow, that's a classy gesture from the banker and his wife. Makes me feel more part of the town and I've lived here my whole life."

"I think that's the idea. I have two more arrangements in the van."

"For us?" Zach echoed again, clearly shocked by the outpouring of sentiment. "People really sent three guys a bunch of flowers? For real?"

"You'll probably get even more," Drea said, spinning on her heels to walk back to the vehicle she'd left parked at the curb.

"I'll help you with those," Zach offered.

"Good because I could use an extra pair of hands." She went to the back door of the truck, swung it open. "This is from Hayden," she said as she picked up the braided money tree and held it up. "For prosperity and for good luck. And this is from Lilly and Wally."

Zach eyed the European garden basket with a Mylar balloon attached that said 'Congratulations' in silver and purple. "I hope like hell we can keep all these plants alive."

"Should I plan to make a house call?" Drea asked.

"It wouldn't be a bad idea. Unless Ryder or Troy has a green thumb I don't know anything about, the greenery is subject to neglect, especially with our busy schedules. Maybe I'll talk Ryder into taking one home to Julianne."

"So you're okay now with Troy marrying Bree?"

Since Troy was his business partner and would soon become his brother-in-law, Zach had done his best to put things in perspective. But no matter how much time went by, he still couldn't get used to the idea his kid sister would soon be married. To him, she still seemed like the little girl who used to bug him to take her wherever he went. Now, Bree was busy getting her own tour business up and going while at the same time planning the wedding.

Zach blew out a breath. "Not really. This summer I was convinced the relationship was moving way too fast to suit me. They're so young. I remember when I was twenty-two, I sure wasn't thinking about settling down back then."

"You aren't that old. Besides, everyone's different. It doesn't take a whole lot to see that Troy is crazy about her and that she feels the same way about him."

"I came around to that a couple of weeks ago. What can I do about it anyway? Don't get me wrong, Troy's a great guy. That goes a long way to how I feel. He makes her happy. I have to accept that."

"Is that your main objection, the fact that they're so young?"

"Yeah. My only objection really. But despite their ages, those two are go-getters—Troy with our boat business and Bree with the tours."

"Has she decided what to call hers yet?"

"Tours by Bree. She's keeping it simple. She's already started taking B&B guests on hikes in the area so essentially she's open and money's already coming in."

Drea stared at the man holding greenery in both hands. He had the sharpest eyes and cutest smile. But if she waited for Zach to get around to asking her out, she'd no doubt be waiting for another several years. So she garnered her courage and blurted out the invitation. "Would you like to go out sometime? Keep it simple. Maybe grab a burger at the Diner?"

"Really? Sure. Okay." Zach turned to go back inside, carrying the flowers, got halfway to the dock and stopped. "I think I can do better than the Diner. How about dinner and a movie in Santa Cruz this Saturday night?"

"It's a date." With that, she closed the doors to the van and watched him disappear into the boatyard. And just like that she pumped a fist in the air. "Yessssss!"

It was only after she did a happy dance no one else could see that she climbed behind the wheel.

"So you're going out with Drea? I thought you were interested in Izzy?" Troy asked from below the hull he was shaping.

Zach shook his head. "There's something off with Isabella. I'm not sure what it is other than she's a little too stuck up for my tastes. A couple of times I tried to have a conversation with her but she doesn't seem to want to answer a direct question."

"She does seem like something's bothering her."

"All I know is I did my damnedest to get a few details out of her and she closed off. I just didn't get a good vibe that the two of us would ever click that way."

"What about Drea?"

"What about her?"

"Do you get a vibe around her?" Troy said with a grin.

Ryder laughed. "Oh, I think our friend here gets more than a vibe."

"Fuck you both," Zach said in jest. "What do you say we get this keel shaped and the cutaway done by tonight."

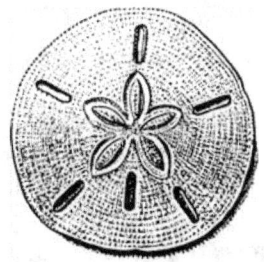

Chapter Four

At exactly three-fifteen, Thane waited outside the school on the sidewalk for Jonah to appear among what seemed like a hundred other little heads. But he could spot his exuberant son in the midst of all the others. For one thing, Jonah was tall for his age. For another, he had a tendency to exude energy wherever he went. He'd have to rein some of that in around Isabella.

Thane waved at a couple of the other parents, talked to a few of the mothers, before Jonah ran up to him and threw his arms around his legs.

That never got old, thought Thane.

"Hey, Dad. Um, you know what happened at lunch?"

Leave it to Jonah. He was always good for a story about his day. "No, what?"

"Kelly Kendall threw up and it went all over Merilee's shirt. And Kelly got sent home. And Merilee's mom had to bring her clean clothes."

"Sounds like you had an exciting day. What happened with your spelling test?"

"I got all ten words right. But I messed up on the word *frog*. I forgot to put in the *R*."

"Then how did you get all of them right, Jonah?"

"Um, I missed one. *Frog*. F R O G."

"That's right. I guess we'll have to work harder on the list over the weekend. Look, I need for you to be extra good while I take food over to a neighbor. I have to pick up a prescription for her too."

"Why does he need food and medicine?"

"She. It's a she. She hurt her head and missed lunch. We're stopping by the Diner to pick her up some soup and a salad."

"Yuck. Soup. I don't want to eat any."

"You don't have to. I'll pick you up something else." He slid Jonah's backpack off his shoulders, slipped it on his. "Brought your Legos to entertain you for a couple of hours. Do you promise to be really good while we're at her house?"

"But I wanted to play games on the iPad."

"The iPad is for backup. You love your Legos, remember?"

"Oh yeah, I do."

"So right now just promise to be on your best behavior and we're good to go. Can you do that for me?"

Jonah's head finally bobbed up and down. He scrunched up his forehead like he was thinking really hard. "Is the food for Miss Donnelly? 'Cause I like her. Is it for Miss Dickinson? 'Cause I like her, too."

"No. It's for Miss Rialto. She lives up on the cliff and you haven't met her yet."

"The cliff with the lighthouse on it? Awesome. Can we go up to the top so I can look out over the ocean? Can we?"

"We'll see. First, you have to promise to be on your best behavior because she's not feeling as good as she could be. Her head hurts."

"Okay. Did she fall?"

As Thane drove over to Main, he relayed the story to his son about how Isabella had hit her head on the pavement.

"That's why we wear a helmet when we bike. Right, Dad?"

"Exactly right."

The druggist, Ross Campbell, filled the meds while Max got their food order ready. By the time he and Jonah reached the keeper's cottage, Thane looked over and saw that his son was bouncing in his seat. As soon as the front door opened and the boy spotted the woman waiting on the stoop, little Jonah blinked in surprise. "Is that her? Is that the bicycle lady? She's pretty."

"You have good taste, my man." Thane helped his son out of his safety seat before Jonah bounded out of the car. Thane went around to the back and shot a look over at Isabella. She'd changed out of jeans and into a pair of yoga pants and a tee. She'd obviously taken a shower because her hair was still wet. But even with her olive complexion, Thane could tell she still looked pale from the exertion.

"Shouldn't you be off your feet?" Thane asked as he removed the carton of groceries from the rear storage area.

Isabella ignored his concern. "What's all this? You went shopping for food? You said soup. You shouldn't have gone to so much trouble."

"No trouble. We went in the Market to pick up fruit and Murphy said you didn't get the stuff on your shopping list. Murph tried to remember what you had in your cart when you dropped like a rock. Because he couldn't remember it all, we had to improvise."

"You hit your head," Jonah said as he rounded the front of the SUV.

"Well, hello. Yes, I did. And you must be Jonah. Hi, I'm Isabella. Or, if you want, you can call me Izzy."

"If he gets to be your friend and call you Izzy then I should've let him pick up the tab for the groceries," Thane called out.

"You can both call me Izzy, especially since you brought food, because I'm starving. How's that?" Isabella countered, reminding herself she needed to answer to the nickname.

Father and son followed Izzy into the stone cottage, old-fashioned on the outside but open, spacious and modern once they stood in the middle of the room.

"Wow! Look at this place, Dad. It's all clean and shiny."

"Are you saying our place isn't clean and shiny?" Thane wanted to know.

Izzy laughed. "I'm not really used to having company, other than an occasional visit from Logan and Kinsey. You guys make yourselves at home. From what Logan said the remodeling went really well."

"Are you kidding? Not that long ago this cottage used to be a dump. It sat vacant for more than forty years, rundown, neglected. In high school we used to come up here to…" His voice trailed off as he realized Jonah was within earshot.

"To what?" Izzy asked with a grin splashed from ear to ear.

Thane waved her off.

"Maybe it was haunted back then," Jonah suggested as he cautiously peered into the other room.

"Look out this way, Jonah. From this angle there's a perfect view of the lighthouse next door," Izzy said, distracting him from exploring such topics.

"Can I go up there, Dad? Can I? I want to go up and see the lighthouse at the top."

"Not by yourself. Maybe after we eat," Thane promised. "We have to put the groceries up first. Remember we bought gelato. Maybe you can get Izzy to show you where it goes before it melts. And Izzy should get off her feet."

"Come on, follow me," Izzy said as she led the way into the roomy kitchen. "Logan did a fantastic job in here, didn't he?"

Thane took in the stainless steel appliances, hooded range, the wine bar and other modern accoutrements and stated, "I'll say. I wonder if he could renovate our old dated model. Or put me in touch with the people who can."

"Who's doing the work on your pizza parlor?"

"Same crew that worked on the school—Ryder, Zach, and Troy. They've formed this remodeling company outside the boatyard they dubbed Razor Team."

"Because they're lightning fast and work as a team?"

"Yep. They do fantastic work. Everyone's lining up to put them to work. But I hesitate to throw more their way because those three are just crazy enough to take it on. They're already swamped with so many jobs around town—my restaurant, River's museum, and their own boatyard—the nonstop grind is bound to wear thin. The commercial appliances are due in tomorrow. You wait and see, they'll have them installed by Sunday night. I don't know when they sleep. They seem to work round the clock on automatic."

"They can't keep that up for long. Especially since two of them have weddings on the horizon. Troy and Ryder are tying the knot soon."

"I heard about that. I think Julianne, or rather Miss Dickinson broke Jonah's heart. I'm pretty sure he had a little crush on her when school started."

"I did not!" Jonah protested while he helped empty the sacks. "I just like her is all. I think she's pretty."

"Like your new classmate, Heather Campbell?" Thane quipped.

"Heather likes to surf," Jonah added.

"Always good to have activities in common," Izzy said as she started to help put away the produce and fruit.

But Thane stopped her. "Sit down." He pulled up a bar stool from the counter, patted the seat so she would sit.

"Do you have an opening date yet for your eatery?" she asked.

"Not yet. I haven't even settled on a name for the place."

"Right now, we like Full Sail Pizza," Jonah piped up.

"That's good. Original," Isabella said.

"To be fair, we've also considered Schooner Pizza, Seaside Pizza, and Dockside, in keeping with the coastal theme," Thane explained. "If only we could settle on a winner."

"I like all those. You guys are creative. I'm curious. Why pizza?"

"Because it's Jonah's favorite food and there's not one in town. You figure it out. It's gotta be a win-win for more than just Jonah."

"Will you deliver?"

"I always deliver." Thane cracked with a wide grin at the exasperated look on her face. "And yeah, I knew what you meant. And the answer is I have no idea. Probably. I still have a ton of things on my to-do list, things to work out, like getting my liquor license nailed down and obviously deciding on a name so I can put up my sign." Thane took out a container, then another. "I picked up some of Max's soup for you."

"On Friday the choice is clam chowder or...or...I forgot the other one," Jonah said, scratching his head.

"Lobster bisque," Thane offered.

"We got you both kinds even if they do smell kinda fishy," Jonah added as he scrunched up his nose and climbed up on a bar stool beside Izzy at the island. "Where'd you hit your head?"

"At the back."

"Dad says you have a headache."

"A little bit, yes."

Thane smiled. "Jonah?"

"What?"

"How about a little less chatter?"

"He's fine," Izzy said. "I don't mind the questions."

Thane shook his head. "Now you've done it. You've opened up that trap door to Jonah's chatterbox persona. It's bombs away, anything goes now. Don't say you haven't been warned."

Jonah giggled. "Dad says that a lot. Sometimes I get in trouble for talking too much in school."

"I thought you were encouraged to talk in school and participate."

"Oh he participates all right. The problem is he participates when he's supposed to be quiet and doing his work," Thane pointed out. "Jonah has a hard time with quiet."

"I like a man who can carry on a conversation," Izzy stated. "You can talk to me anytime."

"Really?" Jonah said, bouncing up and down on his stool. "We can be friends?"

"Sure."

"Can I see the lighthouse now?"

"We eat first then I'll take you on a tour of the lighthouse before we leave," Thane promised.

"I'll take some of that soup," Izzy said. "Feel free to make yourself at home in the kitchen to fix Jonah whatever he wants."

"I want ice cream."

"Gelato later. Right now, you get Max's mac and cheese instead." With Izzy's direction, Thane got down plates and silverware, set them out on the counter. After dumping the soup into a bowl for her, he piled the ready-made, gooey pasta onto a plate for Jonah, and fixed himself a mile-high ham and cheese sandwich.

They ate with banter going back and forth, until details revealed how badly Jonah yearned for a dog.

"I've been thinking about getting one myself," Izzy confessed. "I went so far as to ask Logan, my landlord, if he had any objections to it."

"What did he say?"

"That it was okay by him."

"I want a black and white one," Jonah admitted. "Tommy's dog had puppies. The mom dog had a bunch of them." The first grader sent his father a pleading look. "They need homes. Bad."

"And a boy does need a dog," Izzy declared with a grin. "Or so I've heard. It's a classic for a reason."

"See, Dad? Told ya. I need a dog."

"You'd have to feed it, give it a bath, and take it for long walks. Just a bunch more stuff added to your other list of chores."

"I'd do it."

"You say that now…"

"What's the list of chores?" Izzy wanted to know.

"You're up, buddy. Go ahead, now's the time to tell Izzy how hard I am on you."

"I pick up my toys after I play with them. I take out the trash and dump it into the big can outside. I dust the furniture with old underpants." The boy thought for a moment before adding with pride, "And I load the dishwasher after supper."

"Uh, Jonah, that underpants thing you should probably keep to yourself. He uses the old ones, the ones he's outgrown."

Izzy chortled. "I see. I'm so glad you straightened that out for me. At the mention of 'used underwear' I went a whole other direction. But that list of chores sounds like a lot of hard labor. I think as soon as I'm a hundred percent we should check out Tommy Gates and see what kind of dog he has, see if he has any of those black and white ones to pick from, as a reward for both of us."

"Tomorrow?" Jonah asked with hope.

"Thanks for encouraging him," Thane grumbled and shook his head again, reluctant to give in. "A dog is a big responsibility. It isn't like I don't have enough to do already with the pizza place opening." But he'd have to ask around. From what he remembered Tommy was Archer Gates's kid, a man with a drinking problem. Or so went the rumor.

"I've been thinking about a name for your restaurant too. You guys like to surf, right? You surfers use shortboards, longboards, bodyboards, so what if you called your place, Longboard Pizza?"

Thane and Jonah stared at each other for about two seconds before blurting out at the same time, "That's it!"

"That's perfect. Now I can get Lilly Pierce working on the sign," Thane offered. Reaching out, he took her chin, stared into her eyes. "They don't look as glassy as they did before when I dropped you off. But you should probably still lie down, get some rest."

Izzy looked over at Jonah. "Is he always such a worrywart?"

"Yep. He worries about me a lot. When I'm sick with fever, he stays by my bed all night. Do you have fever? He'll sit with you if you do."

At that image, Isabella's heart did an erratic sputter. "No, I don't think I have fever."

"Just a concussion," Thane charged.

"Dad used to get 'cussions all the time," Jonah explained, patting Izzy's arm. "Being quiet helps."

"That's right, peaceful and quiet," Thane reminded his son, holding one finger to his lips.

"You'll feel better soon," Jonah assured Izzy in his six-year-old voice that tried for a low whisper. "You won't ever get sick like my momma did and had to go away. I didn't know her."

Thane swallowed hard at the sentiment, stared at his son before looking over and meeting Izzy's eyes. "Jonah, if you're done eating let's go take that tour of the lighthouse. Whaddya say?"

Just as he'd hoped his son refocused on that and clapped his hands.

"Let's go!"

"I'd go with you but…"

"That's okay. We'll clean this mess up and get out of your hair so you'll finally take it easy."

"Thanks for the food."

As he started putting away leftovers, tossing the containers in the trash, and wiping down the counter, Thane said, "No problem. Thanks for not suing me."

Izzy glanced over to see if Jonah was preoccupied. When she saw that he had gone to the window to stare up at the lighthouse, she whispered, "Will Jonah be okay?"

"Sure. For the record, I told him his mom got sick and died and that's it. He doesn't know any more details than that. As far as I'm concerned that's the way it stays."

"I agree. He's far too young for details like that."

"Exactly. Besides, I'd rather keep him thinking that Alyson wasn't a bad person, simply misguided in her choices."

"Sounds like a basic plan to me."

"Then I'll see you tomorrow."

Even though it was still light outside when Thane and Jonah headed for home, Isabella went about her normal routine getting ready for bed. Her knee and head hurt so much that she downed one of the pills Doc had given her.

She'd just slathered cream on her face when she heard a noise that sounded like it originated from outside. Her instincts went on red alert. She opened the bathroom drawer and took out a large kitchen knife she'd stashed there. Truth be told, there were others hidden all around the house, including a semi-automatic weapon tucked away in the nightstand. Walking out to the bedroom gripping the handle of the blade, she almost dropped the thing when she spied a familiar image.

Scott Phillips eyed the sharp instrument dangling from Isabella's hand and responded by sticking both hands in the air. "Sorry, I didn't mean to startle you. No need to be scared of me. I just want to talk."

Who knew when she'd set foot in Pelican Pointe thinking to find the perfect sanctuary to recover from her past, she'd be having conversations with a dead guy. In this idyllic setting, Logan had never once brought up the fact she might spend her evenings doing so. She'd have to ask her friend about that.

"I'm having a conversation with a ghost, a man who died in Iraq. There's a park named after you, posthumously."

"I know. Haven't you heard? I'm fairly famous around these parts."

Isabella couldn't help it, she snorted with laughter. "Full of yourself much?"

"Only on Fridays. You're safe here."

"Oddly, it isn't you who scares me. I've seen you walking around…outside. To my knowledge this is the first time you've wandered into the house." She cocked a brow and tilted her head to send him a well-deserved scowl. "Seems to me if a person did that, just came inside when another person wasn't even home, that would be incredibly rude of that person."

Scott grinned. "Who me? I'm a gentleman to the core." All of a sudden his face went serious. "Brent Cody's a good cop. Remember that when you're ready. There are plenty of people here who'll protect you if he comes after you."

Isabella winced. She didn't have to ask who the "he" was. But the reminder still made her ill. "I'm sure Brent knows his stuff but he might be out of his league with Henry Navarro. The man's family has enough money to buy the entire town."

"Makes no difference. Brent might be a small-town cop now but he wasn't always. It'd be a mistake to sell him short. Not only that but I'm well aware of what you and Logan have cooked up." The statement was said simply, with understanding and compassion.

Isabella sucked in a huge intake of breath. Her spine stiffened in denial. "I don't know what you're talking about."

"Sure you do. Can't say I agree with what you're doing but… People often go to extreme lengths to…"

Her attempt at denial turned to cold dread. Had she and Logan made some mistake, some misstep that would send an alert to the wrong person? "How could you know that? Are we wearing some kind of sign?"

"Not at all. But for me it comes with the territory. I just want you to know…" Scott's parting words before he vanished were short and sweet and to the point. "You can trust me."

Later, as she crawled into bed, his vow stayed with her. Even though he'd tried to be reassuring, Isabella wasn't completely sold. Trust meant coming up with faith when she wasn't sure she should rely on anyone but herself. Best she remembered that. She was well aware she couldn't afford to let down her guard.

Cautious and wary to a fault, she had yet to go out of her way to make friends or become part of the community. So far, she'd been content to keep to herself, tending the keeper's cottage with minimal interaction toward anyone else. Getting her life together was a damned good excuse to keep her distance. Thane and Jonah, and even Scott, seemed determined to change that.

Whether or not she stayed on the sidelines, it remained an option. Low-key is what she'd sought and what she'd found. Getting dragged into someone else's dynamics wasn't high on her to-do list. But she knew firsthand such things were rarely predictable and were difficult to avoid in such a small town. She'd best remember that, too.

As she drifted into sleep, it wasn't that mantra on her mind at all. Her last subconscious thought flashed a clear image of ripped Thane Delacourt and his adorable son, beaming as bright as the lighthouse in her front yard.

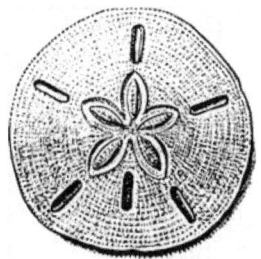

Chapter Five

After years of economic downturn, Pelican Pointe was making a comeback, slowly, bit by bit, store by store. With each storefront that filled up along its streets, with each new business opening its doors, with each dollar plunked down within its city limits, the townspeople gained and profited.

From Janie Pointer's Snip N Curl to Drea's Flower Shop to Ferguson's Hardware, stores along Main had already dragged out their Halloween decorations. Images of ghosts and goblins, witches and ghouls, adorned the windows and doors of new businesses and old. Julianne Dickinson had yet to open her resale shop next door to the church. But while some residents were still in the planning stages, there were others who were eager to have their own pizza parlor in the works.

Reopening the school had brought an influx of new people into town. Parents of all different ethnic groups had moved in, enrolling their kids in hopes of nurturing a diverse and vibrant community, a foundation for the future.

What better way to establish that than fostering a new band of community spirit?

Tucker Ferguson knew all too well about community spirit or lack of it. Over the last five years, his father had managed to alienate much of the hardware store's customer base. Old age had made a cranky man out of Joe Ferguson. Now retired and living in Florida, Tucker's parents had handed him the reins of a store with a major drop-off in profits. Tucker knew that his dad's prickly "me" attitude had contributed to the decline in revenue. Men like Logan Donnelly and Nick Harris had gotten fed up with his father's "what's in it for me?" outlook and had threatened to drive to San Sebastian for all their lumber and hardware needs. Taking over the day-to-day operation of Ferguson's Hardware, Tucker had an uphill battle if he intended to change attitudes.

He had a boatyard that required a steady stream of lumber, a new pizza restaurant undergoing a gutted renovation, and residents who wanted to take on remodeling their older homes. He'd be an idiot if he didn't recognize that the business was right under his nose if someone bothered to nurture it. Tucker was no dummy. He wasn't about to run anyone off. No one could accuse him of not understanding the benefit of helping people in his own customer base. A lumber and hardware store couldn't survive for long with a habit of pissing off its clientele. The other half of that equation was working to establish a rapport with other business owners and encouraging goodwill among them.

Tucker intended to do everything within his power to right the ship, to correct the image his father had left him. Going over the books, the first thing was to increase sales and get regulars coming back into the store. He'd already met the owner of the pizza place, reached out to the triad ownership at Tradewinds Boatyard and to Cooper Richmond, who had opened his new enterprise across the street and called it Layne's Trains.

From the moment the train shop had opened a week ago, Tucker had done his best to mentor the man who'd made his living as a photographer before coming back to Pelican Pointe. For seven days, Tucker had watched with curiosity as people stopped in to reconnect with Cooper. While his own business lacked that friendly, welcoming spirit, Tucker took note. If Cooper could get a train store to do such a brisk business in a short time, then there was hope for Ferguson's.

Inside Layne's Trains, Cooper could have set Tucker straight on that score.

In the week he'd been opened, it had been mostly the curious who had dropped in to shoot the bull. Old-timers who'd known him as a child wanted to see how the boy had grown into a man. No doubt they'd felt the need to see firsthand just how Layne and crazy Eleanor's son had turned out. Cooper discovered that early on. The nosy ones had pushed him for details about his mother's arrest for killing his father so many years ago.

Such was his life these days. He'd have to get used to it. But fortunately for him, there were others who had stopped in to meet and greet and pick out a few early Christmas presents. Those shoppers made up for the significant number who hadn't actually bought anything.

With such measured success thus far, Cooper decided he'd better be able to fall back on his photography skills to pay the bills. So in a corner of the shop, he'd created an area he turned into a portrait studio. For the past week, he'd grabbed his camera more often than he'd gone near his trains.

Kinsey Donnelly had coaxed him into taking portraits of her babies. A string of other moms had persuaded him to snap shots of their kids. That idea ballooned when the principal, Julianne Dickinson, had drafted him into becoming the official photographer for school photos. He'd done a number of passport pictures, and a couple of engagement shots for Bree Dennison, which had led him to offer to shoot her nuptials. Strange thing was, he actually looked forward to the event. Did that make him a wedding photographer? He didn't care what people labeled him as long as he could make a living and pay his bills doing what he enjoyed. And so it seemed after years of avoiding his childhood home, Cooper Richmond had come back and fit comfortably into its way of life.

His brother, Caleb, and his sister, Drea, were an integral part of the reason why. All three had tried to put their twisted childhood behind them. Most in town seemed to understand that and had given them space, didn't ask a lot of stupid questions in the process. Then there were the little old ladies like Marabelle and her sister, Ina Crawford, Myrtle Pettibone, and Ethel Jenkins, who had lavished him with gifts for the little house he'd rented. Within a week, they'd shown up at either the shop or home to bring him an assortment of handmade quilts, crocheted tablecloths, knitted pot holders, and hand-sewn dish towels. But with their generosity of spirit, the women brought a measure of meddling. Cooper knew with each question the guild meant well. He wasn't convinced all newcomers were treated with the same dose of kindness. Of course, Cooper had an advantage. Most of the women had known him as a kid, known his father and mother. Such was the laidback pace and atmosphere in a small town.

Cooper looked out the plate glass window onto Main and beyond to his sister's flower shop. He caught sight of Bree Dennison as she strolled out with a big smile on her face holding a varied bouquet of flower samples in her fist. Somehow, he knew the redhead had already segued from waitress to business owner. A good sign, he thought now as he studied the comings and goings on the street as people began to mill around.

This early on a Saturday morning Bree was surprised to catch sight of Cooper already inside his shop. She waved in greeting and dashed along the sidewalk to where she'd parked her car.

With a packed house at Promise Cove, Bree anticipated a busy but fruitful weekend. Eager and willing to put in the hours to make sure Tours by Bree succeeded year-round, she had to hustle to make her nine o'clock excursion out to Treasure Island—a trip that had her taking two nerdy geology students from San Francisco State across the water to the little patch of local island so they could take soil samples.

It had felt so good to give up her job at McCready's. She'd forever be grateful to Flynn for giving her a job, but after two years of slinging drinks, she needed to move on, to start the next chapter in her life.

Her upcoming wedding to Troy had kept her hopping. There was a part of her that just wanted to run off and elope, to forego the more formal ceremony for a simple stand-up routine in front of a Justice of the Peace. But that urge didn't last for long. Bree wanted the whole romantic package, the long white gown, the candlelight, the fuss, the ceremonial rite itself and the pomp that went with all the circumstance. She'd even figured out how to cut corners on some of the expense. Her friends were pitching in where they could by offering to help make place cards and other incidentals. She'd opted for getting Emma Colter to make her dress. There were still a dozen things on her to-do list and so far Troy had been a good sport about her obsession with each one.

By the time she reached the old Victorian that doubled as the town's only B&B, she rumbled down the long driveway going over the plan she'd formulated.

She hoped Nick and Jordan would go for it because it would keep her from having to go on the hook for an added expense of signing a lease in town. Getting married, planning a wedding, and redoing the house, meant she and Troy were on a tight budget. They'd actually sat down and mapped out logistics for their future together—down to the penny.

During the summer they'd put in the sweat equity on the little bungalow on Athena Circle that needed so much work. In between the jobs that paid the bills they installed cabinets, changed out hardwood flooring, replaced tile, and plumbing fixtures. Bree hoped the work would be done by the second Saturday in November. Their wedding day was fast approaching and they were feeling the pressure. Running out of time wasn't an option. If they somehow missed the deadline, they could always bunk at the house she shared with Zach—the house their father had left them—not exactly ideal conditions for newlyweds but still doable.

Scanning the sprawling grounds of Promise Cove, she spotted Nick and Jordan in the back playing with their kids, five-year-old Hutton and two-year-old Scott. The two were busy kicking a ball around the yard and chasing after it.

Gathering up her satchel from the front seat Bree headed around the side of the house to the back.

Nick and Jordan Harris were pretty much like most busy couples with children. They worked hard during the week—Nick at the bank, Jordan waiting on demanding guests at the inn. They tried to use the weekends to cram in as many activities with the kids as time permitted.

As soon as the toddlers spotted Bree, they surrounded her with offers to join in the fun until Nick put a stop to their persuading. "Bree can't play with you because she has a tour this morning."

"Can we go?" Hutton asked. "Take us."

"Maybe another time," Jordan answered for her daughter. "You wanted to plant seeds in the egg cartons to grow your own beans, remember?"

"Oh, yeah. I forgot."

"And you were going to help your brother make moon sand," Nick added with a wink.

Bree shook her head. "I don't know where you guys find the time. Lately it seems like I'm running from place to place with no time to catch my breath."

Jordan smiled and nodded. "An upcoming wedding and a new business tend to make you feel stretched to the limit."

"It's fun putting together the wedding, but at the same time, a lot of hard work. I barely get to see or talk to Troy without us both falling asleep during the convo, which brings me round to my idea." A little breathless, she blurted out, "It's a bit unconventional but I need for you to hear me out before you say anything at all. After the wedding, when Troy moves out of the studio over your garage, I'd like to turn that space into my office for the business and pay you rent. That way, I would be here, onsite to ferry passengers out to the shipwreck and the island as well as take them on hikes in the area. It would save me money from having to go on the hook for a lease along Ocean Street and keep me out here on a full-time basis."

Nick and Jordan exchanged looks. "You don't have to convince us. It sounds like a plan."

"Good. I've already approached a few of the stores along the boardwalk near the pier to let me leave a stack of my business cards next to their cash registers. Malachi Rafferty thinks I should be able to pick up a few bookings each month that way by word of mouth. Most businesses in town seemed excited about spreading the word."

"Did someone give you trouble about leaving the business cards?"

"Just one. But he's left town now anyway."

"Let me guess. Joe Ferguson."

"You got it. He refused to let me leave a pack of cards. But his son, Tucker, called me a couple days ago and said it was okay if I still wanted to put them on the counter. So I said sure, left a tall stack there yesterday just to shove it in the old man's face."

"Tucker called me yesterday, too," Nick admitted. "It seems the son understands his father might've left him a huge PR problem in his own backyard."

"It sounds like Tucker's taking action before it gets too big to overcome," Jordan added.

"If you ask me, it's already pretty far out of hand," Bree stated. "I know Joe pissed off Troy and Zach. They're both willing to give Tucker a second chance if he realizes the opportunity. What Joe didn't get is that Tradewinds Boatyard will turn out to be a valuable customer."

"Everyone in town should be treated like a valuable customer," Nick declared. "This was a sore spot with me. I could never get Joe to understand that."

"And believe me Nick spent a lot of time trying," Jordan said with a smile. "Nick had more run-ins with Joe than anyone else in town. Dealing with that man became tiresome for both of us."

"Then I guess we'll reserve judgment until we see if Tucker does anything to improve," Bree finished.

An irritated River Amandez Cody looked around at the morning surf as it clawed its way into the shoreline, ripping into beach, eating away the landscape. Because it had gotten worse over the summer, she'd shut down the dig site and watched her team pack up and move on. She'd known Julian and Laura for years and already missed her buddies. But she'd come to terms with keeping in touch with them via email. Her family took priority. Not only did she have a son to raise she had another on the way.

No doubt, she had a lot on her plate. Since Marcus had put her in charge of running the Chumash Museum in town, due to open next month, she'd find a way to work around her duties there. She had seven and a half months to get ready for the new addition. The clock ticked toward that family she and Brent wanted. Even though they hadn't yet announced the news to the world, they would, probably this weekend at the barbeque they planned. From there, town gossip would do the rest.

Brent came up behind her carrying Luke. "I see that look on your face. You're worried that you caused this erosion. You didn't. The storm we had in August contributed to the drop in sea level."

"I know, but I started this. When I got here it was such a beautiful spot. It breaks my heart to see the water this high."

"Give it time, it'll recede. But Dad put a call in to the conservation group out of San Francisco. They'll be here next week to evaluate the best way to handle it."

"That's something, I guess."

"Feeling okay?"

"I'm fine. Stop worrying about me," River said as she rested her head on Brent's shoulder, which had him in turn resting his hand on her still-flat belly.

"The next few months are sure to be busy but since crime is almost nonexistent in this town, I can help you with the museum."

She looked up into his deep brown eyes so like her own. "Never let it be said that the top cop doesn't know how to use his angles. I wouldn't mind having your help but I was thinking about getting the word out that I needed an assistant, someone who knows their way around cataloging."

"What about Isabella Rialto? Word has it she used to work in some type of art gallery."

River ripped out a laugh. "I thought she was a former ballet dancer. That story came from Hayden who got it from Myrtle Pettibone. I suppose the only way to know is to go right to the source."

"Now there's a novel idea, the direct approach. Is that a polite way of telling me I don't qualify as your coordinator?"

"Nope. Your input is crucial. Even with both of us though, I'm afraid I could use help getting ready for the opening. Besides, I don't want to get accused of taking the police chief away from his duties in an official capacity."

"Ah, there is that. Okay. Then go see Isabella. Who knows, maybe the real story is even more interesting and exotic than the one the wagging tongues made up?"

"Ah yes, real life usually is."

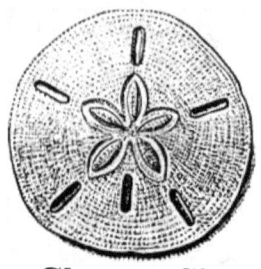

Chapter Six

Over the years the Delacourt home on Landings Bay had seen its share of kids come and go through its doors. The Spanish Colonial where Thane had grown up with his younger sister, Tessa, had acted as the popular hangout on the block. Friends often gathered in the front yard, got into mischief in the treehouse built in the back, or watched cartoons in front of the TV set early on Saturday mornings.

It became routine for Thane and Tessa to share their after-school cookies and milk with classmates. In summer they'd gulp down glasses of cherry Kool-Aid with Little League teammates celebrating a victory or sulking over a loss. Both were hosts to countless sleepovers, created enough batches of s'mores in the old kitchen to delight every chocolate lover within forty miles.

Even though Millie and James Delacourt had moved around a lot during their early years of marriage, once the couple settled down in Pelican Pointe, they put the focus on raising their kids. James hired on as a shrimper on one of the trawlers while Millie got a part-time job as a teller at the bank.

With a growing family some months the Delacourts had struggled with their finances, but for the most part, James and Millie had provided their kids with a typical upbringing. After a year on the job, Millie approached Milton Carr and talked him into giving them a loan to buy the single-story, three-bedroom stucco they'd been renting.

As Thane remembered those years, he looked around at the outdated kitchen cabinets and beyond to the interior in the great room. Early morning light fanned through the open sliding glass door and onto the Spanish tile flooring. His parents had long ago yanked out the old carpeting throughout and put in a stylish substitute with colorful inlay. At his mother's insistence, they'd replaced the dark paneling with a coat of cranberry-red paint and white crown molding that gave it a festive air.

He knew the outside needed another shot at repairing the cream-colored stucco and its brown trim, which he planned to get to first chance he got.

Labor Day weekend, the last time Tessa had visited she'd given him grief about the peeling exterior. He'd almost shoved a sandblaster in her hand and then challenged her to get it done herself and quit her bitching. He laughed at the image of his sister, or rather Dr. Tessa, as she was known to her younger patients, slapping on a new surface coat. Tessa the pediatric surgeon lived in Portland, Oregon. She'd never been a big fan of manual labor.

Thane threw coffee beans into a grinder, dumped the contents into a filter, and while it brewed placed a call to Lilly about the outside sign for the pizza parlor. When he learned she could get on it immediately, they agreed to meet later at the restaurant to go over ideas.

After he hung up the phone he filled a mug with caffeine. While sipping his first cup of the day, he glared at the ancient cabinets. He really did need to find out if it was feasible to install new by Thanksgiving when Tessa was due back in town.

He checked the clock on the wall and wondered if it was too early to call and check on Isabella. He shook his head at the eagerness he felt to hear her voice.

That wouldn't do, he decided. There were a lot of reasons he didn't want to find himself attracted to her. Namely, she was a distraction he didn't need right now. Tessa would surely bitch at him about that. But he had a kid to raise, a restaurant to open, a houseguest due in town in a couple of weeks. He didn't have time to devote to getting a woman into bed. All that aside, he'd learned it was difficult to have an active sex life when he had a six-year-old for a roommate.

He tried to remember the last time he'd made love to a woman. Then it came to him. When they were still living in New York, the night Fischer had babysat Jonah two weeks before the move here.

As he finished his cup and poured another, he formulated a plan to do something about the drought. But this morning he had to quash his lust. He had a kid to roust out of bed, even on a Saturday.

He crossed through the great room and headed down the hall to what used to be his room from childhood. The very same bedroom that now belonged to Jonah. From the doorway he eyed his rumpled, still-sleeping son who had kicked off most of his covers. He sat down next to him, ran a hand over his head where dark blond hair stuck out every which way.

"Time to get up, partner. Time to wake up. Want to go surfing with me or eat breakfast first?"

Jonah rolled over in a sleepy groan. "Wanna surf," he mumbled as he attempted to sit up, but in the same motion he slunk back down into the pillow, rubbing the sleep out of his eyes.

Thane went over to the closet and pulled out the miniature wetsuit hanging on the peg. "Then let's get you out of those pajamas and into this. Raise your arms up."

Jonah knew the drill and obliged, wiggling out of the top that went to his Batman PJs. He let his dad help him get into the body-hugging outfit. But before Thane zipped him up, he tapped him on the shoulder. "Better go pee first."

While Jonah busied himself in the bathroom, Thane got dressed. Afterward, he grabbed towels and sunscreen and watched as Jonah dashed out to the garage to get his boogie board. They walked to the end of the block, crossed over to Ocean and down to the beach.

With a six-year-old in tow Thane knew to avoid the deeper water and stick to the shallow part of the bay. After all, Jonah would never know the difference. As long as the little guy got to get in the water and splash around on his boogie board, spend a little quality time with his daddy, his little boy would be a happy camper no matter what.

After forty-five minutes, Thane paddled the short way in, waded onto the beach with Jonah following him like a baby duck.

Flipping his surfboard up, Thane scooped it out of the water, and caught his son doing the same with his mini board. Tucking it under his arm, Thane bent to unfasten the leash strapped to his ankle and with his free hand shook the water out of his dark blond hair. Again, Jonah mimicked his father's gestures down to the headshake. From behind, his son ran up to him and clapped his hands, stretched one up in the air for a high five.

Thane promptly reached down, tapped his son's palm with the celebratory gesture the boy had come to expect after a job well done.

"Let's do it again, Dad! Do it again!"

Thane slicked back the mass of locks that curled to the top of his wetsuit and planted his board into the sand so that he could snatch up his son, who was bouncing on his toes.

"That was awesome," Jonah yelled. "When do I get to do that again?"

"We'll do it tomorrow. How's that?" Thane reached for the towel they'd brought and threw it over Jonah's head to soak up the excess water.

"It's been a long time since we surfed."

"Jonah, you went surfing last weekend the same as you did just now."

"Oh. That's right. I forgot. I'd remember better if I had my own surfboard like yours."

Thane already knew that. He'd been listening to that same plea for the past several months. "Maybe Santa will bring you one for Christmas. How's that sound?"

Jonah's shoulders slumped in little boy disappointment. "But why can't I have it now?"

"Because you're six and I'm the daddy in charge. And because your boogie board works just fine for you."

As he always did, Jonah changed the topic of discussion in his rapid-fire way without much warning. "I like Izzy. Can we go over there today and check on her head?"

Thane ruffled the kid's mop of wet hair so like his own. "Sure. That's probably a good idea. I've worked up an appetite. What do you say we grab us some breakfast? What sounds good?"

"Waffles. And bacon."

"Now we're talking because I was thinking the same thing."

From the dew-covered grass in front of Sea Glass Cottage, Isabella still wasn't used to having the vastness of the ocean as a front yard. She had only to look out over the water to take in the power and awe at the water's unrelenting force and beauty.

She was about to hobble back inside the house out of the morning chill when something in the waves to the south caught her eye. Looking down at Smuggler's Bay she watched the byplay between Thane and Jonah. From the height advantage of the cliffs, the two surfers might've been mere dots in the sea of foamy crests and breakers, but she found herself unable to turn from the scene. Even from where she stood the sport looked like it took precision and balance along with a healthy dose of adventurous spirit.

While the waves churned, she continued to stare at Thane as he timed the break to perfection so that his son could pop up on his smaller board. She noted he saw to it that the little guy rode the barrel, such as it was, through to its end. Izzy envied such skill and dedication. But that didn't complete the whole picture. Something about the way father and son interacted with each other tugged at her emotions. It wasn't the first time the yearning had stirred inside her. The same thing happened whenever she spent time around Kinsey's and Logan's babies.

It didn't take a therapist to understand the feelings were not-so-subtle reminders of what might have been. Reminders that included how much time she'd wasted with the wrong man.

These last several years, time had somehow gotten away from her. Pretty soon another birthday would mark the calendar and she'd have nothing to show for it.

She shook off the gloom and proceeded to tug at the weeds outside the front door among her patch of fragrant angel trumpets and sturdy ice plants. She was alone for a reason. Her resolve was to never again allow a man to dominate her, to control what she did, what she thought, where she went. Never again would she allow anyone to keep her from doing what she wanted to do. Not ever.

The problem now was to explore the things she wanted to do with her life. Too bad she had no idea what they were. That's why she wouldn't quit until she happened upon that key that would unlock her passion for something.

She could only hope she'd recognize it when it did.

Somehow settling on a name brought the restaurant idea full circle and into the "this is really gonna happen" zone for Thane. As he and Jonah sat inside the future location for Longboard Pizza at a makeshift table—a sawhorse with a hunk of plywood on top—the sounds of whirling drills and swinging hammers soon became difficult to overcome.

As father and son went over ideas for the sign with Lilly, Thane raised his voice and asked, "I guess this wasn't the best place to do this. We can barely hear a thing."

"It's okay. I have kids, which means, I don't need silence to work," Lilly said, never looking up from her sketch pad, pencil in hand.

"I know how that is. I don't trust anyone who needs complete quiet to work." Thane watched as the talented wife and mother drew a rough draft of what they'd discussed earlier on the phone.

"It has to have a longboard on it," Jonah prompted. "This long," he added, holding out his arms wide, hoping to show length and width. "The surfboard's the most important part of the name."

"I won't forget," promised Lilly with a smile, still engrossed in her design.

"You don't think the pizza is the most important part?" Thane questioned. "I'll remind you of that when you're begging me for pepperoni."

"I like pepperoni."

"Who doesn't like pepperoni? Am I right, Lilly?"

"I guarantee you the whole town can't wait for their pepperoni fix," Lilly promised. "You'll be so busy the line will snake out the door and into the street. Wait and see. I hope you hired plenty of help."

Thane hoped so too. He'd talked to Fischer after breakfast. His longtime friend had already signed the papers to sublet his Lower East Side loft and make the move west. Fisch couldn't wait to pack up the car and make the drive cross-country, which was good news for Thane. It meant things were going as planned, staying on schedule. Once Fisch arrived, he could bunk in the spare room until a new place surfaced. It would all work out.

"Everywhere I go around town, people seem excited to have us open. I hope you're right," Thane said to Lilly.

About that time Perry Altman came through the door and walked up to where they were sitting on crates. The owner of the elegant fine-dining establishment, The Pointe, stuck his hand out and introduced himself over the hum of an electric saw in the background. "Hi, Lilly. I came to check out my competition."

"You serve New York-style pizza?" Thane wanted to know with a grin. He already knew the dish wasn't on Perry's menu.

"No, but I should have added it a long time ago. You have a great idea here and a perfect Main Street location to boot, right across from the church will get plenty of action."

"I'm not here to take business away from you," Thane stated.

"Oh, I know that," Perry said with a friendly smile. "If anything you'll cut more into McCready's business than mine. He serves the microwave cardboard stuff that makes people want to puke. When do you think you'll be open?"

Thane thumbed a shot over his shoulder in the direction of Ryder, Zach, and Troy. "If these guys have anything to do with it? Hopefully in about four weeks."

"You're lucky. When I remodeled that old fish hatchery of mine, I didn't have the advantage of hiring local talent. I had to hire a contractor out of San Sebastian and rely on his carpenters. Ryder, Troy, and Zach are a cut above the ones I used." Perry looked around at the space, the size of the kitchen, and the dining area. "This isn't that roomy but you've utilized every inch of space."

"Logan's doing," Thane explained. "I consulted him with an idea and he drew up a plan. Ryder, Troy and Zach followed through by stretching it into what we hope works on a daily basis. At least, I hope my chef thinks so too."

"Who'd you get to cook?"

"Fischer Robbins from Café Papillon near the Bowery."

Perry nodded and smiled knowingly. "French background to Italian pizza, that's a crazy chef for you. I've known a few in my time. Look, if you need anything at all, you let me know."

"You shouldn't offer that because I'm sure I'll bug the hell out of you."

"Bug away." Perry turned his attention to Lilly's drawings. "Longboard Pizza. Great name. I like it."

"Izzy thought it up," Jonah said, pointing to the figure standing in the doorway.

Thane followed his son's stare and said, "Hey, we were just about to come over and check on you." He looked her up and down in a thorough inspection. "Should you be out riding your bike with that bum knee of yours?"

"I'm fine. I had to get out. I felt too cooped up to stay inside. It's such a pretty day I walked here. Besides, exercise is good for the circulation, works out the soreness. What are you guys up to?"

Thane made the introductions to Perry and Lilly. "Lilly's working on my sign and Perry's here to offer his critique."

"No critique. I like what I see so far," Perry said, turning to Isabella. "I hear you thought up the name."

Izzy lifted one shoulder. "Seemed appropriate, what with these two loving to surf as much as they do."

"Well, it works. What you want is a catchy name that stands out. People will easily remember Longboard Pizza, those coming up from L.A. or over from San Sebastian. How many tables are you planning?" Perry asked, making a mental measure of the room.

"Six inside and three out."

"Outside? Where?" Isabella asked in surprise skimming the stingy amount of space. "On the street?"

Thane got up and walked over to the south window, shot a thumb in the direction of a weeded lot through a side door. "It doesn't look like much I know. But it came with the property. My plan is to take advantage of every square inch by pouring concrete in the eight-by-twelve-foot area and turn it into a garden-like setting with a few plants."

Isabella and Perry went over to inspect the overgrown weed patch but it was Perry who noted, "It has potential. String some lights overhead. Give it an Italian sidewalk café feel and it'll be perfect."

"That would be one way to go," Isabella offered in disagreement.

"What would you do?" Perry asked, leaving Thane out of the discussion.

"Just because you're serving Italian dishes and pizza, doesn't mean you have to play up the sidewalk café or bistro motif, especially here in a small town. People like the idea of something that stands out."

"Go on," Perry prompted.

Izzy opened the door and stood on the dirt surveying the overgrown lot. "For starters out here on the patio you'll need more than a few plants. I'd say, start with a simple bed along the building to the border of the cement. Play up the outdoor setting with various herbs, like rosemary. It grows taller than you think and is often used as a hedge. And you'll need an overhang in the event of bad weather."

"Oh, I like this girl," Perry decided. "So, no bistro angle then? It is a tiny space. What does he do for the inside?

She hobbled back into the place, tilted her head to study the windows and walls. "You'll have tourists in the summer, but the locals will be your bread and butter. Play up the name of the restaurant, Longboard *and* Pizza. Make it a tribute to what you love to eat, what you enjoy doing, and that's living by the ocean, making your life here." She turned in a circle but then stopped short when she thought of something else. "Oh. Wait. I'm forgetting you obviously do love football. You *are* a former jock."

"That's okay," Thane said with a grin. "Everyone will expect a former player to cram his restaurant with football memorabilia. There's a ton of players who do that. Let's do something different, go another direction. I grew up here surfing long before I ever started playing football. I taught Jonah how to dog paddle out in the bay on one of the visits to see my mother. This will give customers a glimpse into the new me. I've moved on from football, they should too."

"Are you sure?" Izzy asked. "Because we can certainly think up a name that reflects your time spent with the Giants."

"Nope. I like the surfing idea. What about you, Jonah?"

"Yeah, I like that, too."

"Well, I happen to think the girl knows her stuff," Perry said in delight. "You should listen to her. I can't wait to hear what else she has on her mind."

"Really?" Isabella said, a bit astonished.

"Absolutely. What about the tables? If you lose the sidewalk café feel, what's left for the tables?" Perry wanted to know.

"No tablecloths, that's for sure, too formal and predictable. Instead, once again, play up the surfing angle." She chewed on her lower lip and finally added, "You could buy old recycled tables, use old surfboards for the tabletops. Laminate them, that way it would be a lot less maintenance. Laminate is durable and keeps its gloss over time. Just wipe up and go."

Thane's mouth dropped open. "That's...brilliant."

"I don't know if I'd go that far," Isabella said. "But I do know that just because you offer casual dining, it doesn't mean that it has to look tacky or predictable."

Perry nodded in approval. "Nice touch. My guess, though, is you'll have a lot of takeout, the casual diner. Picture the phone ringing off the wall, especially on Friday and Saturday nights. It won't hurt to be prepared for the weekend dine-in crowd though. And you'll obviously stay busy during weekdays at lunch. Maybe you could create a few specials for that, offer smaller pizzas during the week. Then there's the after-church crowd on Sundays. You will be open then, right?"

"Sure." Pleased that they took such an interest in how the place looked, Thane took advantage of their expertise and presented them with another problem he'd been mulling over. "I hate leaving the walls white. But I have no idea which way to go in here. All I know is that I want it to pop. What would you suggest for the interior décor?"

Isabella thought for a moment. "To stand out, I'd go with a map on the wall depicting all the legendary surfing spots up and down the California coast." Not waiting for a reply or reaction to her suggestion, she went on, "You could do actual surfing photos or a mural."

Thane laughed and looked at Jonah, ruffled his hair. "Okay, I guess we know where to go for the best advice on decorating." He glanced over at Lilly. "Could you do a mural like that if I provide a few pictures?"

"Absolutely. Or anything else you come up with. Everything you do in here sets the tone for the restaurant."

"I'm excited, Daddy," Jonah admitted.

"Me too, Jonah. Me too." And for the first time since coming back home and starting this crazy project, he really meant it.

After Lilly and Perry left, Ryder, Zach and Troy broke for lunch, leaving a serene, peaceful cloud hanging in their wake.

Thane took the opportunity to turn to Isabella and opened the laptop he'd brought with him. He logged in, hit a few keystrokes to get to the website where he stored the pictures online he'd taken himself.

"You mentioned surfing photos and it got me to thinking. There's this trip I took up the coast with a bunch of guys in high school. We went to a place known as Mavericks near Pillar Point Harbor." He angled the screen where she could see the photo. "Would this do for a focal point on the wall?"

She studied an image of a young man about seventeen, but even then he sported muscular shoulders. He wore a wetsuit, his hair wet and long and he stood smiling holding his surfboard. "This is perfect. This is exactly what represents that glimpse into your history and your link to California and ultimately your ties to the town."

"You think so?"

"Definitely. People will love seeing this on the front wall. The great Thane Delacourt as a teenager before he made it to the NFL." She began to hit the arrow keys which revealed more of his personal snapshots. When she landed on an aerial view of the Brooklyn and Manhattan Bridges that spanned the East River, she looked over at him. "These are stunning shots. You're a good photographer."

"I took most of these the first year I played for the Giants." He chuckled. "I remember walking around the city like a tourist with a Nikon strapped around my neck. It was fairly embarrassing because I wouldn't go anywhere without it. Back then, I must have taken a picture of anything that moved and a whole lot that didn't."

Aw, how endearing was that? she decided as she continued to click through the string of albums. Studying each shot, she focused on the panoramic view of Manhattan and the Brooklyn Bridge lit up at night. One in particular caught her eye. "You must have taken this photo walking across the bridge toward the city."

He enjoyed watching her eyes sparkle as she flicked through each folder. It was almost like touring New York with her by his side.

When her eyes landed on a view of the skyline at sunset, her enthusiasm burst out, "Oh, my God, this is beautiful."

Thane peered around, smiled. "I took that from the terrace at The River Café, first-time diner and nervous about getting an invite to a black-tie private party to eat with the mayor. That's the New York Harbor and across that is Manhattan in the background."

"The River Café, that's the restaurant under the Brooklyn Bridge, right?"

Thane laughed, "Yeah. It was fairly impressive. But that was before Hurricane Sandy hit and closed the place down. It took them fifteen months to remodel the place to get it back to the way it had been. It only reopened this past February. But the memories I have of the night I took all these pictures are still with me."

"Well, the view is absolutely spectacular. You captured the exact amount of light. It offers the best of both daylight and dusk." She turned in a circle, faced the side wall. "You've come full circle here, haven't you, Thane?"

"I guess I have. Look, if you're free tonight, how would you like to come by the house and have a meal with Jonah and me? It won't be River Café fancy, but you won't go away hungry. I'll pop *Despicable Me*, which is Jonah's favorite movie at the moment. That changes with the tide..." His voice trailed off because he could see the invitation put her off. "Obviously, you aren't interested. Sorry I misread all this, what we're doing now, as interest."

"I have to go," she said with enough frost in her voice to form a small iceberg.

Nonplussed at her change in attitude, Thane watched her pivot on her bum knee and all but bolt out the front door as fast as she could manage to walk.

A couple of minutes later the guys came back in to finish up their work for the day.

"What happened with Isabella?" Zach asked Thane.

"What do you mean? Why do you ask?"

"Because I just saw her storm out of here."

"She did, didn't she? Damned if I know why. We were having a normal conversation about the images to use as wall décor and when I asked her if she wanted to come over to the house to have dinner and a movie, she couldn't get out of here fast enough."

"Hmm, I guess it isn't just me then. She's snobby like that to everyone."

"Told you it wasn't personal," Troy tossed out as he went to pick up his drill to get back to installing shelving and cabinets.

"What are you guys talking about?" Thane wanted to know.

"Isabella. She's been standoffish for months now, ever since she got here," Zach grumbled.

"Ah, well, I didn't know you two had a thing going on," Thane stated.

"Not a thing at all, not with me anyway," Zach said in denial. "I've tried to have a couple of conversations with her though. She's always polite but...clearly reserved and not interested."

"You called her snooty," Troy corrected.

"Yeah, Zach took her attitude personally," Ryder explained.

Zach skewed up his mouth. "I guess I did. But I'm taking Drea over to Santa Cruz tonight for dinner and a movie. I'm not interested in pursuing Isabella, although she is a looker."

"No argument there," Thane agreed.

Zach slapped Thane on the back. Then the door's wide open for you, my friend."

"I don't think so. I have zero time in my life right now for a woman with an attitude, let alone a high-maintenance one."

"High-maintenance? She doesn't strike me like that," Ryder said. "I've known women who were. But then, what do I know about the ways of the female mind? All I *do* know is that Julianne invited her to a barbeque on Memorial Day and she took a pass. There've been other functions where she did the same thing."

"That day she rode her bike down the hill, stopped for two minutes to tell us she had somewhere else to be," Zach added. "I guess she had other fish to fry."

"We assumed she was headed over to Logan and Kinsey's house at the time," Troy offered. "Gotta be a logical reason she's keeping to herself so much."

"I've seen women act that same way after they've spent time in an abusive relationship," Ryder proffered. "My mother's a nurse, dragged me to one of those women's shelters a couple times where she forced me to volunteer to put on a new roof."

Thane started to disagree with that but then thought of yesterday at the doctor's office. There had been something odd about Doc Prescott's reaction to finding him there waiting when she came out of the exam room, something that seemed off. Doc's attitude had bordered on chilly. At the time, he hadn't thought much about it. But now it made him wonder, not just about Doc but about the woman with the sultry green eyes. Could that be it? Could Isabella have been physically abused? Maybe she wanted nothing to do with men.

"If that's true, it's a shame she'd put up with that," Zach said. "Makes me want to find the bastard and give him the same type of payback."

Troy nodded. "I could get on board with that."

"Make it three," Thane admitted. "With no problem whatsoever."

"Well, if we find this guy he'd be surrounded and outgunned, that's for sure," Ryder noted. "No offense, Thane, but I don't even think the three of us would need your muscle."

"None taken, but you can't leave me out entirely. Do you suppose it's true? Or are we jumping to a conclusion where there's no proof?"

Troy made a sound in his throat that had Thane eyeing him with open interest. "If you know something about her past now would be a good time to mention it." Thane said with an edge to his voice.

"Nothing definite, but I did overhear a conversation once when I stopped by Logan's house. I was there to pick up a set of plans he'd done to redo my kitchen in the house I'm remodeling. When he left the living room to get them out of his study, I heard him talking to someone. It was Isabella's voice talking about a guy by the name of Henry. It was obvious by the tone of their voices neither one of them cared for this guy too much. It was odd. As I stood there waiting, Kinsey walked through the door and called out that she was home. Right away, Isabella and Logan stopped talking and came out to the hallway, dropping the subject entirely."

"That doesn't mean much," Thane pointed out. "Isabella often goes over there to babysit the kids."

"I guess you had to be there. It was like the two of them had a secret they didn't want Kinsey to hear. Not only that when they came out of the study, Logan had forgotten to bring the blueprints. He had to go back and get them."

"Maybe Logan's stepping out on Kinsey. Maybe they're having an affair," Zach volunteered.

"Whoa. I'm not prepared to go down that road," Thane said. "That's a huge leap."

"Me either," Ryder proclaimed. "First of all, I don't think Logan would ever do that to Kinsey."

"That's not the kind of secret I meant," Troy said, throwing a glare at Zach. "Don't you dare go out of here repeating gossip like that, understand?"

Zach held up his hands. "Okay. Okay. Just thinking outside the box here, offering suggestions, reasons why she'd act like she does."

"Well, don't go down that path," Thane warned. "I know how rumors get out of control enough to cause major damage, especially if it's nothing more than speculation."

"I'm not out to hurt anyone," Zach said in his own defense. "I guess I decided last spring, Isabella might be gorgeous but she's just too complicated for me to handle right now with everything else. That's all I'm saying. I might've wanted to ask her out, but something always held me back. I'm glad now I didn't." Zach shrugged and added, "Sorry but I'm just being honest. I think I'll knock off early, go get ready for my date with Drea. Hopefully my self-imposed abstinence has an end in sight."

"Thanks for planting that image in my head," Thane grumbled as he watched Zach pack up his tools and disappear out the doorway. "Is it just me or does Zach enjoy stirring things up?"

"It's his specialty," Troy clarified. "If it weren't for the fact that he's about to become my brother-in-law in November, I might try and take him down a peg."

"His attitude doesn't cause rancor between the three of you?"

"Not really," Ryder answered. "Troy and I are used to all the different personalities that come together on a construction job. But with Zach, it's true you never quite know what will fall out of his mouth."

A little nervous about the night ahead with Zach Dennison, Drea did something she rarely did, even when business was slow—she closed up her flower shop three minutes early. After turning the closed sign around on the door, she made her way upstairs to shower and get ready.

The year she'd opened her business, to save every penny she could, she'd turned the industrial space directly above the store into an open, livable loft. What had started out as a cost-saving measure ended up being the best decision she'd made since high school. She loved the fact that after a long day dealing with customers and filling orders, sometimes playing delivery driver, she could simply walk up a flight of stairs and into her own personal, sunny space.

Once she reached the landing, she opened the front door and crossed over the polished hardwood floor to the bank of windows. From her vantage point, she looked out on the grounds of The Plant Habitat, the garden center her aunt and uncle owned. The nursery supplied all of her inventory.

She'd grown up in a household where the exchange of bad, cruel words had been the norm. It had taken a traumatic event to change all that.

Her brother, Cooper, had reverted to his birth name, Richmond, officially changing it over the summer. She and her other brother, Caleb, had talked about doing the same. But it seemed a rude gesture to the people who had taken them in and given them a home. In Drea's mind, taking in three kids that no one else wanted at the time could only fall into two categories. It was either incredibly brave or incredibly foolish. However anyone chose to classify it, her mother's brother, Landon, and his wife, Shelby, had done the impossible. They'd given three kids from a dysfunctional home the only stable environment they'd ever known. Going to court to ask for the Richmond name back made for an awkward situation she wanted to avoid if at all possible.

Not that she didn't support Cooper's decision to honor their father she did. Caleb felt the same way. Layne Richmond deserved better than having a manipulative shrew for a wife and dying at the hands of said shrew. Eleanor Jennings Richmond had taken a .38 and aimed it at her husband's heart. It wasn't every florist that could say her mother had killed her father. Drea could. Several weeks back, Eleanor had even called collect from the Santa Cruz jail and wanted to talk. Drea had declined to take her mother's call.

She was still chewing on the name change issue when she went into the bathroom to turn on the water for her shower. While the water got hot her mind shifted to Zach. They'd known each other forever, gone to school together. Which made her wonder why they had never gone out before now.

"Because he's never seemed one bit interested in you," she muttered aloud, answering her own query. Stripping off her jeans and shirt, she added, "That's why you had to be the one to ask him out."

But grousing wasn't what had gotten her a date, audacity and brashness had.

Later, after spending an inordinate time on her hair, she decided she could only work with the attributes she'd been given at birth—wild hair that couldn't be tamed unless she used something to take out the curl along with alabaster skin that didn't bode well in the sun.

Dressed in her burgundy cocktail dress, she stood in front of the mirror and turned in a circle. When the buzzer sounded downstairs she conceded that the outfit showed off her dark mane rather well and even managed to flatter her contrasting milky skin tone.

The thought of Zach Dennison waiting on the other side of the door gave her just enough incentive to take the steps two at a time. The man had always been a bit predictable, if not staid in his attitudes, even back in middle school. She wasn't after altering that about him, mainly because she saw his hardworking persona as a major plus. Her brothers were much the same in their work habits. But was it wrong to want to be the one to add a layer of whimsy to Zach Dennison's life? To decorate that otherwise bland canvas he seemed to tote around with a splash of color? Like arranging white daisies in the same vase alongside an array of dazzling fall mums, a flash of red and gold might be just the ticket to chisel away his industrious veneer.

Making a mad dash to the door left her breathless. "You're right on time," she sang out.

"It was a light day. I was able to knock off early."

"I'll just get my wrap."

"You look amazing, Drea."

"Thanks. I'm glad you noticed."

"Hard not to in that outfit."

"You work entirely too hard."

"I don't have much of a choice. The pizza place has a start date. Thane's counting on us to finish the work so it will open on time. Same with Ryder and Troy, they depend on me to carry my fair share of the load. I won't disappoint them."

"What's on the agenda for tonight?"

"There's a place in Santa Cruz that plays live music. I thought we could eat dinner first and drop in for a drink and a little dancing."

"Why Zach, I do believe you've captured my interest," she said with a laugh. "Remember that play we put on in sixth grade?"

Zach's face broke out into a wide grin. "The one with the old-time square dancing? How could I ever forget that I never got the hang of swinging my partner around the old haystack? It made me feel like I had two left feet."

As they walked to Zach's truck, Drea leaned in and boldly kissed him on the mouth. "I thought I'd get that out of the way first thing."

He pulled her into him—the biting and nipping escalating to a frothy steam. Caught up, the energy of the kiss pulled them into a maelstrom, one full of gusts and gale.

Out of breath, Drea took it one step further. "Did you really want to make that long drive to Santa Cruz tonight?"

Zach sent her a knowing look. "Not really. What do you say we go back inside and find something else to do?"

"I thought you'd never ask."

Chapter Seven

Jonah insisted on macaroni and cheese for dinner. Instead of making it out of a box, Thane spent almost an hour rummaging through drawers and cabinets in the kitchen looking for his mother's recipe. He finally found it stuck inside a pocket folder mislabeled desserts.

He picked up the beer he'd opened and guzzled down a good long drink before going over the ingredients, making sure he had all the necessary stuff on hand.

As a single dad, Thane wasn't that different from most parents. He worried about providing a healthy diet for a six-year-old picky eater who had a long list of things he refused to eat. He was pleased with himself when he decided to substitute low-fat cheese and milk in place of his mother's higher calorie version.

While waiting for the elbow macaroni to boil and the oven to preheat, he got curious and rifled through a treasure trove of old Betty Crocker cookbooks he found under the cabinet. Thumbing through the pages, he discovered other recipes that might fall into the "Jonah will eat" category he could use for later meals. Things like homemade spaghetti and eggplant parmesan. As he read the instructions, he marked the pages for future reference, wondering where anyone found the time to make their own whole grain pastas from scratch. Not that it wasn't a sound idea, he decided. But it had him questioning how his working mom ever truly found the time to do anything else outside the kitchen.

Maybe instead of a nanny he needed to hire a cook. Thane knew his friend Fischer would surely take over kitchen duties as soon as the man got here, but that was a short-term fix and didn't solve the problem of creating wholesome meals on a long-term regular basis.

"Is it ready yet?" Jonah said, boosting himself up on one of the bar stools at the island counter. "Can I have an Oreo? When do we eat?"

"Soon. And no. You wanted mac and cheese and it still has to bake. Set out the milk and cheese for me, will you? And the butter." Thane got down a casserole dish and removed the pasta from the stove. He used a colander to drain the pasta, scooping a third of it out and into the bottom of the stoneware dish. He cubed the butter Jonah handed him and set it aside. "You want to layer the cheddar slices for me?"

"Sure. I like doing this part." Jonah peeled off the squares of cheese from the stack and, one by one, placed them on top of the macaroni.

Thane reached over his son's shoulders, added a dab of butter to each piece before spreading another layer of macaroni on top. They repeated the process until it formed a mound above the rim.

After slipping the concoction into the oven and setting the timer, he began to put together a salad. He got out the fruits and veggies—lettuce, apples, jicama, red peppers—he knew Jonah would eat.

"How long do we wait now? Can I have a cookie?"

"Not long, and no you can't have a cookie before we eat. Don't ask again. It won't take that long. This just has to melt so it'll get gooey and cheesy and brown on top the way you like it."

"Why did Mimi have to die?"

The jicama slicing came to a halt in mid-chop. Thane stopped the motion of the knife, let out a sigh. "Because she got real sick."

"Cancer, right? Tommy says lots of old people get it."

Geez, thought Thane, how was he supposed to explain to a child that anyone could get it, young or old. He didn't want his son getting nightmares every time a sore throat made it difficult to swallow. He took the simple path. "The cancer made her really tired so her body didn't work the way it was supposed to anymore."

"Oh. Can we buy her flowers and take them to her like we did before? Tommy says you should do that at least once a month."

Geez, who knew Archer's son would turn out so all-knowing. But Thane kept that to himself. "Sure. Tomorrow we'll go out and buy some of those lilies she liked, take them out to the cemetery to put on her headstone. How's that sound?"

"'K. She liked those."

"She did. Anything else you want to talk about?" Thane wanted to know while he continued to slice and dice. When that was done he handed Jonah several pieces of apple to tide him over before moving on to blending together their own favorite dressing. He peeled and smashed garlic, grated fresh ginger, drizzled olive oil and squeezed lemon juice into a bowl along with salt and pepper. He plopped in a carton of Greek yogurt, whisked it all up. He stuck his finger in the bowl, swiped enough to taste, shook his head "Needs honey."

"I wanna taste," Jonah sang out as the timer dinged, which had him clapping his hands. "Food!"

The casserole came out of the oven. While it cooled, Thane poured a glass of milk, set it in front of Jonah. He dished salad on two plates before adding the pasta to the side. "Here you go, buddy. Dig in."

They both dug into the meal with a zestful appetite until the doorbell rang. Thane got up, strolled to the front door with his napkin still in his hand.

He was surprised to see Isabella standing on the porch. Looking around for her bike, he didn't see it anywhere. "Did you walk here? You really need to stay off that leg. Doctor's orders."

"I've interrupted dinner. I'm sorry. But I wanted to apologize for abruptly leaving this afternoon."

"It's okay. Come on in. Have you eaten?"

"Uh. No. But I couldn't impose like that."

"Sure you could. But I'll warn you it's nothing fancy."

He led the way back to the table where Jonah had cleared his plate. "Izzy! What are you doin' here?"

"Hi, Jonah. I needed to talk to your dad."

"Want some of Dad's mac and cheese? It's his special recipe that my Mimi used to make."

"Sure. What makes it special?"

"It doesn't come out of a blue box," said Jonah and chortled with laughter. "Wanna see my Ninja Turtles?" The boy didn't wait for an answer but took off running to his room.

"He's a livewire, isn't he?"

Thane piled a plate high and handed it off. "And then some. Want a glass of wine with that?"

"You read my mind."

From the small refrigerated wine cooler at the end of the counter, he picked a bottle that promised a rich black fruity flavor with vanilla and got down two glasses. "You know, for Jonah's first four months of life, he cried a lot, his body withdrawing from the drug."

"Thane, that's horrific."

"Oh, it was, and very difficult to watch. Here, let's sit down and eat." They settled around the table and he watched her take her first bite, waited for her reaction.

"Ohmygod. This is fantastic. It melts in your mouth. There must be a thousand calories on this one plate."

"Focus on the salad," he said with a grin, picking up his wine.

"This dressing is delicious."

"I made it myself."

"You're kidding?"

"Nope, I do have some basic cooking skills." He took her through the simple recipe.

"I'll have to try it. Tell me more about Jonah's early years."

"Well, I couldn't take him home from the hospital until he'd kicked the goddamn stuff. Sorry, but that's the way I still feel to this day about watching him go through that. To make matters worse, he only weighed four pounds when he was born. So he was in an incubator. Even though I couldn't actually touch him, I used to put my hands through the mitten things and make sure he knew someone was there for him."

She could picture his big hands reaching in to swallow up the infant. "When did you get to take him home?"

"At eighteen weeks. And that's when he started to thrive. Don't get me wrong, it wasn't a walk in the park even then. We had some close calls with his breathing. And there were times when I worried about the SIDS thing. I was scared he might forget to breathe and die in his crib."

"It must've been scary for a single father."

"It'd be scary for anyone. I think I might've gone crazy if it hadn't been for the help I got from my parents and my sister. Tessa was in the middle of her residency at the time. She was a tremendous help to me."

"She's a doctor?"

"A pediatric surgeon. Anyway, Jonah didn't mind being held like some crack babies do. All of us took turns holding him to make sure he got used to a human touch after spending so much time in the incubator. Then later, we worked extra hard on his speech and motor skills. It wasn't an easy time, let me tell you. And when he was around three the doctors thought he might have ADD because he had so much energy. My mom and I started working with him and his symptoms seemed to even out. We decided he could focus just fine. Given his rough start in life, I'd say he's a pretty normal kid. Or maybe I'm just used to his boundless energy and motor mouth," he added with a grin.

About that time, Jonah came back in with his arms full of Ninja Turtles and an assortment of action figures. "Here, look, see, I brought a van for them to ride in and everything." The bright green vehicle slipped out of his grasp and crashed to the floor with a clatter.

"Jonah," Thane said using a firm tone. "Did you get enough to eat?"

"Uh-huh."

"Okay, then let Izzy finish eating and then you can show off your Captain America. How's that sound?"

"O-kay," he said in a downhearted voice. But it didn't last long until the boy had switched gears. "Want to watch *Despicable Me* with me after supper?"

Izzy shot Thane a knowing look and smiled. "I'd love to."

"Cool." With that, Jonah dropped the action figures and watched as they scattered every which way which meant the little guy had to scoot between the chairs to retrieve them underfoot.

"Welcome to my world," Thane said, raising his glass again. He peeked down at Jonah, rooted to his new encampment under the table and then looked over at Izzy. "One thing you can say about this house, we have something going on every minute of every day."

Surprisingly that sounded appealing to Izzy. Drawn to the havoc Jonah created, she admitted, "I used to hide under the table during thunderstorms." She giggled and added, "But I finally outgrew that by the time I turned eight."

"See, it's a phase." But about that time Jonah bumped his head on the table, which prompted Thane to augment the statement. "At least I hope it is."

"I'm sure it'll run its course before he gets to middle school."

"Great. Thanks for that image. It's like that old Robin Williams skit where he says that every parent has two visions when they hold their child for the first time. One, you see your kid as an adult thanking the Nobel Prize

Committee. The other one is he's asking, 'Do you want fries with that?' It was hilarious the first time I heard it. But I didn't have Jonah then. The thing you learn is that it's absolutely true." He met her eyes and asked, "Did you ever want kids?"

"I did once."

"What stopped you?"

"I married the wrong man."

Since Jonah sat within earshot, Thane's reaction came with some degree of restriction. Instead, he simply chewed the last bite of macaroni and sat back. "It hurts doesn't it? That moment you realize you've made a horrendous misjudgment and hooked up with a person you thought you knew but didn't."

"Emotionally and physically it takes a toll, especially when you pay for it several hundred times over."

"I'm sorry."

"While Jonah made boisterous booming noises with his action figures, Izzy stood up to clear the mess off the table.

"You don't have to do that. I'll get it later after I put Jonah to bed."

"I eat your food, I clean up. Them's my rules. Besides, it goes faster if we form an assembly line. I'll rinse and load the dishwasher, you hand it off."

"Linebackers usually don't hand off. If they had good hands they'd be playing on the offensive side of the ball instead. But I see your logic."

She poked a finger into his ribs. "You're a funny guy, Thane Delacourt."

"I always try to keep my sense of humor while doing my household chores, especially vacuuming. That's really a mindless job where your brain tends to lock up on you and wander if you let it."

Jonah finally crawled out from under the table. "Daddy, you promised I could have popcorn with the movie."

"You just got done with dinner. Okay. Sure. Pick up all your toys and take them to your room first though. Remember? That's part of the rules."

"Oh yeah, I forgot. Then popcorn and Minions!" the boy yelled, skidding off to grab his toys and pack up the mess he'd made.

"At least he attacks his chores with gusto," Izzy noted.

"He does, but they mostly center on him keeping the floor of his room picked up enough to walk around and get to the bed. You're catching him on a good day."

As the three of them settled in front of the TV the smell of freshly popped corn drifted in the air. Jonah took up a position between the two of them. For the next forty-five minutes, Minions ruled. But the familiar movie Jonah had seen so often before wasn't enough to hold his attention for long or keep him awake. Not even Margo, Edith and Agnes could keep him from nodding off during the kidnapping or Gru's boldly stealing the moon.

Thane looked at his sleeping son then over at Izzy. Since supper he'd been stewing about something that wouldn't let go. Truth is it had been bothering him for two days straight. Something about Izzy alluding to her past meant she might be ready to unload the truth.

"What did you mean earlier when you said you paid several hundred times over for marrying the wrong man?"

"He liked to settle an argument the old-fashioned way. His way meant force, force equaled loyalty and no argument about anything."

The implication sank in and explained her bully comments the day before. It also went a long way to figuring out why she'd kept her distance. It answered the big mystery Zach had put forth. "Where is the bastard now?"

"I finally wised up and divorced his sorry ass. Last I heard, he lives somewhere in the south of France with the poor, unfortunate woman who crossed his psychotic path." Izzy leaned in and whispered the rest so there was no chance of Jonah waking up and overhearing. "She's welcome to the brutal son of a bitch."

Thane chuckled at the way she said it. "Good for you. But don't you sometimes live in fear he'll find where you are and show up out of the blue?"

She looked away without raising doubt, her answer firm. "Nope. He's too cowardly to pick a fight with another man. Logan would beat his ass into the ground if he comes anywhere near me."

"Logan?" Zach's accusation reared its ugly head and began to circle Thane's head like a pack of vultures.

"Yes, Logan. Long story. The man's like a brother to me."

For some reason, relief moved through him, putting Zach's words back in the garbage where they belonged.

"Sure, there was a time I spent my fair share of sleepless nights worrying that somehow my ex would find me and kill me for leaving him. Because he'd promised that's what he'd do enough times. Look, if you don't mind, I'd like to talk about something else. I really don't like talking about him."

"No problem. I need to put Jonah to bed. Will you wait here?"

Their eyes met, green to blue. The look ignited heat simmering just below the surface, rousing desire in both long gone dormant.

"Sure." She watched as Thane scooped Jonah up and carried him into the bedroom. As soon as he disappeared into the hallway, a case of sweaty palms and nerves hit Isabella. She fanned her face with a hand, all the while wondering if she should bolt for the door. That would be the chicken way out, she decided.

She drew in a timid breath, resolved to see this through, even if it meant making an ass out of herself. Rudeness had been what brought her here to apologize. Sharing a meal hadn't been part of her equation. But then neither had lust. She couldn't very well dash out the door while he was tucking his son into bed.

"Don't look as though you're about to swallow nasty-tasting medicine," Thane said from the doorway of the great room. "I'm really not that bad."

"But I am." She grimaced at the memory of making love to a man she'd grown to despise over the years. "I always was a disappointment to him, my ex, about so many things."

"Shhh. None of that. You don't have to talk about him." He sat down, picked up her hand and took her chin. "I'm pretty sure I remember how this goes." He moved in, measured and slow, determined not to spook her. But when he realized she was trembling, he backed off, putting a good foot between them. "Isabella?"

"What?"

As much as he wanted to kiss that mouth, he heard himself say, "We'll wait until you aren't repulsed or shaking at the thought of being near me."

"I... I'm not repulsed." She reached for her wine glass, knocked back the contents.

He took the glass out of her hand, let out a solid laugh. "Now there's good news. Knowing you aren't repulsed by me. That's the best newsflash I've heard in three months. But getting you drunk is hardly the route I'd take to talking you into bed."

"I believe in full disclosure which means you should know it's been a long time for me. And I wasn't all that great at it before so... I doubt I've improved over time without any practice."

"Shh," he murmured again as he moved to her mouth.

Right before their lips touched, she couldn't seem to keep her mouth from moving. "Three months, is that how long it's been for you?" Appalled at her own boldness, her hand flew to her mouth, her fingernail scraping his chin. "I'm sorry. See, I'm nervous... I had no right to ask such a personal question... I didn't mean to be so nosy. I didn't mean to scratch you."

He stilled her nerves by telling her, "Take a breath. It's been longer than that for me. And you? How long has it been for you?"

"I don't even want to think about the last time."

He watched as she made a face and then uttered in disgust, "Okay, three years. I don't even miss it. At least not with *him*."

Thane tugged her closer, put his arm around her shoulder in a casual way, picked up the remote with the other hand to turn the channel. "Then let's find something to watch on cable. Let's try to remember, it's Saturday night. Somewhere in the world two single adults went out on a normal date for dinner and a movie. Remember those days of old? Anyway, people do this all the time. Let's see if we can emulate them."

"It doesn't have to be a chick flick. I like action and thrillers too," Isabella said, trying to pretend his arm wasn't wrapped around her. "But maybe nothing too horror-related since I do live alone."

"Got it, so we'll avoid serial killer themes this late at night." The selections onscreen were pitiful but when he landed on *Fargo* he stopped. "How about a little Marge Gunderson to lighten the mood?"

"Sure. A lot can happen in the middle of nowhere," Isabella quipped, repeating the tag line as the credits rolled.

But with sexual attraction hanging in the air, neither one was in the right frame of mind to stay glued to the familiar plot points for long.

Isabella wondered how long she intended to deny herself human contact. She needed someone to touch her, to hold her, to make her feel wanted. Midway through the film, she turned to him, a huge furrowed brow on her face. "Earlier I wanted to kiss you. I wanted you to kiss me. I didn't mean to tense up like that."

He ran a long, lean finger down her cheek. "I'm new at taking things slow. Life for me, outside of Jonah, has been a fast ramp up to getting what I wanted."

"And?"

"It's just as well because I don't want to be attracted to you—for a variety of reasons. It isn't personal."

"That's blunt. Okay."

He shook his head. "I'm a healthy adult male. Something would be seriously wrong with me if I wasn't attracted to you."

That statement had her scooting closer. "So you are?"

"If you have to ask, then I must be losing my touch." Hands still in his lap in a nonthreatening gesture, he leaned in, met her lips with his.

For her, it took a moment for his taste to seep in. When it did, an ember flamed up. This was arousal, pure and wild. It ripped through her like a brush fire igniting the soul. She clung to him, a fierce need pulling, tugging, leading her straight into the searing blaze.

When they finally pulled apart, she wasn't sure what to do next. But Thane did. With his hand he guided her head to his shoulder, kissed the strands of golden-brown hair falling over her eyes. "Relax. We'll take this slow."

"But Thane Delacourt isn't used to taking things slow," she pointed out.

"Does it look like I'm living the fast life here with a six-year-old?"

"I guess not."

When Izzy glanced down at her watch, the dial read twelve-fifty-five. She jumped to her feet. "Oh my God, it's almost one o'clock. I didn't mean to stay this long. I need to get out of here and let you get some sleep."

"Isabella?"

"What?"

"I can't walk you home because I won't leave Jonah in the house, even for ten minutes alone, even if he's sleeping. He's been known to wake up in the middle of the night and come get in bed with me. If I'm not here or he can't find me…"

"It's okay. I wouldn't want you to do that anyway. I'll be fine."

"You don't understand. I don't want you walking home by yourself in the dark. For one, your head is still not a hundred percent. Two, your knee isn't either. If you had to run, you'd have a hard time of it."

"Thane, this is Pelican Pointe. What could happen here?" But even as she said it, her mind drifted to Henry. And Thane saw the expression on her face full of apprehension too.

"How about crashing in the guest room tonight? It's all ready for when Fischer gets here, clean sheets on the bed and everything."

"I couldn't do that."

"Why not? I'm not going to jump you in the night after you fall asleep."

She grinned. "I know that. But it's silly to bunk here when I have a perfectly nice home on the hill."

"Okay, give me a minute. I'll go wake up Jonah and carry him with me while I walk you home."

"That's a sneaky way to get me to stay and you know it. I won't let you wake up Jonah just so you can see me home safely. That's ridiculous."

"It's the linebacker mentality. We fight dirty and we're the most stubborn people you'll ever want to meet on the planet. If you'll follow me, Ms. Rialto, I'll show you to your room for the night."

"Thane?"

"What?"

"Thanks."

"No problem. Let me know if you need anything."

"I'll be out of your hair first thing in the morning."

"What's your hurry?"

"I don't want my staying here to confuse Jonah. Then there are the tongues wagging at the coffee shop. News travels fast around here like the speed of light."

"Bright and early it is then. How do you like your eggs?"

Chapter Eight

Birthdays were meant for indulgences. Hers started out like most other festive celebrations were supposed to— a nice dinner out at a five-star restaurant with a few close friends complete with presents—little gag gifts that were both funny and heartfelt.

The wait staff had even sung Happy Birthday to her while holding a slice of sugary cake and rich ice cream topped with a single candle.

The night had held such promise. He'd arranged it all, acted cheery during dinner, almost jovial over his dessert and coffee.

It was the blood and smashed face that came later.

But even during the drive home she'd known he was ramping up into one of his dark mood swings. There were times she marveled at the way he could transform himself from a funny guy one minute into a raging nutcase the next, especially when he consumed alcohol. Sometimes, of course, he managed it without the booze.

"You were all over Allan tonight."

"No, I wasn't. Allan was seated next to me at the table. The closest I came to being 'all over him' as you suggest was leaning in so that I could hear what he had to say. The music was so loud in there. I merely..."

"Excuses. You always give me excuses. You were the center of attention tonight and wanted him to put his hands on you. I could tell."

"You know that's ludicrous. Allan's wife, Maureen, was sitting on the other side of him within earshot. I've known Maureen since we were children."

The familiar allegation was like an old refrain that refused to go away. He went on and on for miles. There wasn't enough wine in the city to insulate her from his usual tactics. Tonight she refused to bolster his ego. In fact, she was fed up with all the effort it took to get it done and the trap he invariably set to get a reaction out of her. Well aware of the pitfalls and the consequences of argument, she reached over and simply turned up the volume on the CD player. Vivaldi soared from the speakers filling the car with stormy strings—a shift in moods—a precursor to what was to come.

By this time, he'd pulled into the driveway of their suburban home. As soon as the car came to a stop in the garage, she grabbed her keys and got out of the car. She circled the hood to unlock the door and hurried inside, knowing he was right on her heels.

She tried to move quickly down the hallway but he cornered her in the kitchen.

The slap knocked her back a step. But it was the fist to the face that sent her reeling backward. Off-balance, she tried to run, but he grabbed her hair and dragged her into the bedroom. He spun her down to the bed and crawled on top of her. She turned her head to avoid the next punch— which is why it connected to her cheek and not her eye. She did her best to fight him off, but he got tired of the struggle and pinned her arms down to keep her from the defensive gesture. She kept turning her head back and forth, back and forth to dodge his next blow. But he kept slapping her and anywhere he could reach, refusing to let up. She attempted to roll off the bed but the repeated blows kept coming and coming and coming...

Isabella floated out of the toxic dream in layers, eventually rousing fully awake. The wet sheets were the first indication she was sweating like she'd run a mile in the heat of summer. Her body felt like it had been punched, the bruises fresh.

An unfamiliar room greeted her as she glanced around at the four walls. Then she remembered she'd agreed to sleep in Thane's guest room. Her eyes landed on the clock radio next to the bed. The time told her she hadn't been asleep longer than a couple hours. A wave of nausea hit her and had her crawling out from underneath the covers. For one brief moment she had difficulty remembering which direction to go to get to the bathroom. Making a mad dash down the hallway, she reached the toilet just in time to lose the contents of her belly.

Empty now and feeling drained, she draped her arms over the sink, splashed handfuls of cold water on her face. She didn't even bother with a towel to dry off. Instead, she plopped down on the rim of the tub and patted the beads over her face and neck with a washcloth. Little by little, the nausea subsided. But her throat felt like she'd crossed the Mohave. She ran water into the cup of her hand several times and drank until she began to feel better.

Wide awake now, she plodded back to her room, decided what she needed was fresh air. She made her way outside to the porch where she dropped down onto the steps. Lifting her face to the breeze, she felt the cool air.

From this spot, she could hear the waves bumping up against the rocks near the pier. All she had to do was turn her head to look up at the massive lighthouse sending out its beam across the bay. The sight reminded her that she should have passed on Thane's generosity. She should have walked home by herself. If she'd been tucked into her own bed maybe the ugly dream wouldn't have manifested and intruded on her sleep.

The glimpse of a shadow to her right interrupted her misgivings. She jumped and started to dart back into the house when she recognized the man taking shape several feet away. The moonlight revealed a familiar face.

A shaky sigh escaped her lips. "You really have to stop doing that."

"Sorry. Are you all right?"

"Sure."

"Bad dream?"

"What makes you say that?" Before he could answer, she rolled her eyes. "Oh. I forgot you're all-seeing, all-knowing."

"Hey, it's four in the morning. You're sitting here on Thane's doorstep, which means this time I pretty much figured it out without using my superpowers."

"Let me ask you something. When you were in combat did you ever face situations that made you feel powerless, vulnerable? Of course I know you were getting shot at, but did you ever see things that…stayed with you long afterward that were impossible to shake?"

"Sure I did."

"And did that vulnerability ever cause you to have bad dreams?"

"You bet it did. I'd say things happened beyond my control on a routine basis. The inability to deal with the situation is deflating at times. That environment causes recurring nightmares."

"Then you can identify with how I feel."

"Did counseling work?"

"To some degree. But having lived through a combat zone, all the talking in the world doesn't help relieve what I experienced firsthand, doesn't address the elemental fact it happened for so long."

Scott nodded. "I get it. You can't un-see all those times he put the bruises on you. Those memories haunt you but not enough to turn you off men completely."

"Just one man, the man responsible for hurting me. Even when I begged him to stop, he wouldn't."

"Thane's a good man."

"I know that. I have only to watch him interact with his son to know it. Despite Thane's career success in the NFL he's been through a lot with Jonah."

"Life always presents challenges. Even when Thane was just a boy, I've never seen a more talented football player, and yet, he's had a period in his life when everything crashed down around him. Money's not an insulator from life's problems or its difficult times. You of all people should know that."

She stared at him. "It's a little spooky realizing you know so much about me. I...I hadn't counted on you." From several feet away, she watched a white-toothed grin spread across his face.

"Then I must be doing something right."

"Did you say it was four in the morning?"

"Almost four-thirty now. Why?"

"I'm wired. I'll never be able to get back to sleep now. Could you do me a favor?"

"If I can."

"Will you walk me home?"

"Right now? What about Thane?"

"I wanted to be gone before Jonah got up anyway. I already talked to Thane about it. Is it tacky if I just leave a note now?"

"Maybe."

"I'll go back inside and write a terrific note reminding him why I had to leave. Wait here. I'll be right back."

She crept back into the house, did her best not to make any more noise than necessary. On the kitchen counter she found a pad of paper and pen next to the phone. Before she lost her nerve, she quickly jotted down her message.

Thane,

I left at 4:30. I had to go. I hope you understand why.

Thanks for one of the best nights I've had in a really long time.

Isabella

Chapter Nine

Her disturbing dream and her talk with Scott had Isabella up doing busywork until almost seven. She scrubbed the kitchen floor that didn't really need cleaning. Her knee was recovering nicely but not enough to get down on all fours so she used a mop she dragged around the tile.

She dusted the entire house, put away the books she'd bought and intended to read before moving on to tackling her closet. Since she'd only been here a few months there wasn't much to straighten or organize and yet she did it anyway before finally dropping into bed, the nervous energy drained out of her.

Several hours later when her eyes fluttered open it was to hear someone banging on her front door.

Instinct had her reaching into the nightstand for the gun inside the drawer. Hastily she threw on a robe, headed out to see who it was, gripping the nine millimeter. Somewhere between her bedroom and the entryway she realized it was more than likely Thane and Jonah. Peering through the peephole to be sure, she was disappointed to see Logan. Without bothering to hide the pistol, she turned the lock.

"I was about to kick in the door or call Brent to do it for me," the sculptor asserted with some heat. He angled his head to eye the weapon. "Glad I didn't."

"And you would do that why?"

"It's almost ten o'clock. I got worried when you didn't answer my text messages. I made up a story to drop in on Thane thinking maybe you'd spent the night there."

"Oh, for God's sakes." She swept her hair back and blinked more awake. "Obviously you need to slow down. You're way ahead of me. If you want a decent conversation, I'll need several shots of caffeine. I've been up for hours and I haven't even had…"

"I can take care of the coffee."

"Good, then I'll go get dressed." She carried the firearm back to the nightstand, easing it into place, before heading into the bathroom to splash cold water on her face. Her image in the mirror told her what she already knew. The cold water didn't make her look any less tired or haggard.

After throwing on a pair of jeans and a sweater, Isabella followed the smell of fresh-brewed beans to where Logan had made himself at home at the kitchen table, sipping from his own cup.

"What's on your mind?" she wanted to know as she got down a mug.

"I heard from Inspector Cosford."

She blew out a loud sigh. "And?"

"It's official. He's lost track of Henry."

"Again? Damn it. Why does that not surprise me? How is it one man can slip through what amounts to an international net that's supposedly looking for him?"

She sat down at the table across from her landlord, took the first sip of strong brew. "We always knew that was a possibility though, that Henry could disappear off the radar and we'd lose the upper hand."

"I know, but I'm still not prepared to accept the incompetence of the cops. Is it too much to ask that they ought to know where the son of a bitch went? The authorities keep acting as though he's normal when he's anything but."

"Maybe someone in his family paid them off. Did you consider that?"

"Of course I did. But it's my belief what's left of his family is slowly losing patience with him. If he's getting assistance at all it's more than likely coming from Henry's rogue buddies in the terrorist community. They'd no doubt go the extra mile to protect him."

Isabella nodded. "To keep Henry's family's money flowing into the ETA organization, even though they've officially disbanded. I get it. You do know that Henry was never actually a terrorist himself, don't you? He simply likes to think of himself as one. He's more into exploiting others for personal gain. Devoting energy to anyone but himself isn't in his nature."

He stared at her over the rim of his cup. "You know him pretty well. But it doesn't matter if he's active or not. He still contributes heavily to the Basque cause despite their ceasefire and agreement to end the violence. For Henry it's a status."

"Exactly. He still has friends who are active in the separatist group and willing to do whatever it takes for him in friendship."

"That's why it makes the most sense they'd be the ones getting him in and out of the country whenever he gets an itch to leave."

"So what do we do about picking up his trail again? Stick to the initial plan or alter our course?"

"Why deviate now?"

"Because it isn't working."

"Maybe you've changed your mind. Maybe you like Delacourt more than you're willing to admit."

"So what if I do? You have Kinsey, a family you treasure. What do I have?"

"Sorry. You're right. Losing track of Henry has me...irritated. To answer your question about what we do, we tighten things up around here. The tourist season in town is virtually over. So any strangers coming around will stick out from the norm. I've decided to install a gate at the foot of the hill."

She tossed him a dubious look. "That's a little extreme even for you, don't you think? And totally unnecessary, not to mention fairly ridiculous. Henry would simply find a way around it." Eyeing Logan's stubborn set to his jaw, she went on, "You know it's true. Think about it. He could just as easily drive farther up the Coast Highway and veer off to the west, come through the woods near the B&B, make his way up to my front door in a roundabout fashion. You can't very well make this place a secure compound, Logan. It just isn't feasible."

"I can try."

"Don't. I'm a big girl. I'm not that same woman I was three years ago either. I'm stronger." She discounted her fear last night at not wanting to walk home alone in the dark. Taking away the panic then, she was determined to put up a strong front. "I'm armed and not afraid to fight back, remember?"

Logan rolled his eyes. "Sometimes that isn't enough. Maybe we should go see Brent. Get him in the loop."

"Since you know him better than I do that's your call, I suppose. But the fewer people who know, the better chance at success we have." She paused and said with a bite of humor, "Scott knows. I don't think he'll blab though."

"Scott? You're kidding?" Logan sent her a lingering glare over his cup. "So he's been skulking around here like a—"

"Ghost? Yeah. Don't knock it. Scott makes me feel a lot safer."

Logan dropped a shoulder. "Women. I'll never understand the female mind. Which brings me to ask the question. What's the deal with Thane Delacourt anyway?"

"Sheesh. Really? It's no one's business but my own. Not even yours. How's that for an answer?" After several long seconds, she added, "The whole town knows I went over there last night to apologize? How? Never mind. Look, I was rude earlier in the day. I felt the need to explain my behavior. I had dinner, watched a cute, animated movie, and stayed later than I should have. That's it."

"Sure it is."

Isabella sipped her coffee, looked over the rim. "If the government could only harness the power of small town gossip we'd have a decent shot at world peace."

"Ain't that the truth. You like this guy?"

"What's not to like? His kid is fairly adorable, too."

"Getting attached wasn't part of the plan."

"Neither was losing track of Henry."

Thane had been up for hours, restless and moody, with a nagging sense he needed to call Isabella and check up on her.

The note hadn't surprised him nor had it explained a lot about her state of mind. He should probably go up to the cottage to see how she was doing, use some made-up excuse. But first he had to come up with one. The fact that he wanted to see her again, spend time alone with her, and eventually take her to bed didn't seem like the right fit.

To get his mind off that, he took Jonah to the beach as he'd promised. Their trips had a ritual that went with the fun. Before ever getting in the water, sunscreen went on first. Next, they took the time to wax their boards to assure better footing. They spent fifteen minutes stretching the muscles and loosening up. Then they made sure the fins were set depending on the surf. This morning the waves weren't high or intimidating but surfing with a six-year-old, Thane had to be cognizant of where the boy was at all times. He let him slap the leash on his ankle by himself and the two paddled out, side by side.

"He's pretty good for his age," Malachi Rafferty said from eight feet away as he watched Jonah dip into a barrel and soar through it.

"He's improved a lot over the summer. He's able to maintain his balance for longer," Thane admitted, feeling a pride he didn't know was there.

"I bet you can't wait for him to be old enough to play football."

"Actually, I'm not sure I want him going anywhere near a field that requires him to put on a helmet and pads."

"Really?"

Thane stared at the familiar face. He knew Malachi used to play with the band, Bridge Omega, but not many in town knew Malachi's secret. Malachi had been a major part of Bridge Omega's selling millions of CDs. Thane had no intentions of ratting out the stellar guitarist or asking what had brought him to a place like Pelican Pointe.

"Yeah, really. I've seen too many head and neck injuries to get excited about my son taking up the game. It'll be up to him, of course, if he wants to try and make a team later on when he's older."

"By the way I'm supposed to ask you, if you ever need a sitter, I have two teenagers who are both eager to earn some extra spending money."

"Are they old enough to babysit?"

Malachi shrugged, not very excited about the prospect of his daughters taking on responsibility with someone else's kid. "Sonoma's the oldest at fourteen. Sonnet's thirteen. They just had a birthday last week. They're eleven months apart. You hire them, you get the pair."

"Let me think about it. Jonah's very…energetic."

"I hear ya," Malachi grumbled, wading out of the surf. From over his shoulder, he added, "You think it's tough now with a six-year-old, wait until he's a teenager."

Even wearing a wetsuit that thought gave Thane chills. Because he knew Malachi's wife, Melody, had died three years earlier from cancer, Thane had something on his mind. "Could I ask you a question single father to single father? It's sort of personal."

"Sort of? Sure, as long as I don't have to talk about my years in the band."

"It isn't that. How exactly do you date with kids?"

"That's easy. I don't. Every Saturday night I close the shop and head to Santa Cruz to play live music at a little dive off the Coast Highway. There's a woman there who I've known for a couple years. She waitresses at the bar. If the girls tag along with me, then daddy doesn't get any that night, if you know what I mean. If the girls stay at home, I go back to my friend's place for a few hours but I never spend the night."

"How does this waitress handle that arrangement?"

"Thankfully she isn't looking for a commitment and neither am I."

"And if she were?"

"Then I'm afraid I'd have to break it off."

"Why?"

"Because I'm not serious about her and my girls deserve better than that."

"Thanks for the honesty, Malachi. I'm grateful."

"No problem. I'd like to add something if I could."

"What?"

"Don't let the wagging tongues set the parameters."

"Good advice. I know a lot about wagging tongues."

"I know you do but tabloids are nothing compared to the gossip in a small town."

Later, father and son were standing knee-deep in bay water, when Jonah looked up at the cliffs and pointed. "Look Daddy, there's Izzy at the top."

Sure enough, he gazed upward and there she stood at the edge of the cliffs looking like an exotic goddess surveying her domain from high on the hill. The image forged a searing reminder that his libido needed a fix.

On their way back to the house, Thane passed by Tradewinds Boatyard. From inside he heard the sounds of guitar-busting hard rock beating a competition with whirling power tools. An idea formed.

"Come on, Jonah, let's go in here and see these guys for a minute."

The place was jumping. Ryder was in one corner working on a spinnaker, Zach in another laboring over a galley module, while Troy shaped a piece of teak wood.

To be heard over the deafening racket, Thane had to shout. "Hey guys, could I ask you a question?"

All three stilled their hands; silence descended.

"I know you guys are busting your asses in here, but I was wondering."

"What?" asked Zach, looking up at the ex-jock and removing his safety goggles. "Is there anything wrong with the work we did at the restaurant yesterday?"

"Nope, not a thing, going in an entirely different direction here. I don't know if you overheard our discussion yesterday about the restaurant's décor, but Isabella had this idea that I could use old surfboards for tabletops. I like the idea and was wondering if you knew where I could find enough broken surfboards to make that happen."

All three men started talking at once. Thane had to hold up his hand to indicate one at a time. It was Troy who was trying to talk the loudest. "First, you'd have to find the tables you want repurposed so we'd know what kind of top to make, round, square, or anything rectangular. We can put a new top on any shape."

"He's right," Ryder added. "I know a salvage yard that sells all kinds of stuff you can recycle. It has tables galore. Logan stumbled on the place when we rehabbed the school. It's the old Atkins farmhouse between here and San Sebastian. There's a lot of junk to sort through but there's also a lot of hidden gems to be had."

"Sounds perfect," Thane noted. "So if I find the tables, you'd be able to put new tops on them, make them stand out and unusual to Longboard Pizza?"

"You bet. I'd love to be the one to work on a project like that," Troy said. "How many are we talking about?"

"I'd need enough surfboard pieces to finish out at least ten tops for starters, the more colorful the design, the better."

"What a unique idea," Troy proclaimed. "If you want unique, don't let the different sizes of tables throw you. I can tie them all together with the design and it won't matter if they're round or square."

"Just what I wanted to hear," Thane said. "I'll start looking around for the tables this week."

"In case you were wondering we plan to get started installing your appliances this afternoon after we spend some time in here. Shouldn't take that long," Zach assured him.

"On a Sunday? I don't expect you to do that."

"It's okay. It's the only spare time we may have in the next week."

"Then I hate to add to your workload but is there any chance you guys could make me a couple of surfboards when you get the time? Something bright and attention-getting for the restaurant—a focal point to hang above the counter with the logo on it—and then there's the one I'd like to order for..." Thane nodded his head toward Jonah who was too taken with the design of the boat the guys were building to pay much attention to anything else. But Thane lowered his voice anyway. "It's for him, for Christmas, a shortboard maybe?"

"That's right up Troy's alley," Ryder said. "He's been itching to get a guinea pig for experimentation."

Thane laughed. "Really? Well, I guess Jonah and I don't mind becoming your guinea pigs."

"Excellent, then I'll create you something guaranteed to cause a buzz for the restaurant and another that you'll be proud to show off to your friends," Troy pledged in a voice tinged with excitement at the prospect. "What design did you have in mind?"

"Lilly's creating the sign. I have some of her sketches at the house. I'd like to coordinate that with what you'll come up with."

"Sounds like a plan. Let's go into the office."

For the next thirty minutes the two men disappeared into a stark hole-in-the-wall room in the back of the shipyard to talk surfboards. They went over a series of ideas until it soon became obvious to Thane that Troy had a passion for his work.

"When could you have something ready for me to look at?"

"Give me a week."

Thane offered his hand to Troy. "Good deal. Let's try to keep the one pegged for Jonah between the two of us. It's okay to show me what you come up with for the restaurant as soon as you can get around to it though."

As Thane turned to leave, Troy thought of something. "Would you like to come to my bachelor party?"

"Sure. When's the wedding?"

"Not for weeks yet. But Logan's throwing me a bash at McCready's the night before. I'd love it if you could stop in and have a beer with us."

"Great. Let me know when it happens. I'll have to get a sitter."

Thane and Jonah left and were almost back home when the boy wanted to know, "Can we go see Mimi now? And bring her the sweet-smelling flowers we brought last time?"

It occurred to Thane that maybe he should be concerned his son had an apparent fixation on visiting his grandmother's gravesite. But then he'd picked up a book in Hayden's bookstore about how to talk to young children about death and the grieving process. Thane didn't want to overreact to what was easily becoming a frequent request to go out there. "We'll stow our surfboards, change out of our wetsuits and go get those lilies."

An hour later father and son were strolling among the headstones at Eternal Gardens heading toward the Delacourt family plot. At times, Jonah would stop to pick up little pebbles or rocks along the way and put them in his pocket. Thane would have to remember to go through them before he tossed them in the washer, otherwise he'd have a clogged mess on his hands.

When they reached the patch of grass with the gravestones, Thane pointed to one. "You never knew your grampa but he was good man."

"He got cancer too and died when I was a baby."

"That's right." Thinking he had his son's attention, Thane was surprised when Jonah pointed across the lawn.

"Who's that guy standing over there?"

"What guy?"

"That guy," Jonah said, pointing to a man who stood in front of another memorial on the other side of the cemetery.

Thane followed Jonah's gaze and spotted a man wearing tan shorts and a button-down shirt over one of the brightly-colored tees Malachi sold in town emblazoned with the Pelican Pointe logo. Even though the guy looked like a tourist, Thane recognized Scott Phillips.

"Well who is he?" Jonah repeated.

"That's..." Not a real man, Thane wanted to say. How did one handle the topic of a ghost when it wasn't even Halloween yet? Isabella had been right after all. He and Jonah were both staring at a guy who'd been dead for years. When Scott caught sight of them, Thane watched in amazement as he waved at them. Thinking on his feet, Thane looked over at his son. "That's a... His name is Mr. Phillips."

"I've seen him before."

"Where?"

Jonah shrugged but then decided to divulge more. "The man surfs, like we do. I see him catching a wave. I see him at home too...sometimes."

Thane did his best to keep his voice level without freaking out about that little tidbit. "How long have you been seeing him at the house?"

"Since we first got to Mimi's. Can I put the flowers down now?"

"Sure."

"Grampa can have some of my rocks," Jonah stated as he started digging in his pants pocket for a variety of stones and pebbles. "I'll pick the best ones. Are we gonna go see Izzy again?"

"How about we ask her to a picnic on the beach?"

"Yeah, I'm hungry."

"Figured you were getting there. Let's go, buddy." As they walked back to the car, Thane glanced over his shoulder. Not surprisingly, Scott was nowhere around. He took out his cell phone, punched a number on speed dial.

Three thousand miles away in Manhattan, Fischer Robbins answered the call with a snark. "What did you burn this time?"

Thane ignored the sarcasm as he often did when it came from the man he considered to be more like a brother than a friend. "Not a thing, smartass. Haven't you heard? I'm becoming a regular Rachael Ray in the kitchen. I do have a question though. Let's say I wanted to create the perfect picnic basket, what would I put inside?"

"Before I answer that, I sense a female somewhere in the picture. If it were just you and Jonah, you'd find a way to brown bag it with a turkey sandwich. Am I right? You've met someone."

Thane ignored the question. "Hey, you can't argue with the fact that Jonah loves his turkey sandwiches. How about I make wraps, some type of meat and cheese?"

"It's obvious you aren't going to answer me. That's okay. I'll see for myself when I get there next week. In the meantime, buy some of Perry's crab salad, make sure you keep it cold enough. Pick up a few fresh turkey slices and serve them on ciabatta bread with melted mozzarella, and a smidgen of honey mustard. Are you writing this down?"

"Yeah. How do you spell smidgen again?"

"Bite me."

"Next time. Hey, I gotta run now. Jonah's starving and I still have to line up the woman."

"Sheesh, most men do that before they start making plans. You're always getting lucky on your fame, Delacourt."

"Yeah. Probably. But you love me anyway. See you when you get here. Drive safe." Thane disconnected and then turned to fasten Jonah into his safety seat in the back. "Let's go get some chow. Izzy can't say no if we already have the food in hand, right?"

Jonah bobbed his head. "Right. 'Cause she's probably hungry, too."

Once Isabella opened her front door and saw the eager faces on both man and boy, she didn't have the heart to turn them down.

So, on a stretch of sugary sand they'd set up their blanket and picnic area near water's edge. Thane handed Jonah his turkey sandwich while Izzy forked up a bite of Perry's crab salad, a better bet than the wrap idea.

"So you aren't mad about my leaving this morning?"

"No, I figured as jittery as you were about the whole thing you wouldn't last till breakfast. You weren't afraid to walk home at that hour?"

She decided to tell him Scott had taken care of that little problem and watched his face for a reaction. "You don't seem surprised."

Thane stole a glance over at Jonah who was busy woofing down his sandwich before telling her about the conversation at the cemetery.

"But you didn't see him?"

"Sure I saw him, big as life, standing in front of another headstone. It's just that I was surprised to learn Jonah has been seeing him around for several months."

"Seeing who?" Jonah asked, done with his sandwich. In typical child fashion, the boy segued into another topic, one that had nothing to do with Scott. "Izzy, did you know we don't have to worry anymore about people following us with big cameras?"

"You don't? That's good to know."

Thane stretched out on the blanket and watched Isabella do the same, unfurling her long legs to get more comfortable while Jonah sat between them and every now and then peppered the conversation with a random display of his six-year-old wisdom.

"There aren't many paparazzi hanging around here in Pelican Pointe," Izzy noted.

"It isn't that. Dad doesn't play football anymore so he's not one bit famous. No one wants our picture."

Izzy let out a belly laugh, looked over at Thane. "Your son has a way of putting things in perspective that gets to the heart of the matter."

"He definitely keeps it real."

Tugging at her shirtsleeves, Jonah said, "Izzy, Izzy?"

"What?"

"Um, wanna hear a joke?"

"Sure."

"What did the turkey say to the computer?"

"I don't know. What?"

"Google, google, google."

She cracked up again. "I see Jonah got most of the sense of humor in the family. What's your favorite sport? Do you like football as much as your dad does?"

"We usually watch the games on Sundays together, except today, today Dad wanted to have a picnic with you instead."

Izzy sat back, stunned. "Wow, you're both missing football because of me? I'm... Wait, what time is it? You still have time to catch the second game of the day."

Thane threw his arms out wide. "We're devoted fans but we aren't without our ability to commune with nature. Look at this place. It's a gorgeous sunny day and we're in the company of a beautiful woman. Aren't we, Jonah?"

"Right. Dad said you were hot."

"Jonah! Do you have to repeat everything I say?"

"Well, you did say that," Jonah stressed.

"But you don't have to share every single thing I say with every person you meet," Thane pointed out.

"But she is pretty."

"Hey, if he said it, it's clearly worth repeating, right?" Izzy teased Jonah.

"Lesson learned about watching what I share around Jonah," Thane said ruffling the kid's hair. "I have yet to invoke the spirit of the male bond ritual—what happens at home stays at home."

"What does that mean?" Jonah challenged.

"It means you can tell me anything," Izzy whispered, leaning over Jonah's ear.

"I heard that," Thane confessed. It gave him a jolt to see that his son had already begun to bond with her in such a short time. How did he feel about that? Was Jonah that needy, that desperate for a mother figure in his life that he'd attach himself so easily to the first woman who entered his life? That gave him pause.

With no idea what was on Thane's mind, Izzy made an offer. "Why don't you guys come over to my place tonight for dinner? I'll fix chicken tacos, guaranteed to fill the tummy. You guys can even watch football."

"Yay tacos! I love tacos." Jonah squealed.

"We need to work on your spelling for next week," Thane said in a voice that caused an awkwardness to hang in the air.

Izzy met Thane's eyes, an understanding passing between them. "Then I guess we'll have to make it another time."

That afternoon, Thane settled in front of the flat-screen to catch the last half of the game between the Giants and the Vikings. But his brain couldn't focus on either team's defense. Instead, he kept replaying the confused look he'd seen on Isabella's face when he'd dropped her off. He'd asked her to the beach for a picnic and she'd returned the favor. And what had he done in response? He'd pulled back. Even Jonah had acted puzzled by his abrupt behavior.

So how could he fix this situation he'd created? He glanced at the clock and decided it wasn't too late to mend fences.

He picked up his phone, texted her number.

Is your offer for dinner still open?

It seemed like an eternity before he got a reply.

What gives? Are you sure you trust me enough to fix your son a meal?

I deserved that. But I panicked. I'd like to come for dinner if you haven't changed your mind.

It's tacos on the menu.

That's fine.

Then I'll see you around six.

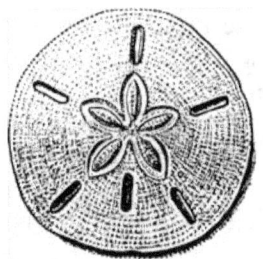

Chapter Ten

The aroma of onions and poblano peppers laced with a heavy helping of chili powder and chipotle wafted through her kitchen as she tossed the Spanish rice while it warmed in the skillet. Running a spoon around the creamy chicken, she checked its consistency before adding generous dashes of turmeric and cocoa to her simmering sauce.

It had been a very long time since she'd cooked for anyone but herself. It felt odd and yet she enjoyed going through the familiar tasks.

She turned to the counter, began chopping the ingredients for her own blend of Pico de Gallo. For fresh guacamole she pitted two avocados, mashed them up in a bowl, and added a splash of lime and salt.

When the doorbell rang, she wiped off her hands and headed for the front door, while the TV blared the beginning of the Sunday night game between the Colts and the Dolphins.

As soon as the door opened, Jonah held up a bag. "We brought more ice cream!"

"It's my belief that you can never have too much ice cream," Izzy pronounced taking the grocery sack out of his hands. "I'll go make sure this doesn't melt. The game's on. Make yourselves comfortable while I finish up. Dinner's almost done. I just need to set the table."

"We can take care of that, can't we Jonah?" Thane offered.

"Yep. I'm good at putting out the spoons and forks and napkins."

"Then, be my guest," Izzy directed. "It's great to have an extra pair of hands, or in this case, two extra pairs in the kitchen when making a meal."

"Uncle Fisch says too many cooks make a mess," Jonah tossed out.

Thane laughed. "He does. Fischer is one of those typically moody chefs who love to have the kitchen all to themselves."

"On certain days that wouldn't necessarily be a bad thing," Izzy said as she brought in serving dishes full of meat and rice. "Now, I'm taking drink orders. What will it be?"

"Beer for me if you have it," Thane said. "Milk for Jonah."

"I have an amber Belgian ale I'm fond of, will that do?"

"In Pelican Pointe?"

"I was surprised that Murphy carries it."

"Works for me."

Izzy returned to the kitchen, got down a glass for the milk and two beers.

Thane took his first sip, commented, "Creamy, a little sweet, but woodsy."

"That's what I like about it."

The trio gathered around the table, in the dining room with walls painted a cheery cranberry-red. This was different than Friday afternoon when they'd shared soup and sandwiches or when they'd dug into a plate of macaroni. Somewhere along the way a comfort zone had sprouted.

"I made a mild version for Jonah and a spicier one for us."

"You shouldn't have gone to so much trouble, what with your leg still bothering you."

"Don't be silly. I have to eat. I have crunchy tacos or soft. Which do you prefer, Jonah?"

"Crunchy. Even though my tooth is loose. See?"

He tilted his face up to her and opened his mouth, wiggled the tooth back and forth with his fingers. Sure enough Izzy spotted the culprit.

"That's pretty loose. Let's hope it makes it through the meal."

"I get a dollar if it doesn't."

Thane forked over tender chicken, dipped it into the mole sauce. "Oh this is good, really good."

"I make a mean chili, too."

"If it's anything like this, you can cook for us anytime, right Jonah?"

With his mouth full of taco, the boy simply nodded and then let out a loud belch.

"What better compliment is there than that," Izzy said as Jonah broke out into howls of laughter. Yes, she thought, the three of them were so much more at ease than before.

"Are we ready for dessert? The sea salt caramel gelato will go with the double fudge brownies I made."

"Oh boy, sugar here we come," Thane said.

"Okay, maybe that is too much. We'll pass on the brownies and just have the ice cream."

"No way."

"Brownie a la mode it is then."

The meal ended with a flurry of kitchen cleanup. Pots and pans went into soak-mode. Plates clinked together as Jonah helped load the dishwasher.

"Can I play a game on my iPad now?" the boy asked as the last plate slid in between the prongs.

"Sure. But before you do that, thank Izzy for fixing supper."

"Thanks for supper, Izzy. You make good tacos."

"You're very welcome. Thanks for coming."

Thane watched him take off for the living room and then bounce into one of the comfy chairs. "That boy is only still when he's asleep."

"But you wouldn't have it any other way."

"I suppose that's true."

He moved to where she stood at the island, pulled her into him. Touching his lips to hers, he let her sweet and spicy taste sink in and ramp up before boosting her up on the counter. He began a slow nibble along her jaw and down to her neck. "You have beautiful, soft skin," he stated as he left a string of kisses to prove it.

She held on to his muscled arms, locked her fingers behind his neck. She scooted into his hard abs, locked her legs around his toned torso. From the living room she heard Jonah let out a whoop during his game, which had her breathing out, "What about Jonah?"

Thane backed up a step, putting a halt to the make-out session.

"We need a time and place where we can be alone," he whispered. "I want you, Isabella. But right this minute I have to head home to get Jonah in the tub and ready for bed. I want you to start thinking about us spending time together." He tilted her chin up, met her eyes. "Are you up for that?"

"I'm definitely game."

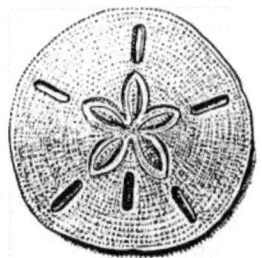

Chapter Eleven

Monday morning, a little after nine o'clock, Isabella answered the door and was surprised to see River Cody standing on her front porch.

"Hi, I'm River Cody, Brent's wife. I don't mean to drop in on you like this but I'd like to talk to you about something."

"Sure, come on in. Would you like coffee?"

"No, I'd better pass. Had a cup of decaf already." River made a face and launched into a detailed account of why she was cutting back on caffeine. The story revealed her pregnancy.

"Congratulations. Well, I have orange juice containing lots of folic acid good for the brain," Isabella said in response.

"I'll take it," River said following Isabella into the gleaming kitchen. "Wow. I saw the 'before' pictures but I prefer the 'after.' I used to walk up here with Luke, that's my son, to show him the lighthouse. I peeked into the windows once or twice after Logan got this place whipped into showplace form. It's what inspired us to redo our old place."

Isabella poured a tall glass of juice, handed it off. "Logan definitely has a flair for bold design and using vivid colors."

"I love that he made it open and airy."

"And got rid of the body," Isabella quipped.

"I heard about that. Carl Knudsen's work. You're not spooked living here are you?"

"Not really. I think Scott Phillips watches over me."

"Honey, Scott watches over all of us."

"You didn't even blink at the mention of his name. You believe I see him?"

"I'm Native American, Pueblo specifically, so of course I believe in spirit guides. That's what he is, you know."

"Spirit guide? Hmm, I hadn't considered that. Ghost absolutely, but spirit guide? That actually makes me feel...more in tune with him."

"He was instrumental in helping Brent find my son, our son," she corrected. "Long story."

"This I have to hear. Take a seat."

"My ex abducted Luke when he was six months old. I didn't get him back until a cop in Wyoming confronted him in this out of the way café. He'd gone all woodsy— my ex, not the cop. Anyway, by that time, Luke was nearly three years old. Between Scott and Brent's detective work, we were able to home in on that area, stay focused in the right direction in order to bring my baby back home to me." River looked up from her glass. "On numerous occasions Scott's even helped save lives here in town."

"How?"

River thought of the story Cord Bennett had told her. "Like saving people from suicide, stuff like jamming guns so they won't fire. Other times he's warned people away from dangerous situations right before something terrible happened, like sniper fire. That happened to Brent. Just a few months ago it was a lightning strike. Don't believe me? Just ask Ryder and Julianne how they barely escaped getting struck by lightning. And he woke Nick Harris up in time to prevent Kent Springer from setting fire to Promise Cove."

"See? That's why I feel safer having him guarding the cottage."

River narrowed her eyes in a frown, considered that info. "Is there someone after you?"

"I have a crazy ex, too."

"Ah, ever wonder why there are so many out there?"

"Crazy seems to have become the new norm. What did you want to ask me?"

"The Chumash Museum opens in a month. I'm looking for an assistant, someone who might be familiar with cataloging items for display. A little bird told me that you have experience working in an art gallery."

Isabella's mouth dropped open. "How could anyone besides Logan possibly know that?"

"Small towns," River said by way of explanation, wiggling her eyebrows up and down. "If you're thinking he broke a confidence, I didn't hear it from Logan, although I can't reveal my source. So don't ask."

"It isn't that. I'm just amazed at the flow of information—or rather disinformation. Some so outlandish I don't know where they get their ideas. One day last August, Myrtle Pettibone confronted me at movie night, certain that I'd once danced for the Bolshoi Ballet but was forced to leave because I was involved in a sex scandal."

River cracked up laughing. "A sex scandal? And you've been keeping that to yourself? Unfair to hold back details like that. Okay, it was the hubby who mentioned the art gallery connection. But if it comes up in conversation, you twisted my arm to get that out of me. I'm not sure exactly how Brent heard. So is it true?"

"No, I never danced for the Bolshoi," Isabella admitted with a grin. "And yes, I do have gallery experience."

"Perfect. Then what about coming to work for the Museum? I promise I'm not a slave driver, not much of one anyway."

To add another enticement, River tossed out the salary. "I know it's not what they pay in Paris but…"

"I'll take it," Isabella blurted out. "And for the record my gallery experience comes from my college days where I spearheaded a private art collection. Not sure what that has to do with Native American exhibits but I'm willing to expand my horizons if you are."

"As long as you're familiar with the boring side of data entry and the importance of description in a computer database, I'm willing to stretch your hands-on experience."

"Then we have a deal. When do I start?"

"Is tomorrow too soon?"

"Tomorrow's perfect."

At ten o'clock recess, Jonah filed out to the playground with the rest of his class. As soon as he reached the yard, he did what he always did. He made a mad dash for the slide, getting in line behind several others. Just as he was about to climb up the ladder, a voice belonging to third grader Bobby Prather yelled out, "Hey, Delacourt, why doesn't your mother live with your father?"

Another third grader, Bobby's cohort Doug Bayliss, tossed out, "Jonah doesn't got no mother."

"That's because his mother was a druggie and a whore," Bobby declared. "My dad says that people who do drugs are stupid. That makes your mother dumb and stupid."

"I heard he never had a mother," another boy chimed in.

Jonah stepped back from the slide and shouted, "I do too. She's just dead is all. And she wasn't a whore!"

"She was and I say that makes Jonah Delacourt a bastard," Bobby proclaimed to everyone.

"I am not. You take that back," Jonah said, clenching his fists, ready to fight.

Tommy Gates, a stocky boy, moved in beside Jonah, prepared to show support. "You cut that out, Bobby. Stop picking on Jonah. He never did nothin' to you."

More ugly words flew back and forth causing the other kids to gather round to watch the fracas build up into a full-blown fight. The shouting got the attention of more and more kids as an inner circle formed around the five boys involved and grew out from the center.

From the stoop near the door, Olivia Brach spotted her favorite troublemaker, Bobby Prather. After teaching third grade for five years, Olivia recognized a boy with a disruptive home life. The Prathers were known far and wide for having a tumultuous marriage. They lived on Athena Circle and couldn't stop yelling and screaming at each other long enough to get much else done. Neither one was willing to give an inch in a fight or walk away to stop the verbal battery. Since the start of school, Olivia had seen Bobby cultivate a foul mouth. His friend, Douglas, didn't help matters. The only thing the two boys excelled at more than name-calling was picking on younger classmates.

Olivia leaned back inside the doorway, called out to another teacher in the hallway. "Go get Ms. Dickinson. I want her to see this. And hurry. Tell her Bobby is at it again."

Olivia darted off the porch and headed toward the group of children. Pushing her way through short little bodies she reached the fray about the same time Bobby drew back his fist to punch Jonah.

Focusing all her efforts on Bobby, Olivia missed the Delacourt boy behind her about to make his charge toward his tormentor.

Good thing the principal grabbed Jonah around the waist in time to prevent a full-out brawl.

Julianne Dickinson raised her voice over the din. "Boys, stop this! My office. Right now, this minute! No argument." To the other children, the principal instructed, "Recess will be over soon. Go back to playing or you'll miss the opportunity before you have to go back to class." With that, she marched both boys into the building and straight into her office.

"Now, you want to tell me what started this?" Julianne demanded, looking first at Bobby for an explanation. "I want the truth."

Bobby hung his head, unable to take his eyes off the floor.

Turning to Jonah she hoped for enlightenment. "Tell me what happened."

That was all the prompting Jonah needed to repeat the ugly things Bobby had said about his mother.

Julianne stared at Bobby, tilted his chin up to meet her eyes. "Is that true, Bobby? Did you say all that about someone else's mother? How could you say those things? What if someone said that about your own mother? How would you feel then?"

"I didn't say anything. Jonah just wanted to fight," Bobby muttered swinging his feet back and forth under the chair.

Julianne sighed at the boy's stubborn resistance to the truth. Knowing Bobby's reputation for dishonesty she pressed further, "You should probably know that I heard you taunting Jonah from the steps. So there really isn't any point in denying it. Besides that, you're two grades ahead of him. Why is an eight-year-old picking on someone who's six? If that wasn't enough, now you're lying to me. I'm calling your parents in hopes they'll put a stop to this behavior of yours. We have a long school year ahead of us. I don't want to have to haul you into my office every day because you've been acting out like this with your classmates."

Julianne turned to Jonah. "And you, fighting isn't the answer. I'm also calling your father. He'll probably want to come get you."

When his cell phone dinged, Thane stood in the middle of his restaurant talking to a potential supplier. The phone number ID that came up on the digital readout said Pelican Pointe Elementary. Never a good sign, thought Thane as he excused himself to take the call.

"This is Thane Delacourt."

"Mr. Delacourt, this is Julianne Dickinson. There's been some trouble at school."

"Is Jonah okay?"

Thane listened as the principal caught him up on what had happened.

"It's my belief that it's this sort of thing that brings out an opportunity where you have the power to turn negative, ugly words into a positive by reinforcing the image of his mother," Julianne offered. "It's a critical time to listen to his concerns and hear what he has to say about what happened."

"I agree. I'll see you in a couple minutes."

It took him less than ten minutes to finish up with the supplier and make the short drive to school. In days past, he'd spent his fair share of time sweating it out in the principal's office, waiting for one of his parents to walk through the door. It brought back memories when he spotted Jonah wiggling in what looked like a very uncomfortable chair in the outer office area.

"Hey, buddy. You okay?"

"Daddy! What took you so long?"

"I got here as soon as I could." At the sound of his voice, Ms. Dickinson came out of her office to greet him, so he turned back to Jonah and said, "You stay put while I talk to Ms. Dickinson, okay?"

"O-kay." A hangdog Jonah sat back down, impatient with the turn of events.

Thane disappeared through the doorway and into the principal's domain.

"Thanks for coming," she said.

"Thanks for calling me. I won't try to pretend I'm not upset because I am, especially since it involved an altercation with a much older, much larger kid than Jonah. I try to make sure I'm here every day after school to walk him home, mostly it's to let him know I'm around, but if this becomes a recurring issue, you can bet I won't miss an afternoon where I'm waiting on the sidewalk for him."

"Mr. Delacourt, I don't blame you for feeling that way. You should know Bobby Prather has a bit of a past. He got expelled last year from the San Sebastian school for exactly the same thing. Here, Bobby's been in trouble since the first day he walked through the door."

"You're telling me a second grader got expelled for using this kind of language about another boy's mother?"

"Yes, and for egging on another student to fight. I've already informed the Prathers that if there's another incident like this one, they'll have to consider getting their son into counseling."

"Let's hope this was an isolated thing and the parents heed your advice, get the boy some help and this Prather kid gets the message."

Later as father and son drove back to the restaurant, Thane quizzed Jonah. "Is there anything you want to ask me?"

"My mom wasn't a whore."

"That's an ugly word, Jonah. I don't want you using it, okay? Not ever. And no, your mother wasn't that. She had problems. She got sick and she died because of those problems."

"Drugs, right?"

At that moment, Thane wanted to wring the little playground bully's neck himself. He didn't like the kid who'd planted these ideas in his son's head. But that sentiment wouldn't do Jonah any good now. "Sometimes when a person is unhappy they resort to taking medication to feel better. Your mother was hurting so she went that route. It's never a good solution and it always leads to other problems."

"Did you ever take drugs?"

How was he supposed to answer that minefield of a question? To keep it simple, Thane lied. "No, and you shouldn't either." He switched gears again. "Jonah, this kid, this Bobby Prather, he's done this same thing to other kids before."

"So he's just mean?"

"Yeah, and probably unhappy at home."

Done with it for now, Jonah was the one who segued into another subject. "Can I have a puppy? I'll take good care of it."

Grateful for something else to discuss, Thane spared his son an eager glance. "You really know how to milk this for all it's worth, don't you?"

"I just want a puppy of my own."

Thane let out an audible sigh. "I guess we should go call Izzy and invite her along to check out those puppies Tommy has. Maybe she can help you pick one out. Whaddya say?"

"Really, Dad?"

"Yep. As I see it, it's the only thing to do." He picked up his phone, sent a text. "We'll see if Izzy's afternoon is booked."

Twenty seconds later, the response bounced back.

"What did she say?" Jonah wanted to know.

"Looks like it's a go. She's free and would love to help you find the perfect dog."

Jonah pumped a fist in the air. "Yay!! But Tommy's still at school."

"Then we'll wait until school is out."

At three-thirty the two were waiting for Izzy on the porch when she sailed up the Delacourt driveway on her bike. "Hey, guys. How's it going?"

Bouncing on his toes, Jonah ran out to greet her. "We're ready to pick out a dog."

"You should get one too," Thane pointed out with a wry smile. "You'd be less alone way up there on the hill. Just think how happy you'd be when the dog greeted you at the door every evening."

"Hmm, there is that. But working on me ahead of time might be fruitless. Tommy might have only one left."

"True. We'll soon see. The Gates house is just around the corner on Cape May. We can walk and talk while Jonah figures out a name."

"I'm gonna call him Leo."

"What kind of dogs are these exactly?" Izzy asked.

"You mean breed?" Thane replied. "From what Archer told me when I called earlier, they're all mutts of indeterminate origin, a product of his Labrador mix meeting up with the Campbells' golden retriever."

Thane caught sight of the rambler-style single-story house that looked straight out of the fifties. The grass had been cut. The shrubs neatly trimmed. It reminded him that Tommy's father, Archer Gates, had moved back to Pelican Pointe from Fresno bringing his son with him. The forty-year-old had gone through a contentious and costly divorce. Archer's mother, Prissie, had opened the door to her home so that her son and grandson could get back on even footing. Because of the breakup, Archer had been struggling with depression and alcohol. Tommy had been caught up in all of it.

Today, Tommy sat in the yard surrounded by four energetic furry balls of fluff and one adult female dog that looked on. Thane had a ray of hope Jonah might pass when none of the pooches turned out to be a black and white combination. But as he had to concede, the adorable angle might prove to be too much.

"Hey, Jonah," Tommy yelled from his position on the lawn. "These are the ones I have leftover. My gran's been working on getting them housebroken. They're really good about not pooping in the house."

"There's good news for anyone who's ever tried housebreaking one," Izzy announced. "That's a huge plus in my book. You should snap one of these bad girls up, Jonah."

Almost immediately, one in particular, the one with a soft gold and white coat, spotted Jonah and pounced. As Jonah squatted down to get a better look, the dog jumped up and began to lick his face. The boy rolled on the grass giggling at the liveliness of the pup. Completely captivated by the pooch, Jonah seemed to have forgotten about his previous stance on color preference.

"This one, Daddy. I want this one," Jonah said, sneaking out a series of belly laughs. "This one's Leo."

"Uh, Jonah, that's a girl dog," Thane pointed out.

"Girls are all we have left," Tommy informed them. "We had seven but the three males all went first."

"Any backup names for a girl?" Thane asked his son. Maybe, just maybe, Jonah had his heart set on a male and would take a pass on these. But when the boy wrapped his arms around the dog's belly and hugged tighter, Thane knew they'd be leaving there with a new member of the family.

"Then how about the name Jax?" Jonah offered.

Thane smiled, shook his head. "You sure about that? Jax still sounds like a male name…sort of."

"I like Jax."

"Jax it is then." About that time Thane looked over at Izzy who was dealing with a lively puppy of her own nipping at her knees. The pooch shared her sister's coloring and features but bore deeper shades of brown with swaths of white on her feet. "Whatcha got there, Isabella?"

She grinned and sat on her haunches. "I believe I've found the answer to my lonely nights."

"Now that's a shame but definitely a challenge if I ever heard one," Thane said with a wink. "Looks like you two have bonded. You gotta name picked out?"

"I think I'll call her Jazz."

"Jax and Jazz. I have a feeling that's a sister combo that spells trouble."

"We'll find out sooner rather than later if we don't stop by the market and stock up on treats and food for both."

"Good idea. I'm glad someone's thinking clearly," Thane said as he steered them toward Murphy's.

Once he got back home, Bobby hadn't fared as well as Jonah. When he'd reached his house, both his parents had been in a snit. But then that was the usual atmosphere at the Prather house.

Life for Peggy and Greg Prather had become a bitter pill they both were forced to swallow daily. It seemed they'd accepted their acrimonious union as an everyday occurrence. They both knew they were in a rut but refused to do anything but disagree.

Peggy didn't like her husband any more than he liked her. The two had long ago realized happiness was for other people and not for them. From the day they'd said "I do" until this very afternoon, everything had turned out wrong. Peggy made sure she reminded Greg how worthless he was and Greg returned the favor. Day in and day out, the same tune played and never changed.

Once upon a time, the daughter of a doctor from the Mission District in San Francisco, Peggy had rolled the dice and married a talented but struggling design student. During those first months together it soon became clear she had neither the patience nor the commitment to stand by Greg until he got his art degree. When she'd become pregnant with Bobby, that fact had sealed the couple's fate. Peggy forced Greg out of school and into the first of many menial jobs he took to pay the bills. Peggy didn't care for the day-to-day struggle so she finally encouraged Greg to leave behind the high cost of living in San Francisco for some place more affordable. That move led them to Pelican Pointe.

Nothing over the years quite humiliated Peggy like the realization she'd hooked up with a man who couldn't make enough money to support his family in the lifestyle she wanted and expected. The fact that everyone in town knew her husband was a failure seemed somehow even more of a crushing blow to her ego than anything else.

When it came to blame, Greg wasn't that much different in pointing the finger. He grumbled about the jobs he did manage to find. Whether it was a stocker at

Murphy's Market or cleaning the cages at the veterinary clinic for Bran Sullivan, Greg groused about his lot in life. No matter how hard he worked, he never seemed to bring in enough money. Money contributed to ninety percent of the couple's arguments.

Today was no different.

Angry about his low-paying jobs and his inability to work at what he loved, Greg had been the one to answer the phone when the school had called. Discovering his son was in trouble again had pissed Greg off. He didn't like having to face Ms. Dickinson about Bobby's behavior for the fourth time since school started.

"It's your fault Bobby's the way he is," Peggy insisted, pointing a finger in Greg's face.

"Oh really? All you can think about every single day of your life is yourself. 'Why don't we take trips, Greg? Why don't we have a decent car, Greg? Why don't you make more money, Greg?' I'm sick of your bitching. I'm fed up with you. Maybe if you'd get off my ass for just one freaking day and not be such a bitter old hag, Bobby might not be such a problem."

"Don't you dare blame this on me, don't you dare. You're the one who can't get a job and keep it. You know damn good and well that kid doesn't like anything I do for him. You're both draining me dry so much that I can't think straight half the time. You can't stand it because Bobby's turned out just like you are—argumentative, aggressive and worthless. He's just like his father."

"Worthless? I'm out every day working two jobs. I stock shelves at night at the market and then I go shovel out crap from animal cages. You think I wanted to do that for a living? Think again. I'm gone all night long and today was my only day off. Instead of relaxing, how do I spend it? I have to go drag Bobby home from school because you won't do it. He's picking on some first grader and all you can think about is yourself. You sit here on your ass watching reality TV shows all day long, making sure you get your hair done once a week. If you'd stop buying useless shit for yourself you see on TV and take care of your kid more, maybe this family would be a lot better off."

"Are you kidding me? Bobby never likes what I fix him for dinner. He gripes about everything I cook. He complains that he doesn't have the toys that the other kids have…"

In his room, Bobby put his hands over his ears in an attempt to muffle the ugly words. While he listened to the accusations bounce off the walls, he just wanted to be somewhere else, anywhere else but in this house with these two people who hated each other and him. He was fed up with it all, which is why after an hour or so he decided he'd heard enough. He decided to do something about it.

He grabbed his knapsack, began to stuff the candy bars he'd hoarded down into it along with a can of Coke. He grabbed an empty plastic bottle and went into the bathroom to fill it up with tap water. He went through his dresser drawers, picked out an extra T-shirt and a pair of shorts, crammed both down into the bag. He found his sketch pad, the one where he liked to draw cartoon characters and opened the window.

Climbing outside he fell into the bushes under the sill. He picked himself up and made his way across the lawn. Once he got to the sidewalk, he took off running, heading east to Main Street and then south out of town. His plan was to walk out to the 101 until someone picked him up and gave him a ride.

He'd show Ms. Dickinson he didn't need school. She could kick him out whenever she wanted and he didn't care. It wouldn't make a whole lot of difference to him because he had no friends anyway. But most of all his leaving would show his parents he didn't need to listen to their stupid arguments all the time. They didn't want him? That was fine with Bobby Prather.

As he took off toward the Pacific Coast Highway, eight-year-old Bobby decided he was done listening to anyone.

It wasn't until five o'clock that afternoon that the Prathers noticed Bobby wasn't in his room.

"That damn kid, where is he now?" Peggy ranted, tearing from room to room. "Bobby, you stop this nonsense this minute and get out here where I can see you."

"Bobby, you listen to your mother. You hear me, get out here now," Greg shouted. "I don't have time for this bullshit. I have to get to work in thirty minutes."

But after hunting throughout the house twice, they found no sign of their son. He wasn't in the garage or the shed in back. When they walked up and down Athena Circle calling his name, they got nothing but stares from the neighbors. Even after widening their search along Ocean Street, they still couldn't locate Bobby.

"Maybe he walked over to see the seals. He does that sometimes," Greg suggested.

After looking everywhere she could think of, Peggy gave up. "We don't have a choice. We'll have to call Brent and tell him we can't find Bobby,"

"Okay, okay. I'll put in the call. But when I find that kid, I'm tanning his hide for sure for making us worry like this."

Thane and Isabella were playing with Jonah and the dogs on the front lawn when they spotted Brent Cody pulling up at the curb in front of his brother Ethan's house just a few doors down. The police chief got out of his truck and met Ethan on the sidewalk.

Because both brothers looked harried and tense, Thane called out, "What's going on?"

"Bobby Prather's gone missing, ran away most likely. But I've issued an AMBER alert just in case because of his young age. Any eight-year-old out there on his own is in danger until we locate him."

"Bobby Prather got in trouble today at school," Jonah reminded his dad. "He's the one who said nasty things about my mom."

Thane relayed that back to Brent.

"That's what I understand from his parents," Brent said. "They punished him once they got him home from school and sent him to his room. But he hasn't been seen since. The parents got into another fight and apparently lost track of the boy."

"Need any help?" Thane asked. "I'm here to help anyway I can."

"You bet. All I can get. What I need right this minute is for people who know what the boy looks like to cruise up and down the streets, see if we can spot him that way. I'm taking Ethan out to look along the Coast Highway."

"You guys get moving and I'll round up everyone else I can to start the search."

As Brent and Ethan jumped into the cab of the pickup, Brent turned back. "Text or call if you should find him."

Thane turned to Isabella. "You stay here with Jonah and the puppies. I'll take my SUV and check the pier and the beach along Smuggler's Bay."

"I'd like to help too," she offered.

"Then start making calls, round everyone up. Use my phone." He handed off his cell. "I have just about everyone in town listed under my contacts. Start with Ms. Dickinson and Ryder first. Then move on to Nick and so on down the list."

"Got it. I'll call Logan, too." She traded phones with Thane. "Take mine. That way you can keep us up-to-date with text messages."

Once word got out, people wanting to help began to gather at the school parking lot. Murphy took out a street map of town and began marking up grid sections. Nick formed teams and assigned each one a section of town to search while Tucker Ferguson handed out flashlights. Men and women and children volunteered to spread out along Tradewinds Drive to Ocean Street looking in every alleyway and behind every business location sorting through every dumpster and trash bin along the way.

Despite their best efforts, by seven-thirty there had been no sightings of Bobby anywhere.

Back at Thane's, a hungry Jonah persuaded Isabella to fix chicken fingers and mashed potatoes for dinner. Underfoot, Jax and Jazz looked on as she worked in the kitchen. With each step she took, the puppies seemed agitated and worried, perhaps picking up on the underlying tension of the situation.

While she prepared dinner, Jonah attempted to play a game of baseball in the living room by batting the ball around. When it went flying into the ceiling fan with a thud, the dogs went wild.

"Are you supposed to be doing that in the house?" Isabella wanted to know. By the droop in Jonah's shoulders, she already had her answer.

"No, ma'am."

"Then maybe you should put the bat up for now." To give him something to do, she suggested, "Why don't you get out the food we bought for Jax and Jazz and scoop some into the dish? They're probably as hungry as you are."

"Sure," Jonah said with zeal. "I'll give them water, too."

When the timer dinged signaling the potatoes were done and ready for mashing, she let Jonah help with the prep. They got out milk and butter and she let him plop in both before putting her hand over his. Together they ran the mixer around the bowl, working the texture into the right consistency.

"That's the first time I've ever used a blender," Jonah beamed with pride.

"Mixer," Isabella corrected. "You just made your own mashed potatoes, something to tell your dad about later."

"I can't wait to tell Uncle Fisch, too!"

During the meal, once things settled down somewhat, she was bombarded by twenty questions every other bite from the anxious six-year-old.

"Have they found Bobby yet?"

"Not yet."

"Is he dead like my mom and my Mimi?"

"No, I'm sure he's scared, but he'll be fine. They just have to find him."

"Is he in trouble?"

"I'm sure his parents are worried sick. They'll be so glad to get him back they won't think about punishing him."

But by the time she put Jonah to bed at eight-thirty, there was still no word about the third grader. Thane had sent several text messages back and forth without adding much hope. He'd driven as far north as Promise Cove, scoured the area around Taggert Farms, and searched the woods near the lighthouse.

With every hour that passed, a sick feeling invaded Isabella's heart and stayed there. Even the dogs couldn't provide the comfort she needed. She decided to turn on the TV for a much-needed distraction.

But the local news anchors only confirmed what she already knew. Bobby's disappearance had become breaking headlines all over the area.

When Jax and Jazz started whining, then barking, then going crazy, she followed their gaze only to gape in astonishment as Scott materialized next to the fireplace.

"Shush," she commanded the puppies, snapping her fingers to get them to settle down. It was then she heard Scott utter the words, "Tell Brent to stay on the 101. Tell him to go to the turnoff to San Sebastian, south of town. Tell him Bobby's at the intersection there hiding in a ditch on the southeast side. Bobby's scared. He's cold. And he's crying."

Still clutching Thane's phone, Isabella hunted for Brent's number and keyed in the information just as Scott had relayed it to her. When she was done she said, "You're a godsend, you know that? Thank you."

A few seconds later, the cell phone rang and the digital readout told her it was Brent.

"Hello?"

"Is this Thane?"

"No, I have his phone though."

"Did you just send me a text? How do you know this is where the Prather boy is?"

Isabella didn't even hesitate. "Scott Phillips says that's where you'll find Bobby. I believe him."

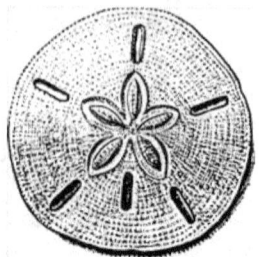

Chapter Twelve

Thirty minutes later, the front door burst open and Thane walked in, looking spent and haggard.

"Is Jonah okay?"

"He's sound asleep, has been for two hours."

Thane ran a hand over his face. "It wasn't even my kid out there tonight but I have to tell you, I was scared to death that we wouldn't find Bobby or that maybe we would, and he'd be…somewhere near the water, washed up onshore. I don't know. Brent finally found him all the way down the 101 near the junction to San Sebastian. How in the world do you suppose an eight-year-old goes ten miles on foot and gets that far from town on his own?"

"I'm sure he was very motivated."

For the first time in several hours, Thane let out a shaky laugh. "I suppose that's true. Makes you wonder though."

"Want food?"

"I guess. Yeah. My appetite's coming back." Snatching her around the waist, he covered her mouth, worked out his worry and frustration. "I needed that."

"No problem. Were you able to get a look at Bobby?"

Thane cut her an odd glance as he took a seat at the table to eat what she'd warmed up. "I saw Bobby when Brent and Ethan pulled up at the school where we were all gathered. I've never seen a kid that afraid. I can't get over the fact that little boy didn't want to get out of the truck. I mean his parents were right there and instead of yanking the door of the car open and running back to them, he just sat there in the backseat."

"You mean he didn't want to go home?"

"I don't think he did."

"What did the parents do?"

"They started yelling at him."

"Oh, Thane. No."

"Brent took them aside to have a talk with them. God, I'd hate having his job, the things he has to deal with. I'm not sure what Brent said to them but the Prathers pulled it together after that. I think maybe that one impression of Bobby bothers me more than his running away does."

"What?"

"The look Bobby gave Brent when he caught sight of his parents. It broke my heart," Thane confessed, digging into the leftover chicken. "Julianne mentioned to me this morning the boy's homelife wasn't the best, but I had no idea he'd rather be somewhere else, anywhere else, including hiding in a ditch, than back at home with his mom and dad."

"That's a sobering thought. Were the Prathers worried sick?"

"I'm sure they were."

She noticed the evasion. "That's not what I asked."

Thane blew out a frustrated breath. "I don't actually know the answer to that. Greg was more interested in how Murphy would surely dock his pay tonight and Peggy wanted to know if Janie Pointer would do her hair if she had to make a statement on TV."

"You can't be serious?"

"Unfortunately, I am."

"Thane, that's pathetic."

"Yeah, well, real life isn't always a bowl of cherries."

"I'd better get home."

"I should walk you there."

"Look, let's not go through this again. You need to stay here with your son. Besides, I have Jazz now. She'll be my guard dog. And there's always Scott nearby."

Thane looked over at the ball of fur sound asleep in the corner. "You start work tomorrow, right?"

"Yep." The light bulb went off in Izzy's mind. "Oh no. What will I do about Jazz?"

"You might as well drop her off here on your way to work."

"Really? You'll dogsit for me?"

"Why not? How much trouble can sisters be anyway?"

While Thane and Isabella were bringing their Monday night to a close, Henry Navarro's day had just gotten started. Everything he did these days centered on one thing. The motivation for him was to get back anyway he could at the woman who had not only defied him but had done the unthinkable. She'd divorced him.

This little trip out of the country reminded him that their ties went back years, ties that had been bound and sanctioned by a priest, something that couldn't be severed by a silly piece of paper.

Henry knew that no matter what Isabella did, she couldn't negate the fact that their families had known each other for decades. Both ancestries could be traced back to the fifteenth century. The Rialtos branch belonged to a Spanish nobleman named Marqués Carlo Frederico, a landowner who settled in the present-day area near River Turia. While impressive, Henry liked to boast that his lineage went all the way back to royalty and a series of Spanish dukes and duchesses who'd hailed from Barcelona.

Whichever one had the strongest ties to wealth and position, it didn't seem to matter. The two families were so close the lineage had long since blurred. They'd forged a bond so tight they'd gone into business together in the 1920s, buying and running the prosperous Castle de Vega Winery located in the fertile, rolling hills near the border of France. It still did a brisk business today despite the death of its owner and operator, Isabella's father, Javier Rialto.

A pity Javier had to go, thought Henry, as he scurried through the airport with a single task on his plate.

It had been Isabella's roots as much as her beauty that had captivated Henry. He'd figured their pairing would be a match made in financial heaven. Too bad Isabella had possessed an independent spirit, one that had been difficult to break. God knows, he'd tried. As for now, he refused to accept that all the time they'd spent together had been for naught. He would continue his effort to keep her in line until his last dying breath.

Through his family's connections he used the services of a skilled private detective who had managed to track down his wife's solicitor in London. The man, Alistair Chatswick, would pay dearly for providing Isabella with such misguided advice about ending their marriage. Henry would see to it personally. Instead of sending anyone else to do his bidding, this chore he would carry out for himself.

After sneaking out of his current country, Henry had made the best use of a friend's passport. He'd worn a convincing hairpiece over his own thinning hair and added a fake moustache to the disguise. Landing at Heathrow in the middle of the day, he'd hopped into a cab and taken it to the five-star Cornelius Piazza Hotel and checked into a luxurious suite. Even if his trip was short, only for one or two nights, there was an image to maintain. Henry was good at maintaining that haughty air that came so naturally to him. But make no mistake, like any common criminal, he could and often did circumvent the law to get his way.

Once he'd settled into his studio, Henry ordered steak from room service, ate the rare meat in an ease of leisure while he waited for the cover of darkness.

Once the sun went down, he dropped the pretense and made his way around the corner to the Bristow Law Firm. Dressed in black, Henry used the back entrance and the access card he'd paid dearly for to gain entry to the

building. He held his nose while taking the service
elevator to the fifteenth floor. There, he used the same key
card to slide through the reader. Because the law offices
were empty, he was able to take his time going through
file after file until he found what he was looking for.

According to the paperwork, he discovered that since
their divorce, Isabella had settled in some disgusting
backwoods community called Pelican Pointe, California.
As Henry read the words, he realized he should have
known she'd go running to that bastard, Logan Donnelly,
for comfort and help.

"Typical bohemian behavior," he muttered under his
breath as he shoved the file back into its slot in the drawer.

The urge ran through him to set fire to the entire office,
watch the whole building go up in flames from the street.
But Henry had a better idea. He'd take that brilliant plan to
Alistair's own back door, the place where the solicitor and
his family felt the safest. He'd show him the power of
Henry Navarro.

Henry took the elevator to the basement, walked out the
way he'd come in. On Stratton Street he hailed a taxi and
directed the driver to drop him off near the intersection of
Abbey and Wellington Roads.

With traffic, the drive took twenty minutes. At the
appropriate spot as instructed, the cab driver pulled to the
side allowing Henry to pay his fare.

There was a moment of hesitation before Henry
reached across to the front seat, waved two fifty pound
notes under the man's nose and told the driver in a heavy
Spanish accent, "Forget you ever saw me here. Got it?"

"Whatever you say, mate."

From there, Henry got out and footed the half mile into
the trendy neighborhood of St. John's Wood carrying a
tote bag. On a tree-lined street, the address went with a
spacious red-brick, three-story mansion. Studying the
opulent digs only increased the fury he was already
harboring. It seemed Isabella had contributed to the

solicitor's success. Apparently the divorce business was a worthwhile occupation.

From the inside of his satchel, he drew out a pair of mini binoculars and surveyed the building for a security system or camera setup. He was unable to spot one. The gate persuaded him he'd have to scale the brick wall at the most advantageous position. After breaching the perimeter, he circled around to the back of the property. Once there, he brought out a flashlight. Slicing his way through a thick line of hedges, he missed his footing and stumbled over the stone statue of a cherub near the entrance to the garden. Like an idiot, he swore and kicked the ugly thing with his foot.

Even with the beam of light it was difficult to see in the darkness. He had trouble locating the circuit board. But when he did, he flipped each breaker to the "off" position just in case. From there, he made his way to the backdoor where he took out his lock pick.

When he heard the mechanism click, he pushed open the door and strolled inside. Taking out his flashlight again he slipped past the kitchen and prowled through the first level collecting small items he could carry away in the pockets of his jacket. His scavenger hunt continued as he moved into the study. There he pilfered a Montblanc pen set. From the living area he took a platinum figurine in the shape of a bird adorned with a ribbon of diamonds and rubies. In the library, he perused the bookshelves, decided the first edition copy of *The Velveteen Rabbit* by Margery Williams would fetch a fair price on the black market and pay off a few of his debts. He shoved the loot down into his bag. On his way out of the room he picked up a silver Cartier cigarette lighter. This he would put to use in about ten minutes. He moved upstairs with a purpose, finding the nail polish remover he needed in the second floor bathroom.

He went out into the hallway, stood with pride on the landing near the bedrooms and the singular staircase. He opened the small bottle and emptied its contents onto the carpeting. He took out the fancy lighter belonging to the solicitor. Flipping open the top, he triggered the flame. With one toss, he pitched the entire thing on the floor and watched as the spark flared then burst into a full-blown blaze. Calm and satisfied with his work, Henry walked down the stairs and out the front door, escaping into the night with the feeling of a job well done.

Back in Pelican Pointe something caused Isabella to jolt upright in bed. The unease had her reaching for the gun in the nightstand drawer. At the foot of the bed, the movement caused Jazz to raise her head in a foggy gaze.

"A lot of watchdog you are," Isabella grumbled, staring at the pooch. "Or is it me? Am I imagining things that go bump in the night?"

Jazz yawned in response and crawled closer until the pup was right up next to her master.

"Good idea. We'll go back to sleep huddled together. I won't let him hurt you or anyone else," Isabella muttered to the dog. But she knew those words were a weak reminder of what Henry was capable of doing.

"We'll go back to sleep," she repeated, rubbing Jazz behind one droopy ear. "We'll kick his ass if he shows up here, won't we girl?"

But there was one problem with that plan. Years earlier she'd gotten a glimpse into what true evil looked like. She knew him to be an attractive man who showed up often bearing a smile and most times, gifts or trinkets geared to impress his quarry.

Good thing she was no longer interested in anything Henry Navarro had to offer.

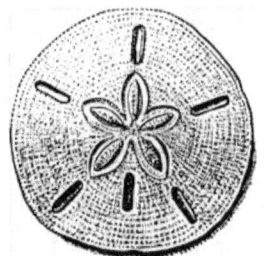

Chapter Thirteen

From a haze of sleep, Thane heard a series of yips and whines coming from somewhere in the room. He rolled over to see that it was barely four-thirty. His first thought centered on Jonah. Was that the boy moaning in his sleep? Was Jonah sick? Maybe it was the ice cream and peanut butter he'd eaten before bedtime.

After he'd eliminated everything else, Thane remembered the puppy. That thought had him zeroing in on the end of the bed. Movement caught his eye as the dog bounded over and started licking the hand that stuck out from under the covers. The action told him she was either missing her sister or needed to go outside. With a reluctant but resigned motion, Thane got up, wandered over to the patio door in his bedroom and slid back the glass. He watched as Jax scampered out into the backyard and into the darkness.

He stood there on the cold floor, his toes curling as he tried to keep an eye on the canine while she sniffed every blade of grass in the yard.

"Come on, hurry up. It's chilly out there."

A few minutes later the pooch came back obviously pleased with herself by the constant wagging of her tail.

"Good girl, Jax," Thane said as he rubbed her ears. "If you promise to do that every morning instead of peeing on the tile floor, I'll treat you to bacon and eggs for breakfast."

In total agreement with the deal, Jax woofed back.

Thane flopped back down on top of the mattress hoping to catch more shuteye. Without an invitation the dog hopped up next to him, burrowed into his body. He didn't have the energy to make her move and fell asleep with the dog nuzzling the side of his face.

The next time he opened his eyes, Jonah was shaking him awake. "Daddy, I'm hungry."

"What? Oh. Sure. Eggs. I'll fix eggs."

"But I don't want eggs. I want cereal," Jonah said stubbornly, standing next to the bed, clutching his puppy. "But Jax wants eggs."

Thane threw back the blanket, stared at his son's hair sticking straight up from sleep and his Spiderman PJs. He looked at the clock, noted they had overslept.

"We need to hustle. This is your fault," he said to Jax as he scrubbed a hand behind the dog's ears.

"Do I get cereal?"

As a father, there were times that called for strict guidelines and a stern hand. But after last night's ordeal with Bobby Prather, Thane decided giving in on a simple request for breakfast was hardly worth a major battle. "Is a bowl of Cheerios more to your liking then?"

Jonah pumped a fist in the air and took off for the kitchen, sliding down the hallway with his dog in the process.

Thane followed and found Jonah scrambling up on a stepladder so he could reach the bowls. Two dishes clattered on the counter.

After searching the pantry for the box of cereal Thane took out the milk and waited for the right time to discuss what he wanted to address before Jonah headed for school. They both were well into digging into the food when Thane said, "I want to talk to you about Bobby Prather."

"Did you find him?"

"I didn't but Mr. Cody did."

"He's the chief of police. He's coming to the school next week to talk to our class."

"Great. Look, I need to ask you something. Since school started has Bobby always said mean things to you?"

"He says mean things to everybody."

"But he didn't bother you before school started, right? I mean, we've been right here in the same neighborhood since June. Yesterday on the playground was the first time Bobby singled you out, right?"

Jonah bobbed his head up and down, slurped his milk.

"I need to ask a favor. I want you to try to hold your temper when dealing with Bobby, okay? No matter what he does or says, I want you to try and ignore him."

"Why? I want to bash his face in."

"I know you do. But fighting him won't help you or Bobby. Besides, he's older and outweighs you by a good fifteen pounds. Let's try another approach."

"Like what?"

"Let's try one that's a lot more difficult, a harder one. I want you to do your best to make friends with him. You and Tommy should ride bikes with him or something."

"No, Dad! Bobby's mean. He says nasty things."

"Bobby says those things because he's not happy at home."

"Why isn't he happy? He has two parents."

"He just isn't. Sometimes it doesn't matter if two parents are in the house. Families are made up out of happy people and sad people. Sometimes sad people rule the day and turn out to be the meanest. Trust me on this, okay? So how about we try and help Bobby out. Why don't we start slow. How about you invite him over here this afternoon after school?"

"Do I have to?"

"No, you don't have to. But it would be a nice thing if you did. Who knows? You might actually find you have something in common. You might actually like each other. Think of it as an experiment."

"Sounds like no fun to me," Jonah muttered.

"If it doesn't work, we'll try something else. How's that sound?"

"Like no fun at all."

Inside Sea Glass Cottage, Isabella woke to a wet, sloppy tongue slicking the side of her face. Jazz looked ready to go for a potty break. The puppy didn't mind letting her master know it either. It was the dog's persistent jumping that had her throwing on a robe.

"Okay, okay. I'm getting up as fast as I can."

Isabella moved over to the French doors and flung them open. The pooch raced out into the sunshine and Isabella followed out onto the terrace, watched as the pup explored her new terrain.

A little nervous about the day ahead, Isabella stood there and realized how long it had been since she'd last held a job. Before her ex, that was for sure. The idea of starting to work again after all this time made it difficult for her to build up any real excitement. But she'd already committed to River Cody. That meant someone was counting on her to show up on time. Because of that she'd go through with it. After fifteen minutes waiting for Jazz to finish her business, Isabella gave up on the dog and went into the kitchen to start coffee.

As she listened to it drip through the automatic brewer, Isabella found her thoughts drifting to Henry Navarro. She considered calling Logan or Thane to talk things over with them but decided she didn't want to interrupt their regular routines. After all, Logan had twins to help care for and Thane had to get Jonah ready for school. It didn't make sense to complain to them about her ex and the uneasiness she felt. Where was the careful prep she'd done for the past several years? She'd taken enough self-defense courses for six people, learned to shoot a variety of weapons, and trained her head to defeat the ex who had such a hold on her.

But despite all that, during quiet, peaceful moments like this morning, memories often overran her thoughts. Maybe because this time of day, when she'd had trouble sleeping the night before, she'd think back to times when her life hadn't been this serene.

Annoyed with her focus, she called the dog back into the house, turned the locks, and went into the bathroom to shower. While the water sluiced over her body, she thought about Thane. He was so unlike her ex. Thane exuded self-confidence without the haughtiness and malice she'd rarely seen that combination in a male. In her mind, Thane brought out masculinity in an attractive way each time he interacted with his child.

Out of the shower, she fiddled with her hair, tried a new style by putting it up in a bun and decided it looked ridiculous that way. She let it trail down to her shoulders.

Moving into the confines of her closet, she suddenly realized if she rode her bike, she had to pedal down the hill to the museum—a fact that impacted her choice of outfit. Standing among a sparse selection of jeans and dresses, she sifted through hangers and wondered what ensemble would work best. River hadn't mentioned a dress code and she hadn't thought to ask.

She decided to play it safe and settled on a longish flowered skirt, paired it with a pink crop top and a bold orange jacket.

Over two toaster waffles with maple syrup, Isabella sipped her coffee, enjoying the solitude—except for the slurping sounds coming from the corner of the kitchen. She chuckled at the way Jazz had taken to her water dish and food. "Nothing wrong with your appetite," she noted in the dog's direction.

When it came time to leave, she grabbed the leash she'd picked up at Murphy's Market from the peg in the entryway and checked her image in the mirror. At the last minute she decided to tie her hair back instead of leaving it down. Pleased with the outcome, she grabbed her purse and called to the dog.

"You'll have to stay at Thane's today," she told Jazz on the way to where her bike was propped up at the side of the house. But then she stopped in her tracks. "What am I thinking? I can't ride my bike. You'd have to follow me and you're too little for that. You'd never be able to keep up. We'll walk to work." She started down the hill with Jazz at her heels. "Today, you'll get to spend time with Jax and then I'll pick you up after I get done with work. You'll see, the time will pass quickly."

Once she reached level ground, she thought long and hard about buying a car. But the day was so beautiful with the water glistening in the bay that it signaled all the advantages of being able to walk such a short distance to a job.

For a Tuesday Ocean Street seemed busier than usual. People were out and about early. Flynn McCready stood on his stoop holding a broom and grunted as she strolled by. She waved to Dan Jenkins at the bait shop who was in the process of helping a customer load bags of ice into his pickup.

Malachi Rafferty, owner of the T-Shirt Shop, said hello as he dragged his sign out onto the sidewalk. The ad made sure everyone knew that if you bought three shirts he'd give you a nice price break for the money.

Jazz had to stop several times to sniff each tree along the route and, at times, fought the leash. Near the pier the pup wanted to bolt toward the bay. Isabella couldn't figure out why until she caught sight of Scott standing at the end of the wharf. That explained Jazz's reaction just like the night before, she decided.

It was the smell of crab cakes cooking inside The Pointe wafting on the breeze that made her remember she hadn't bothered to pack a lunch. Ah well, she'd get back into the rhythm of going to work soon enough. She'd run over to the Diner whenever she got hungry.

When she spotted Thane at the end of the block walking Jonah to school she waved for him to wait. She and Jazz caught up with them just as Jonah darted off to talk to his friend, Tommy.

Thane cocked his head and eyed the golden-brown hair pulled back in a ponytail. "Hey there, you look beautiful and all ready for your first day on the job I see. Love the skirt."

"Thanks. The Archers must be great at potty training a dog. Jazz didn't have a single mishap overnight."

"Same with Jax. We'll have to find a way to repay their efforts."

"Agreed. Well, she's been fed and shouldn't give you any trouble. Oh, look, Thane, there's Bobby Prather."

"I'm about to head inside now to talk to Julianne Dickinson." He told Izzy about his plan to befriend the troubled boy. "If it goes well this afternoon, I'd like to see if Bobby's parents will let him come to a sleepover this weekend at my house."

Isabella stared at him. "You know what? You get more and more handsome every day that passes."

"Really? Why?"

"Because you're an amazing human being, Thane Delacourt, add in the fact that you're completely in tune with who you are as a father, and it makes me want to..."

About that time a voice from a nearby house broke up what promised to be an interesting offer. Logan came running up. Instead of finishing her thought, she waved over her shoulder.

"Gotta get to work. Take good care of my dog. See you guys later..."

He watched her walk away and glared toward Logan. "Did anyone ever tell you that you have rotten timing?"

"Hey, you heard the woman. She has to get to work. She has no time to play kissy face with the likes of you standing in the middle of the street."

Thane shot him a sarcastic look. "What would the town do without that artful bulletin from Logan Donnelly?"

"It's a gift, I know. I wanted to thank you for your help last night looking for the Prather boy. Did you see the way the town came together in such a short time?"

"Yeah. I kept thinking about that while I drove around. We might be a small dot on the map to many but the people who live here show up for each other."

"I've traveled the world and never experienced that sort of thing before I came here."

"I guess that says it all about why I came back. I want this for Jonah. Every child deserves to grow up knowing the people around them care." Thane thought about Bobby and it made him more determined than ever to crack the kid's veneer.

A few minutes before nine o'clock Isabella reported for duty inside what looked like a warehouse. But she already knew the place had once been the town's newspaper office. She liked to think that with the mural on the outside of the building next door, this part of Pelican Pointe held the beginnings of an art district, small but starting to come around.

Once she stood inside the entrance looking up at the focal point—the tomol hoisted up on display that River and her team had unearthed—that feeling doubled. The plank canoe had been positioned to look as though it had just washed up onshore. The exhibit popped with realism. The Chumash craftsmanship was evident as she took a tour around the vessel encased in glass. With nothing more than flints and sharpened shells, the early people had built their boats with redwood logs, tied the slats together using wooly milkweed fiber or hemp, and filled any cracks in the design with yap, or pine pitch before stretching shark skin over the shell to make it even more resistant to water.

"On time. I like that," River said with a glint in her eye from the opposite side of the room.

Isabella stood back, tilted her head admiring the display. "This is an amazing representation of skill and workmanship."

"I had this idea to make it look as though the canoe rested on the rocks just like we discovered it, like it had been swept onto shore with the tides. Since this baby is our primary focal point, Logan took it a step further with the design. He's in the process of building an authentic-looking beach scene complete with a series of faux boulders to make the exhibit really work. He'll add that in layers in a couple weeks."

"It already pops. I'm guessing you couldn't actually get boulders through the front door so his design works as the next best thing."

"We could, but it would be a lot of wasted energy bringing in big rocks when Logan managed to solve the problem."

"Exactly. Where's the rest of your inventory?"

"There's a *lot* more in the back. Follow me. We'll have the main exhibit room and then several anterooms or halls holding the smaller items."

She followed as her boss led the way into a storage area packed with relics waiting to be cleaned and tagged for show. Isabella spent the rest of the morning listening to River spin a tale about each individual Chumash artifact. With each story, she got a better idea of the Native American people who had lived and thrived in the area for more than eight hundred years.

As she analyzed each piece, Isabella became more and more fascinated with the lifestyle. "I'm impressed with what you've done here, River. People will definitely line up to get a look at all this."

"That's what we're hoping for—an 'if you build it, he will come' *Field of Dreams* type of moment."

Isabella continued to skim through the assortment of shells and beads used to make jewelry, the crude pieces of pottery, the numerous steatite carvings of animals in grayish green or light brown. There were pretty ornaments in soapstone, many different animals of various shapes. Bears, wolves and deer showed off their creative use of paint. She picked one up and dangled it at her earlobe. "These are beautiful. You do realize they'd make fantastic earrings."

"I know. The temptation is definitely there. Look at this." River held up a rock with a colorful drawing of village life depicted on it. She waved her hand over a table replete with stones. "There are enough arrowheads and simple shells here to fill up several baskets."

"All this came from the beach below the cliffs?"

"Every single piece dug out of the sand and grit. What you see here is two years of my life's work."

"You must be so proud of what you've discovered here and brought out into the open for the rest of us to enjoy."

At noon Thane showed up at the museum with Jax and Jazz on leashes to take Isabella to lunch.

"Hey River. Any chance I could borrow your slave, feed her, and then bring her back to you ready for a brutal afternoon?"

"Sure. Isabella, get out here. There's a hunky guy standing near the display willing to take you to lunch. I have to run home anyway to see if Brent remembered to feed Luke."

"You're kidding?"

"Yeah, I am," River said with a grin. "Brent's probably waiting with tuna sandwiches at the ready."

"The ones with apples and pecans in the mix?" Thane asked.

"This guy knows his way around the kitchen," Isabella said with a nod of her head when she appeared from the backroom.

"I just like to eat," Thane admitted to the women.

"I'll have to try that combination," River told them as she locked up for lunch. "In the meantime I don't expect culinary genius from the town's top cop. I know my guy. Just as long as he remembered to throw together a ham sandwich or an omelet, I'll be happy."

The three took off walking until Thane and Isabella turned the corner on Pacific Street to head to his house.

"What's on the menu?"

"Nothing as fancy as tuna sandwiches."

Once he unlocked the door to his house, the dogs bounded inside ahead of them. She noticed he'd tidied up quite a bit from last night. Standing in the great room, she caught sight of the table already set for two with a snappy white tablecloth and crystal. A smile broke out on her face. "This is above and beyond what I was expecting."

"It's never too early in the day for ambiance." He lit two candles for a centerpiece.

"Why Thane Delacourt, I do believe you're a romantic."

"I never said that I wasn't. I know how to wine and dine with the best of them. Today, I picked up one of Perry's specialties, crab cakes, fingerling potatoes and a broccoli-cabbage salad."

"That is so funny. I've smelled those crab cakes ever since I left home this morning. You're a mind reader."

"Take a seat. How about a glass of wine?"

"Absolutely. In celebration of my first day on the job, how can I refuse? I'm sure one glass won't prevent me from cataloging artifacts."

"How's that going?" he asked as he pulled the cork out of a bottle of Chardonnay.

"It's interesting work because it's directly related to the history of the area which makes for a fascinating real-life walk out of the past." She went into a detailed account of some of the relics, saving the best for last. "You saw the canoe. Logan's creating a base that will give it a natural setting so that when you walk in the whole thing blows you away. Imagine, that piece buried under all that sand for hundreds of years."

"It's an impressive piece. But then I always thought the Chumash were talented. If you haven't been to the Santa Barbara Museum of Natural History, they've dedicated an entire exhibit hall to the Chumash way of life."

"River mentioned it. I believe her goal is to make this one as notable one day. Not changing the subject but I'm curious. What did Julianne say when you suggested that you'd like to help Bobby Prather?"

"She was totally onboard with the idea. I just hope befriending him helps the kid, you know?"

"It's a shame his homelife is so chaotic. But maybe by reaching out to him you'll at least find out the reason."

He picked up her hand and kissed the palm. "You're an understanding soul. For one so young, you seem to have come to terms with your past, your trouble with the ex you've put behind you. Not everyone does that."

"There's an old saying or maybe it's a Chinese proverb, I forget which. 'Make friends with your misfortunes, otherwise you'll always be angry.' I made friends with my past about three years ago. I've moved on from the past and I'll never go back to living that way ever again," Isabella admitted.

"To a certain extent, that's what I've learned, you pretty much better accept the things that have happened and move forward, give up clinging to the past, otherwise you're bogged down in making the same mistakes." When he saw that she'd finished her meal, he took her hand and led her over to the sofa.

Without a word, he snatched her around the waist and brought her onto his lap.

Throwing her arms around his neck, she latched on to his strong shoulders. Like gripping a lifeline to keep from going under for the third time, she held on. For a brief moment, a tremble of doubt ran through her. But that dissipated once his lips met hers.

Somewhere inside, a force kindled to life within her. It built slowly like an ember glowing along a dark road. She felt herself warm, then get burner-hot. With each of his kisses, the past slipped farther and farther into the distance until the wound had seared closed.

He nudged her shirt aside, undid her bra so he could nibble on her bare breast. The sucking motion had her calling out his name. He lifted her up slightly, slid his hands up her skirt, dragged down her panties. He shifted her position slightly to gain better access. Her breath hitched while his fingers traveled to wet folds. As his mouth worked its way around curves, the climax slammed into her. A state of bliss she'd never known before swallowed her up, healed her completely.

A liberating freedom moved through her. She pressed him to lift his hips so she could help him out of his jeans. Leveraging herself up, she climbed onto his lap and straddled him again. Opening, moving as he moved, like two souls stirring to dance—two connected as one. They formed that one link as old as time.

Pleasure took hold, erupted and slipped into every nerve and core, overriding everything else. The air sizzled around them with sensations. They let loose like two teens in the backseat of a car on a Saturday night. Clinging to each other and dizzy with the fervor that built up, they raced along the edge of a cliff. When she shattered again it was into a million brilliant shades of red like sparkling sea glass scattered on white sand.

Breathless, she rested her head on his. "You're good, I'll give you that." She threw out her arms, raised her voice and announced, "The drought's over."

"In a big way. You were phenomenal. What happened to 'I wasn't all that great at it'?"

"You think I was great? Really?"

Thane chuckled even though he didn't really want to let go of her hips. "Yeah. I opt for a replay. Give me twenty minutes and I'll see what I can do."

She laughed and slapped his hand away as it wandered up to her breast to toy with a nipple. "I don't have twenty minutes. I'm late getting back to work on my first day as it is. I'll probably get fired."

He finally released her and watched her shapely form extract from his. "You've got some body there, Rialto."

Grabbing her underwear, she wiggled into them, and caught Thane staring at the showy movement.

He grinned and patted her ass. "Next time I promise to last longer."

"You lasted just fine."

"Come on then. I'll zip up and drive you back. It'll be a lot faster than walking."

Once back in the main room at the museum, Isabella's assignment was to log each artifact into the computer. There was a folder for weapons—harpoons, bows and arrowheads. There was one for tools, which included those items used in the day-to-day running of the village. River's team had found an abundance of rudimentary utensils used in the communal cooking chores. Most were made from the hard natural substances like quartz and obsidian that were prevalent in the area. Some were used to scoop out the meat from abalone shells while others were honed and sharpened and used in place of knives. A variety of bones from deer, bear, swordfish and whale were used in the same manner.

Which meant Isabella had a fair share of data entry to complete. As she got down to her work, she wouldn't allow herself to rethink how she'd spent her lunch hour. Instead of second thoughts, she decided to ride the tidal wave Thane had provided for as long as it lasted.

That's why she was stunned to see Drea walk through the door carrying a huge vase full of two dozen purple and white orchids.

"Who are those for?" River asked from across the room where the glass cases would hold the weapons display.

"These are for Isabella, with a card."

River turned to stare at her employee. "What kind of lunch did you have anyway?" River teased.

"Uh, the usual," Isabella said getting up out of her chair to take the bouquet. She read the card, which thankfully held no indication of what the two had spent their lunch hour doing.

"Brent didn't send me flowers, but then marriage tends to take the romance out of everything."

That comment brought wide-eyed looks from Isabella and Drea alike.

"Just kidding," River said with a wink. "How's the dating thing going with Zach?"

"Oh. Well. Zach's been super busy with everything he has on his plate and I'm swamped with homecoming approaching and helping to plan two weddings. That's why it isn't easy to find time to get together. Plus, I've never been both the florist *and* part of the wedding party. That creates its own challenges."

"Both Bree's and Julianne's? That's a lot of pressure for you," Isabella noted.

"It is." Drea tilted her head to study the newcomer. "Thanks for that, not a lot of people understand that flowers are a big deal to the bride-to-be."

"Flowers are a big focal point of the ritual, getting it right will be a reminder for years to come that you did a great job," Isabella offered, remembering her own unfortunate, misguided nuptials where she'd wanted to toss the pictures into a roaring fire and obliterate the bad choice she'd made.

Drea blew out a breath. "Tell me about it. A lot of people don't understand what work it is to make sure the bride, in this case two, both Bree and Julianne, get the perfect flower arrangements that reflect who they are on the big day. And then if I do a lousy job, the photographer is right there to capture it all in pictures."

"For the bride and groom to revisit over and over again," Isabella finished in empathetic mode. "After all, every woman has her favorite flower she wants to see in the background."

Drea smiled. "I hope you like orchids."

"Oh, I do," Isabella said, inhaling the fragrant buds. "It's a romantic gesture I appreciate more than he could possibly know."

"Then don't forget to tell him that."

"When exactly are Julianne and Ryder getting married?" River wanted to know as she leaned over and took a whiff of the buds.

"Two weeks before Christmas so I've got more time to prepare for theirs. But Bree's is closing in fast at six weeks. And she's so busy getting her new business off the ground that it's been a challenge."

"Well, just for the record, if Brent ever asks you, my favorite flower is tulips or maybe sunflowers. Yeah, sunflowers are cheaper."

Drea burst out laughing. "Okay, I'll give him a head's up and a nudge the next time I see him. If you ask me every man needs to keep that kind of info available in the data bank."

Chapter Fourteen

That afternoon on the playground, Jonah and Tommy looked on as Bobby Prather and his buddy, Doug Bayliss, ran roughshod over a group of second graders. The scene frightened the onlookers so much it had Jonah admitting, "Can you believe my dad wants me to invite him over to my house? No way am I doing that."

"That's because Bobby's *mean*. Look at him over there. He's picking on Brennie Davis."

"I know you like her."

Tommy lifted his shoulders. "She lives right next door to me. I've known her my whole life. Uh-oh, Bobby's spotted us. He's coming over here."

"What are you two jerkwads lookin' at?" Bobby demanded.

"Nothing. We're just standing here talking," Jonah stated.

"Well, knock it off or I'll flatten your nose."

Intimidated, Jonah chewed his lip but managed to sputter out, "Want to come over to my house after school?" Jonah heard the words and couldn't believe they'd come from him. He hoped this wasn't a huge mistake but took comfort knowing it would make his dad happy.

"Why would I want to do that?" Bobby asked. "You're in first grade. I don't want to hang out with a six-year-old. That would be lame."

"Okay. Fine. Then don't. Only reason I asked in the first place is because my dad told me to."

"Your dad? Stop lyin' to me you little shrimp."

Jonah shook his head. "I'm not lying. I get in trouble if I lie."

About that time the bell rang, signaling that recess was done. The boys rushed off to line up with their respective classes before going back inside.

The next two hours dragged by as Jonah struggled to create a collage with the letters of the alphabet. He had to pick a word that started with each letter which seemed to take forever, especially with x, y, and z. So when the final bell sounded no one was more ready to go home than he was. In the hallway, he hefted his backpack and started running toward the exit.

He skidded to a stop when he saw that Bobby Prather stood outside on the stoop, guarding the door and waiting to make trouble.

"Hey, did you mean it when you said I could come home with you after school?"

It took Jonah a few seconds to answer. "Um, sure. But you said it was lame."

"I don't have anything else to do so...let's go. I've already spotted your dad over there at the curb. He's always waiting for you. He's got dogs with him."

"Yeah. When we lived in New York it used to be my grandmother who picked me up from school until she got sick and died and then we moved here. That's my dog, Jax with Izzy's dog, Jazz," Jonah explained as he went running up to his dad and immediately hunkered down to rub his pup's ears. "Bobby's coming over to play at our house."

"So I see. Hello, Bobby. Have you asked your parents if it's okay to go home with Jonah?"

"No, but they won't care."

Thane shook his head. "Sorry, but that's not good enough. Let's walk over to your house and talk to your mom or dad. How does that sound?"

"Do we have to?" Bobby moaned. "My dad's probably at work already and Mom doesn't mind what I do as long as I stay out of her hair."

Out of the mouths of children came the most unflattering sorts of information, Thane decided. "'Fraid so, buddy. Your mom needs to know where you are at all times. It won't take that long since your house is just around the corner from ours." When he saw the downhearted look on the boy's face, he added, "Don't look so worried, I'm sure they won't mind."

On the walk to the Prather house, Thane turned to Jonah and wanted to know, "How was school today?"

"My teacher said I had trouble with my math worksheet. She gave me homework and problems to add and subtract," Jonah grumbled.

"Okay, we'll work on that tonight when we get home. How about you, Bobby, are you any good in math?"

"We're learning our multiplication tables. Ms. Brach says I do okay."

By that time they'd made the shortcut through the alleyway to Athena Circle and stood in front of a country-style cottage that needed a little upkeep on the outside trim. But then it was a reminder that the stucco on his own home could use a refresh.

Bobby ran up to the porch and opened the door, keeping Thane and Jonah from ringing the doorbell. Bobby hollered into the living room, "Mom, Mom, I'm going over to Jonah Delacourt's house to play."

By the time Thane stepped to the door, he realized why Bobby had to yell. The volume on the television was cranked up so loud it was almost deafening. From the doorway he took in the room and the female form sprawled on the sofa.

"'Bout time you got home. You know what Brent Cody said last night..." The woman's voice trailed off when her eyes landed on Thane. She unrolled herself from the couch and said, "Who's this? What have you done now?"

Thane held out his hand, introduced himself. "And that's my son, Jonah, standing on the porch. I was one of the men who went looking for Bobby last night. I thought he might like to get to know Jonah better, one on one, that way Bobby might stop picking on him at school. Is your husband around? I'd like to talk to him if he is."

"Already left for work. You want Bobby to come over to your house for real? You should know he can be a handful."

"That's boys for you, always into something."

"You're the one opening that pizza joint on the corner, right?"

"That's me."

"You used to play for the Jets, didn't you?"

"Giants," Thane said with a grimace, and correcting the woman with a grin. "Big difference."

"Okay. Sure. I guess it'll be okay. Bobby, do you have homework to do?"

"Did it already."

"Then sure, I guess. But you be back in time for supper though," she told Bobby as he flew out the door to where Jonah stood keeping the dogs in hand. "You be good," she shouted to her son's back. "I don't want Mr. Delacourt telling me you gave him trouble, you hear me? Boy never listens."

"I'll see that he's back home on time," Thane said, heading out the door on Bobby's heels.

Once outside on the sidewalk, Thane directed each of the boys to take a dog leash and watched as they sprinted ahead, the pups scurrying beside them.

As soon as they reached the house, Thane swung the door open. What had been a romantic, quiet rendezvous point only hours earlier at lunch turned into a world of bedlam.

The dogs skidded across the floor with their nails clicking. Jonah tossed his backpack on the bench in the entryway with a thud while Bobby took a tour of the living room filled with excited chatter. While Bobby marveled at the slew of sports trophies and photographs of Thane with celebrities that lining the wall, Jonah acted like it was all no big deal.

Thane offered the standard milk and cookies and Jonah's personal favorite, the peanut butter ones Max made at the Diner. While the boys climbed up on the bar stools at the island and dug into the treats, Thane kept an ear on the conversation. He wasn't stupid. He realized Bobby was light years from Jonah in worldly knowledge and devious cunning, especially after the language tossed around on the playground. To Thane the boy acted as if he had a pent-up temper flowing just under the surface. For that reason, he had no intentions of leaving them unsupervised for longer than a few minutes. But if he could get the kid to open up about what was making him so angry, he might be able to keep Bobby from picking on other kids, namely his own.

"Wanna take turns playing Angry Birds on my iPad?" Jonah asked, stuffing his mouth with a glob of gooey dough.

"Nah, let's play Legos. I like to build stuff."

In the great room, Thane supervised their play without butting in, letting them roughhouse with the blocks as boys do.

From out of the blue, Bobby picked up a photograph sitting on the end table and asked, "Who's that in the picture?"

"That's my mom."

Bobby glanced over with a hang-dog look on his face. "I'm sorry I said those mean things about her. She looks nice…and pretty."

"I never knew her," Jonah admitted as he crashed into the tower of blocks he'd built and sat back as the whole thing tumbled down around him. "She died like my Mimi did."

"My sister died."

"You had a sister?" Jonah asked.

"Yeah, she came down with a disease and died when I was in kindergarten. It made my parents fight all the time."

Ah, there's hope yet, decided Thane. As he listened to the two boys go back and forth it occurred to him that

Bobby was simply acting out in response to the negativity going on at home. If only death and misfortune didn't have to touch those so very young, thought Thane.

Because he couldn't wait to tell Isabella the turn of events, he sent her a text message.

In the back room at the museum, Isabella was knee deep in Chumash pottery when her cell phone dinged from inside the depths of her handbag. She dug it out, and read Thane's words.

I think I found out why Bobby's parents fight.
Why?
They lost a child. They're very unhappy together.
Sounds like a reasonable explanation. But their anger is obviously affecting Bobby in the wrong way.
I feel sorry for the kid.
Me too.
Are you ready for that replay? For good measure, he thumbed on a smiley face.
Bring it on. But make sure it's your A game.
Good thing I'm an A game kinda guy. He added another smiley face.
Gotta get back to work. See you tonight. Btw, thanks for the flowers.
My pleasure. I'll have dinner waiting. Any requests?
A repeat of earlier is fine with me. Hard to do with Jonah, I know.
But that's what I wanted to hear.

Isabella gave herself a minute to steady her heart. About that time River walked into the room, startling her back to reality, a reality that headlined one sad fact. She was way out of her league with a man like Thane Delacourt.

"I need help finding tables for the restaurant," Thane mentioned over the Swiss steak dinner he'd thrown together with a side of rice. "Ryder says there's a place south of town before the cutoff to San Sebastian. Will you go with me this weekend to check it out?"

Isabella smiled. "Sure. But you should know ahead of time that I have this thing for sturdy, solid wood tables, like country French."

He made a face. "Is that the ornate stuff with the curvy legs?"

"Cabriolet. That's what they're called. And no, I'm not talking about French provincial. What I like is the farmhouse look, a table with a trestle and an attractive skirt. A lot of the time the design includes tables with drawers and clever knobs."

"Are we still talking about tables?"

She rolled her eyes. "I am. I'm not sure what you're imagining."

"Why not just use surfboards for tables?" Jonah asked his mouth full of rice. "You can eat off one. I've seen surfers at the beach eating their lunch on top of their boards."

Izzy looked over at the boy and contemplated his visionary use of fiberglass, considered how they could make it work. "Wow, that's not a bad idea at all. You know that side wall you have, the one with no windows. What if you took a longboard and used it like a counter, affixed it to the wall? You could put bar stools underneath and you'd easily get four more seats."

Thane's lips curved up. "I'm surrounded by geniuses. I bow to the superior decorator's intellect."

Izzy held up her hand to Jonah for a high five. "We rock our superior decorator intellect, don't we?"

"Yeah, we rock!" Jonah said tapping her palm in reply. "I want to eat my pizza at the surfboard counter."

Thane picked up his glass of Cabernet. "I'll have to ask Troy if it's doable. If it is, I like the idea of continuing the surfing theme on that bare wall, not to mention the novelty of it."

They went over the details while scrubbing pots and pans and loading the dishwasher. They got down to basic accessory ideas, like fixtures and paint. While they worked and talked, Jonah played outside with Jax and Jazz until it got too dark to see. He came in sweaty and smelling like puppies.

One whiff and Thane said, "You need a bath. Bad."

"I want Izzy to read me a story."

"Afterward. You can't go to bed smelling like that."

Getting Jonah in the bathtub and then getting him in pajamas was Thane's job. Hers was to read the boy a bedtime story and tuck him in, kiss him goodnight while Thane called Troy to discuss the feasibility of the counter idea. So she delved into the world where fairies and pixies made their home in a magical woodland that reached all the way to the clouds. Jonah fell asleep before she got to the "happy ever after" part. Leaning over him, she placed a kiss on his brow, pulled up the covers and went in search of Thane.

She found him sitting on the sofa finishing off the bottle of wine with the dogs curved around his feet. He'd taken off his shoes, propped his long legs and feet up on the coffee table.

"Those dogs are as worn out as Jonah was. I didn't even get to the end of the story before he conked out."

He smiled at her, patted the seat next to him. "I love this time of night. Just listen to that," he said. "Peace. Quiet."

She laughed, sat down next to him, took the glass of wine out of his hand. "You've done an amazing job with Jonah. You should probably know, I think I've fallen for your son." She sipped the Cabernet, draped the other hand around his neck, following that up with a nip to his jaw. "And his father has these incredible blue eyes that just draw me in, make me want to do things I usually don't think of doing."

"I like the sound of that." Toying with her lips, he took her under in a deliberate play of tag and tongue. Tender persuasion led to him cupping a breast, fondling the shape and curve.

"This time when I make love to you I'll do it in a bed," he promised as he got to his feet, led her down the hallway to his bedroom. He shut the door, went over and took out his iPad, thumbed through his playlist. The violin strings of Vivaldi sailed from the speaker.

"Who would've thought you were a fan of classical?" Isabella said as she started to undress.

"After today, I'm a fan of you." He eyed the way she took her time undoing each button on her blouse and letting it drape seductively from her hand before falling to the floor. She undid her bra, reveling in the reaction on his face.

The urge to touch those breasts was too great. He pressed against her as she started shimmying out of the skirt. Running first one finger along the rim of the lacy panties then using two, he ripped them off in one yank.

She returned the favor by gripping his shirt, jerking it down his arms, helped him get rid of his pants. She angled, pushed him back on the mattress and sprawled on top. A gradual glide up his body had her fisting her fingers in his hair. Drawn to his mouth, she fused her lips to his.

They feasted, groped, then rolled, changed positions, rolled again, bringing her back on top. They bumped. She rode. Bodies locked in blinding speed with one thought in mind.

Pleasure ratcheted up as they headed into a dazzling halo of light. The room seemed to shake like a rocket racing headlong toward the sun.

They built to eruption like the first steam in a volcano before lava burst to the surface. The heady rush had their hearts pounding.

She went lax, draped herself onto his body.

Neither one moved. They lay spent, exhausted, the smell of sweaty sex lingering in the air.

"Just so you know, I'm a big fan of the replay," she whooshed out.

"Duly noted for future reference. You just keep getting better."

"Imagine that."

When he was able to get his breath back, he reversed their positions, shifted to bring her body into his. From above he looked down at her, tugged at her lips. "You are beautiful, you know that?"

"So are you."

"That's a first. I'm not sure anyone's ever called me beautiful before."

"Don't let it go to your head. Your ego's big enough without adding to it."

He ran a long, lean finger down to her silky thigh and then on to her calf. Spotting the ink on her ankle, he brought her leg up so he could make out the design. "What's this? I missed that this afternoon. You have a tattoo. Interesting, a four-leaf clover with two crossed swords in the middle. Not exactly the usual choice you pick right out of the catalogue."

"It's…special…personal."

"How special? How personal?"

"Something between…two…very old friends."

"I have something special for you between two new friends. Wanna see what it is?"

She giggled and rolled over him. "Don't you need like twenty minutes to 'recover'?"

"Probably. But there are so many things I want to do to you it'll take me that long to get around to all of them."

"Sounds promising. You'd better show me what you mean so I won't miss one."

"No problem. Good thing I'm detail-oriented."

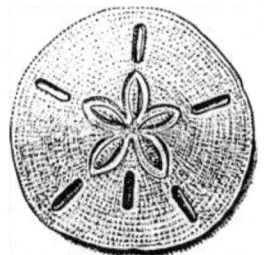

Chapter Fifteen

Saturday morning they found the Cleef Atkins place among the gentle rolling hills sloped toward San Sebastian. The farm itself went on and on for acres and acres over a messy jungle of junk. The bumpy pavement gave way to a field of golden blooming fennel. A patch of carob trees became home to old Chevys and tractor tires, long put out to pasture and a slew of broken, discarded furniture that had seen better days.

"Wow! Look at all this stuff!" Jonah exclaimed from the backseat.

As soon as the three of them got out of the car an old man appeared, walking through the wildflowers that grew among knee-high thistle and purple milkweed. He had to be in his late eighties.

"You the people looking for tables?"

"That's us," Thane said, making the introductions.

"Got quite a few to choose from, any particular kind?"

"Not really as long as they're sturdy and durable."

The true hidden treasures were found inside the barn. Isabella spotted a fifteen-foot outdoor theater marquee and rows of auditorium-style seats. Thane noticed a stack of tables that looked as though they'd been used in a restaurant.

"Those came from the old inn located south of here. It used to be out on the main road that went to Scotts Valley. But when the county built the alternate route, the hotel was forced to close down. That was in the late '70s," Cleef recalled.

"These are nice," Thane said running his hand across the dusty top. "They'd be ideal for re-sanding and repurposing, don't you think?"

Instead of answering, one glimpse at Jonah climbing up a tower of weathered lumber, nails poking out of the wood had Isabella rushing over in that direction. "Uh, Thane…should Jonah be up here like this?"

He followed her eyes and let out a warning. "Jonah, get down!"

Hustling over, Isabella managed to grab the boy just as he teetered and lost his balance.

"I'm not sure four pairs of eyes are enough to keep an eye on him all the time," Thane said. "Thanks."

"No problem. That was close though." She turned her attention to the stockpile of tables, all different sizes and lengths. "If it were me I'd avoid the commercial ones from the inn, stick with these made out of solid wood." She went over to examine one. "See, this has a decent support skirt and this one has a sturdy apron. Both would be an asset when Troy puts on the surfboard tops that will add weight."

Thane stood back, decided the woman knew her stuff. "Okay, let's see if we can locate ten like these."

"Better make it twelve," she suggested. "Just in case one isn't as well-made as we think it is."

That afternoon at the corner of Tradewinds Drive and Pacific, Nick surveyed the empty lot, the same spot where Bradford Radcliff wanted to put his used car lot. The thirty-year-old was the brother of Nick's business associate back in Los Angeles and was hoping to make a fresh start somewhere else.

Bradford liked cars and wanted to turn that passion into his own business. Nick just wasn't sold on the idea that Bradford could make a go of it in such a small market.

"You have yourself a nice little town here, Nick," Bradford said. "I'd like to be a part of it."

"We'd love to have you. New business is always welcome," Nick returned easily.

"I don't need a loan from the bank. I have money I've saved over the years and my brother is willing to put in the startup costs. What I need from you is advice on how best to get this up and running. It wouldn't look like your usual rundown used car lot with a mobile trailer on it either. I'd like to put up a small, tasteful permanent building. I'd like to sell reasonably priced, reliable transportation. People always need a ride."

"See, that's what I don't understand. You'd have a much better chance with that idea in a larger market near Santa Barbara or Santa Cruz. Why here? If your plan is to target a more upscale community this isn't the place. Most people hereabouts are hardworking and don't have a lot of money to waste on exotic cars."

"I know that. I want to provide them with a place to buy a used car without getting taken. Remember when Dave suggested I come up here to the B&B and bring my girlfriend for a romantic weekend getaway? Well, I did and left the smog behind in L.A. I ended up loving the area."

"And the girlfriend?" Nick asked with a grin.

"Is long gone," Brad answered. "Anyway, I wandered around the town that trip. I admit I wasn't too impressed with the place. But by the third trip—"

"Each with a different girlfriend, as I recall."

"Well, yeah. But by the third trip I noticed this town has started coming back from the dead. I began to wonder if it might just be the place for me to put down roots. I've fixed up a lot of cars over the years. I'm better at working with my hands than sitting in a cubicle all day. I'd like to bring my inventory up here, such as it is, along with all the ones I have yet to get running. I'd need a good mechanic."

"Wally Pierce is one of the best. Thane Delacourt also likes classic cars. He drives one of those old Range Rovers he and his dad fixed up when he was a teenager."

"I've already talked to Thane. His car caught my eye when I was here last month."

"So you don't work on engines at all?"

"I mostly work on the body but I've been known to tinker with a carburetor a time or two. My shop would be in the back of the property. I talked to Dave already and he thought the whole thing had potential. I think at this point he'd just like to see me happy at something."

"And? What are you not telling me, Brad?"

Brad blew out a breath. "Look, I just want out of L.A. I have my reasons. For one, I'm tired of the commute to work that takes sitting in bumper-to-bumper traffic for two hours every day just so I can sit behind a desk staring out the window of a thirty-five-story building. I want to do something I enjoy before I get too old."

Nick slapped him on the back. "Then welcome to Pelican Pointe. You'll need carpenters to help with the building. You'll also need a sign. It just so happens I know where you can get both. If you need anything else, let me know. We help our own around here."

Over the summer at Taggert Farms the newcomer, Gavin Kendall, might've assumed the role of overseer from Ryder McLachlan but he still had a lot to learn about growing crops. While he and his wife, Maggie, had done all they could to settle into the caretaker's cottage—homelessness no longer an everyday occurrence for them—there were challenges. Gavin had his hands full helping to work the farm and learn the ropes. Milking cows hadn't come easy for him. He hung out with Sammy and Silas as much as time allowed trying to pick up the basics of everything from planting the seeds to packing up the final product. Insecure in that knowledge, he worked hard each and every day to overcome that deficit.

Incentive to succeed came easy. After spending six months living out of the family minivan going from place to place, no one wanted to make a go of it at the farm more than Gavin did. What he faced working the land was a piece of cake compared to not having a place for his family to live.

That's why Gavin tried hard not to make waves. But as the months progressed into fall, something wasn't right.

Once a week, Ryder stopped in to check on things. Today was one of those days.

"Why don't you just spit it out and tell me what's wrong?" Ryder asked after Gavin had spent an hour hemming and hawing.

"Look, I don't want to lose this job."

"And I sure don't want you to do that either because I might have to go back to farming. Believe me I'd rather work with boats. Now tell me what's bothering you."

"I'm pretty sure we're running out of growing space here."

"What? That's a joke, right? That's the last thing I expected you to say. What makes you think that?"

"I may only have a high-school education, but I can do math. The numbers don't add up." Gavin took out a map of the farm, unrolled the paper and flattened it out on the table so Ryder could see.

"If you break it down per acreage, we're using every inch of available dirt. Seven acres of lettuce, up from five, five acres of kale, increased by two." Gavin went on to describe each plot of vegetable in detail and the space each took up. "If you want to maintain output and production and keep up the pace, there's a problem with the projection."

"What are you saying?"

"That we will, as farmers, eventually run out of land to plant and keep up production."

Ryder rubbed the back of his neck considering that. "Wow, Nick and Jordan decided to expand two years ago by merging the land they already had with the Taggert property."

"Silas mentioned that. But I saw right off that we have the cliffs to the west, the road to the east, which means we're locked in on the other two sides."

Ryder shook his head. "I take it you've gone over the numbers?"

"Three times. I came up with the same thing."

"Then let's check them again. If we come up with it the fourth time then one of us will have to meet with Nick and Jordan and plan to give them an update as to how things stand."

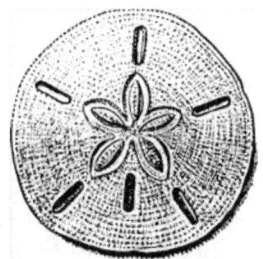

Chapter Sixteen

October arrived the same day Fischer Robbins rolled into town driving his Volvo station wagon. After a trip cross country and a few dozen text messages to get him to Pelican Pointe, Fisch pulled up to Longboard Pizza to a welcome committee. Thane and Jonah were standing on the sidewalk eager for Fischer to get out of the car.

"Man, it's good to see you," Thane said, throwing his arms around his friend in a hug.

"Same here."

"Uncle Fisch!" Jonah yelled, jumping into the man's arms. "Are you gonna stay with us?"

Fischer fell back a step as if weighted down with more than he could handle. "That's the plan. But who is this big guy? This can't be Jonah, or he's grown ten inches since I saw him last."

"I did not," Jonah claimed. "Daddy measured me this morning. I'm still the same size as I was before."

"That can't be," the man insisted. "The Jonah I know is this little bitty guy who is so ticklish he squeals when I do this." To prove his point, Fischer proceeded to tickle the boy wildly in the ribs before setting him back down on the sidewalk. "What's new with you, shrimpster?"

"I got a puppy named Jax. And she has a sister named Jazz. Jazz is Izzy's dog. We're dog sitting for Izzy while she works. Wanna see them? The puppies are around the corner where the patio is. Wanna see?"

"Sure. Jax is the name for a boy dog," Fischer noted as they started around the other side of the building.

"Not in our house," Thane stated. "Tell me, how is it that it took you three days to make the drive here anyway? Seventy-two hours when it usually takes about forty-five."

"Maybe if I'd paid better attention to directions the last time I was here I might've cut several hours off the trip."

"Don't give me that. You could've shipped your car and flown like Jonah and I did. That drive along I-80 is so boring I started to wonder if you'd fallen asleep at the wheel and got lost. I know you. What side trip did you take?"

The big man sighed. "No big deal, just a little unplanned excursion outside Salt Lake City, a little detour to Wendover, Wyoming."

"What on earth for?"

"There's this sculpture there by a Swedish artist, Karl Momen, I wanted to see." Fischer took out his cell phone, slogged through a ton of images until he held the device out to Thane. "See, it's an eighty-foot-high tree out in the middle of nowhere."

Thane stared at the photo, shook his head. "This is what you wanted to see? An ugly cement tree? You worry me sometimes, Fisch. You know that? Who else would drive out of their way to capture a picture of such a weird-looking monument? If you wanted to see something really unique, why not set your sights on the big ball of twine?"

"Hey, laugh if you want but Momen's sculpture is a kitschy, quirky abstract that shows what one artist decided to do to liven up an otherwise stark stretch of landscape in the middle of the desert."

"It's a tall slab of cement with balls in the air."

"Such a critic. It's more than that. It commemorates the desolation of the Great Salt Lake Desert using tons of native rock and minerals from the same area where the Donner Party once got stuck before they headed into the Sierra Nevada."

"I'm surprised you didn't try to follow the path." Thane stared at his friend. "You did, didn't you? You took off into the wilderness and that's why it took you so long to get here."

"Not all the way, no. I wanted to see Momen's *Metaphor*. He's been compared to Kandinsky."

"Who?"

"Kandinsky, the great Russian expressionist. Sheesh, you know nothing about art. I suppose you could do better?"

"No, I wouldn't even know how to top a concrete tree out in the middle of nowhere."

"Smartass."

About that time, Jonah came through the gate and dropped to his knees to hug the dogs. "See, Uncle Fisch, this one is Jax and this one is Jazz."

"Good-looking mutts. I can't believe you sprang for a dog. Living here has turned you into a total Mr. Mom. If I hadn't known you for ten years I wouldn't recognize who you've become."

Thane slapped Fisch on the back and said, "You don't know the half of it. Come on in. I'll show you your new domain." Holding the door for Fischer and Jonah, the three made their way inside and the bickering came to an abrupt halt when Fisch got a look at the restaurant.

"The guys finished out the interior paint job yesterday afternoon. They used that quick-drying stuff. Troy hung the surfboard this morning." Thane motioned toward a brightly colored red and yellow striped longboard suspended over the counter. He turned to Lilly as she worked on the wall with her paints. Thane introduced the two. "Lilly's still in the process of working her magic on the mural and she's just the person who might appreciate your photos of that *Tree of Life* in Utah."

"You have pictures of that, the one near the Bonneville Salt Flats?" Lilly asked, clearly impressed. "I urged Wally to take the kids out there this winter break on an adventure."

Fischer grinned. "I have a feeling I'm going to love the people in this town."

Fisch moved past the artist and near the counter area to stand under the hardwood surfboard with the logo and the words, "Longboard Pizza."

"Wow! What a difference. It's hard to believe this is the same place I saw when I was here last." Fischer took in the gleaming floor, the colorful walls, the rehabbed kitchen area and exclaimed, "This was nothing but an empty shell. These guys you hired must be miracle workers if they got this place ready on time."

"Pretty much. How do you like the work and prep areas? What do you think of the commercial range and refrigerator? Do they meet Your Highness's long list of requirements?"

"Hey, Delacourt, my pickiness is what's going to save this joint from ruin before it ever opens."

They'd been friends long enough that the sarcasm between the two men was expected. Still, Thane was pleased when Fischer gave his nod of approval and turned to wrap him up in a hug.

"This joint's going to rock this town," Fischer boasted.

"Yeah, that's what I hoped you'd say."

As soon as Isabella got off work she dropped by Longboard Pizza to pick up her dog. Her goal was to do a quick in-and-out and head home. But that turned out to be impossible as soon as she spotted Jonah playing with the puppies on the patio.

The boy greeted her with a hug.

"Was Jazz any trouble to watch?"

"Nope, she was good, like Jax."

"How was school? Any trouble out of Bobby or Doug?"

"Nope. Want to come in and meet my uncle Fischer?" Without waiting for a reply, Jonah took her hand and tugged her inside making an announcement of her arrival as soon as he hit the door. "Izzy's here."

Meeting Fischer Robbins caused her to stick around longer than she intended to get acquainted with the new chef in town—or try to. Despite his "just-arrived" state of mind, Fischer seemed already in his element. The guy had to be six-foot-three, almost equal in height to Thane. But as fair-haired as Thane was, Fischer was just the opposite. With coal-black hair and huge warm brown eyes, he evoked the typical, brash New York attitude in voice and demeanor.

She'd heard chefs could be quite temperamental. Fischer didn't disprove that. But it seemed the man had taken to his new kitchen like a duck to water. She stood by watching him busy himself in his galley, organizing cookware and utensils. "Talk about hitting the ground running, you're already getting organized?"

Thane laughed and answered for his cook. "We got a shipment delivered ten minutes after Fisch pulled up to the curb. What you're seeing now happens to be a Fischer Robbins trademark."

"He doesn't like people to touch his stuff," Jonah threw in.

"That's a fair statement," Fischer said in agreement, turning to get a good look at the woman who'd captivated his friend.

"He refuses to let anyone lift a finger to help put anything away. He has to have everything arranged just so, and refuses input from anyone else," Thane explained from the sidelines where he'd been relegated. "The earlier you accept the fact that this guy's a control freak when it comes to his cooking, the better off you'll be."

"I see that. Like the rest of the town, I can't wait to sample your New York-style pizza, especially your crust. I'm fairly picky about the texture."

"Since I'm a culinary genius, I'll dazzle you with my dough. No pun intended," Fischer shot back.

"Have you thought about where you'll get your supply of herbs and vegetables? Will you use fresh or frozen?"

Fischer sent her a haughty stare. "I always use fresh. When I was here over the summer I checked out this farm out on the highway, north of town. That is, I think it was north of town. Anyway, it has a reputation for quality."

"Taggert Farms. And they're organic," Thane added.

Isabella frowned. "But isn't most of what they grow targeted for commercial use already headed to grocery stores? What you guys could use is a place to grow your own ingredients."

Thane exchanged looks with the chef.

Fischer raised his eyebrows in agreement. "I like this woman. She obviously recognizes the costs involved in running a kitchen. Not a bad idea at all."

"Maybe when you get your own place you'll hunt for one with acreage," Thane tossed out in jest.

"I'm no farmer," Fischer shot back. "Do you garden, Isabella? If I remember correctly, you're the one who has all that room up on the cliffs."

She thought of her former life, the ex that used to go ballistic if she so much as ruined a nail from weeding. "I used to be able to grow things. I'm a little out of practice now though. I do know the value of using seasonal veggies to lower your costs. And that land on the cliffs isn't mine. It belongs to Logan Donnelly."

"Ah, yes, the sculptor. I bet he'd appreciate my stopping to take pictures of the *Tree of Utah*."

"Karl Momen's *Metaphor*? That *Tree of Utah*?" Isabella queried.

Fischer flashed an "I told you so grin" in Thane's direction and walked over to hand her his cell phone. "Take a look at these photos. I snapped the very treasure of a monument that embodies the pioneer spirit."

"Out in the middle of nowhere," Thane said, unable to resist yanking Fischer's chain.

Isabella's lips bowed up in a smile at the two who couldn't seem to keep from giving each other a hard time.

"You're an interesting sort of renaissance man, Fischer Robbins."

"Ain't that the truth? You know what they say, looks can be deceiving. Here's a woman of obvious style and substance who appreciates a man of many talents," the chef said.

After that, a discussion broke out about the best available property around town suitable to growing a vegetable garden.

"It would have to be larger than the norm to meet the requirements of a restaurant," Isabella pointed out.

Armed with an idea, Isabella got up to leave.

"Do you have to go?" Jonah asked.

"Right now, I do. I need to go see someone. But what if this weekend, we spent some time nosing around the train store down the street?"

"Yay! I'd like that."

"Good. Then be sure to ask your dad if it's okay." Isabella went outside to get her dog and hurried off knowing she'd left the little boy slightly downhearted. There was something about Jonah that tugged at her heartstrings. Was it his cute dimples or something much deeper?

She tried to brush off the glum mood on her way over to Landings Bay. She texted Logan, told him she needed to talk. When she discovered he was still at his studio, she headed over to Ocean Street and his newly designed gallery next door to the museum.

When he met her at the door, she looked around at his barebones surroundings. He hadn't bothered with anything more than a concrete floor and the basics. "It's a shame the lighthouse didn't work out for your studio. I'm still not sure what you found wrong with it compared to this rustic atmosphere."

"That's what Kinsey says. But I discovered that I create better in a stark environment. In fact, half the town thinks I'm crazy for going to the trouble to renovate a lighthouse only to abandon it to make this my place to work."

"I suppose as your friend I should remind you that it's no one's business where you decide to create."

"There you go."

"By the way, thanks for letting me get Jazz. Having her has made a real difference in my life."

"Don't be ridiculous. It's a good idea to have an extra layer of protection, especially since you won't let me put up the gate."

"That's because I'm telling you it would be a waste of money. Not to mention, a total put-off to anyone wanting to get a good look at the lighthouse."

"I hate to remind you, but that lighthouse is no longer on state property. The land's private. That's why I put up the sign to keep tourists out of there."

"But the lighthouse provides such a gorgeous view. Maybe you should think about giving tours to school children."

"Actually that's not a bad idea."

"Let's hope I'm on a roll then because I have another. What if we took the stretch of land next to the lighthouse, that clearing from the road you paved to the copse of woods and turned it into a vegetable garden—a big one, one that could be used to feed people, like a co-op?"

In typical Logan fashion, he grunted. But then she stood back, folded her arms across her chest and could see the wheels turning within the artist.

"You *are* on a roll. That's a good use of that land and fairly…brilliant. What brought this on?"

She told him about her conversation with the new chef in town. "It would take some time, of course, to get the kind of yield we'd need to feed anyone and some expertise to do it. But think about how great it would be for the town if people took turns tending the land, harvesting the crops."

"They'd get to eat fresh vegetables on a routine basis. I like it."

"So do I. Now we just need to make it happen."

"You know anything about farming?"

"Not on this scale. We'd need someone who could help us figure it all out."

"Even with the dog there, I still want to put in that gate."

"I know you do but let's not overreact and ugly-up such a beautiful spot for defensive purposes when there's no need."

Later, after Thane had cleaned up the kitchen—and the mess that Fischer had made throwing together pasta primavera for dinner—he'd gotten Jonah to bed for the night.

Thane and Fischer were sitting in the living room watching Thursday night football, the dog sleeping on the floor between their feet when Fischer finally wanted to know, "Okay, so tell me about Isabella."

"She's…amazing."

"Pretty name. And the body to go with it."

"Like the statue of a goddess."

"And you've worshipped at this particular monument a time or two, I take it?"

"Not often enough. In case you haven't noticed, I'm a little busy. What with the restaurant and Jonah and the fact that she's now working a nine-to-five job herself, we haven't been able to spend a whole lot of time together. And last night was open house at school."

"Thanks for the update."

"I'm trying to use that as an example. I haven't had much of a chance to be with her because I've been hopping all week at the business and then last night I had to come straight home to make Jonah dinner. While I went to school, she stayed here, got him ready for bed. But then by the time I got back it was after nine and the phone rang…"

"Cry me a river, why don't you? At least you have someone. Do you know how difficult it is on my crazy schedule to keep a relationship from heading south?"

"I intended to ask. What happened with Chelsea?"

"Same thing that happens in all my relationships…eventually. Chelsea got tired of spending her Saturday nights home alone. She wanted to go out and party and she didn't want to do it solo. I've always worked Saturday nights. Women don't like that."

"There's a lot of breaking up in New York."

"There's a lot of that everywhere."

"Maybe not so much here. You'll find that out for yourself. It's a strange little hamlet with its own eccentric denizens." When Thane noted the worried look on Fisch's face, he added, "You haven't changed your mind about moving here, have you?"

"Nah, just a bunch of flop sweat about starting over again in a new place."

"Then stop worrying. You'll fit in here just fine. You'll see."

"I don't know. The long drive caused me to have some doubts. I mean what's a New York boy, born and bred, doing living on the West Coast like a fish out of water. You'll probably have to draw me a map so I can find my way around."

"You're kidding, right? It's pretty much a grid. I showed you around in July. Think of it like a borough, Staten Island for instance, but on a much smaller scale."

"Like five hundred thousand versus five thousand?"

"Half that. There aren't even twenty-five hundred people living here yet."

"And you think we can make a go of a pizza joint in a small town like this?" Fisch shook his head. "I hope you know what we're doing." Fisch drained his beer and got up to get another. "I guess now's a good time to ask one thing. What are you still doing here with me when you have a woman up on the hill?"

"It's your first night in town. I thought I'd be a good host and stay home, prevent you from going all nervous-Nelly on me because you're having second thoughts."

"I'm fine. Go get yourself laid."

"Are you sure you don't mind me ducking out on you?"

"For a woman like Isabella?" Fischer placed a hand on his heart, the other he waved up and down. "She sizzles. No problem. You know I have this thing about love in the fall. She's an amazing person, witty, intelligent. Who knew you'd move here and find a gem like that?"

"You just met her," Thane pointed out. "She could be hiding the fact that she's a terrible human being."

"Not the woman I talked to this afternoon." But then Fischer frowned. "Has she shown you a dark side? What's bothering you?"

"No. No, nothing like that." Thane ran a hand through his hair. "I'm just... I don't know exactly. Obviously Isabella's made a fan out of you. I know she's made one out of Jonah."

"And that worries you?"

"No, it's a good thing." He didn't want to dwell on any misgivings, not tonight. "So I'm taking your adoration to mean you don't mind watching Jonah for me tonight?"

"I told you I would." He gave Thane another once-over, beginning to wonder what was going on. "Okay, what's eating you? For a guy headed out on a date with a beautiful female, why are you so grouchy? I've never seen you act this jittery over taking out a woman before. Unless..." Fischer stepped back, eyed his friend a second time. "My God, Thane Delacourt has feelings for her. Real feelings."

"Who says you aren't a genius? Of course, I have feelings for her. I'm getting ready to spend, what I hope, is a special evening ahead for both of us."

Fischer cut him a look that said he knew exactly what kind of night his friend had planned. "Take your time and do it right."

"I don't recall getting many complaints over the years."

"Then I've got Jonah covered," Fisch repeated. "Go. You won't have to be back until morning. Just remember though, this is different."

"Different? How so?"

"Think about it. This isn't you banging a fan that happened to show up at the hotel the night before a game. Nor is it the wired, crazy female looking for a thrill by hooking up with an athlete. This is a down-to-earth woman who's been through a lot."

"Yeah, I get that."

"And Thane?"

"What?"

"You just spent the evening reminding me that this is a small community. If you break a heart here, it may not make the tabloids, but it will affect people like the ripples in a giant pool."

"Yeah. I know that already. If the lecture's over I'd like to leave before I'm late and she sends out a search party."

"Very funny. Then go forth and enjoy all that love has to offer. But don't forget to wear a condom. There are some things love offers that's best not to pass on."

In response, and with Jonah tucked into bed, Thane reacted using the same salute he had for years between the two. He lifted his middle finger and strolled out the door.

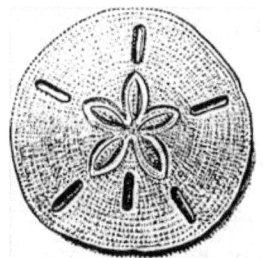

Chapter Seventeen

Isabella had changed out of her work clothes and taken a long luxuriant shower. Hair still damp, she worked fragrant oil into her mass of long locks, slathered perfumed lotion over her body.

She took out the black teddy she'd purchased online in anticipation of just such an evening with Thane. When the doorbell rang, she threw on a silky matching robe over the lingerie and strutted out to the entryway. She checked her image in the hall mirror, made sure it was Thane before turning the lock.

They grinned at each other, as the sound of ocean meeting the rocks below belted out a cadence in the background.

"Hi," she said in a sultry voice. "I went Internet shopping. Do you like?" She twirled to give him the full treatment.

He walked through the doorway, eyes glued to the outfit and the woman. "No wonder I've been looking forward to doing this all day." He kicked the door shut before one hand flew to her waist while he bent to scoop her up into his arms.

"What? No foreplay?"

Carrying her into the bedroom, he dumped her on the mattress, untied the belt on the negligee so he could get a better look at the racy outfit.

"I really like the lace but not enough to leave it on." Sliding a thin strap of silk off her shoulder, he nipped her flesh with his teeth. He worked his mouth down to a breast. She tasted like sweet ripe cherries or maybe a juicy peach.

"Lingerie is kind of a weakness of mine," she admitted. "I haven't indulged though in some time."

"You should do it more often. Red or black makes your skin tone pop."

"Or orange or blue?"

"Now you're getting the hint. Any color will do as long as there isn't much of it."

"Men appreciate underwear but..."

"My preference is you wear nothing...nothing at all. Let me show you."

"You need to lose the shoes," she commanded, reaching to shove up his shirt, yanking it over his head. She began to unbutton his pants, ran the zipper down. Strumming her fingers down his lean abs and up his chest, she reared up to ravage his mouth.

He shoved her back, found the center heat, and gorged himself on the core of it. They collided in fiery union, merged with one thought in mind as he climbed on top and dove into her, fast and hard.

Eager bodies moved in sync, picking up rhythm and pace. As he drove them higher, she locked her legs around his waist. Torrents of pleasure flowed into untouched chasms. Ecstasy circled and soared. Like fireworks bursting with color and awe, the thrill shot up. It spun out in a wild whirlwind streaking across in blue and gold, blinding their vision.

Hunger for each other clawed at the fringes. Just when triumph loomed, she called out his name. He felt his hold slipping, slipping, about to erupt, until finally he sent them rising up and up as high as he could fly. With everything he had he brought them into glorious freefall and into a rush of hot, glorious light.

Heart beating a double time, she wrapped her arms around his body to keep him where he was. She gnawed his jaw, slicked back his hair, soaked in the afterglow.

Empty and spent, he collapsed. His body slick, his breathing heavy, he kissed her mouth before rolling to the side.

"Is it just me or is this getting better and better?"

"It gets any better and I won't be able to walk."

"Are you staying the night?"

"Just try to get rid of me."

"Want some water?"

"Sure." He watched her crawl out of bed bare-assed, disappear out the door. He got up to go to the bathroom, stood in front of the mirror realizing for the first time since coming back he'd traveled full circle. There was something fulfilling about that. He knew it was primarily due to having Isabella in his life. Even Jonah seemed to have taken to her right off the bat. There was a moment when his mouth went dry at that. Was he ready for that kind of relationship, ready for Jonah to get attached? When his lips felt parched and chapped, he went looking for lip balm. Opening one of the drawers to go rummaging, that's when his eyes landed on the butcher knife, out of place in a bathroom. "What the hell?"

When he heard Isabella come back into the bedroom, he stood in the doorway, cocked his head. "Is there a reason you have a kitchen knife in the bathroom drawer?"

"It's probably the same reason I have a Smith & Wesson next to the bed."

"Really? You say that so casually."

"You don't own weapons?"

"No, not with my kid in the house."

"Ah, well if it makes you feel more comfortable I'll lock it up whenever Jonah visits."

He wasn't sure that was it. But something troubled him. Once they settled in under the covers, he picked his words carefully. "I was thinking earlier about how I've traveled the globe but ended up right back where I started. Where did you start out, Isabella?"

"I've lived lots of places. I'm of the belief that you have to see the world to expand your horizons, to be able to fully appreciate where you end up."

As he drifted to sleep he realized she'd evaded the question. The dodge didn't sit well with him. He went to sleep in a near-huff.

As morning light filtered through the blinds, she woke to see Thane standing next to the bed putting on his pants.

"What, no breakfast?" she muttered sleepily.

"I know exactly what I'd love to have for breakfast," he professed with a grin. "But I have to get moving so that I'll be home when Jonah gets up to get him ready for school. I'm sorry."

"No problem. It's endearing the way you take care of your son. You're a good dad."

He sat on the edge of the mattress to tie his shoes, then leaned back, hovered over her mouth to place a kiss there. "You know I'd stay if I could."

"I know. Let the dog out will you?"

"Sure." He started for the door until she called after him, "I promised Jonah I'd take him to the train store this weekend. Is that okay?"

"He mentioned it. You know it will probably entail his friends tagging along, too. At this point, Tommy and Bobby go wherever Jonah goes."

"I don't mind. It never hurts to have friends. It's better than Bobby trying to bully him or beat him up."

"That's what I thought." He walked back over to the bed and covered her mouth, ran a hand down to her breast. "This could get to be a habit."

"Mmm, if you don't get out of here I'm gonna toss you onto your back."

"I'd love to see that. And just so you know, if I had the time, I'd totally let you."

The Delacourt house on Landings Bay was quiet when he entered through the laundry room. His first stop was the coffeemaker where he added a filter to the basket and dumped in enough coffee for a strong result.

After the night of lovemaking spent with Isabella, he was running on empty. His stomach growling, he took a loaf of bread out of the pantry to make toast and set out the ingredients for scrambled eggs.

He was in the process of cracking the shells when Jonah sprinted in. "Hey, Daddy!"

"Hey, buddy. Eggs okay this morning?"

"I guess."

"Want to handle the toast for me?"

"Sure. Is Izzy gonna be my new mom?" Jonah asked as he stuffed bread into the slots and shoved down the handle on the toaster.

The question had Thane's hand stopping in mid scramble. "Why do you ask that?"

"You kiss her and stuff. Tommy says that's what moms and dads do. Bobby says his mom and dad never kiss each other anymore, they just yell at each other a lot. So I figure it's better if you kiss Izzy than yell at her."

From the doorway Fischer shook his head. "I think that's a cue for me to take my coffee to-go."

"No, it's okay. I'll be honest with you, Jonah. Izzy and I are just getting to know each other. We like each other. A lot. We enjoy doing things together."

"You have fun together. You laugh. I've heard you."

"Yes, that's true, we do. But it takes time to get to know a person to make sure that she likes us as much as we like her, that she fits in with our life because, let's face it, you and I will be together for a long time. Whereas couples…"

"They break up and get divorced," Jonah finished. "You have to make sure Izzy isn't crazy like the others."

"What others?"

"You dated crazies before."

Stunned, Thane shot a glance at Fischer. "How does he know these things?"

"Obviously your son is a wise, worldly soul who listens to what grownups talk about much more often than you think he does," Fischer said, getting down a mug from the cabinet.

"I've dated a few women who were…" Unable to find a word that fit, he went on, "Yes, couples can end up divorced. That's why it's my responsibility to make sure Izzy is the right woman for us…and not one of the crazies."

"Okay." Satisfied with Thane's answer, Jonah went on to something else. "Can I have orange juice with my eggs?"

"May I and I'll pour it," Fischer said. But then he glanced over at the glop of yellowish mixture in Thane's skillet. "On second thought, you pour. Let me at those eggs before they become the consistency of rubber."

Thane ate his breakfast in silence and got Jonah ready for school without saying much more on the subject. But when he came back to the house after walking Jonah to school, Thane went in search of Fischer and found him outside sitting at the patio table drinking his third cup of coffee.

"What did you think of Jonah's question this morning?"

"More importantly what did you think of your answer?" Fischer fired back.

"I thought I was upfront with him."

"Then don't overanalyze the situation. Don't let your head get in the way of your heart either."

"The one thing my experience with Alyson taught me is the need for caution. I don't have the luxury of letting my heart lead the way to the wrong woman."

"Is that what you think Isabella is?"

"I don't know. I can't put my finger on it, Fisch. But she's hiding something. She pulls back if I ask detailed questions about her past. Things like, 'where have you lived?' should be pretty simple enough to answer. At first I thought it was because she'd been in an abusive relationship."

"If you think she's being deceptive that might be a big red flag."

Thane nodded. "That's just it, the abusive relationship doesn't account for those long, drawn-out, ambiguous ways not to answer a question. So until I get her to open up more to me, the jury's still out."

"I guess I don't blame you for being cautious. But try not to be so much that you close yourself off to something wonderful."

"Yeah, I got it. I'll do my best."

Bobby Prather and Doug Bayliss had become fixtures around the Delacourt house. So often that Thane liked to think he'd succeeded in giving the boys something else to do other than make trouble wherever they went. In addition to them, Tommy regularly stopped by to play with Jonah.

Today all four boys were over, eager to get into some mischief. Izzy was more than willing to spend her Saturday overseeing and carting around the troop for a little fun while Thane and Fischer got Longboard Pizza ready for the grand opening.

One of the places Isabella promised to take the gang was Layne's Trains. Cooper had offered to demo all the new engines and gadgets he got in for the holidays. She didn't have to make the offer twice before Jonah and his friends were scrambling to get there. With the dogs on leashes, they walked over two blocks to Main Street.

On the way Jonah chattered like a motormouth to the other kids and to Izzy about anything and everything that popped into his little head. He went through his week at school citing a list of information. His spelling words had been really tough. His math problems were hard. But he'd made a puppet for Halloween that he really liked that he'd displayed on the refrigerator.

Maybe that's why listening to the ordinary ramblings of a six-year-old boy, it surprised her when the bombshell rolled out of Jonah's mouth so easily.

"Daddy says we have to be careful and make sure you're the right woman for us."

She stopped walking. "What did you say?"

"Daddy says there's a lot of crazies out there. Guys have to be careful."

"Jonah, are you certain your father said that?"

"Yep. Daddy's dated women before who were really— out there. That's why he kept me away from them." He took her hand. "But you seem okay to me. I'll put in a lot of good words for you so Daddy won't think you're crazy."

Unable to think of an appropriate response, she simply uttered, "Gosh thank you, Jonah. I feel so special now."

She tried not to let that jolt cloud the outing. But the disappointment she felt could only be cleared up by asking Thane.

When Isabella noticed Bobby Prather hanging back from the rest, she could only wonder what had the boy sulking in a train store. "Bobby, are you okay?"

"My mom and dad are getting a divorce. My mom's moving back to San Francisco to be with her family."

"And she's taking you with her?"

"Nope. She never liked me, she liked my sister best and when my sister died, she really acted like she didn't want me around."

Isabella shuddered at the coldness of the child's words. She tried to find a bright spot but after several long seconds, she simply said, "So you'll stay here with your friends instead of changing schools. That's good news, Bobby."

"I guess, but my dad doesn't know who'll look after me while he's at his jobs."

"We'll figure something out, okay?"

"No one wants me."

"That isn't true."

"Sure it is. Jonah doesn't even have a mother and yet he has you."

"I'm your friend, too. Are you sure you didn't misunderstand what your mom and dad were saying?"

"No. I heard my parents arguing about who I would live with but it wasn't about who would take me, it was about which one *had* to take me."

"Oh, Bobby, I'm so sorry they hurt your feelings." No child should ever hear anything so hurtful, she decided, trying to come up with something else to say. Grasping at straws, she added, "Believe it or not, I know how you feel. I was married to a really bad man once. Even though he didn't like me very much he didn't want me to leave either. I felt stuck, trapped."

"What did you do?"

"I left on my own, kind of like you did the night you ran away. For you, that wasn't the answer, to try to leave. What I'm trying to say is that I know what it's like to feel unwanted. Believe me, when I tell you that we'll work on your parents. I want you to know Thane's door is always open. If you should need a place other than that, so is mine. You remember that when things get tough at home, okay?"

"You mean that?"

"I do. Now why don't you go over there with your friends and play with the trains and try to enjoy the rest of your Saturday while you're here." She watched the boy saunter over, his heart not really in the activity.

Later, she told Thane about the conversation.

"He actually said his parents didn't want him?"

She nodded. "I wonder if it's true. Someone needs to go talk to Mr. Prather and find out."

Thane wasn't stupid. "I take it that 'someone' is me."

"Man to man, father to father, it's better than me approaching him, especially since I've already formed an opinion of him that isn't very flattering. Same goes for Mrs. Prather."

"I hear that. Okay. I'll go see him first chance I get."

"There's something else." She went into what Jonah had told her earlier and waited for his reaction. It wasn't what she expected.

He started laughing. "I did say that. But that was before you. That was back when we lived in New York. I didn't bring women around Jonah. You understand that, right? I went out, left him with my mom. My dates were never part of the mix. But apparently in talking about you Jonah decided to lump you with them. You should know that you've been given access to Jonah more than any other woman I've ever been with. Do you honestly believe if I didn't think this was serious between us, I'd let you near Jonah on the level I have?"

"You could just feel like I'm nothing more than a babysitter."

He frowned. "I hope you're joking. I was under the impression you wanted to spend time with Jonah to get to know him better."

"Of course, I do. That's the reason I took four boys to the toy store today. It's the reason I got upset when he told me."

"He didn't mean to upset you. Sometimes I need to watch what I say around him. He picks up on a lot when I think he's distracted. Stay here tonight and I promise I'll make it better."

"I suppose I could live with that."

"That's my girl."

Thane had to pick the best time to approach Greg Prather. The man had a weird schedule. Four times a week Greg worked second shift at Murphy's Market stocking shelves. Five nights a week, he showed up at the vet clinic to clean out the cages of the animals recovering from surgery or other ailments. He performed those same duties as needed at the Fanning Marine Rescue Center for Keegan and Cord Bennett.

From what Thane could tell, the low-paying jobs kept Greg in a foul mood most of the time. When he rang the bell it was a couple hours before school let out. As he waited on the porch, Thane didn't really expect much in the way of cooperation from Bobby's father.

Greg opened the door glassy-eyed and annoyed.

"Sorry to bother you, Mr. Prather, but since our kids have been hanging out together for several weeks now, I thought it might be a good time to stop by and connect."

"Look, I don't have a lot of time for socializing. My wife packed up and left me this past Wednesday. She went back to her fancy family in San Francisco. She didn't bother to take her son with her either. So if you don't mind, I think I'll pass on *connecting*."

"Okay. I just thought..."

"Doesn't matter what you thought. I know who you used to be, some hotshot ballplayer in the NFL. I doubt we have a thing in common. What I can't figure out is why a big deal like you wants to live in this town?"

His attitude just made Thane sink his teeth into the conversation even more. "I grew up here. My parents have a house on Landings Bay. We have two boys that attend the same school and hang out together. I know how it is to be on my own when it comes to raising a child. My boy lost his mother when he was a baby. My mom used to take care of him but when she died of breast cancer I retired from the NFL and became Mr. Mom."

Greg let out a loud, weary sigh. "Well, come on in then, maybe we can wallow in a vat of self-pity together. Name's Greg."

"Thane Delacourt." The two men shook hands to sanction their meeting.

"Want something to drink? I've got a pot of fresh coffee I put on not fifteen minutes ago."

"Sure, that'd be fine."

Thane followed him into a small kitchen where he watched Greg get down a cup. "How do you take it?"

"Black with plenty of sugar."

"So, you're a regular Mr. Mom, are you? You're opening that pizza place at the corner of Main and Pacific," Greg said as he took a seat across from Thane at the kitchen table.

"Which means I'll be hopping whenever it opens. I don't know how to say this but…"

"I knew you had something else on your mind when I opened the door and saw you standing there. Might as well spit it out."

"Bobby told Jonah about his sister dying, so I know it's been a rough few years."

"Ah, little Ariana. Leukemia took her."

"I'm very sorry. But that's not all. Before your wife left, Bobby heard you two fighting."

"That's not news. He often heard us fight because that's all we ever did."

"He overheard you both arguing about how neither one of you wanted him."

Greg lowered his cup, met Thane's eyes. "Do you know what that woman did? She packed up and took off in the middle of the night while I was at work, left him alone in the house sleeping in his bed for hours. I know you more than likely have good intentions even though it's not any of your damn business but… I don't mind telling you I don't know what I'm gonna do with the kid while I work my three jobs."

"Maybe you should look for a day job while he's at school. That way you'd only have to worry about a couple hours in the afternoon."

"Gee, that sounds great but there's just one problem with it. In case you haven't noticed there aren't a lot of jobs around town. I took what I could get to pay the bills. We all can't be rolling in dough like you."

"Would you be willing to give up at least one of your jobs if I could work something else out?"

"I'm not an idiot. You come up with a decent job for me that brings in as much as all three are doing right now and I'll give up the night work."

Thane extended his hand. "It's a deal. What is it you enjoy doing?"

That sent Greg into a fit of laughter. "I had this notion once upon a time that I'd become an artist, not the kind Logan Donnelly is, but rather… You see, I liked to design jewelry. I know it sounds kind of odd for a guy. But I went to school for it until I had to drop out. We had Bobby and that put an end to that."

"Really?"

"Surprises you, huh? I had this stupid notion I could make money at it." Greg shook his head. "I was young, idealistic, and foolish. Turns out, I couldn't, not enough anyway."

"Do you have any computer experience?"

"Not for years. I don't even own one now. Look, I barely get by. This house was paid for by my in-laws. Who knows how long I'll get to keep it once Peggy gets around to filing for divorce."

"That isn't the way it works. In California it doesn't matter who pays for the house, everything is considered community property, split fifty-fifty, unless there's some type of legal doc like a prenup that says otherwise."

"No shit? I never signed a prenup and neither did Peggy, didn't even consider such an option."

"Plus, your wife left you."

"And abandoned her son," Greg finished. "I may like you yet, Delacourt."

"Yeah? I may like you, too."

After Thane left, he mulled over the job dilemma. The man was right. Jobs around the small town were definitely few and far between.

That night he reported back to Isabella and together they tried to brainstorm a solution.

"Right now the only thing I can come up with is that Julianne Dickinson has yet to get her resale shop off the ground. She'd planned to have it opened by now but she hasn't found anyone to manage it."

Thane chewed on that news. "Wonder how much she'd be willing to pay?"

"Not sure but she makes a good side business with all the stuff she finds to recycle. She certainly doesn't have time to run it nine months out of the year and take care of her duties as principal. It's worth a shot."

"Okay, it's a place to start. I'll approach her at school tomorrow and see if it's something she'd be interested in doing."

The next morning Thane walked Jonah to class and then went in search of the principal. Tapping on the open door to her office he found her sitting behind her desk surrounded by a pile of paperwork.

"If this is how you start every day you have my sympathies. Going through all those folders would drive me up the wall."

"It isn't as bad as it looks. Besides, the school board increased our budget and I'm getting an admin to help me with a lot of the filing and correspondence."

"Good for you. That's kind of what I wanted to talk about. A job. Isabella tells me that you wanted to open up a resale shop on Main Street but couldn't find anyone to manage it."

Julianne nodded, waved her hand over the file folders. "This is pretty much the reason Reclaimed Treasures has taken a backseat. I'm considering giving up the idea because I just don't have the time to set up, tag every piece of merchandise let alone take care of the day-to-day operation."

"What do you think about Greg Prather as your manager?"

"Bobby Prather's father? Oh, I don't know, Mr. Delacourt, the Prathers are going through a really rough patch right now."

"Call me Thane. Peggy Prather's already left town. My take is their rough patch is about to get a whole lot rougher. The couple's headed for divorce. Mrs. Prather didn't want to take Bobby with her and Greg didn't want him to stay."

"Oh, no. Does Bobby know this?"

"He overheard every word of the knock-down, drag-out fight."

"When will parents realize arguing in front of the kids…?" Her voice trailed off and she let out an impatient sigh. "Listen to me, dishing out advice when I don't even have kids. I'm not even married yet."

"In theory I suppose it's not a bad rule for parents to live by though. Anyway, I sat down yesterday with Greg, got to know him a little better. He's trying to hold down three jobs, all of them at night. He pointed out to me that it's difficult to find a job here. He can't give up his night jobs if he wants to put food on the table. Taking that into consideration, how is he supposed to look after Bobby when he isn't home at night?"

"So, as a solution you want me to give Mr. Prather a chance at the resale shop that hasn't even opened its doors yet?" The principal sat back as if deciding what to do, all the while chewing on her bottom lip. After several long seconds she said, "Tell you what, let me talk to Ryder first before I dive headlong into making a bigger mess of Bobby's life than it already is. It's a good idea, Thane, doable. Once we talk, Ryder and I'll be able to figure out how much I can pay him and go from there."

"That's all anyone can ask. You know he says he wanted to design jewelry. He went to school for it."

"Greg Prather, a jewelry designer? Really?" She shook her head again. "The old adage is true. Never judge someone from afar. But that's interesting…about the jewelry I mean. Over the years I've found some gorgeous silver pieces for next to nothing that would make lovely bracelets or rings. For that matter I've found pieces of clunky metal that would make cool necklaces."

"Then maybe Greg's your guy."

"Imagine that."

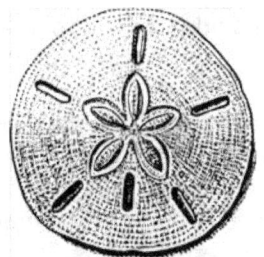

Chapter Eighteen

Saturday night, the welcome dinner for Fischer Robbins turned into the opening of Longboard Pizza. Sort of. The place was packed with those residents who couldn't wait for the official grand opening in two days.

While traditional pepperoni would no doubt win out as the most popular item, there was a long list of gourmet concoctions for the adventurous types who wanted to build their own.

The restaurant offered every kind of cheese you could think of—gorgonzola to smoked gouda to the standard mozzarella, and every veggie to go with all that cheese and crust. You could mix it up any way you wanted including an array of herb toppings to add to the varied meat choices, like tender roasted chicken, crispy bacon, hot capicola, and the traditional Italian sausage.

Tonight the wait for a pizza was zilch unless you ordered a pizza to-go. For the crowd that dined inside, Fischer had spent several hours making up an assortment of extra-large pies served buffet style. But the wait for a table was another matter. Maybe that's why it seemed like the entire town had begun lining up at six o'clock to get inside for a sample.

Thane had managed to squeeze two more tables into the eating area, which made for seven inside and four on the side patio. With the counter on the side wall, it brought his maximum occupancy up to a grand total of forty-eight. Not bad for a tiny eatery. It didn't sound like a lot, but when the throng included elbow-room-only it meant one thing. The advertising and word of mouth had paid off.

Lilly's mural grabbed the attention of all who came in, as well as the photograph of a young, teenage Thane that dominated the front wall. She'd drawn a map of California using light blues and greens, added famous surfing spots, painting them in complete with foaming whitecaps. From Stinson Beach to Mavericks all the way down to Baja, the places she'd highlighted made patrons want to dive into the water, right then and there, and catch a wave.

For the time being Thane had hired only one other employee to help out. Tonight, pretty Madison Colter, daughter of Emma, sister to Gerald, helped him jot down customer orders. As people continued to sail through the door, Thane tallied up their bills and worked the register, while Madison took drink preferences, either beer or soda, filling pitchers to the brim and handing out glasses. After placing their food requests, patrons could then move on to grab a table and wait for their pie to be brought out to them.

Because seating was scarce tonight, every table taken, many were getting their orders to-go. The busy crowd kept them all hopping. Isabella had volunteered to help with orders. And Jonah's role was to meet and greet or hold the door open or bus tables if people didn't clean up after themselves and left the table messy.

Logan and Kinsey pitched in to keep the line moving and organized, while Murphy and Carla Vargas helped with crowd containment.

The party atmosphere rocked until it began to wind down four hours later. Everyone had been fed and those that remained were die-hard friends who stayed to help with cleanup.

Ryder and Julianne's group had stayed on, sitting with Nick and Jordan. Gavin and his wife Maggie and their kids had been latecomers, but they now clustered around, pulling up chairs to eat their pizza. When the festive mood began to die down and taper off, the talk turned to more serious subjects. It was Ryder who brought up the Taggert Farms issue of limited growing space.

By that time Thane, Isabella and Fischer had joined the assemblage as Ryder took the lead, trying to figure out what to do about the problem.

"After Gavin mentioned it, the two of us sat down and looked at the subject from several different ways. For the past few weeks we've kicked it around and found there's no way around it. The farm is slowly running out of growing room," Ryder explained. "We've increased production so much that there's a real chance in five years we'll be at a limited capacity."

"I guess that's my fault," Nick admitted. "I thought adding more products would be a good thing."

"It is a good thing," Gavin said in response. "The farm provides jobs for more people in town than any other business. So don't spend too much time beating yourself up about your decisions. It runs like a well-oiled machine and that's because of you and Jordan."

"Thanks for that," Nick said in gratitude.

"What do you suggest we do?" Jordan asked. "There's no available land between the B&B and the farm to expand. Nick's already checked several years earlier."

"There might be an alternative," Logan prompted from the end of the table. "Recently, Isabella brought me an idea. I'll leave it to her to tell you about it."

"But it's your property," Isabella pointed out.

"That doesn't matter. It's a solid plan," Kinsey noted.

"Okay. There's the piece of land at the lighthouse, at least three acres, between the road and the forest to the north. The space is just sitting there wasted. It could certainly be utilized as a secondary site to grow quite a number of vegetables. The stipulation would be to keep the yield right here in town instead of shipping it to other parts of the state. In that way it would benefit the people here in town."

Jordan and Nick exchanged glances. It was Jordan who said, "That's it, that's the solution we've been missing. It's a win-win for the town. That's brilliant, Isabella."

"I'm no expert but I've read about other places that started a successful co-op by growing things on rooftops. I figured surely we could take that available land and do something worthwhile with it."

Heads turned, eyes got big, until Thane said, "If the residents helped work the land, it would keep costs down, significantly."

"We should all thank Logan for his generosity," Fischer suggested.

"But *Logan* had nothing to do with coming up with this idea," the sculptor replied with a grin. "Isabella is the generous one. That's what makes this town work, why I'm proud to be a part of it. We have people here who care what happens to one another. They care about the town as a whole. You can't get any better than that."

Fischer raised his glass of red in a toast. "Then here's to all of us who had the presence of mind to move here and put down roots."

After the other guests left, Isabella lingered behind. She wandered outside to the little strip of patio. She was looking up at the starlit sky when Thane joined her. "I never thought I'd feel this comfortable in a little town like this. It never occurred to me people could accept a stranger so willingly without bias."

"Bias? You mean like racial bias? Jonah goes to school with all different types of kids. It's one reason I feel the way Logan does. I'm proud to be part of a town that comes together in a crunch."

"No, I wasn't really talking about that kind of bias. Sometimes outsiders find themselves shunned starting over in a small place among strangers. For months, I've been keeping my distance. Now, I'm beginning to settle in, get more comfortable, get a better feel for the people."

He was tempted to pursue why she'd been so aloof. But one glimpse into her eyes had him offering, "Fischer's watching Jonah for the night. Let's go back to your place and take advantage of it."

She glanced up at his tall form, hooked a finger in the loop of his jeans and tugged him over to her. "Take advantage of me, Thane."

"You bet. Several times."

"Promise?"

"Watch me."

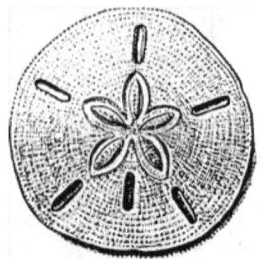

Chapter Nineteen

For four decades, April to mid-November, the Taggert Farms fruit and vegetable stand stood on the side of the road to town, open rain or shine, enticing travelers to stop and sample the produce.

Any resident over the age of five knew you could fill your basket here with crisp apples, tasty pears, or sweet cherries. In the mood for a salad or fresh kale? No problem. They offered five different kinds of lettuce to pile on your plate.

This year, parents themselves, Gavin and Maggie Kendall had made a few changes to the traditional fall event. With Nick's and Jordan's approval, they'd added a slew of activities for the kids. An inflatable bounce house in the shape of a magic castle offered the kids several hours of jumping up and down. Gavin had talked Cord and Keegan into providing whatever animals they could spare for a petting zoo. The Bennetts had shown up with a goat, a couple of lambs, a litter of piglets, and plenty of rabbits to play with. They'd provided a pony from a nearby ranch so parents could snap photos of their little ones on a horse. For babies, parents could choose the pumpkin patch as a backdrop. Maggie had persuaded Abby Bonner into setting up a face-painting station.

Izzy took in the scene, looked up at the tall scarecrow at the entrance and announced, "It's like fruit-stand-meets-fall festival."

Thane agreed. "I'm sure somewhere outside Manhattan they grow pumpkins but there's nothing quite like this. Jonah will go wild here."

This morning they'd left the house, dogs included, with one goal in mind—to help Jonah search for the best, the fattest, the biggest pumpkin he could find. There were so many to choose from though that the six-year-old ran from pumpkin to pumpkin unable to make up his mind.

"Which one? Which one should I pick?"

"Tell you what," Izzy suggested. "How about we take a stroll through the corn maze first so you have time to consider your options? After that you can take your turn inside the castle and bounce until you're able to come to a major decision."

Jonah responded by pumping his fist in the air. "Yessssss!"

Thane watched his boy take off in a rush and head straight to where the animals were located surrounded by a circle of hay bales.

"You have a way with him," Thane commented. And should he mention that it triggered a memory of his own mom's enduring patience? Probably not.

"I like kids. They're usually the most honest and boldest little souls around."

The couple watched as Jonah shifted gears into the farm pen where he ran around like a wild man tagging after a baby pig. When the boy grew tired of that, he segued to getting his face painted and then went on to wander through the maze before finally getting to bounce around in the castle.

"He's a ball of energy and cute as a button."

"Mischievous."

"That too."

When the bundle of energy came running up, Izzy suggested, "Let's pick out that pumpkin and head back to your house. How about we pop in a movie? Maybe one with a Halloween theme to keep the topic consistent?"

"Shrek, I want Shrek," Jonah said.

"Then Shrek it is."

The last day of October Bradford Radcliff took down the chain on his car lot next to the bank and made it official. His place was open for business. He'd re-paved the lot, transported his ten-car inventory up from L.A., and had a small four-hundred-square-foot prefab house delivered to use for an office. The little clapboard building sat at the corner of the property, and now for the first time that morning, Brad walked outside to take in what was happening on Main Street.

Brad didn't have to wait long before Thane Delacourt brought him his first customer, a beautiful woman with a good eye for detail and color. The couple had a little boy with them who ran around opening all the doors so he could crawl into the interior and sit behind the wheel. Brad didn't mind, he liked kids. Besides it was Halloween. He'd be pretty lame if he didn't have candy on hand for the kid.

Brad went back into his office, picked up the bowl full of mini Snickers and Milky Ways, and brought it back outside.

"Is it okay if the boy has candy?"

Thane called to Jonah who hadn't yet put on his costume. "One, you can pick one and eat it before lunch," Thane cautioned.

"Yay! Chocolate! I get more tonight when I get dressed up," Jonah told Izzy as she rubbed her hand across the hood of a 1970 gold Karmann Ghia, a vintage ride to be sure.

"Ninja, right? You plan to wear the ninja outfit tonight?"

"Ninja!" Jonah said as he sent several karate chops through the air.

"What do you think of this one?" Thane asked, standing beside her at the Volkswagen. "Brad says this one he restored himself."

"I really like the style."

"The style is classic with the bug headlights and rust-free," Brad pitched. "I can vouch for the engine and the drivetrain, starts the second you turn the key." Brad dangled them in front of her. "Take it for a spin, judge for yourself."

"Let's go," Thane said, opening the driver's door for her. "Let's see how it handles. Hey, Jonah, climb into the backseat. Isabella's taking us along for a ride."

They cruised through town, made a turn at Crescent, headed over to the pier and circled the block. By their second trip down Ocean Street, Isabella declared, "Oh, I love how it drives!" She looked in the rearview mirror and asked Jonah, "What do you think?"

"It's a lot smaller than Daddy's car."

She guffawed with laughter. "It certainly is, maybe a tad too impractical."

"No such thing if you like it," Thane said eyeing the joy on her face. "Just out of curiosity, how long has it been since you've driven?"

"He wouldn't let me have a car. I mean, I had a car when I married him, but he made me get rid of it. Some days I felt like I was barely getting permission to breathe."

"How did you put up with that? And why did a woman like you let yourself be controlled like that?"

"Lack of self-confidence, I suppose. I don't know."

When she pulled into the lot, Brad was waiting for them. "Well?"

"I don't have a trade-in. What's the best price you can give me?"

Brad threw out a figure.

Isabella countered with a thousand dollars less.

"In honor of you being my first sale..." Brad shoved his hand toward her and said, "We have a deal. Let's do it."

They went into the little office—a tasteful clapboard building with white trim on the glass-paneled door that matched the shutters—to sign the papers.

To celebrate car ownership and before taking Jonah trick-or-treating, they stopped in at Longboard Pizza to grab a bite to eat. While stuffing his face with pepperoni, Jonah announced he'd changed his mind about dressing up as a ninja.

"I wanna go as Dracula and wear a long black cape and fangs."

"What about the ninja? It's more appropriate for a first grader to be a Ninja Turtle than a Dracula," Thane pointed out.

But Jonah shook his head.

Somewhere between lunch and dinner he'd gotten it into his head that Halloween was all about scary and the ninja wasn't terrifying enough. In order to make a convincing Count he needed a long black wig on his head. He claimed the costume wouldn't be complete without smearing his face with white face paint so that he'd look "dead."

Thane wasn't all that convinced about the white makeup, especially since it denoted the "lifeless" look. But Isabella persuaded him not to make a big deal out of it.

Fischer backed her up. "He's at that awkward age where he wants to make sure he isn't a baby and emulate the older kids."

"And I'll need drops of blood dripping out of my mouth, too," Jonah proclaimed.

Thane stared at Jonah. "Did someone not like the Ninja Turtle outfit?"

"It's a little kid costume."

"Uh, I hate to point this out to you but you are a little kid," Thane told him.

"But I want to be so scary that the other trick-or-treaters run when they see me."

"I run when I see you now," Fischer retorted.

"Ha. Ha. Just wait till you see me all made up and you'll run all the way to Santa Cruz," Jonah fired back.

"Good one, sport," Fischer said, rubbing the kid's head. "What do you think, Izzy?"

In a voice that resembled Count Dracula, with her hands held out toward Jonah, fingers moving like she intended to weave a spell, she mimicked, "I see the night ahead. I see Jonah's carrying a bag weighted down with lots and lots of candy. I see it's cloudy with a chance of Halloween. Bwaahahahahaha!" With that, she began to tickle his belly and ribs until he roared with giggles.

Once they got back home, Thane decided to compromise. "I'll tell you what. You can make up your face but since we've already bought the ninja outfit, you have to wear it tonight. Deal?"

"O-kay."

Thane took out the pumpkin they'd bought for carving. While he cut out the top, scooped out the goopy guts, he turned to Isabella. "Why is it I get this messy job when there are three of us here?"

"Uh, because it involves a sharp instrument and one of us is six," Isabella tossed back. She watched as he whittled out a pair of eyes and a nose. "You do know there's a way to do that without all the slicing and dicing."

"Now you tell me. Take over here, will you, while I go check to see if he's getting into his costume."

She did a mock salute and said, "Aye, aye, sir. I'm on it, sir. You betcha, sir."

"Funny, very funny," he countered, wiping his hands before heading into Jonah's room. Thane found his son struggling to get into the ninja top and pull-on bottoms.

"You gotta take your shoes off first."

"Oh, I forgot. Is Izzy ready to make up my face?"

"Just about. I wanted to talk to you about trick-or-treating. You know we're going to businesses only tonight. And you have to stay with us and not go darting across the street by yourself. Understand? There's traffic out. The sidewalks will be crowded and a lot of people milling around town. So, stick to us like glue. Got it?"

"I got it."

Later, Thane watched from the bathroom doorway as Isabella spent half an hour coating Jonah's cherub face with a film of milky-colored grease paint. While his little boy disappeared before his eyes and slowly became a walking monster, Thane couldn't help noting the easy way Jonah responded to Izzy.

"I hope that stuff comes off," Thane groaned as the paint began to cover up skin.

"The label promised it would easily wash off with soap and water." She hoped that was true. After smearing red tint in the form of drops at the corners of the boy's mouth, she went to work on his hair. Using gel to make it stick up at the top, she sat back, turned him around to face the bathroom mirror. "There. How's that look?"

"I look…fierce. Don't I, Dad?"

"You look absolutely terrifying."

"What do you think, Izzy?"

"You look like the scariest Ninja Turtle I've ever seen in my life or maybe a mad scientist. I'm not sure which."

"I do?"

"Yep, you look positively ghoulish."

"Do I get to wear the fangs?"

"Trust me, you won't like wearing them because they make your mouth feel funny," Thane told him. "But go ahead stick them in your mouth."

Sure enough, after five minutes having them clamped on his teeth, Jonah made a face and spat them out into Isabella's hand.

"We have to go. We have to. I'm meeting Tommy at the corner."

There was something about the little coastal town that had gotten Fischer Robbins to move three thousand miles from his beloved New York. It wasn't simply the fact that he'd followed his friend to get here. No, there was more to it than that.

While he and Madison manned Longboard Pizza shorthanded until Thane and Izzy showed up with Jonah, Fisch took the time to get to know the residents, one by one. Each neighbor who came in seemed to be genuinely glad they could get a freshly made pepperoni pizza. That appreciation translated into a friendliness it took years to build in other places, especially in and around Manhattan.

Like all the other businesses in town, Longboard Pizza handed out candy to the kids.

"Been busy?" Thane asked when they came through the door.

"Swamped. How was the candy gathering?" Fisch asked the kid.

"He scored big-time when he hit The Pointe. Perry gave out these giant-size chocolate chip cookies."

Jonah dumped his take on the counter and crawled up on one of the stools to go through his bounty. "Look at this, Uncle Fisch. I got a load of Snickers, not the little ones either but the regular size."

Thane peered over his son's shoulder. "There's enough sugar floating around to send cruise ship passengers back to port in diabetic shock. Dentists must love this time of year."

"Where's Izzy?" Fischer asked.

"The dogs were worn out so she headed home. Jonah wanted to show you his stash before bedtime or he would've gone with her. And no," he said when he saw Jonah's mouth start to pop open anticipating the boy's plea. "No more candy or the cookie. It's too late," Thane added. "I'll be sure to pack the cookie in your lunch tomorrow for dessert. That's the best deal you're getting this close to bedtime."

"Better take it," Fisch counseled.

"O-kay."

Relieved it would be his teacher's problem at lunch the next day, Thane began to help bus the dining area. "Dump all that candy back in the sack, okay? It's time to help clean up and get home to bed."

"Can't I have just one more Snickers bar?"

"What did I just say? No. You've already eaten one and one's enough. Now go help Uncle Fisch count the change in the register. You can practice with the nickels and dimes and pennies while I gather up the trash." He watched his son move to the back, head down, clearly disappointed. Thane shook his head, hating the idea of all the head-butting they'd do until all that Halloween candy was out of their lives.

A couple days later, the first Friday night in November found Isabella and Jonah at home making their own fun while Thane headed to McCready's for a rare night out and Troy's bachelor party.

Isabella had fixed hearty chicken nachos, made a huge bowl of popcorn, and brownies for dessert. Now, in the living room, Izzy set everything out and put in the DVD *Lilo and Stitch*. "You'll love this one, it's about a little girl who surfs, who thinks she's found a dog, but it's really an alien from a faraway planet who's stuck on earth."

"Is it a girl movie?"

"No, it's a kid movie and you…" Isabella poked a finger in his belly. "Are a kid."

From the first roll of the credits she knew it was a good choice for Jonah. The music kept his attention up front and had him on his feet, hopping and swaying to the beat. But then she'd known that no one could sit through tunes with a Hawaiian beat and a series of Elvis songs, not even a six-year-old. In fact, she took his hand and they danced around the room to "Burning Love," laughing at the silliness of

Stitch playing guitar and surfing a wave. After several songs, they flopped down on the sofa, out of breath.

"I think someone likes to dance," Isabella noted.

"Mimi liked to dance too."

"She did? She danced with you?"

"Yep. All the time until she got sick."

"I'm sorry she died, Jonah. What was her favorite song?"

"I don't remember the name but it was some old song by this old group called The Bugs."

"You mean the Beatles?"

"Yeah, that one."

"You miss her, Mimi?"

"Yeah, she was the closest thing to a mom I had."

"You can talk to me about her anytime you want."

"I think it upsets my dad when I talk about Mimi."

"I'm sure that's not it. Your dad just doesn't want you to be sad. He wants all the best for you. Would you like to see if we can find your Mimi's favorite song so you can dance to it before you go to bed?"

"You'd do that?"

"Sure. Let me get my iPhone and we'll go through the music list together until we find the right one. How's that?"

"Super."

They went through at least twenty-five Beatles tunes before they hit on the right one.

"That's the one!" Jonah shouted when he heard the first notes of "Here Comes the Sun." "Mimi used to sing it to me. Sun, sun, sun, here we come!" With that the boy sang and spun around the room in time to the music.

They played it six times before Isabella decided it was time to get him ready for bed.

"Aw, I'm having fun. Do I have to?"

"'Fraid so, but why don't we do this. I've downloaded it to my iPhone and you can listen to it after I read you a story until you fall asleep. How's that sound?"

"Okay, cool," he said and went running off to change into his pajamas.

Getting him ready for bed proved he had an imagination. He offered up several scenarios in order to stay up. But when she discovered he had a fondness for dragons and pulled out a rhyming book that he loved, the last surge of his energy waned. After reading the last words on the page, he put his head on her lap. "I like you, Izzy. You're as fun as my dad."

She couldn't help it. At the declaration, her heart felt like it flipped in her chest. "That's such a nice thing to say, sweetie. You're a lot of fun to be around."

"Will you sit here till I fall asleep?"

"Sure." And she did. It didn't take long for him to wind down once he stopped talking. She couldn't believe the boisterous boy with so much get-up-and-go earlier could be so still now. When her cell phone dinged, she stepped back into the hallway to take the call, a call from a concerned dad.

"How's everything going? Did you get Jonah to go down without a fight?"

She laughed. "You are a worrywart. Bedtime was World War I all over again but this time with dragons. Just kidding," she added. "Jonah's asleep and we didn't wreak havoc all over the house to get there."

"I don't know why I was worried."

"Neither do I. Now go have a couple of drinks with your friends. See you later."

"What will you do?"

"Start that new romance novel I've been putting off. Now go."

"Thanks Izzy. I'll be home in a couple hours."

"Go have fun. Take advantage of the night out."

After closing down Longboard Pizza, Thane walked into McCready's with Fischer in tow to find the joint crammed with a rowdy Friday night crowd.

Fisch took one look at the décor, the sign behind the long scarred mahogany wood that read "Drink More Beer" and stared at the giant of a man who owned the place. The ex-boxer and former Dubliner, Flynn McCready, stood behind the bar working the taps. The jukebox was cranked up—the Traveling Wilburys singing about going to the end of the line. "This place is every cliché there is known to man to describe an Irish dive except for maybe the blaring country."

"Yeah, that's why I figured you'd love it."

"Thanks, makes me feel right at home."

Thane waved to Troy and his group of friends—at least twenty guys he recognized—who were already drinking and shooting pool at both tables. He could hear the smack and roll of the balls, make out some of the good-natured ribbing that flew back and forth between players.

"You're buying the first round," Fisch reminded him.

"Why me?"

"Because you're the one getting laid regularly."

"I knew you were jealous of that." Thane returned.

"I wouldn't say jealous more like envious. Get me a Guinness will you? I see a little blonde over at the end of the bar. Those chimis of hers make me want to get to know her changas a whole lot better."

"You get lucky, drinks are on you," Thane reminded him. He watched Fischer move through the crowd and waited for Flynn to fill the order for a round of brews. After loading up a tray with the mugs, he toted the beers over to his friends standing at the pool tables.

"Hey, you showed up," Troy said, stretching out his hand.

"I said I would. Sorry if I'm late but I had to wait to close tonight, brought Fisch with me. Hope you don't mind."

"Nah, the more the merrier. I'm not much of a drinker," Troy said, leaning in. "But I admit I've had a few already tonight."

"A man about to tie the knot tomorrow deserves one last hurrah before taking himself out of the game for good."

Troy hooted with laughter. "Logan said almost the same thing. You ever been married, Thane?"

"Not me. I've managed to avoid matrimony. Now Fisch, he's gone that route before."

"He didn't bring her with him to Pelican Pointe?"

"God no. The marriage lasted about ten seconds. Oh, sorry. I don't want to rain on anyone's wedded bliss."

"That's okay. Sometimes it happens. Logan's first marriage didn't work out either. He married one of those high-maintenance, narcissistic screamers."

"Huh, maybe Fischer and Logan hooked up with the same female? Count yourself lucky you didn't."

"I do. Bree and I have so much in common."

"That's a good start." He glanced over, saw Logan and Nick edge up, both holding pool cues.

Logan asked, "How about a little eight ball, Delacourt? We play teams, the two newcomers against the two of us?"

Thane looked over at Fisch who was still standing at the bar, chatting up the blonde. "Fisch seems to be otherwise occupied at the moment." He shot Troy a look, changing the roster. "What do you say, Troy, we take these guys on?"

"Rack 'em up," Troy said, putting down his beer. "These guys are toast."

"I'll break," Nick offered.

For the next two hours Thane and Troy won three games in a row from the banker and the artist. From there the team took on all comers.

After Troy banked another shot, he sipped his beer. "All that hanging out here waiting for Bree to get off work must've paid off. And you...? You're smooth as glass."

"I played in this bar when I was underage," Thane said, tapping the solid red into the corner pocket.

When Fisch finally wandered over to the group, he and Thane took on Cord and Ryder. The former army rangers proceeded to run the table.

"You're bad news, Robbins," Thane grumbled. "Never switch partners in mid-strike."

Ryder chuckled as he banked the next shot. "Cord and I've played together before in dives seedier than this."

"We had a long winning streak back in Georgia," Cord boasted as he chalked his stick getting ready for the next challenger.

"In case you haven't noticed this ain't Georgia." Four young locals had sauntered over expecting to pass the time in their usual haunt, doing what they normally do when they normally do it. One of them, a tall, lanky fellow with tattoos all over his neck, couldn't seem to keep his mouth shut. "How long you guys gonna be? 'Cause we've been waiting for almost an hour."

Earl's pal, a thick-necked man with the same colorful tattoos, moved to stand at his friend's elbow. "We don't like to wait. That means it's time for all you old guys to head back home to the wife and kids and let us get on with our game."

"Look, Earl, we don't want any trouble," Troy said. "This is my bachelor party tonight. Flynn knows we've been planning this for weeks. That's why we got here early."

"Then Flynn shoulda said something. We come in here three times a week, regular like. This is our bar. Ask anyone."

Another one of Earl's punks sidled up. "That's right. Friday nights at this same time is our time. Go play in someone's basement."

Nick lifted his mug, wondered how Jordan would react if he came home sporting a bloody nose. The idea didn't prevent him from throwing in his two cents. "That so?

Never known Flynn to take reservations before now, that's a new one."

"That's because he doesn't. Never has," Thane pointed out.

"It's first come, first serve. Everyone knows that," Cord added taking up a position next to Thane.

Troy set down his beer, moved over to where the others lined up. "That's right. Been that way for years."

In the middle of calculating his next shot at the second table, Zach stopped what he was doing long enough to size up Earl and his friends. "I recognize you now. You're the guys who come in here and like to give the waitresses a hard time."

The scruffiest of the lot, a man sporting a mile-long ponytail and beard, began clenching his fists in a show of strength. "What's it to you who we give a hard time to?"

Zach and Troy exchanged knowing looks but it was Troy who stepped forward. "We do. His sister, my girlfriend, worked in here five nights a week, carting trays left and right for the likes of you. Not only is your little posse used to verbally abusing the waitresses, you're lousy tippers."

Thane saw the blow about to fly, stepped in front of Troy in time to block the attempt at a punch. Thane shoved the ponytailed man back, watched Earl readily take his pal's place. Thane drew back a fist, rammed it straight into Earl's nose. "I can't very well let the groom show up with bruises on his face tomorrow for his big day, now can I?"

Zach agreed and tackled the next scruffy loudmouth sending him to the floor. Ryder took out the churlish tough guy, leaving Cord to level the last punk.

By the time Brent walked through the door, the melee was already over.

Out at Promise Cove where Julianne had thrown Bree a bridal shower, things were far more serene. Wine flowed while the bride-to-be sat in the living room and opened a stack of gag gifts along with her real presents. Cocktail sets, engraved serving trays, pitchers, cookbooks, a waffle iron, and the like were stacked in a pile around Bree's chair.

"The idea is for Bree to sit back tonight and take it easy, to relax and take advantage of a little 'me' time before she walks down the aisle tomorrow."

"If not tonight, when?" Keegan noted. "The week running up to the wedding is the most stressful without adding on a lot of unnecessary boring activities that no one is interested in doing."

"So don't expect the toilet paper bridal gown game tonight," Kinsey hinted.

Bree held up her champagne glass. "Thank goodness for scrapping that idea. Splitting into teams and trying to come up with a design is too much pressure for me right now, although it might keep me from worrying about the weather. I check the forecast every day every hour to see if it's changed. Tell me I'm not crazy for planning an outdoor wedding in November."

"You aren't," Jordan said, patting her hand. "And if it opens up and pours, Nick and I have you covered. So stop worrying. This very room will turn into a gorgeous place where you and Troy can exchange vows. You'll see. So just relax."

"No one does a wedding better than Nick and Jordan, outdoor or indoor. Ethan and I can attest to that," Hayden said. "How many does this make now?"

"At least twenty. I believe we're starting to make waves with Reverend Whitcomb. But then the man never did really warm up to Nick or me. I have no idea why. I do think it had something to do with Sissy Carr though. Milton has been a deacon in that church for almost forty years."

"He was a tad standoffish when he performed our vows. Now it makes sense because Brent and I opted for Promise Cove, as did just about everyone else in this room," River noted. About that time her cell phone rang. "Oh sorry, I need to take this. It's Brent. I hope it isn't about Luke. He had the sniffles earlier." River disappeared into the dining room to take the call. But two minutes later she came back out.

"You won't believe what happened." River glanced around the room at each face. "I guess this pretty much concerns everyone here. Brent just busted up a fight over at McCready's. Looks like Troy's bachelor party turned into a brawl."

"Oh no. Is Troy all right?" Bree asked, concern lining her face.

"Don't worry. Brent said Troy was fine. In fact, thanks to Thane, he kept Troy's pretty face free of black eyes and bruises for tomorrow."

"What?"

River held up her phone showing a digital image taken at the scene and Brent's latest text message. "See, not a scratch on any of them. Now the other guys weren't so lucky." She passed around the phone with Brent's second text. "Looks like these four got the worst of it."

Keegan and Julianne exchanged looks. But it was Keegan who put the incident in perspective. "What kinds of idiots take on two former army rangers and an NFL linebacker the size of Cord, Ryder, and Thane?"

Jordan peered at the picture Brent had sent and recognized Earl right away. "I guess some men have no regard for the shape of their faces. That one will need stitches."

Studying the photo, Hayden snorted out a laugh. "Oh yeah, brings back memories of my first time in McCready's, a whiskey bottle to the head of some guy named Sal. Flynn really needs to consider finding a way to attract a better clientele."

"That's what Troy and I keep telling him," Bree pointed out. "That's the very reason I'm glad I don't have to work there anymore. I'm grateful Troy didn't get his face bashed in. Because it suddenly hit me, this time tomorrow night, I'll be Mrs. Troy Dayton."

The women raised their glasses in salute. "Then here's to a dry and sunny forecast."

Chapter Twenty

It had taken weeks for Pastor Whitcomb to finally get over his annoyance knowing Troy and Bree planned to hold their nuptials at Promise Cove instead of at the church.

But on a beautiful Saturday afternoon just before the sun dropped over the horizon, the preacher couldn't argue with the spectacular outdoor venue.

Nature had brushed the soft blue sky with hues of orange and tinted the backdrop with glowing accents of velvety purple.

High on the cliffs, Troy stood a bundle of nerves and sweaty palms under an archway draped in organza and lace, the pergola intertwined with baby's breath and lavender. The groom looked around, turned to his best man to ask a question. Logan patted his pocket, assuring Troy for the third time in an hour that he had the ring. On the platform Troy had built for this occasion, Ryder took his place next to Logan.

This day, Zach Dennison had a dual role. He would act as both a groomsman for Troy and before that, would take his sister's arm and lead her down the aisle.

In the audience there was no bride's side or groom's side, not at this wedding. Early on, it seemed as though each guest had no preference as long as they got to watch the young couple exchange their vows.

So, at exactly four-thirty, Sonoma, Sonnet and Malachi Rafferty began the first strings of music that signaled to the bridesmaids that it was time, which meant Abby

Anderson went first, followed by Drea and lastly, the maid of honor, Julianne. As the women lined up taking their places on the stage, all eyes turned to the rear where Bree waited for the first notes of the wedding march to begin.

Standing on the terrace Bree heard her cue. She wrapped her arm around her brother's and stepping together let Zach guide her along a pathway strewn with rose petals.

Emma Colter had designed Bree's off-the-shoulder satin gown with a beaded and lace bodice that swept down from her waist into a feathery chiffon train. It made Bree look like a red-haired princess. She'd curled her hair, woven ribbons into the auburn locks and left it down to drape her shoulders. As Zach handed her off to Troy her tresses swirled in the light breeze. Troy met her halfway and helped her make the climb up the dais to stand next to him.

Elliott Whitcomb began the ceremony with the age-old words, "Dearly beloved…" In the end, it took less than fifteen minutes to exchange vows, give each other rings and declare their love so that with the pronouncement Troy and Bree became husband and wife.

Once the Reverend looked at Troy and stated, "You may now kiss the bride," the groom didn't need to be told twice. Troy met Bree's lips in a tender showing of both heat and longing.

The pastor had to wait a beat before announcing, "Ladies and gentlemen, it's my great pleasure to present, Mr. and Mrs. Troy Dayton."

When the couple turned to face the guests, applause broke out. It swept through the audience about the same time the Raffertys began the recessional with a guitar riff and a splash of violins.

Bree took Troy's arm and together they walked back down over the rose petals to a standing O.

At the last minute Logan, Troy's best man, switched places with Ryder so Ryder could escort Julianne down the aisle. About midway down the rows of chairs, Ryder turned to Julianne and whispered, "I feel like I just had a run-through of our own wedding and it wasn't nearly as impressive. I can't believe we let them beat us to the punch. How do we top this?"

She elbowed him in the ribs. "That wasn't your worry two months ago when you were swamped with work and put the wedding off until the week before Christmas. Now the pressure's definitely on us. We'll have to up our game."

"Maybe we should focus on just closing the deal," Ryder muttered with a kiss near her ear.

"Agreed. Besides, your mother's determined to help pay for her only son to have a wedding to remember. Despite how many times I've told her I'm perfectly capable of…"

"My mom's been a bit over the top since she found out about you."

"We need to have our heads examined for getting married this close to Christmas. Maybe we need more time. Do you want more time?"

"No. Look, think of it this way, while everyone else is unwrapping their presents, we'll be in honeymoon-mode enjoying Waikiki to the fullest. Just keep picturing a hotel room for seven days with no interruptions, no work-related issues to deal with, and no school-related activities, just us, room service, and time to make up for."

"You're right, center our energy on making that happen and enjoy the winter break to the fullest. I like the way you think."

"That's my girl." About that time Ryder caught sight of a quick make-out session between Zach and Drea. "Do you see that? I've never seen Zach this…happy. In fact the word 'happy' doesn't really jibe with him."

"Forget Zach, word around town is that no one's ever seen Drea this enamored…with anyone. You know what that means? Those two show all the signs of heading toward matrimony."

Ryder barked out laughter. "I'd have to see that, maybe if a brick falls on Zach's head but that would be the only way."

As the couple continued through the back entrance of the B&B where other guests were gathering, they noted the flurry taking place with food prep. Jordan and Perry were busy directing the caterers. The two had gone in together with Troy's and Bree's friends to plan the sit-down reception. Everyone had pitched in to set up tables on the quad for guests to dine on roasted chicken or tender roast beef served by waiters carting trays back and forth.

With her mind on playing cupid, Hayden Cody had dragged her sister, Sydney Reed, to the event, even though Sydney didn't really know anyone. But then that was the point, to introduce the ER nurse around, get her to mingle. After huddling with her best friend, Jordan, Hayden had decided the situation called for a little switcheroo in the seating department. So the women had manipulated Sydney next to Malachi Rafferty at the same table with his teenage girls.

"Don't you think she'll suspect something when she isn't sitting next to you and Ethan?" Jordan asked while watching Nick and Ethan transfer the wedding cake from the counter to a pushcart for serving later.

"Probably, but the girl needs to circulate."

"Sydney's only been here a week," Jordan pointed out.

"That's what I told Hayden," Ethan said. "But did my wife listen to me? No. Sydney starts at Doc's on Monday. She's getting settled into the house she rented on Tradewinds Drive. If you ask me, the woman has a full plate without trying to fix her up seven days after she gets here."

Hayden peered out the window; her eyes lit on the table in question. "See, look at that. She's laughing at something Malachi said. She's enjoying herself."

Ethan chuckled and shook his head. "Of course she is. It's a festive occasion. I'm just not sure throwing her into a dynamic with two teen girls is a fair thing to do to your own sister."

"I admit I was desperate. My choices were Cooper, Fischer, Malachi, or Archer Gates. Abby Anderson seems to have set her sights on Cooper so I didn't want to interfere there. And Fischer seems a little too busy with the pizza place to start something new right off the bat."

"And we all know Archer's still mired down in his divorce enough that he can't seem to let go of the bottle for long," Jordan added. "Not a good mix for a new relationship."

"Exactly. Speaking of new relationships, what do you make of what's happening between Thane and Isabella?"

"It's always tough for someone to date when they have kids. I've seen the three of them around town. Jonah seems over-the-moon with her, which is important to a parent. I know Hutton fell for Nick right away."

"That's because I'm fairly irresistible," Nick threw in.

"You spoiled her then and you know it," Jordan claimed. "That is, after you got over being afraid to hold her. Oh, look at that. Thane and Isabella are really getting down on the dance floor."

"Hmm, according to River, she didn't learn that move at the Bolshoi."

In the middle of expounding on that thought, Ethan grabbed his wife around the waist. "That's it. There's music and merriment here. Ricky Oden's band is just getting warmed up and since we paid for a sitter, I intend to enjoy the rest of the evening without fixating on Sydney's future dating status or how another couple is having a blast at the same party where we are."

"Okay, okay, point made."

Ethan led her outside to the wooden platform set up for dancing.

Nick watched them go, turned to Jordan with his hand held out. "Mrs. Harris, that sounds like an excellent call to action to me. I'd like to dance with my wife. What do you say?"

"But I have to…"

"No, you don't," Nick stated, calling out to the other host for help. "Perry, get the cake in position. I'm taking my wife for a spin around the floor, maybe several times."

"We should all do that," Perry suggested, pointing a finger at his partner, Alec, a young Stanford grad student whose parents owned a winery in Napa Valley. "Come on. Let's show them how to shake it."

Outside, Thane and Isabella dropped into chairs at their assigned table to take a breather. After bumping and whirling to the beat, Thane mopped his brow and looked over at the alluring woman next to him. Her green eyes sparkled, accessorizing the emerald green strapless number she had on. Thane leaned in over the noise, nipped her bare shoulder. "Did I tell you how stunning you look in that dress?"

"You brought it up once but that was hours ago. I could use a reminder."

Openly flirting, he took her hand and nibbled her fingers. "Stunning with clothes on, stunning without, I like you better though when there's nothing at all between us."

She fanned her face. "Like it wasn't hot enough out here without a visual of that."

"That's the idea."

For the first time, Thane noticed Malachi and turned to his neighbor. "If the babysitting offer is still open, I'd like to take you up on it. I need someone to watch Jonah next Saturday night. I'd like to take Isabella out for an evening where it's just the two of us."

"Not that we don't find a six-year-old highly entertaining because we do," Isabella chimed in with a grin.

Malachi grinned back and drew his daughters into the conversation. "What do you say to having spending money, girls?"

The teens exchanged glances. Sonnet pumped her fist into the air, but it was Sonoma who sat up straight, all businesslike and announced their going rate. "If that's acceptable, then we're in. It's a go."

"This is my boy we're talking about here. If you have any problems at all, I won't be that far away. Do you think this is too much responsibility?" Thane asked, turning to Malachi. "You're their father, do you think your girls are up for the job?" a curious Thane wanted to know.

Malachi slapped him on the back. "Between the two of them, I believe they'll do a good job for you. But I don't leave for my gig until eight-thirty, which means I'm available to drop in on them if it will make you feel better."

A mortified Sonoma insisted, "Dad! We can do this job by ourselves." The teen glanced over at Thane, the potential customer. "You have nothing to worry about, Mr. Delacourt. We won't let Jonah watch R-rated movies or anything like that while he's in our care."

"Good to know," Thane said as Isabella laid a hand on his arm.

From the other side of the table, Sydney smiled at the conversation, joining in. "At twelve I was babysitting three kids down the street from me, one of whom was just a baby. I'm pretty sure these girls should be able to handle one six-year-old for three hours."

"I suppose that's true," Thane noted.

When Ricky Oden went into a rendition of "Black Mountain Rag," Thane took Isabella's hand and stood up. "It might not be my kind of music but we should make the party last as long as we can before I have to pick up Jonah from Tommy's house. One more time around the dance floor ought to get my mind off worrying about him."

"You could have let him sleep over at Tommy's," Isabella said as they moved back into the throng of dancers.

He held up his phone. "Jonah was supposed to call by now if he wanted to stay over. He hasn't."

"It's early enough that he still might," she pointed out.

The words had no sooner left her lips than the phone dinged. It was the Gates's phone number displayed on the readout. Isabella started laughing. Thane tugged her hand in his and moved off the dance floor so he could take the call where he could hear better. Jonah was on the other end, begging.

"Please, Dad, please Tommy and I are having fun. I want to stay here. I packed my pajamas and my toothbrush and we're going to bed right at nine o'clock."

Thane knew the likelihood of two boys going to bed on time was virtually zero. "Okay, but you'll call me if you want to come home, right?"

"Sure. But I won't."

"Okay, then let me talk to Mr. Gates."

Archer got on the phone and the fathers settled on a time that would be good for Jonah to get picked up in the morning.

"It's his first sleepover," Thane said to Isabella when he hung up.

"I know. It must be tough. But think of it this way, he's made a friend. And we get to stay longer at the party." She lifted her eyebrows up and down. "And then there's later..."

"I like thinking about later. Would it be rude to leave now?"

She roared with laughter. "Before cutting the cake? Yes. But after that..."

In another corner of the terrace, Julianne cornered the social worker, Carla Vargas.

"You know, it looks like I finally got a dozen students enrolled in sixth grade next year. The only problem is they don't have a teacher yet."

"That sounds wonderful," Carla noted. But when the principal continued to stare at her, Carla asked, "Why are you looking at me like that?"

"Because Murphy says you could put your four-year degree and master's to better use and teach my sixth graders. The upside is that you wouldn't have to travel all over the county from house to house doing spot checks. Instead, your experience and expertise with children could have a greater impact on that difficult age group."

"You can't be serious."

"You'd need your state certifications, of course, but I can help you with those."

"But I'm a social worker. I'm not a teacher."

"All the more reason you'd bring an excitement to the new position."

"I wonder if this has anything to do with Murphy wanting me to move in with him."

Julianne beamed an innocent look in Carla's direction. "I'm sure it's just a coincidence." When she spotted Thane, she told Carla, "At least think about it because you'd be an asset to the staff. Right now I need to go talk to Thane. If you could let me know by December first, we'd have time to get all the documentation done."

When Julianne reached Thane and Isabella, she went into an entirely different pitch. "As you know Ryder and I are getting married in five more weeks."

"Congrats," Isabella offered.

"Yes, well, after tonight, I admit inspiration struck. What with work I haven't had much time to plan anything. Ryder's mother has tried to help but she's doing it all from back East. She doesn't get here for another three weeks. Anyway, after seeing what a phenomenal job Bree did on her wedding, Ryder and I decided we needed to think outside the box. I know this is a huge favor but I'd like to hold the ceremony on the cliffs, next to the lighthouse. Of course, we'd come back to Promise Cove for the reception."

Isabella waved off her concern. "It sounds like a fantastic idea but I keep telling people I only rent the property from Logan. It's really Logan's decision."

"Logan said that we should ask you. So here I am."

"Me? It's fine by me. I think it'd make for a wonderful, romantic setting. And you know what? If the weather's bad, as backup, there's the huge antechamber at the bottom of the lighthouse where light filters down from the top into the middle of the floor."

"Oh my. That does sound romantic."

"It is. You and Ryder will love it. Why don't you plan to come by tomorrow and take a look."

"We will. And Thane, I talked to Greg Prather about your idea…about his working at the resale shop."

"Actually it was Isabella's idea. And?"

"I think Greg's a good fit. Turns out, he's a lover of junk, someone who collects and fixes up old necklaces and other jewelry he finds and sells online. When you think about it, it's really an uncanny fit."

"So you'll go ahead with the store."

"Yes, but not next to the church, only because the Springer family still owns the property and it's tied up in some sort of litigation. So Ryder's come up with a solution and it's much cheaper rent. There's this slip of a space next to Ferguson's Hardware. At one time, Tucker's grandfather used it to stash old water heaters and any other items he thought might resell for a buck. It's rundown and shabby but the guts and support structure seem sound."

"I'm sensing a 'but' here," Thane noted. "What's wrong with the space?"

"Other than it's small and cramped? Well for starters, it's full of junk, I mean to the rafters. Like most of the storefronts in town it's in sad shape, too. But Greg assures me if I hire him, he'll help Ryder and me shovel the stuff out and clean it up so it's habitable. And of course, my dad's willing to pitch in on weekends whenever we need him."

"Is Tucker giving you a problem with the lease?" Isabella wanted to know. "Even in the short amount of time I've been in town, everyone has an opinion about Ferguson's ability to run off customers."

Julianne smiled. "It's true. But Ryder's done some major negotiating in that regard and used his leverage, the kind that only a Ferguson seems to appreciate. In fact, Ryder's offered to take it off Tucker's hands, keeping the hardware store as the boatyard's major lumber supplier, if you get my drift."

Isabella burst out with a laugh. "Oh, it's brilliant. That kind of leverage tops an entrenched position in negotiations every time."

"You bet. Ryder and I want you to know how much we appreciate getting to use the lighthouse for the wedding."

"No problem. Come by tomorrow and get a feel for how best to work with the setting and the lighthouse itself."

"We will. I can't wait. And again thanks to both of you for the kick in the pants we needed to get the resale shop opened. Greg starts in two weeks after he gives notice at all his jobs."

"I bet Murphy's not happy about losing his stocker," Thane said.

"Maybe Archer Gates can get on there. He's been looking for work. I heard that from Tommy the other day when we were at the train store," Isabella reported.

"I'm seeing Archer tomorrow when I pick up Jonah. I'll send him to Murphy."

"Good idea. Looks like the reception's starting to wind down." Isabella nodded her head toward the house. "It tends to do that when the bride and groom disappear upstairs to their honeymoon suite."

Thane chuckled and watched as people began to drift homeward. Those designated as cleanup crew collected trash and bussed the outdoor area. In the kitchen, the wait staff washed dishes and plates before packing up and loading their vans to head back to Santa Cruz.

To Julianne, Thane offered their goodbyes, using the opportunity to whisk Isabella out of there and toward the car.

As soon as they reached his Range Rover, Thane scooted the seat back all the way to a recline position to make more room in the cramped front between his body and the steering wheel. He grabbed her around the waist, brought her onto his lap and covered her mouth. "Just a taste to hold me over. I've wanted to do this all night."

"Mmm, what you need is a huge reward for your patience and perseverance," she said as their bodies wrapped like tangled vines.

"I was hoping you'd see it my way. Your place or mine?"

"Whichever's closer."

"Fischer's at my house."

"Then Sea Glass Cottage here we come."

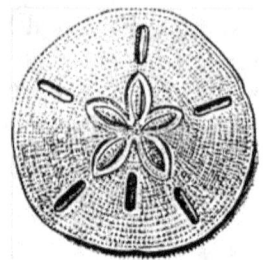

Chapter Twenty-One

At 14 Lighthouse Lane, Thane threw back the front door as they fell into the foyer draped all over each other. The frenzy continued as they bumped along shedding clothing as they went.

Fumbling with the zipper on the back of the cocktail dress, he finally slid it down enough so that he could peel it over her hips. They dropped where they were, causing the tapestry rug on the floor to skid with them sprawled on top of it. Jazz leaped out of the way in time to witness them tearing at each other, ripping off any obstacle that got in their way.

"Look at you. I've been saving this all day," he said as he feasted on her mouth. He savored curves with one purpose in mind, pleasuring himself as much as he did her. He slicked along her body savoring sweet flesh. He used his tongue to linger over her belly. He tasted silky thighs.

He was doing things to her body no one had ever done before, the pace surging her along into a furnace-like heat. Fast and heady, she dug her nails into the smidgen of carpet and rode the swell. Stars exploded as shudders rocked through her. Little quakes rippled out, made her toes curl up. When she came, a feral moan escaped her lips. Something wild within her broke free.

Rearing up, she exploited his mouth. The kiss seared, went deep, then deeper.

"Now, Thane! Now!" she begged.

They joined, became a fierce one, bucking and rocking. They moved together, the wild rhythm urging them on. It felt like a tremor shaking the house as they spiraled upward, shattering into a thousand shades of gold.

He dropped on top of her, winded, and tried to pull in air. "I'm not sure I can move."

"That was…incredible. I'm pretty sure I've lost the feeling in my toes."

He finally stirred and moved his weight off her. "How's that? Better?"

"I didn't know sex could be like this. I thought it was just…you know…one-sided."

"You've been with the wrong men."

"Well. Duh."

"That's okay. I've been with the wrong women." He sat up, gathered his clothes.

Sensing things had calmed down, Jazz thought it was safe enough to saunter over. She stuck her nose in Isabella's face, looked up, licked Thane's hand.

"Are you staying or do you have to get back?"

"I'm staying. I'm suddenly exhausted. Let's catch some sleep, work up to round two."

The bed was empty when he woke up. The smell of bacon had him kicking out of the sheets and getting to his feet. After taking a hot shower he found Izzy outside on the patio fiddling with some kind of ivy-looking thing that seemed to be on its last leg. She wore one of his oversized Tees that draped almost to her knees barely covering her panties.

"Hey."

"Hi, sleepyhead. There's fresh coffee."

"Thanks. How long have you been up?"

"About an hour. I puttered around out here so I wouldn't wake you."

"What is that thing?"

"It's called a peace lily. I found it last week at your place in the corner of the flower bed, neglected and almost dead. You know, California might be experiencing a drought but I'm pretty sure it's okay if you spare a few drops of water for a poor houseplant that never did you any harm."

He snorted out a laugh and went inside to get down a mug. "If I'm not mistaken someone sent that plant when my mother died. I guess I forgot about it. Want some eggs to go with that bacon I smell? I'm good at fixing eggs."

"Sure. Do you know where everything is you need?"

"I'll figure it out as I go."

"Okay, I'll work the toaster."

Later when they sat down to a panful of perfectly scrambled eggs, she became acutely aware of how homey this scene was and how comfortable she felt in it.

"What are you thinking?" he asked.

"That this is what I wanted when I got married. Peace. Joy. Normal. I didn't get it."

"You rarely talk about it and I haven't pushed."

"I know and I appreciate it. I don't like bringing it up or thinking about that time of my life. I mean, what's the point?"

"You're very careful not to say too much."

"Is that how it seems to you?"

"Sometimes because you often answer a question with a question."

About that time a car horn sounded outside. "That must be Julianne and Ryder. They did say they couldn't wait to take the tour. I guess they weren't kidding."

Sure enough, when Isabella opened the front door, Julianne was already out of the car and rushing past the lighthouse to take in the spectacular view. Ryder spotted them in the doorway and waved.

"Sorry we're so early but Julianne is excited to see what this place offers so we can make a decision today."

"No problem," Isabella said. "You should check out all your options."

"This is a beautiful spot," Julianne said turning at the edge of the cliffs and breathing in the ocean air. "If we do this, we have to hope for good weather, though."

"Like I said last night, take a tour of the lighthouse. Make sure you walk up the spiral staircase and see the view at the top. Who knows? You might even decide your guests could make the climb to the watch room and have your ceremony up there," Isabella suggested.

Ryder glanced up at the towering structure, took in the catwalk. "That would be so cool, such a scenic place to hold a wedding. We could have the service above..."

"Don't even think about it," Julianne countered. "I'd have to troop up there in a gown with a long train attached wearing heels."

"You could walk up barefoot, put the shoes on when you reach the top." That offer got Isabella a lethal glare from the principal. She lifted a shoulder. "Just saying."

Julianne sighed. "Well, hey, I'm willing to explore the possibilities. How about you guys make that hike with us?"

"Sure. There are sixty-four steps up to the top," Isabella said, turning to Thane. "Are you still in shape from your playing days?"

He grinned, leaned in, and whispered, "I thought I proved that last night. Twice."

"Just checking," she said, grinning back. She took his hand, told the other couple. "If you're ready, I'll lead the way. The view from the top is guaranteed to blow you away."

From the moment they got inside the entrance and walked around the anteroom, Isabella knew this is where the couple planned to hold their wedding. "Even if it rains and you're unable to hold the service between the cottage and the lighthouse, you could easily fit seventy-five people in this room."

While Isabella took the couple on a tour and pointed out each historical fact to them, Thane watched Isabella's eyes light up as bright as the beacon in the lantern room. If he'd wondered about her intentions to put down roots here in town before now, he had his answer. Not only did she glow with enthusiasm about the place, she had Ryder and Julianne so excited about their big day it was almost as if Isabella had planned the event out in her head. She was captivating. She was entertaining. She was everything Thane had ever wanted in a woman.

Then why did he feel like something was missing—that there was an enormous hole in her past? And could he overlook that feeling enough to move on with her? To make it permanent?

For Jonah's sake he had to tread carefully. He had to be ever vigilant that there was no way his boy would get hurt in the process. But how could he do that without delving further into her past, a past she didn't want to discuss?

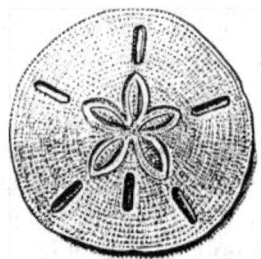

Chapter Twenty-Two

The day before Thanksgiving a Pacific storm roared into the area bringing heavy rain. The gusty wind slammed out of the north, whipping and whistling, shaking and rattling the window panes. The bad weather made for an intimate setting where Thane and Jonah had found a place to spread out with the dogs by the fire. Thane had brought in a stack of firewood for the night and kept tossing logs on the hearth so the cottage had a nice and toasty feel to it.

Isabella had stowed her stash of guns away in a locked safe in her closet. So there was no chance Jonah could get to any of them or reach any of the knives she kept around the house. Besides, what did she have to be afraid of when she had an athletic former NFL linebacker for a boyfriend?

It was enough for her that Jonah was excited to be here, eager about the big meal tomorrow when his Uncle Fisch would show up and spend the day with them watching football.

In the kitchen Isabella had spent her morning keeping busy preparing the menu for tomorrow's meal. She'd discovered she liked the homey duties. Getting a turkey stuffed and ready for someone else to eat seemed like the key to cooking.

She stood at the stove pouring hot cocoa she'd made from scratch into mugs. "Hot chocolate's ready," she called out. Two seconds later, Jonah came darting in and appeared at her elbow, to get his share.

"Yum. You make it better than Uncle Fisch does."

"I do? What a nice thing to say. Thank you. That's quite a compliment. Although let's keep it between the two of us. We don't want to hurt Fischer's feelings."

"Uh-oh, I already told him last time you made me cocoa," Jonah admitted.

Isabella snuck out a chuckle. "It's okay. I'll tell you a secret. I'm a little nervous to have Fischer coming here for dinner tomorrow sampling my cooking."

"Don't be," Thane said from the doorway. "The guy might be a picky perfectionist in his own kitchen when he's at the helm, but I've never seen him become a rude guest when it comes to grabbing a meal at other people's houses."

"You're sure about that? I suppose that makes me feel better. But I wouldn't be honest if I said he doesn't intimidate me a little bit with his skills near a stove. I'm nervous."

Thane watched her check the pot of soup she had simmering for lunch, watched as she opened the oven to test the cornbread she'd baked for what she hoped to use for stuffing. She'd even rolled out dough for a crust and added the pumpkin mixture she'd created from scratch to pour into a baking dish for pie.

To show his appreciation, he went to where she stood, wrapped his arms around her body. Nestled up against each other like this, he felt as though he'd finally found what he'd been looking for his entire life.

"Do you mind if Jonah and I stay here tonight?"

"You have to ask? Of course not. It makes no sense to go out into the pouring rain when there's a perfectly good guest room for Jonah."

He nuzzled her neck and lowered his voice, "Good because after dinner I have this idea where we get naked and…"

From his perch on the bar stool next to the counter, Jonah piped up, "Daddy, help, I can't get the last piggy on Angry Birds. I'm stuck on level four and I can't get past this one mean pig."

Thane kissed Izzy's neck and muttered, "Duty calls. Later." With that, he moved over to join his son at the island. "Let's see if we can figure this out together."

For lunch she dished up vegetable chowder and watched as they went through the whole vat of soup like they hadn't eaten in days.

After spending time with kitchen detail, Isabella went to the closet and took down a game from the shelf, spread out the board, pawns, and dice on the table.

"I remember this," Thane said as he took a seat. "I didn't know they still made Parcheesi."

"I didn't know either. I found this at Layne's Trains going through a stack of Cooper's old inventory. As the only toy store in town you'd be surprised how busy that man has been since getting his business going two months ago. He said his first month was abysmal and slow but now…"

"It's turned around. I know he told me the same thing."

"Cooper also mentioned that there used to be an old theater sandwiched between your pizza place and the police station. I got curious and went by there to check it out."

"Wow, I remember that. It was gone two decades ago. Now that I think about it, I remember being around ten and standing on the corner watching them dismantle the old marquee and truck it off somewhere."

"Well, that's a shame. I checked the place out, the marquee's definitely history, the only thing that remains are the ornate doors on the front of the building. Someone gutted the inside. I know because I scraped off a layer of dirt to get a look inside. Anyway, it's an empty shell now. Remember when we were out at that old barn where you bought the tables? There were all these old theater seats just sitting there gathering dust. It occurs to me that Cleef must've acquired them at some point and stored them there."

"Are you thinking what I'm thinking?"

"That if you own the pizza parlor next door to a movie theater, you could pick up walk-in business when they come out hungry."

Thane nodded beginning to see the upside. "We could bring the place back to its former glory. I'm sure Troy or Ryder or Zach could tell us what kind of money we'd be talking about for a space that size."

"Or if it's even doable."

Thane chuckled. "Are you kidding? Troy will try to tackle anything. Ryder has the presence of mind to see the pitfalls. And Zach is the one who grumbles about their choices. They're an odd group of guys."

After three rounds of Parcheesi the game had them laughing and arguing good-naturedly over moves. Later, she helped tuck Jonah into the guest room with a sense that he had something weighing on his mind.

"Okay, spill it, what's wrong?"

"I like it here in your house."

"That's good. That means you'll come back."

"Tommy says you're almost like a mom. How come you don't have kids of your own? Don't you like kids?"

"I love kids, especially balls of energy and wiggle worms like you," she told him, poking him in the ribs.

From the doorway Thane listened to the byplay. He had to admit his son had seemed a lot happier lately. It had been more than a week since Jonah had brought up his grandmother. The boy hadn't pestered him to go out to the cemetery either. That had to be a good sign that the kid was moving on, didn't it? But Thane wondered what he should do about this thing with Isabella. This was beginning to feel like a real family effort and he wasn't sure the ground was stable enough yet.

And the next words out of Jonah's mouth had him sweating bullets.

"Since you don't have a little boy of your own, I could be your little boy."

Thane saw Isabella get tears in her eyes before she could muster up something to say. "Are you kidding? I'd love that. I'd be crazy not to love you or want you for my son. And we know I'm not crazy, remember?" she said with a wink.

Thane could see it was all she could do to fight back the water that wanted to fall out of her eyes. He understood that it wouldn't do to have Jonah see her start bawling.

"You think you can sleep in here tonight, buddy?"

"Sure. I like it here. I brought my Legos and four of my stuffed animals."

"Okay, then get some sleep. We'll talk tomorrow."

"Can Jax and Jazz stay in here tonight?" Jonah asked.

"Absolutely, they could use the company."

Thane closed Jonah's door and took Isabella by the hand leading her into the bedroom. They sat down on the bed so they could talk. "Did that freak you out in there?"

"Not at all. But I can tell by the way you're acting, it certainly freaked you out."

"A little. It's just that he's so young. I don't want to see him hurt."

"I don't want to see him hurt either."

"Jonah never knew his mother, lost his grandfather early on, lost his grandmother who was basically his primary caregiver. I'm still not convinced that he's completely over losing her either. That's a lot of disappointment and loss for a little kid to handle at such a young age."

"I agree. So you're afraid that things won't work out between us and he'll be left confused and wondering what happened?"

"That's part of it. This whole thing is moving so fast for him. I think he desperately wants a mother or at least a mother-figure in his life. This is hard for him. Me? I'm not a divorced parent. I'm the only parent. I can't call up his mother, my ex, and say, 'what about taking him for the weekend?' It doesn't work that way. I'm a single parent where every decision I make lands on my shoulders, my responsibility, my mistakes."

"Parents make mistakes, Thane. It's inevitable. They aren't perfect. You do the best you can and hope that it's enough. Are you trying to end this between us because you're afraid...?"

He didn't let her finish. "No, not that. I'm hoping with Jonah you meant what you said back there and that you weren't just being kind to him because he put you on the spot."

She narrowed her eyes and stared at him. "I admit I wasn't sure exactly how to handle it. But Jonah had obviously given it a great deal of thought. Couldn't you tell that? I would never hurt him, Thane, never. My feelings for him are as genuine as my feelings are for you."

Thane blew out a heavy, pent-up puff of air in relief. "You have no idea how glad I am to hear you say that. It's a load off my heart and mind."

She ran a hand up his chest. "Then let's go to bed."

The rain had eased up by the time she took the dogs for a walk down the hill and back before breakfast. When she returned to the cottage, she found Thane in the kitchen starting a pot of coffee and Jonah sitting at the table holding a box of Count Chocula.

She took one look at the two stubborn faces and decided a disagreement hung in the air.

"That's way too much sugar, especially after all the candy you've had lately," Thane reasoned.

"But I want it for breakfast."

Thane sent Isabella a smoldering look. "Who buys Count Chocula anyway?"

She lifted a shoulder in defense as she reached down to unsnap the leash on each dog's collar. "It's a seasonal Halloween thing. I sometimes eat it at night after supper for dessert."

"See, Dad. Izzy eats it."

Jax and Jazz bolted toward the boy and slid across the tile floor. Using that as an opportunity to get between the two willful corners over breakfast food, Izzy spread her fingers through Jonah's hair. "Why don't you feed the dogs? You know where I keep the puppy chow, remember?"

Over the past few days Jonah had gotten into a routine. She watched as he dutifully went into the pantry, used the scoop to grab enough dog food to pour into the stainless steel feeding bowls. What spilled over on the floor, the dogs quickly inhaled.

It didn't escape Thane's notice, the way she'd handled the situation. She'd managed to get Jonah's attention refocused on something else while he eased off his stance. That's why he relented and took down a bowl from the cabinet. "Count Chocula today but I don't want to catch any flak when Jonah's swinging from the light fixture above the dining room table because of a sugar rush."

Jonah hooted with laughter. "I'm not gonna swing like a monkey in the zoo."

"You're not? Hmm, sometimes I think you are when I see you jumping up and down on the sofa."

Isabella threw together eggs for breakfast while the banter ramped up. By the time the doorbell rang and Fischer strolled in, the announcers on TV were playing up the pregame between the Detroit Lions and the Bears. The guys huddled over the screen to see kickoff while Jonah alternated his time playing with his iPad or building stuff out of his Legos.

As Thane had promised, Fischer left her alone in the kitchen to prep Thanksgiving dinner by herself. That is, until Isabella begged for help making the gravy. "If I ruin it by using all the turkey stock we end up eating dry mashed potatoes. That's the truth of it. Help. SOS. I'm sending up a red flare here. I'm not afraid to admit gravy scares me."

The chef flashed a grin. "Gravy's tricky." Fischer moved beside her at the stove and added, "But it's the easiest thing to make once you get the hang of it. You have any cognac?"

"For gravy?"

"No, for me," Fisch said with a laugh. "White wine will do in a pinch though."

She tapped him playfully on the arm before handing him a bottle of Sauvignon Blanc she'd picked up at Murphy's. "How's this?"

He took a swig straight from the bottle. "Not bad. This will do fine. I need flour, onion, and all the fresh herbs you have on hand."

She disappeared into the pantry, came back with an armful of stuff. "Don't beat me with a stick but all I have fresh is rosemary. Sage and thyme are in a bottle." She laughed at her own joke. "Thyme in a bottle, get it?"

Fischer's lips curved up. "I may like you yet."

"My other fresh herbs took a nosedive once I went to work. I forgot to water them a couple times. And I had to toss the fresh oregano when Jazz peed on the plant I had growing on the patio. She squatted down and hit that sucker dead-on, which shows you she has a purpose."

"And perfect aim," Fisch added.

"That too," she said with a snicker. "It's one reason I can't wait to get started on making that plot of land a garden."

"It's a huge undertaking. Are you sure you want to make that kind of commitment? To the town?"

She was no longer certain the two were talking about growing vegetables. Before she could answer though, Fisch went on, "So you wanted to be a farmer, did you?"

"Most of all I just wanted to be free, free to be able to do what I wanted, when I wanted. For people who take that for granted, they've never walked in my shoes."

Thane came through the door just in time to hear that last declaration. Skimming his hands up her arms, he nuzzled her neck. "Will he find you and take it away again? Is that what you're afraid of? Is that the reason for all the weapons?"

Fischer turned to gape at them. "Weapons?"

She leaned her head back on Thane's shoulder, relaxed somewhat. She noted Fischer gawking and met his eyes. "He's referring to the arsenal I keep for protection. A girl can never be too careful."

But she saw the men exchange cautious glances at the statement and wasn't surprised when an awkward silence set in. Though it lifted once they grouped together around the dining room table to eat, she remained uneasy. That is, until her guests dug into the food. She watched in fascination as two grown men and one little boy devoured what had been a twenty-two-pound turkey. She'd never seen a bunch go after a meal with such zest. The wine flowed. Thane kept filling her glass until she finally covered the rim with her hand. "No more for me. I hope you guys saved room for pumpkin pie."

"If it's with whipped cream on top, I have some more room," Jonah said with confidence.

"Of course. No one should ever serve pumpkin pie without whipped cream."

The four of them had no problems polishing off a nine-inch pie.

Afterward, there was a flurry of dish cleanup, as the kitchen grew crowded around the sink. Everyone helped with the chore even when it meant stepping over the dogs that were underfoot most of the time to do it.

When Jonah conked out, she watched as Thane gently picked him up and carried him to bed. For the second time in as many weeks, her heart felt like it turned over in her chest. She turned to Fischer. "He's an amazing man."

Fischer nodded. "I'm glad to hear you say that. I watched him go through hell after Jonah was born. He's a special father in ways that no one seems to get."

"You mean the way he won't hire help when he absolutely could afford to? I get that he wants to be hands-on. It's one of the things I love about him."

"Did you hear what you just said?"

She smiled. "I've known it for some time now. I'm hoping you'll keep that to yourself since I'd like to be the one who tells him."

Henry Navarro hadn't counted on bad weather when he'd rented a car at the San Francisco Airport and headed south to the bumpkin town of Pelican Pointe. He had all the maps he needed to show him the way down the California coast to the place where Isabella had found a refuge, or so she thought.

His associates had cautioned him that it wouldn't be easy to go unnoticed in a town this size with one hick cop and a stoplight on Main Street. And yet, he had other concerns. Even though no one knew him in the tiny hamlet, a stranger would no doubt stick out like a hooker during Carnival in Rio. Because of that, he'd have to find a place to keep out of sight for a few days away from prying eyes. He'd done his research of the area beforehand and knew there was only one option for accommodations, a third-rate B&B that offered just six rooms. Even with a disguise he didn't think he could pull off the ruse with the local yokels. So he'd improvise as he so often had in the past and come up with an alternate plan.

As soon as Henry reached the heart of town, he slowed his speed and was tempted to continue on toward the lighthouse. Instead, his foot hit the gas sending him through the darkness of Main Street, his GPS heading southward.

Henry drove until he spotted the isolated farmhouse out in the middle of nowhere. He pulled the rental into the rutted lane, swearing at its bumpy potholes the entire length of the drive. The beam from his headlights landed on a junk heap—old cars and tractors, rusted-out bed springs and plows. He cut the ignition and sat back wondering if perhaps Isabella had gone mad to end up in such a backwoods part of the world. Shaking his head at her obvious ignorance, he rummaged in his bag for the small flashlight he'd brought.

Once he opened the door and unfurled himself from behind the wheel, he took in the surroundings. Rustic didn't come close to describing this dump. But maybe he'd found the perfect out-of-the-way place to crash for the night. If it worked out the way he hoped, he'd hide here indefinitely until his plan came together.

There was a light coming from one of the first floor windows so he headed that way. When he reached the house he stepped through a line of hedges and peered into the main room. From the flower bed, he spotted an old man sitting in front of his TV, the sound so loud he could make out the dialogue coming from the old-fashioned set.

Henry took out the knife he'd stopped to buy at a box store on his way from the airport. Circling around to the back, he took out his pick lock, deciding, once again, that opportunity somehow always worked in his favor.

Inside his living room Cleef Atkins huddled around his own fire in the den waiting for his turkey dinner to get done in the microwave. The drizzle outside made him long for company. On nights like tonight, he remembered his boys. He'd had two once—lost one when his helicopter had been shot down in Vietnam during the Easter Uprising in 1972; the other had succumbed to leukemia when he'd been just twenty-six.

Since Cleef didn't have anyone left, he'd already decided to spend his evening in front of the tube watching the classic John Wayne movie, *The Searchers* while he ate his supper.

When he heard the timer ding on the microwave, he shuffled past the family photographs lining the wall and into the kitchen. That's when he saw the back door standing wide open. Cleef never saw the man slip up behind him to slit his throat.

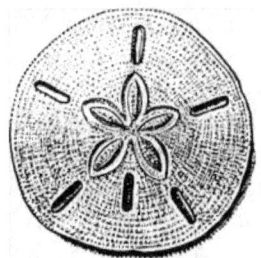

Chapter Twenty-Three

Twenty-one years earlier
Long Island, New York

Since birth, Isabella Rialto and Henry Navarro had spent the long, lazy days of summers basking in the sun along the shores of Oyster Bay. Their families had known each other for years and owned adjoining summer homes along the waterfront complete with private docks and boats.

As babies the two kids had bathed in the same bath water, gone swimming side by side in the bay, waded into boggy tide pools to catch slippery fish, and tried their hand at digging for clams.

They'd played tag among the red pines and oaks, romped over the lush grounds, hidden from each other along the sand dunes and grassy marshes, and roasted hot dogs over bonfires.

When Isabella wasn't tromping behind Henry exploring the wooded hillsides, she tried her best to talk her friend into playing dress up. She'd discovered that if she played five innings of baseball with him, which was his favorite sport, it equaled to getting him outfitted in costume—or whatever fancy clothes she could scrounge around the house—for thirty whole minutes. It was all part of passing the time whenever the two kids grew bored with everything else.

Henry generally went along with Isabella's pretend scenarios as long as he got his way later during rounds of

Candy Land or some other game he liked to play—and win. Izzy had grown used to his bossiness.

Today, they stood inside Izzy's playhouse at the back of the sprawling coastal estate, trying to pretend they weren't sweating like pigs or standing in the middle of four walls that seemed more like an oven in ninety-plus degree heat.

Dressed as bride and groom, Izzy wore her princess gown, a deep purple frock, leftover from last Halloween. She knew brides were supposed to wear white but today the groom, a stubborn Henry, had insisted they wear matching outfits. Ever the obstinate male, Henry had thrown on his purple jacket—another by-product of a costume party the children had gone to the previous month—over much protesting. Izzy decided the oversized coat made the six-year-old boy look like a miniature version of Willie Wonka.

Henry had the Navarro good looks that ran in the family—an olive complexion with warm brown eyes that danced with an equal measure of mischief and merriment. But today, the boy's mass of rich black hair had all but disappeared under the formal stovepipe hat that made him two inches taller than his bride. The height difference was uncommon since Izzy, as he so often called her, was older by a whopping seven days. Besides, in matters of temperament, Izzy usually had no problem sticking up for herself.

This August day so full of prospects for two rambunctious six-year-olds had them pledging to each other for all eternity in front of the "minister," the Rialto's faithful, huge, black Labrador retriever, named Sully. Even though Sully rarely stayed on script and wasn't too much on ceremony, he did bark a couple of times after the bride and groom repeated their vows, vows that were by this time so familiar to both because they'd gone through this same routine at least fifteen times since June.

On this afternoon, they used the same rings they always used. Izzy gave Henry a gold plastic band she'd found buried on the beach and dug out of the sand. Henry gave her a replica cameo ring he'd stuck in his pocket at the variety store in town when no one was looking.

"Are we done yet?" he asked in pent-up frustration. "I'm ready to get back to tossing the ball around. This is stupid."

"Not yet. You promised. Five more minutes because I already spent the whole morning playing baseball with you."

He ripped off the hat and threw it at her face. "I told you I'm done playing this stupid dress-up game. Every time you make me do it, I hate it. In fact, I hate you. It isn't fun for me."

Because she'd seen him go off the deep end over less, Izzy braced herself for the blow. She wasn't expecting it when he knocked her to the wooden floor. As usual, that wasn't enough for Henry. The little boy straddled her and wrapped his hands around her throat.

Izzy thrashed her body up and down, trying to buck him off. But Henry wouldn't budge. The pressure of his fingers increased around her neck.

"Get off her this minute, Henry! Do you hear me?" Jenna Rialto shouted from the doorway. She dashed over and grabbed the boy's arm right before his fist smashed into Isabella's cheek. "You go home this minute and cool off. And don't come back to my house until you can control that ugly temper of yours."

"You can't tell me what to do," Henry yelled out, standing firm, fists clenched at his sides. "You're not my mother!"

"Thank goodness for that," Jenna tossed back. "Get out of here now and go home before I tell Isabella's father what I just saw you do to his daughter."

Izzy watched as Henry disappeared out the doorway in a huff of temper and rage.

Jenna stared at the red marks on her daughter's throat, the bruises forming on her cheek. Taking her daughter's chin in hand, Jenna wanted to know, "Does he do that to you often when you're out playing with him? I've seen bumps and bruises before on your arms and legs. I thought they came from the usual scrapes kids get running around the island. But now…"

"Sometimes. He does it with his mom, too. I saw Henry kick her once. She usually gives in to him to avoid a scene."

Jenna's mouth dropped open. She did her best to pretend as though that news hadn't shaken her to the core. She tried to draw in a calming breath. "Yes, well, I know Mrs. Navarro thinks she's doing Henry a favor. But what she's really doing is enabling him to become more violent. Of course, I'm not his mother and you aren't his family, either. You don't let him treat you like that, Isabella. Do you understand?" Jenna bent down so she was eye level with her daughter. "Do you understand me? Don't let that boy or anyone else for that matter hit you like that or treat you disrespectfully again. You don't have to put up with his meanness."

"But he lives right next door. I love Henry."

"Oh, Isabella. There will be other boys. There's a world full of good guys out there. Don't ever settle for the Henrys because he's…disturbed. Thank goodness he's only here in the summers otherwise I'd be concerned for your safety. This infatuation you have with him has to stop though. I'll discuss it with your father. It's not such a bad idea if we lessen our contacts and visits with the entire Navarro family. It might be awkward at first, but we'll curtail the year-round personal events."

Jenna paused, studying her daughter's face. "The fact he's a boy doesn't give him the right to do that to anyone. From this point forward, if he's mean to you, you let me or your father know. Understand?"

"Sure. But I love Henry. He's my oldest and dearest friend."

"He needs to learn how to treat people better, Isabella, that includes friends like you. Don't let him push you around. Are you listening to me, honey? Do you *understand how important it is not to let Henry keep doing this to you?"*

"Yes. Okay," she agreed after some reluctance.

Even at six, Henry couldn't hide his darker sides. He had several. Yet it was nothing compared to what he would come to be as an adult. Her mother had known that early on.

Marisa Lattimer came out of the dream, grateful it hadn't been real. She remembered the day Isabella had told her the story, reliving it in gritty detail. While it hadn't been the first time Henry had showed his temper to Isabella, it had been the first time the little girl had known fear because of it.

Marisa had listened to Isabella as she'd poured out her story. She recalled now how the fear had come into her friend's eyes at the memory of that childhood incident. Together in group therapy, they'd shared their past at the women's shelter where they'd both found a measure of solace.

They'd gone over their stories, tried hard to better understand why they'd put up with such abusive behavior for so long. If only they had recognized the signs and had the sense to run the other way, far, far away from…

But how could she pass judgment on Isabella or anyone else when Marisa Lattimer had done exactly the same thing? How long had she put up with Garth's violent outbursts before she'd done anything about it? How long had she put up with the bruises she had to cover with massive makeup just so she could stand to look at herself briefly in the mirror?

When Marisa realized she was trembling under the covers, she tried to calm down knowing this time the dream hadn't been about Garth. It was somehow easier to handle a memory when it belonged to someone else.

She and Isabella might've come from the same dark place. But how long would she have to go back in time to relive those days again and again? To be reminded of all the mistakes she'd made, all the days she'd spent fearing the man she hated? Did she intend to let her past haunt her forever? Would she ever be rid of it?

Marisa blinked awake, understood immediately she was nestled beside the man she loved. When Thane stirred beside her, she took the opportunity to latch on to him for security.

But in her need, it suddenly dawned on her. What had she done? She'd fallen in love with a man who didn't even know her real name. How on earth did she plan to fix that?

At breakfast the next morning she could barely concentrate on pouring a bowl of Cheerios for Jonah. She was that upset about telling Thane the truth. Over the last two months, he'd asked about her past, had hinted that he wanted to know all there was to know about where she'd lived, who she'd been before. Today the bill came due. The day of reckoning meant she'd have to come clean.

Edgy and tense, when she went to take the carton of milk out of the fridge, it slipped out of her grasp. The container hit the tile floor and splattered, its contents spilling out onto the cracks of the inlay.

"Wow!" Jonah exclaimed. "I didn't know a carton of milk could explode like that."

As Thane rolled off paper towels to sop up the mess, he noticed her odd, jittery demeanor and sent her a long look. "What's bothering you?"

Like a woman with a secret, she dashed around the counter, hurriedly dabbing at the liquid before it could spread farther under the cabinet. "I'm sorry to waste the milk. I'm sorry for being so clumsy. I'll fix Jonah pancakes instead."

"Isabella, what's wrong with you?"

"Nothing. Why do you ask?"

"Because you're as nervous as a rookie before a big game."

"I am? Hmm, I guess I'm stressing out about…work."

"Work? Is River giving you a hard time?"

"River? Um, no. I think I might've messed up on a couple of entries in one of the categories though. I have to correct it."

Thane narrowed his eyes, unsure about whether or not to believe that lame excuse. Instead, he looked at the clock. "Come on, Jonah. We're running late this morning. Go get your clothes on, grab your backpack. I'll fix you a waffle with peanut butter."

"I'll get the waffles," Izzy offered quickly.

By the time Thane and Jonah left the house to make the walk to school, for the first time ever, she was grateful for the solitude. It helped her think. But there was really only one way out of this situation.

She had to figure the best way to tell Thane the truth.

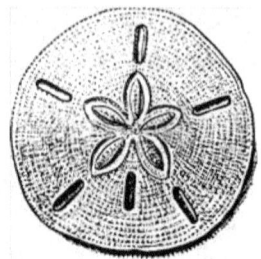

Chapter Twenty-Four

That day on her lunch hour, Logan agreed to meet her at twelve-thirty on the pier so they could talk. While Marisa sat on the bench overlooking Smuggler's Bay, she contemplated the absurdity of what she'd done, how she'd lived for the last several years, the lies she'd told to maintain the ruse. There were so many lies the thought of them all but paralyzed her brain. She couldn't think straight. She couldn't breathe without fear creeping in. What would Thane think of her? How would he react? Would he understand why she'd lived the last three years as another person?

But staring out at the blue water and beyond to the horizon, she realized the source of her fear. If she lost Thane and Jonah because of this she'd never forgive herself.

As soon as Logan walked up, she unloaded on him. "You do realize that when Thane finds out about all the lies I've told, he'll be furious with me. Because that's the way he'll see this, Logan. He'll probably put an end to our relationship, which means I've lost what has taken me a lifetime to find. What the hell am I going to do? I never bargained on falling in love with him."

"Tell him the truth?"

The sarcasm didn't bode well with her so she sent him a seething look. "Please tell me this isn't funny to you."

"No, it isn't funny. I'm sorry. Why don't you tell me what happened to set this off?"

"The dreams, Logan. The dreams keep coming back to me about what happened that night to Isabella. If I'd just been with her at the market... If I hadn't let her go out alone..."

"Stop it! If you'd been with her, Henry would've killed you, too. In your heart you know it's true. And if Thane's feelings for you are real, if they're as deep as they seem, he'll understand your motives."

"Understand?" She jumped up from the bench and began to pace back and forth in front of him. "I'm not sure he will when I'm losing my ability to figure out why I did this in the first place. I'm beginning to forget why I ever thought this was such a great idea. I was motivated before I found Thane. Now, I'm not... Logan, it's been three years. If Henry planned to show up here for Isabella, if he planned to finish her off, he'd have shown up by now. You know I'm right."

Logan blew out a shaky sigh. "Yeah, I do agree with that. As I see it you have two choices—either come clean with Thane and try to explain how and why Marisa Lattimer has been pretending to be Isabella Rialto or keep up the ruse as Isabella Rialto and say nothing After all, who will it hurt? Isabella's gone. And with the death of her father, she had no family left. In the grand scheme of things, the time you spent with her, you two were more like sisters. Who is there left to care about Isabella Rialto but you and me?"

"But I'm not Isabella. I'm Marisa Lattimer."

Now it was Logan's turn to pace. "That's right. And Marisa Lattimer at one time had Garth after her. There's no reason on earth for you to have to go back on his radar, none at all. That's what I'm saying. Think about it. Marisa Isabella Vidalgo Lattimer spent just as many years miserable, living with a bastard who beat her as badly as Henry beat Isabella. Sometimes you tend to forget you two were so similar. She wouldn't want you paying the same ultimate price she did. You know it in your heart that Isabella wouldn't care what name you use. The Isabella you knew, the one I knew, would be eager to have you avoid suffering the same fate. Neither one of us can ever bring her back no matter what we do or how hard we work at catching Navarro. That in no way equates to you going back to being Marisa Lattimer, the woman with zero self-esteem and no will of her own. That is, until she broke free and got out of Denver for good. If it gives you peace of mind we can always go to court in Santa Cruz to change your name legally in this country."

"Like we did in the UK? I don't know what to do, Logan. I'm so confused."

"If you remain off the grid using Isabella's name, Garth Lattimer will never be able to find a trace of you. It's that simple. It's worked all this time so I think it should stick. The name change, that is."

"That's another layer of deception I have to own. But I'm beginning to doubt the wisdom of my choices."

"Like you say, maybe it was a poorly designed idea on our part to go to such extremes to nab Henry. And maybe it's time we forget about it entirely and move forward."

"Is that what you want, to forget about luring Henry here?"

"Don't you? When we hatched this thing up, I didn't have Kinsey or my kids to worry about. For two years we've tried staking you out like a piece of meat—first it was on Long Island and now here. But the slime didn't ooze out of his hole like we thought he would."

"At least not long enough to come sniffing around. Or maybe, if he did, we just missed our opportunity somehow. The coward's still hiding behind his diplomatic immunity. He might be for years yet."

She shoved her hair off her face as the ocean breeze kicked up. "I don't know what to do. What a mess! We don't even know where Henry is for certain." When Logan cleared his throat, she turned to cut a glance at his face and then just stared. "You know where he is, don't you? How long have you known?"

"Since Cosford lost him."

"Be more specific."

"Okay, a couple months. My private detective says Henry's been camped out in Morocco, or was last week. He's masquerading behind that ridiculous Spanish nobility angle he so often uses."

"That would be just like the bastard, wouldn't it? I told Thane the jerk was living in the South of France. It sounded better than telling him the truth that he'd gone into hiding again. You could've told me where he was."

"Why? Henry never stays put for long. He's snuck out of the country twice before, the last time about six weeks ago, took a trip back to Spain to see his dying uncle." Logan snorted. "More like making sure he wasn't left out of the family fortune. Before that he tracked down Alistair and set his house on fire."

"Oh my God, that poor man, is he all right? What about his wife and kids? You might have mentioned that to me."

"I'm sorry. I didn't want you to freak out. Let's face it, if Interpol and the RMCP had done their jobs back when this all happened, we'd already have the son of a bitch extradited back to Canada to answer for what he did to Isabella."

"Well, that didn't happen and neither did using me as bait. Maybe Henry knows she's dead, Logan. That's the only explanation. Did you consider that? Maybe he's smarter than we've given him credit for. Maybe he never fell for the story that she crawled out of that ditch for help and lived. That's the story we planted. But our pretending she recovered hasn't gotten us the results we wanted. We can't touch him for killing Isabella or for the murder of her father. Maybe we should just accept reality and move on."

"I think I can prove he twisted Isabella's arm to turn over her father's insurance money. Once she did that, he tried to subjugate her, control her, and beat the hell out of her at every opportunity."

"You're getting worked up again. You know Henry beat her. We both do. But that isn't the same as being able to prove he murdered Isabella's father. I can make all those same comparisons to Garth. He was a wife-beater. Even though I don't think Garth ever killed anyone, he was a miserable, controlling asshole. But abusing your wife on a regular basis doesn't automatically mean we can prove Henry killed Javier Rialto. We've been over this all before."

"Yeah, well…"

"Listen to me. We'll never be able to get Henry for the murder of Isabella let alone her father. That's the bottom line here. We might as well chuck this crazy idea and start accepting that we messed up."

Logan ran his hands through his hair. "It doesn't take much for me to get worked up and hate Henry Navarro."

"That makes two of us. But that's no reason to keep this up. Maybe it's time to put an end to this whole charade once and for all. Maybe I should start living my life here as Marisa Lattimer."

Even thinking about taking that step made chills run through her body at the notion of coming clean with Thane. "If I do that, not only will I lose the man I love, but the town will think I've lost my mind. Either way, I lose everything I ever wanted in this town."

"They don't have to know. You're divorced legally from Garth. You've put that portion of your life behind you for good. For almost three years now you've been living as someone else, someone who happens to be dead. You can't exactly go back and erase all that." Logan finally managed to inhale a calming breath. "But it's your decision. I'll support whatever you want me to say or do. Just make sure it's for the right reasons. Because as much as I cared and loved Isabella and thought of her like a sister, I can say the same thing about you."

He grabbed her by the shoulders, looked her in the eyes. "It's taken courage to do what you've done. When we started out we had no way of knowing Henry wouldn't take the bait and come after you two weeks after we forged this thing. I think you're one of the bravest people I've ever known."

Tears welled up, started filling her eyes. "You don't have to say that."

"By this time, you know me better than that. I don't hand out accolades or false praise unless I mean it. Just promise me that in the future you'll never sell yourself short like you did with Garth, not ever again. Not with Thane Delacourt or anyone else."

She shuddered at the memory, locked her arms around herself. "If it weren't for people like you and Isabella, I might not have stuck it out enough to become the survivor I am, to get out of my own ordeal and stay out."

"Sure you would have."

"I don't know. Even knowing Garth was so horrible to me, my friends wanted me to stay with him, stick it out. They continued to work that angle while I tried to come up with a plan. Believe it or not, there are people out there who tried to sabotage me every step of the way. It wasn't enough that I had to find a way around Garth's controlling nature but I had to play a character role with my own friends. I'm not sure I can ever forgive them for that, for abandoning me when I needed them the most. I don't want to be around people like that anymore."

"No one's blaming you. You had to keep listening to that sanctity of marriage crap when you needed to rely on them to help you get out. And yet, they weren't the ones getting their face pummeled on a regular basis, or going to the ER with broken bones, now were they?" Logan shook his head. "You haven't spoken to any of them have you? Not since you left?"

"No. And I won't. I'm in this thing just as deep as you are." She rubbed both temples with the fingers of both hands. "I'm so confused, Logan. I don't know what to do. I don't want to lose Thane and Jonah. That's the bottom line."

"Look, it's your decision. I'm just suggesting that keeping Marisa Lattimer permanently on ice might not be such a bad idea for a variety of reasons. One, Garth never knew your whereabouts. After it happened, you immediately began living life as Isabella. Marisa Lattimer simply disappeared off the radar. I'd like to go on record to keep it that way. It wasn't a bad plan, honey. You don't ever have to feel guilty about becoming Isabella. If Thane cares about you as much as it seems it does then remind him that he fell in love with the person you are inside. He didn't fall in love with a name. He fell in love with you. But like I said before, that part of it is always your call."

When their conversation ended, she left Logan, but the doubt and indecision overwhelmed her. Still at odds with what she'd done, she went back to work. But she found it difficult to concentrate. No matter how hard she tried, she couldn't focus.

The fourth time in the last hour she placed the wrong tag on one of the obsidian figurines, River finally looked over at her and asked, "Earth to Isabella, what's wrong with you? It isn't like you to be this sloppy."

"I'm sorry. I need to go talk to Thane."

"Couple trouble? Then skedaddle because you're no good to me in the state of mind you're in now."

Isabella got her jacket and her bike. She pedaled the two blocks over to Longboard Pizza, dreading the encounter the whole way.

Hoping to catch Thane in a lull, she spotted him behind the counter taking orders. Inundated with an after-school rush, he had several phone lines on hold blinking and the phone ringing off the hook. With all that, it didn't seem like the right time to confess her sins.

As soon as he spotted her though, he pleaded, "If you've got a minute, I could really use a hand. I'm swamped. It's been like this for thirty minutes."

"Sure, I'll help take the delivery orders." Tossing her coat off she went to the kitchen phone, pushed the first button blinking on hold.

For the next two hours, she pitched in with more than taking calls. She bussed and wiped down tables, dumped trash, refilled the ice machine. By the time the school rush had dwindled down, the dinner crowd began to show up.

Once again, a steady stream of customers kept her from baring her soul.

About six-thirty the crowd thinned out enough that Thane announced, "Hey, Fisch, I need to head home to give Jonah a bath and put him to bed."

"No problem. I've got it from here," Fischer yelled out, standing in front of the oven.

"Time to go. Grab your backpack," Thane told Jonah. To Isabella, he said, "Walk your bike to the corner with us. As soon as Fischer gets home to sit with Jonah, I'll head to your house. How's that sound?"

"Great, because there's something I really need to talk to you about."

"Okay, does it have anything to do with the way you were acting this morning?"

"Yes. You wanted to know what was wrong at breakfast. I'm ready to tell you."

For several long seconds, they stared at each other. Curiosity and doubt hung like a weight. But then once the trio reached Landings Bay, Thane and Jonah took Jax and went one way while she stood there with Jazz watching them go. A feeling of doom began to sink in. That desperation wanted to take root in her throat.

Instead of hopping on her bicycle, she tried to call out, but the anxiety blocked her voice until she finally managed to get out the words. "Want help putting Jonah to bed?" It might be the last time she'd get to read him a bedtime story, she thought, standing under the street lamp as they walked away.

"That's okay. You pitched in at the restaurant for almost three hours on top of putting in your time at the museum. Go home and get off your feet. I'll be over later when Fisch closes up and gets home."

They were halfway down the block before she called to the dog and took off for Ocean Street, making the turn at the corner. She crossed the street, pedaling toward the lighthouse, the dog able to keep up because of her lack of hustle.

She'd almost reached the pier when she heard a car approaching behind her which meant it had to be traveling on the wrong side of the road.

She tossed a look over her shoulder, caught a glimpse of a bumper as it appeared in her peripheral vision. At the wharf, she steered up on the sidewalk, pedaled faster. The car kept coming, heading right for her. She braked, jumped off the bike, tossed it down on the grass and took off running toward the beach. As she bolted, she dug for the cell phone she'd stuffed in her pocket.

Jazz thought it was a mere playful romp through the night so the dog kept up a steady riot of barking.

With her hands shaking, Isabella punched in the numbers 9-1-1. But before the call could connect, out of the darkness, a man careened into her. The force knocked her to the ground. There was a scuffle. She tried to fight as an arm wrapped around her neck from behind. A handkerchief covered her nose and mouth. Kicking, fighting, she did her best not to take the next breath knowing what would happen. But as she was forced to inhale the sweetish smell, her body began to go numb. Her vision blurred.

And then everything went black.

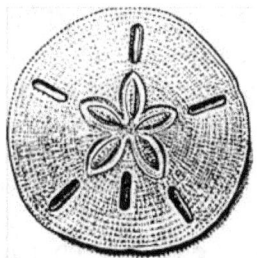

Chapter Twenty-Five

An hour later, after showering off the dregs of the day, Thane left Jonah in the care of Fischer and hightailed it toward the cliffs. The three-minute drive had him pulling up into the driveway in record time. The first thing he noticed getting out of the car was that there were no lights on inside the cottage. The place was dark when he rang the bell. He stood there expecting her to welcome him wearing one of her sexy outfits. But after several long seconds ticked away and she didn't come to the door, he began to pound on the wood. When that didn't get a response, he took out his cell phone, texted her.

But there was no response.

His gut started to do an uneasy slow roll. All at once, he remembered the odd look on her face as she'd stood under the streetlight wanting to help tuck Jonah into bed. She'd appeared... almost frightened. The last few hours at the eatery there hadn't been any time to talk. But something had been bothering her since that morning. That uneasy roll in his gut turned into a full-blown sick feeling as he got back into his car.

Behind the wheel he sat there wondering where she could've gone. He'd been in such a hurry to get Jonah in the tub that he hadn't actually seen her pedal off. As he contemplated the options, he decided that maybe she'd dropped in on Logan and Kinsey just down the street from his own house. He put the car into gear and headed that way, determining that she probably got hung up there helping out with the twins. It didn't exactly make a lot of sense but it was all he had.

At nine-thirty he knocked on the door at the Donnelly house. It took a while for Logan to answer, but when he did Thane immediately realized the sculptor had on a robe over pajamas. It looked as though Thane had gotten him out of bed.

"What's wrong?" Logan asked blinking wildly.

"Sorry to bother you but I thought Isabella might be here."

"Here? Now? Why would she be here this time of night?" But as the question left his lips, Logan's eyes went wide with worry. He held the door open farther. "Come on in, sit down, and tell me the last time you saw her."

Thane went over the last hour, ending with, "She told me she was heading straight home. But she's not there."

"Did you go inside?"

"No. Should I have? I don't have a key and didn't want to break the door in." He sat there a minute with his forehead creased in thought. "Where could she have gone this time of night? And with Jazz in tow?"

"She was on her bike?" Logan asked as he moved to the phone, punched in a series of buttons.

"What are you doing?"

"I'm calling Brent."

The hair began to rise on the back of Thane's neck. "Why?" Before Logan could answer, he narrowed his eyes. "Not an hour ago Isabella said she had something to tell me. Do you know what that something was about?"

"Yeah."

"Is it about her ex? You're starting to scare me, Logan. Start talking."

"Look, I need to wait for Brent to get here because I'm only telling this story once." When the chief of police finally picked up on the other end, Logan said into the phone, "Brent, this is Logan. I think we might have a serious situation in play. Isabella isn't where she said she'd be. Thane can't find her. Could you get over to my house as soon as possible? Thane's here waiting. Okay, see you soon."

After hanging up, Logan started to leave the room but Thane stopped him.

"What is this about? I want to know what the hell is going on."

"I need to put some clothes on before Brent gets here. I'll wake up Kinsey to put on a pot of coffee. It has all the earmarks of becoming a very long night. I'll be right back."

"You have to tell me what's going on. If you know something...I deserve to know. We have to find her."

"And you will. Answer the door when Brent comes, will you? I need to throw on a pair of jeans."

With that one statement, it was like a bomb had gone off in Thane's head. All his questions splintered into a million pieces.

Once Brent arrived Thane stood back and listened as Logan told the entire, unbelievable story.

"So let me see if I'm getting this," Thane finally said, "The woman I know, the one I thought I knew, her name is not Isabella Rialto at all but Marisa Isabella Vidalgo Lattimer? Marisa became Isabella Rialto in order to lure out the man who actually killed the woman in Alberta, Canada?"

"That's about the size of it."

"That's the craziest thing I've ever heard," Thane said, his fury exploding in Logan's direction. "So all this time she was pretending to be someone else. And now, if this Henry guy does have her, what happens when he realizes Marisa isn't Isabella? You want to tell me that? What happens to your plan then? Or Marisa? He'll kill her if he hasn't already. What were you two thinking?"

Thane wasn't the only one having a difficult time controlling his temper.

"It really pisses me off when amateurs try to play undercover cop," Brent said in a huff, throwing a sympathetic look toward Thane. "Then you call in law enforcement and expect us to understand your misguided intentions. I won't even go into the possibility that this Henry might be as unstable as they come. Thane's right, if Henry does have her and this man's killed before, there's no telling what he'll do when he learns he's been tricked."

"Okay, okay, I get it," Logan said, noting the glare from his wife. To Kinsey, he apologized, "I'm sorry. I should've told you the truth. It was a bad idea."

"Yes, you should have told me the truth long before now, and yes, it was a very stupid idea," Kinsey fumed from her stoic position at the kitchen table. "But right now, the most important thing is to find Isabella, or rather Marisa."

Thane ran a hand through his long hair. "Was this Henry waiting at the cottage for her to come in? Or did he take her somewhere along the route home? Wait, I don't remember seeing her bike at the cottage. I drove right here but I didn't see the dog anywhere along the way. Instead of sitting around, I should be retracing her steps from the corner at Landings Bay, where I last saw her, taking the route along Ocean Street back to the lighthouse. That makes sense, doesn't it?" he said, appealing to Brent's cop mentality.

Brent nodded. "That's what we'll do then."

Thane whirled to Kinsey. "Got a flashlight handy?"

"I'll get it," she offered. Opening a kitchen drawer, she pulled out one, held it up to Thane. "I don't pretend to understand their logic. I just hope you find her."

"I'll go with you," Logan offered when the two men started for the door.

As the trio walked outside, Thane shook his head. "You think you know someone. How could she have lied to me like she did? I feel like I've been had, tricked, sucker-punched." He tossed a glower at Logan. "And you, I'm not sure who I'm angrier with, you or Isabella, Marisa."

"I know how you feel but right now we need to find her and fast before Henry…" Logan let his voice trail off at the thought before adding, "You can smash my face in later."

"I'll remind you of that when I'm pummeling you into dust," Thane said with disgust. "Let's get on with this."

The men got into Brent's truck and drove down Landings Bay to the corner.

"This is where she was standing with the dog, holding her bike in one hand, the leash in another." The entire time he talked, Thane checked every house and yard. "Make a right on Pacific, will you? Let me out at the corner."

"Why?" Brent asked.

"Because I need to go over every inch of street until I find her," Thane said, worry and panic beginning to take root in his head and his heart.

Once the truck reached Ocean Street, Brent pulled to the curb. All three got out, Brent stopping to grab a couple more flashlights to light the way. They combed one side of the street before crossing over to the dock side.

Doing his best to see in the dark with a small beam of light, Thane spotted Jazz trotting toward him. While bending down to let the dog lick his face, he caught sight of the bicycle thrown on its side in the bushes.

"I found the bike," he shouted to Brent and Logan. Going over to it, he picked it up, shined the light from front tire to back. "It appears she left it here in a hurry. Someone was definitely after her."

"Maybe she ran down under the pier to get away," Brent suggested. "Maybe we should split up, cover more ground."

They fanned out, walked the stretch of beach from under the cliffs to the south side of Smuggler's Bay, calling her name. It was on their second pass that Logan found her cell phone. Thane snatched it out of his hands, put in her pass code to unlock the device. "Looks like she tried to call 9-1-1 and never hit send."

Thane glanced around at the waves lapping the shore and shouted, "Isabella, Isabella, where are you?" About that time his eyes landed on Scott Phillips. Out of desperation, Thane pleaded, "Point me in the direction where she is. If you know where she went, tell me."

"Check Cleef Atkins' place. Check his farmhouse. She's there. But hurry. Henry's losing it."

Isabella came out from under the effects of the chloroform in a fog and sick at her stomach. She puked up the contents of her stomach onto the floor as Henry stood a few feet away, oblivious to her condition. Instead, he waved a knife back and forth in her direction.

Isabella's eyes rested on the man who looked like Henry. But three years had taken its toll. This man was disheveled and wild-eyed. It didn't help that the images of him kept fracturing in separate pieces and she'd see three of the same face. Once her eyes began to focus better she managed to confirm that it was indeed Henry Navarro.

And Henry kept getting confused.

"You aren't Isabella. I know you aren't. I killed Isabella with my own hands. Where is she? Tell me where she is. Now! I'll kill her again and again until I get it right. I'll keep killing her until the bitch goes away for good."

She let him rant until she thought she could stand up. When her head stopped spinning she got to her feet on unsteady legs. She ran the zipper down on the back of her skirt and let it fall to the floor. If she planned to fight, she couldn't do it in a skirt. Kicking the outfit out of the way, she kept eye contact with Henry as she stepped toward him wearing only her top and panties.

"What are you doing?"

She'd planned this for three years. No way did she intend to blow it now. "I'm getting ready to be with my husband. It's been a long time, Henry. Don't you want me? Isn't that what you want? To be with me? Aren't I pretty, Henry? You always said I was your radiant, refined Isabella. Remember that, Henry? How you used to flatter me and pay me compliments before beating the crap out of me?"

"But it can't be you. Isabella's dead."

"What are you talking about, Henry, my love? I'm right here. I'm Isabella. You know me. We used to play together in the reeds along the marshland near Oyster Bay. Remember the time I talked you into getting my name tattooed on your left arm. Show me your arm, Henry. Show me how much you loved me back then."

A light came into Henry's glassy eyes. He pushed up the sleeve of his pullover, looked down at the writing inked on his upper arm.

Inching toward him a little at a time while he checked out the tattoo, she waited until he met her eyes. By this time she'd closed the distance.

"And what about the four-leaf clover with two crossed swords in the middle that was always our symbol, Henry? What about that? How would I know about our symbol if it wasn't me standing right in front of you now?" She held up her ankle, showed off the ink on the outside of her lower leg. "There, look at our symbol tattooed on my ankle, Henry. Only your dutiful Isabella would do that for you."

"But how? How is that possible? I murdered you."

"How?" She let her head fall back in wild laughter. "I lived, Henry, that's how. The same night you drove me to that remote area outside Calgary and beat me senseless, leaving me for dead, I scratched and clawed every inch of the way up to reach the top and dig my way out. I managed to crawl on my elbows out of that filthy trench to the highway where a trucker found me and got me medical attention. That's how I did it, I crawled out of that filthy ditch where you tossed me, where you left me…and I survived."

Henry stared at her and muttered to himself, "You've changed, Isabella. Your hair's lighter. Your eyes, they're greener."

"Three years is a long time. Maybe you've forgotten how green they were."

"You're still beautiful."

"That's right, Henry. Do you remember that night, the night you kidnapped me from the grocery store?"

"You ran from me. You left me. You ran away to some godforsaken place in Canada. I had to do something. I had to get you back. You were living in a tenement."

"A tenement? Hardly. Such drama, Henry. I see you still have a flair for theatrics. That night you tried to kill me, after you left me there, a truck driver found me on the side of the road and called the police. They took me to the hospital where it took me months to recover from the beating you gave me. But as you can see..." She held her arms out wide. "I'm back now. We can be together now, Henry. If you'll just put down the knife, we can be together for all time. You'll see."

"But you were all bloody and bruised and ugly that night. Your head was bashed in."

"I know, but the doctors made me better, stronger. Look at me now. Once you said I was beautiful."

"You are."

Close enough now to feel his breath on her skin, she brought her leg up and kneed him in the groin. When he doubled over, she put her knee into his face as hard as she could. Even though he fell back, he still gripped the knife.

"You bitch!" He screamed, moving toward her.

She pivoted and threw an elbow into his stomach. She grabbed his wrist, the one that held the knife in a death lock. Leveraging his arm against the doorframe, with all her strength she flung him back and into the wall. He finally let go of the knife. As it dropped to the carpeted floor, she sent a series of karate kicks to the side of his head and whirled to pick up the weapon.

Waving it in the air in invitation, she held out a hand, motioned him toward her. "Come on, you son of a bitch! You know you want to. Come on. Finish me off."

At the challenge, Henry lunged. When she stuck out the blade, she aimed for his chest. As it ripped through flesh and muscle, Henry dropped to his knees. She brought her knee up again and landed a blow under his chin. Reeling, he finally went down, toppling backward.

Still gripping the knife, she ran to the front door, flung it open and walked out onto the porch, straight into Thane's arms.

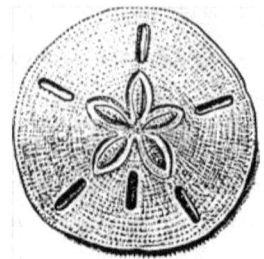

Chapter Twenty-Six

Thane wrapped her up, noting the blood on her face first, the splatter on her tank top, and the streaks of red running down her bare legs. Since she was shivering from the chill, he took off his jacket, draped it around her shaky shoulders. "Are you okay? Thank God you're alive."

"I'm fine," she said. "A little woozy still but... Where's Jazz? Is she okay?"

Before Thane could answer, Brent rushed past them and into the house, leaving Logan standing in the doorway taking in the grisly scene inside.

A man lay on the living room floor in a puddle of blood.

Thane shot an angry look at Logan. "Looks like you got what you wanted. You both did." He sucked in his anger for the time being and yelled out to Brent's back, "Do you need any help in there?"

Brent appeared back on the porch, shook his head, his cell phone already at his ear. "Don't go in there. No one goes in there," he repeated. "I found Cleef's body in the hall closet. Looks like the old guy's had his throat cut, been dead a couple days at least, maybe longer."

"Poor old guy. That must be where the foul smell is coming from," Thane stated, turning to spare a look at Isabella. "Are you sure you're all right? You look pale, like you might faint any minute."

Isabella grabbed her stomach thinking she might be sick at hearing Henry had killed that sweet old man. When she did finally manage to speak the string of words came out scattered. "I'm…I'm okay. It looks worse than it is. The blood isn't mine. It belongs to…Henry. Is he…is Henry dead…did I kill him?"

Brent didn't answer right away but kept to his official call, telling the 9-1-1 operator that he needed an ambulance. As soon as he disconnected though, he stared at Isabella. "Navarro will live. He's coughing up blood which means you probably nicked a lung. The paramedics are on their way, so we'll know something more concrete when they get here."

She angled her head toward Logan. "Looks like our plan finally worked." At that statement, however, Isabella saw the irritation come into Thane's eyes. "This is what I wanted to talk to you about earlier tonight. But you were so busy at the restaurant…"

"Well, the whole thing came unglued before you could, huh? Funny how that works sometimes." Thane took a step back from her, looked over at Brent. "If you're staying here to wait for the sheriff's department to show up, shouldn't someone get Isabella over to Doc's, have him check her out?"

"Good idea," Brent said in agreement. "Since Cleef's house is now a crime scene, use my truck and take Isabella back to town. Looks like I'll be here for hours."

"Are you coming, Logan?" Thane asked as he took Brent's keys.

Logan shook his head, noting Thane's body language spoke volumes—getting in the truck at this point didn't seem like a good idea. "That's okay. I'll call Troy to give me a ride back home."

"Suit yourself." Thane led Isabella to the vehicle, helped her inside. Once he started up the engine, they drove in relative silence until she finally uttered, "If you'll just let me explain."

Thane took his eyes off the road long enough to send her a stony stare. "Sure. I deserve the truth now because you got kidnapped by a crazy psychopath that I didn't know existed until tonight when he almost killed you. Well, thanks for that."

"Just hear me out."

"Hear you out? For starters, your name isn't Isabella. How's that for starters? I'm in love with a woman and, wait for it, I don't even know her real name or anything real about her. The truth is I'm not sure I want to hear some bullshit story or anything you have to say to me right now."

"I know you're angry."

He blew out a breath. "Unless you suddenly became a parent in the last two hours, you don't know shit. Tell me this before you get into your explanation though. How in the world did two smart people like you and Logan ever cook up this scheme and hope to pull off such a crazy plan? How does staking you out like bait work exactly?" He held up a hand before she could answer. "Oh, I know. The nut kidnaps you. You stab him. That's how it ends."

"If you'll just listen long enough for me to explain, I'll walk you through what happened." Before he could object, she went into her detailed story. "My real name is Marisa Isabella Vidalgo. Just after my twenty-second birthday, I married a much older man named Garth Lattimer. Even though we lived in a nice house in Denver, Garth had a horrible, horrible temper and a problem letting go. That is Marisa Lattimer's truth, a truth very similar to Isabella's truth, which you already know about." She took a deep, calming breath to get her balance so she could continue.

"Garth was abusive and controlled my every move. I had to account for every minute of the day; every dime that I spent, he tracked. He kept up with how much time I spent on the computer, where I went, how long I was gone. That day at the car lot when I told you that he wouldn't let me have my own car, was the truth. Marisa's truth. Garth wouldn't allow me to get a job. He owned his own business so he worked out of the house most of the time. I spent my days depressed and my nights miserable and catering to his every whim. After twenty months of that, I started plotting how and when I would get away from him. It took me another eight months to build up the courage to go through with the plan and then to take my chance when the opportunity presented itself."

She shoved her hair out of her face and went on, "It didn't go quite like I thought it would go but I did eventually make it into Canada with the help of a very kind stranger. You'd never believe that part of it anyway."

"Try me."

She'd never seen Thane's jaw as set as it was right that minute so she sucked in another deep breath and fought to control her emotions. "The night I left Denver I crashed Garth's car. The roads were slick. I wandered off into the woods where I was forced to spend the night. The next day I came across this cabin. A man was outside chopping wood. He took one look at my face and realized I'd taken a beating. I'm not sure what exactly he thought, but for whatever reason, he decided to help me. He got me across the border into Canada. I ended up at a women's shelter in Calgary. I'd been there four days when Isabella Rialto walked in. The two of us connected almost immediately. We had the same tastes in food, the same tastes in clothes. We even had similar features—enough that people there thought we were sisters. At times, we pretended we were."

"I'm beginning to see where this is going. Pretending seems to come natural to you. It must be your true nature, what you're all about."

"I don't blame you for being angry."

"Yeah, well, I don't need your approval for that. I knew something was off about you. I sensed it. I should've listened to my gut instincts early on from that first day and stayed away from you."

"What's that supposed to mean?"

"You've been evasive with everyone. But you'd think if you cared so much about me and Jonah, remember Jonah, the little boy you offered to tuck into bed tonight? If you cared so much about us you would've found a way to tell me the truth. You see, that's what I don't understand. You *pretended* all this time to be someone else? Why would a sane person do that? Or better yet, an honest one?"

"You have a right to be upset. If you care for me at all, you'll give me a chance to explain, to explain all of it. Now, where was I?"

"You were back in Canada where the two Isabellas were pretending to be sisters," Thane repeated, his voice laced with as much sarcasm as he could pull off.

"We were a lot alike, Thane. I hadn't been allowed to have friends in such a long time it was like being handed a gift. The two of us had been through so much that very few people could understand. There were times we didn't even get why we put up with the abuse for as long as we did. Anyway, after Isabella got settled at the shelter, Logan started sending her money with the idea that she'd come to Pelican Pointe."

"And you'd go with her."

"Exactly. We couldn't take up space for any longer than necessary there because, let's face it, neither one of us was even a Canadian citizen. Hiding there for me had always been a temporary fix anyway. So Isabella and I started to make long-range plans. Logan put us up in an apartment for a couple weeks until we could figure things out from there."

"Then why not just head to Pelican Pointe?"

"Because Henry knew that's the first place Isabella would go, the same place where Logan had relocated. He knew Logan was very much a part of Isabella's life. It wouldn't do to commit to going there when Henry would surely figure that out in a couple hours and come after her. But that delay cost us...her...dearly. It cost Isabella her life."

She wiped back tears and went on, "The night it happened we'd planned to stay in. The weather was bad, it was snowing like mad. We didn't want to leave the apartment and for safety reasons we'd made the decision to pair up whenever we went out. But that night we decided to make chocolate pudding. We didn't have any cornstarch on hand. Who keeps cornstarch in the pantry, right?"

Tears continued to run down her cheeks at the memory. "The store was at the end of the block, at most, a five-minute roundtrip walk from our place. I let Isabella go out alone and she never came back. Henry had more than likely been waiting for his opportunity to get at her right outside our door. And that night with one bad decision, we handed it to him on a silver platter."

"Look, the tears are a nice touch. But they don't change how angry I am right now at the fact that you lied to me."

Desperate for him to get it, she went on, "I wasn't with her when that bastard tried to kill her with his own hands, when he beat her to death. When she didn't come back I called the police. I alerted Logan. I had no idea at the time that Henry had intercepted her at the market, dumped her in a remote location. Or that he had dragged her out of the grocery store in front of witnesses while no one did anything. If you don't believe me there's surveillance video that shows him doing it."

"You're the one who doesn't get it. I understand Henry's a bad guy, that he murdered your friend. That doesn't explain your ruse, living here day after day lying to me."

She grabbed Thane's arm. "Don't you see? Henry left her there, *alive*. Isabella fought to live that night. She was alive when he left her in that ditch. And I wasn't there to help her."

"But you made up for it tonight when you kicked his ass, didn't you? Kudos to you for hanging in there and getting justice the way you deemed."

"You really don't get it. She died two days after they brought her in. Logan and I managed to keep that information private. At the time we were both grieving and while we wallowed in what might have been, we came up with a plan. What if Isabella had survived? What if she'd lived? Sure it was pure fantasy on our part, but it's a nice one to have. Don't you think? There was all this 'what if' stuff going back and forth between us until finally Logan and I looked at each other and we both knew what we had to do."

"Do you realize how crazy that sounds? Which just proves that smart people have an irrational side to them."

"Crazy? Irrational? Not so much when you realize Henry did show up here. I'd almost given up on it working. But it did. Work that is. By the time we'd cooked up the plan Henry had already snuck out of the country. He couldn't have known how it all ended up because Isabella's death didn't make the papers. We both made sure of that. Wherever Henry was headed, however long he lived, he couldn't be entirely certain, not a hundred percent anyway, that Isabella couldn't identify him as her attacker. If there was one little nugget of doubt in his psychopathic brain, we wanted to foster that, to let it grow into full-blown uncertainty. Without solid confirmation, for all Henry knew, Isabella had survived her injuries."

"And the Canadian authorities went along with this?"

She sucked in a breath knowing it was finally over. "A week after her death, they charged Henry with kidnapping based on the security camera video. But by then it was too late. For the next several years, Henry made certain he hid behind his phony diplomatic status. He's been on the run ever since. Two years ago I sent him a wire telling him that I was alive. I signed it, Isabella Rialto, and added a secret sign that only the two of them knew about, something she'd told me they used as children, a four-leaf clover with two crossed swords in the middle."

"The one on your ankle? That's why you got it? Between two friends you said. You went to those kinds of lengths to carry out this cockamamie plan to lure him, another convincing piece to use as bait, knowing if you were successful, if you played the part well enough, you'd put yourself and everyone around you in danger."

"Please, try to understand. I had to do something. The bastard's been hiding with help from a long list of people on his side. He uses the diplomatic immunity angle, his family's wealth, money from Basque causes. He's relied on them to help him every step of the way. This was the only thing we could think of doing that might draw him out, out of his snake hole."

Thane pulled up in front of Doc's, cut the engine. He ran nervous fingers through his hair and said what had to be said. "Well, if it counts, no matter how many ways you say the same thing it still doesn't make any sense to me at all. How's that? How about coming clean with this? Just how long have you been waiting to give Henry this chance to get to you? A year? Two? How long have you lived like this in actress-mode?"

"Three years. Two primed inside the Rialto estate in Oyster Bay, the last six months here."

Thane's mouth gaped open. "Three years?" His mind ran through the implications until he narrowed his eyes, glared at her. "Logan left you alone at this estate with no backup? My God. It's one thing to spend that long pretending but to fool yourselves into believing that you could have taken on this guy alone is completely unreasonable...crazy."

"I did it, didn't I? I took him out tonight."

"Yeah, sure, you did. But at what price? All this time you've spent lying to me, to Jonah, that's the bottom line for me, Izzy, or whatever the hell your name is. I can't be involved with anyone like that. Someone who has no regard for the truth is someone I want to avoid. I've been through that with other people, a long list of other people. Some irrational person out for revenge willing to sit out three years of her life isn't what I want for myself. It damned sure isn't what I want for my son. This whole thing amounts to a crazy side to you I didn't know existed until tonight."

Instead of calming down, he kept building up to his point. "And you know what occurs to me most of all, other than you putting my son in jeopardy for months? It's one thing for Henry to fall for the trick. You got him here. But it's another to put my son in harm's way knowing you were dealing with a demented killer. You had that information locked away. Logan knew. You think I'm stupid? The Canadian authorities had to know who they were dealing with, too. At any time you and Logan could've dropped this entire thing and let the authorities handle it. From what Logan said, the guy's practically a serial killer. And you think this bolsters your case? Hardly."

Her ire was beginning to take shape and hold. Because of that, she raised her voice. "Look, Thane, justice for Isabella has been nonexistent. Henry's family has helped hide him away all this time. The only thing Logan and I could try to do was to get him to come after Isabella. It might have been a longshot but…"

"I get it, Henry was obsessed with Isabella. You used it to your advantage. Oh, believe me, I get it. And along that path comes Jonah into the picture, your picture. What did you do about it? Did you take me aside and tell me what you were dealing with? No. You chose to keep me in the dark, chose to keep up the charade while Jonah could have easily gotten in this bastard's way to get to you."

She swallowed hard. "But, I took Henry out tonight. I finally did something to stand up for women like Isabella and me. What Henry felt for Isabella is the same kind of sick, warped obsession Garth felt for me, so violent, so controlling. Henry might've loved his mother but it didn't stop him from beating her into a coma when he was sixteen."

"No argument that this man needed to be off the streets and stopped. But for God's sake, that isn't your responsibility."

"Then whose responsibility is it exactly?" she fired back. "RCMP messed up and so did Interpol. Right now my faith isn't exactly with the New York cops either at this point in Javier Rialto's death. So what was I supposed to do, stand by and do nothing, let him get away with murder?"

Thane scrubbed his hands over his face. "Let's face it, we're worlds apart on this, Isabella. Marisa. Isabella. What the hell am I supposed to call you now?"

She tried to reach out and take his hand but he pulled it back from her touch, which had her realizing the depth of his anger. "It's okay to call me Isabella. My parents used to call me that. It wasn't a lie when I told you my friends used to call me Izzy. But Garth changed all that by calling me Marisa because in his mind it was more regal."

The memory of that haughty man brought on a bout of wild laughter until she settled down. "It was just another way to enact control early on. For what it's worth, I always preferred the name Isabella, but of course, what I thought never mattered much to Garth. Back then, I had so little to say in any aspect of my own life… Don't you see? Going to this extreme—pretending to be Isabella—was the only way to beat Henry at his own game, the only way to draw him out of hiding after he murdered her. The only way to take back the power I'd given up with Garth."

Those words were a powerful reminder of the real reason she'd wanted to go to this extreme. "Tonight it was as if Garth was standing there in front of me instead of Henry."

"You're just now figuring that out, are you?"

"If you'll just take the time to see my side, it made sense at the time. No one forced me to take her place. If you've never been through anything so horrific like a daily dose of abuse, mind control, manipulation dished out on a regular basis, it's impossible to understand fully the freedom we felt together when we were in Canada, the bond we forged. For once that brief amount of time was exhilarating. It gave both of us an empowerment we hadn't known for such a long time. Like me with Garth, Isabella had almost gotten free of Henry a time or two, but she always failed. And like me, she'd already let Henry destroy her soul just as I almost let Garth destroy mine. Men like Garth and Henry squeeze the light right out of a person. The light that once shone so bright is snuffed out.

You feel like there's no place to turn. It's a sad reality. How can I make you understand that I was a party to my own self-destruction and didn't even realize it until it was almost too late? It happened to me, Thane, to me. All I was trying to do was to get justice for my friend."

"I just want to know this. You are divorced from Garth, right? Please tell me you divorced that son of a bitch."

"Yes, yes, I'm divorced from Garth. He actually divorced me when he couldn't locate me. But don't you see it wasn't Garth who followed me into Canada. Garth didn't try to kill me there. Henry Navarro succeeded in doing both to Isabella. Henry took her life and I wanted him to pay for it."

Thane shook his head. It still wasn't falling into place for him. "I thought I knew you. I thought I'd found the person I could trust."

For the first time, Isabella took in the resentment in his eyes and began to panic. She began to consider the fact that he really didn't understand her reasoning at all. "Of course you know me. You know the real me. Now. I just went through the reason for all of it. I didn't come to Pelican Pointe to fall in love with anyone. But...I didn't fall in love with just you. I fell in love with Jonah, too. You have to believe that. You can't take all that I love away from me."

"It was your decision to put yourself in grave danger. You pulled it off tonight. But I can't get past the fact that if this asshole had come along when you were with Jonah, what would have happened to my son? How did you intend to handle that? What would have you have done then if he'd gone after Jonah or kidnapped him to get to you?"

When he continued to sit there and scowl at her, she said, "I would never have let anything happen to him. You know that. I took self-defense courses, enough so that I could kick Henry's ass tonight. I learned how to fire a weapon and am fairly accurate at it."

"So now you carry a gun around with you? What were you gonna do if he'd held a knife to my son's throat? You say you care so much, but a mother knows she doesn't put her children in harm's way out of some misguided revenge. Even a substitute mother knows that. If Logan wanted this guy so badly, why didn't he take any of the risks that you took? Through this entire explanation of yours, there's one missing chunk. I don't see Logan putting anything on the line here. He didn't put his kids out as bait. He put you out as bait and along with you he put Jonah. Did that ever come up in conversation? So if you cared so much about Jonah at all, surely you understand why I feel as betrayed as I do. That's the main reason we're done. We're done."

"You don't mean that."

"See, that's just it, I do." And with that, Thane leaned over past her, lifted up the handle of the door, and shoved it open for her so she could get out of the truck.

"But if you'll just…"

Thane shook his head when she started to get out of his jacket to give it back. "Keep the coat on, you'll freeze otherwise. But please, get out now, I have to get Brent's truck back to him and get back home to my son."

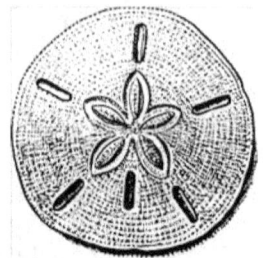

Chapter Twenty-Seven

Her medical exam lasted less than forty-five minutes. Doc cleaned her up, pronounced her fit enough to make a statement to Brent and sent her on her way. When she reached the waiting room, Brent was there to take her to the police station where she went through the story again for the record.

It wasn't until Brent had gone over his final question that she worked up her courage to ask what had been bothering her the most. "Am I in trouble?"

"You were kidnapped and fought back. You stabbed your attacker with one of the knives Cleef had on hand in his own kitchen. There will be an inquest, but you won't be charged with a crime if that's what you mean."

Relief swelled and then ebbed. "What's the latest news on Henry's condition?"

"He's in surgery. He'll no doubt be well enough to face California charges for kidnapping. He has several assaults in his past in other states that stem from an attack on his mother and another on a university campus police officer for battery."

"But what about his going back to Canada to face charges there?"

"Sure. Eventually. Maybe even take a scenic route through New York down the road. There are detectives there interested in talking to him about Javier Rialto's death. But you already knew that."

Brent's tone suggested he was just as put out with her as Thane had been. "You're angry with me, too."

"I think what you did was incredibly dangerous and ill-advised. You could've been killed tonight. Having said that, you got the job done well enough, the job you set out to do initially. Henry's in custody and looking at prison for the rest of his natural life. So congratulations are in order on that score."

"But at what cost? That's what Thane said tonight sitting outside Doc's before he ended our relationship."

Brent blew out an exhausted breath. "Look, I wasn't a father until recently. But after being one for a short time, I know where Thane's coming from. Someone else might have been Luke's sperm donor but—in a Darth Vader moment—I'm Luke's father. I'm the person who reads him stories and tucks him into bed at night. If anyone put him in danger, I'd flip to furious in a heartbeat. Maybe even use my fists to make a point. That's the world of parenthood."

"I would never have allowed Henry to do anything to Jonah, or Thane, for that matter."

"It isn't me you have to convince. Look, it's late. You should go home and get some sleep. But keep this in mind. Thane was frantic tonight until he found you. If it hadn't been for his quick thinking, and heading over to Logan's when he did, things might have turned out differently, even if you did kick Henry's ass the way you did. Do you understand how lucky you are that this turned out the way it did?"

"I'm beginning to, since no one sees what I did as a noble or..."

Brent didn't let her finish. "Now, wait a minute. That's where I draw the line. I understand how you and Logan thought law enforcement around the world had let you down and you had to do something on your own about it. Noble? You aren't a vigilante. It's unrealistic to think otherwise."

"For most people, I guess it is. I thought I could hold my head up now because I'd found a way to stand up for myself, for Isabella. I see that's not the case."

"You did stand up for yourself as soon as Marisa opened the door that night and left and didn't go back to that environment. You got out for good. That was standing up for yourself. Now, come on, I'll drive you home."

"Thanks. Where's my dog? I never got a straight answer."

"We dropped her off at Thane's house."

"Okay. Great. He has Jazz."

"Things will settle down, you'll see. Just give it a few days. Thane's pretty upset. If you just give him time, I'm sure he'll calm down enough to forgive the lies."

Isabella bristled at his using the 'L' word. Lying hadn't been part of her plan. "If you don't mind, I've changed my mind. I think I'll walk home."

"It's almost four in the morning."

"With Henry Navarro under twenty-four-hour wraps, I think I'll be safe enough to walk back home."

"But I insist on seeing you get there safely. If not, I won't sleep a wink. If that's not enough for you, River would have my head if I didn't drive you home and see you safely inside. It falls under the heading of keeping the citizens of Pelican Pointe from crazed killers."

For the first time in hours, she smiled. "Okay, Mr. Chief of Police, be my taxi. See that I get home."

The next morning Fischer woke her up pounding on the front door. He had Jazz on a leash and the dog stretched as far as she could reach to get the chance to dash inside.

"Hey, girl," Isabella said as she dropped down to rub the pup's ears. "I missed you. Did you miss me?"

"Thane thought you might want her around today so I was tasked with bringing her home."

"Isn't that thoughtful of him?" she said, splashes of sarcasm in the words. "Of course, I want Jazz around today. Thanks for taking the time to bring her back to me. It explains his not answering my text messages."

"Look, I don't want to get in the middle of this thing but lying is a big deal to Thane."

"Lying should be a big deal for everyone. Be sure to give him a message for me, will you? I get it. Jazz and I will make sure to stay out of his hair from now on. It might be a small town but he doesn't have to worry about a blow-up scene from me."

"It *is* a small town. I'm not sure how you'll manage that."

"Don't worry about it. We'll be just fine." With that, Izzy closed the door in Fisch's face.

Since Thane had made it clear he didn't want to talk to her or see her or take her calls she spent another rough two nights in misery. But on the third morning she crawled out of bed determined to confront what she'd done head on with Kinsey. The best way to accomplish that seemed to be to sit down with Logan and his wife on their turf for a heart-to-heart.

She fixed coffee, went through the motions of getting dressed, and headed to the Donnelly house around eight. Kinsey answered the door, bouncing Liam on her hip.

"I wanted to tell you how sorry I am for being a party to all this," Isabella said quickly.

"Come on in," Kinsey offered, ushering her into the living room. "You don't exactly look like your usual perky self. Are you okay?"

Logan stood a few feet away holding Leah. He motioned for Isabella to take a seat on the couch. "You look like you didn't sleep last night. I take it Delacourt is still being an ass."

"I'm not sure how much longer I want to spend thinking he's an ass. I've had several days to think it over. I keep going over stuff in my head, the times when Jonah and I were together and… I think Thane might have a point. What would I have done exactly if Henry had come after me with Jonah right there the way he did that night?

Henry would no doubt have found a way to use Jonah as leverage. After all, he murdered Cleef Atkins, an old man who never did a thing to him. I can see why Thane's upset."

Kinsey sent Izzy an empathetic look. "For Logan's part in all this, I did get him to agree that the whole plan was rather outlandish. But no one can argue that it got results. It just took three years to do it, a lot longer than you two thought it would. That's a great deal of time invested in the belief that you could somehow bring this guy to justice, which is exactly what you did."

Isabella's mouth dropped open. "You're the first person to say that to me. I mean, River's been supportive but…Brent's not exactly thrilled with me at the moment."

"My change of heart is Logan's doing. Since my problem stemmed from the fact he didn't let me in on any of this once you got to town, I had a snit. Throw in the fact that it was a conscious decision on his part to keep it all from me and…that hurt. I mean, I knew about his trip three years ago to Alberta. But he lied and told me it was for business reasons, which it clearly was not." Kinsey glanced over at her husband. "He knows he didn't trust his own wife with the truth. No relationship withstands that kind of dishonesty for long."

Logan sent his wife an uneasy look. "I didn't see a reason to tell you and have you worried. Okay, okay, I see the error in that now. My mistake. Maybe I thought you'd try to talk me out of it."

"Which you knew I would have."

"Of course, it occurred to me that your lawyer mind would kick in and I didn't want to be talked out of anything."

"See, we've made up and put it behind us enough to talk it through. Give Thane time and…"

Isabella interrupted her. "How much time do I give him exactly? He won't even take my calls or answer a text. It's possible he even blocked me. He sent my dog back home via his friend. He couldn't even do that one thing. It's as if he doesn't even want to look at me. At least you and Logan were able to deal with the issue and talk it out in the same house, occupying the same space. Not so with that stubborn jock mentality."

Kinsey reached for her hand. "It didn't come overnight. The fact is Logan couldn't see that this stupid idea might have put our own children in jeopardy, too."

"Well, that was Thane's biggest complaint, that I put Jonah in danger. I have to admit, I didn't even consider it. What does that say about me or about my ability to become a mother to Jonah?"

Logan shook his head. "You think having kids— whether they get here by the good old-fashioned way or through adoption or whether you become a step-parent to them—comes with a manual? Think again. It doesn't. Thane knows that. Parents make mistakes along the way all the time." He cut a look at his wife. "Granted, some are dumber than the norm, but still, mistakes are part of the everyday equation. You do the best you can and move on and hope you learn the hard way not to repeat them."

When Leah started to fuss, Isabella stood up to leave, but Logan said, "Stay. You need someone to talk to. That's us. You didn't get into this mess without my help. I have no intentions of letting you stand alone getting slammed with repercussions by a decision we both made."

As he bounced the baby in his arms Kinsey added, "I knew when I married Logan that he had a tendency to shoot from the hip when he makes decisions and deal with the consequences later. He's getting better at thinking as a couple instead of a single guy but... He still does things, makes decisions, without considering all those involved, and that, at times, is what is so maddening for me. A relationship takes work, compromise, honesty."

"I get it. What I had with Thane is so new there's no hope for us at all."

"I wouldn't go that far," Kinsey said. "But it does take time to get over a huge betrayal of trust like this. My advice would be to give him time to...I don't know…maybe get over the feeling of duplicity. Be patient with him. If your relationship is meant to be…"

"That's just it…maybe I'm the one who should realize that it was never meant to be and move on."

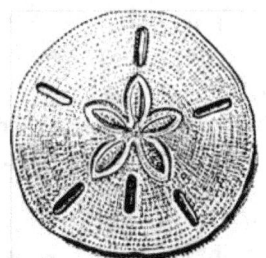

Chapter Twenty-Eight

He'd had three days to calm down and still it bothered him. After stewing for that long Thane had a few choice words for the man he believed in his heart was the responsible party who had led Isabella down such a foolish path. Logan Donnelly.

So once Thane got Jonah off to school that morning, he went looking for the sculptor. He found him working in the studio next to the museum.

Thane strode through the door and for a couple of minutes watched the guy work on a hunk of marble, chiseling away then smoothing out the stone with a grinder.

"What caused you to move out of the top floor of the lighthouse?" Thane asked, looking for an opening. "Isn't that why you renovated it in the first place?"

"Tried it, the space didn't work for me. Besides, I got the lighthouse up and going again because it was something that interested me at the time."

"You know why I'm here. I didn't come for small talk."

"You're the one standing there babbling about my studio choices."

Thane huffed out a breath, got down to it. "How could you let Isabella do something so stupid and dangerous? It came to me last night that it had to be you who fronted her the money for three years in this ridiculous pursuit of getting at Navarro."

"You're certain of that, are you? One of these days when you decide to talk to her, you might bring the topic of money up to her."

"Who else would have that kind of money, the kind it would take to finance this mess? You should know I came in here to flatten you like a pancake."

Logan put down his grinder, stepped away from what he hoped one day might be considered a potential stroke of genius. "Take your best shot. You've wanted to do that for days."

Thane sent him a contemptuous glower, the kind he'd used on Sunday afternoons to stare down an opposing lineman. "I outweigh you by forty pounds and have a much longer reach. You wouldn't last two minutes."

"Probably. And since I don't wish to have broken bones or to have to call Kinsey to cart me over to Doc's just now, I'll simply tell you that I understand where you're coming from. I don't blame you a bit for feeling the way you do—pissed off at the world."

"No, not the world, just you and Isabella."

"That's why I'll give you first shot."

"Now you're being ridiculous. I'm not going to bash your face in. I've had time to consider the fact that you have kids. Not to mention my own. I don't want to spend the night in Cody's jail waiting for my attorney to show up just for taking you out—although it would feel damn good to do it because your actions could have potentially put my son in danger. You and Isabella did a very irresponsible thing without a thought to how it might impact the safety of those around her, namely Jonah."

"For what it's worth, that's been pointed out to me now in a major way by my own lovely, gorgeous wife who was furious thinking that I'd also managed to endanger my own children in the process."

Thane narrowed his eyes in a lethal squint. "The fact of the matter is both of you wanted this guy so badly you would've done anything to get him."

"Am I arguing that point? No. Because I did want Henry to pay for what he did. We both wanted that. Neither one of us is arguing that one point. That's the major reason I allowed myself to go off on this tangent to do it. The week Isabella Rialto died, the two of us were grieving to such an extent that maybe we weren't exactly thinking straight. The nuts and bolts of the plan called for your Izzy to become Isabella, to do whatever was necessary to lure Henry anyway she could. She wanted, no, she needed to do this for herself."

"See, that's where I have a problem with this whole thing. You're supposedly a smart guy. Everyone says so. How does someone like that just sit back and watch while she waits for this guy to come after her? You were nowhere around when she was a sitting duck back on Long Island."

"Okay, point in your favor. But I'm not sure you really understand the loss of power women like Izzy and Isabella experience when they marry a narcissist and a control freak, a man who takes everything away from them, either all at once or chipping away at it daily, little by little, until all the decision process has been taken away from them."

"I understand that. I've watched my share of *Oprah* and *Dr. Phil*. I know about feeling the loss of empowerment."

"Maybe you think you do. I'm not sure I understand it, not fully anyway, not to the degree that women like Izzy and Isabella did. I never gave up my freedom, my power, not like that for anyone or anything and my guess is neither have you. So both of us are already a step behind the curve when it comes to appreciating what one Isabella wanted to do for the other Isabella and why. Not just that, but she convinced me with one thing she said."

When Thane started to speak, Logan held up a hand to stop him. "She said that by hiding out, pretending to be Isabella for a while, Garth wouldn't be able to find her and that he would eventually move on."

Thane frowned. "I…I hadn't considered that."

"Nor had I. But that's exactly what Garth eventually did. She was wise enough to know his traits and take that path. She looked at all the angles and decided the best thing to do for herself, was to somehow convince Henry that his wife had survived the attack that night. She was convinced that by pretending to be his wife, Henry would try it again. I admit, it sounded reasonable enough to me at the time because Henry was so obsessed with Isabella he couldn't see straight. That was irrefutable. I ought to know I watched it happen over the years and did nothing about it."

"You must've known Isabella well. How well?"

Logan's temper finally snapped in full force. "It wasn't like that. Not ever like that. She was a kid to me. It was actually her father I was closest to—Javier Rialto helped me get established in the art world enough that I could grab a foothold and become what I am today. If not for Isabella's father I doubt anyone would even know Logan Donnelly from any other struggling artist."

"Somehow I doubt that."

"No, it's true. Believe it. Javier was an influential presence in my life, a respected collector, who knew his stuff. He also knew the right kinds of people to get me embedded into the scene. Do you have any idea all the talented artists out there who go undiscovered? Thousands. Millions. Javier made sure I wasn't one of them. But the man had one weakness. Javier loved his daughter and wanted to protect her. The Rialtos had been friends with the Navarros for several decades. Javier knew Henry better than anyone did. But on occasion, usually after we'd had too much to drink, Javier would tell me stories about how awful the bastard had been to Isabella over the years. It went back to their childhood. Isabella's mother, Jenna, even caught him slapping her to the ground a couple times. From what I discovered later, Henry was a disturbed individual who never quite outgrew his idiosyncrasies, translation, his meanness, his tendency to lean toward psychopathic bullying. I suspect Henry killed Javier. He either did it himself or had someone else do it for him. But I can't prove it."

"Yeah, that's what Izzy said, and it's one more reason that says your plan was so amazingly ill-conceived."

"Okay, another point in your favor. But think about it. Henry Navarro made Javier's death look like an accident. Her father had been actively encouraging Isabella to break it off with Henry. I wasn't around a lot back then. I'd gone on to spend some time in Tuscany, to work, to create, to add to my inventory. When Javier died on Long Island it took some time for the news to reach me. Even before I had time to digest the loss, to react to my mentor's death, the next thing I knew Henry had taken charge of everything, the money, the estate, and of course, Isabella. Before I could stop it, they were married in a quickie ceremony without any of her family around."

"I hate to point this out to you, but you're not exactly making a case for yourself. Instead, you're making mine for me. If this Henry did all that and you suspected him of it, then why in hell would you allow Isabella to take such drastic measures to bring him out in the open? And for God's sakes, why didn't you at least stand by while Izzy completed the illusion?"

Thane paced back and forth in front of Logan, his anger building up again. "Why not try to get Isabella out of her horrible marriage to Henry while she was still alive, knowing what Javier had told you about this bastard?"

Logan shook his head, sent him a disbelieving look. "You can't be that clueless. You can't help someone out of a marriage, even an abusive one, if that person isn't willing to take that major step to get away. Again, something people who haven't gone through it couldn't possibly understand. If they aren't ready to take that step...if they aren't ready to get away from their situation, it's useless to pound away on them. You can encourage. You can be a sounding board, but the decision to leave is ultimately theirs."

"You mean Isabella wasn't ready? How could that be? Why on earth...?"

"No, she wasn't ready. And the short answer is I have no idea why. Guilt plays a huge chunk of my part in all this."

"Yeah, that's what my Izzy said, that she feels she should've been there for your Isabella that night," Thane tossed back.

"Now you're beginning to get the drift. Guilt. Do you have any idea the lengths Izzy went to, to see this thing through? To make sure it was a believable ruse? How committed she was to its success? She took classes in self-defense. She learned how to fire a weapon. Izzy put her life on hold for three years. Three years of living life as Isabella, breathing in her persona and personal habits just in case Henry had sent his emissaries to spy on her. Those first two years she lived at the Rialto family home on Oyster Bay, she did such a compelling job even the neighbors had no reason to believe it *wasn't* Isabella staying there. They didn't even question her performance. But after time passed and there was no activity on Henry's part, she came out here to try to stir things up."

"And you went along with it every step of the way?"

Logan rubbed his eyes, scrubbed his hands over his face, weary of the discussion. "Yes, I went along with it. Not only that, I didn't say a word about this to Kinsey. So you see I've had a rough couple days with my own problems dealing with my less-than-forthcoming behavior.

"Ah."

"Until three days ago my own wife didn't know the truth. And let me tell you Kinsey was *not* happy with me. So believe me when I say I understand where you're coming from."

"So Izzy's past is just as real to you?"

"You bet it is. It's very real. Garth Lattimer treated her just as shitty as Henry treated Isabella. So you see no one could have played this role more to perfection than Izzy and pull it off the way she did."

Thane started to pace again, to storm back and forth. "And where is this Garth guy now? Maybe I should look him up."

"He's not that hard to find since he still lives in the Denver suburbs in the same house he shared with Izzy. For a year he scoured the country for her and when the private investigator he'd hired couldn't find a trace of her, Garth got the message. He gave up the hunt and filed for divorce. The next year he remarried a woman he met over the Internet."

"Someone should've stepped up and tipped her off, warned her about what she was getting into."

"You think we didn't try? Isabella and I signed up at the same site, found her email address, and sent her several messages as a caution. But some people refuse to see the writing on the wall no matter how large the script is. None of it made a difference. The woman married the son of a bitch anyway."

"You just called her Isabella."

Logan blew out a frustrated breath. "Maybe that's because I don't think of her as Marisa. I've leaned on her as a friend ever since that night in Alberta when Isabella Rialto slipped away from us. She's stronger than the Isabella Rialto I knew. She's happier, more at ease forgetting she was ever married to Garth Lattimer. I have no problems thinking of her as Isabella."

"I'm in love with her. I don't want to be but I'm in love with her."

"I figured as much. You wouldn't be standing here itching to put a fist in my face if it was just lust or a casual fling."

"But what happens when you find out that you've been lied to? Tell me that much."

"You either find a way to forgive or you move on. It's as simple as that."

"That's a helluva choice. It's not that easy."

"I never said either one was easy."

"That's what I was afraid of."

"It's never an easy thing to eat crow either."

"Yeah, especially when I'm in the right. The thing is now I have to figure out how to get over the way I've acted like an ass."

"That's the easy part. Women are used to us acting like asses most of the time. The deal is to know you were right but still be able to pull off the big apology."

For the first time in days, Thane grinned. "I guess I could work on that."

The rest of that day Thane walked through his routine in a fog. His anger hadn't completely subsided and probably wouldn't. He knew himself well enough to know it still simmered just beneath the surface and at the slightest provocation might go volcanic.

Inside his little office at the restaurant, he got into it with Fischer over ordering meat supplies. When he waited on customers he was a tad on the short-tempered side. Not a good habit to get into when you were trying to get a new business up and going. When he had to fix the soda machine, he used words he hadn't used since his playing days to no one's benefit but his own. But no matter what he did, he couldn't seem to get past the way he felt about Isabella.

Later that afternoon when Brent brought his family in to order a large pepperoni pizza, Thane couldn't help but ask River how Izzy was doing.

River rolled her eyes at the question. "She's maintaining the status quo for miserable heartache. If you're so worried about her why not pick up a phone and ask her yourself?"

Brent sent his wife a knowing glare. "We discussed this, remember? Stay out of it."

"Fine. But is being right worth being alone? That's really the question," River reasoned, lifting a shoulder in an unbiased gesture. "I've heard the ability to forgive is a virtue."

After that exchange, the Cody family moved to a table and got Luke settled into his booster chair. They sat down to wait for their pie. Sitting across from each other, Brent whispered, "I'm so glad we agreed that you'd stay out of it."

"I simply have an opinion and voiced it. That's all. I'm entitled to do that you know. In case you haven't noticed everyone's picking a side. Most women think what Izzy did was nothing short of incredible while the men are taking a 'she lied and I'm not forgiving her for a minute' stance."

"And yet, I'm supposed to be pleased that the women in town endorse what Isabella did."

"I'm simply saying that there are people willing to get in the middle of the issue and not think twice about it."

Thane overheard the discussion and knew River was right. He'd heard all the rumblings firsthand. His friend, Fischer, the worldly New Yorker, hadn't had a problem weighing in. Fischer had already counseled Thane to distance himself from the woman who'd been so dishonest.

Thane had gotten an earful from each and every customer who'd walked through the door at Longboard Pizza. Everyone it seemed had an opinion. Ryder, Zach and Troy seemed to be firmly in his corner while their significant others held slightly opposite viewpoints. He'd listened to more sentiments than he'd bargained for from Julianne, Drea, and Bree.

But it had been Jonah who had added the most poignant thing of all to the debate. His son didn't care so much about opposing perspectives. The boy just wanted to know why Izzy wasn't coming around anymore.

"Did you two have a fight?" Jonah asked while practicing his spelling words sitting at one of the tables next to the Codys.

Thane hated being put in this position, which only made him resent Izzy all the more at the moment. That feeling, in turn, prevented him from eating the crow he'd discussed earlier with Logan. "Grownups disagree sometimes. It's the nature of adult relationships. We're having a disagreement."

"Could you have it somewhere else so she could read me a story tonight? She promised to read me the one about the baby dragon."

Thane ignored River's snicker coming from the next table. "I'll talk to Izzy tomorrow about it, how's that?"

About that time, Thane heard Brent's cell phone ring, listened while the top cop dealt with an obvious law enforcement issue; the problem, an apparent BOLO, was something about a roadblock and an escape.

Brent pushed back his chair and said to River, "I have to go. Box up the pizza when it comes out and take Luke back home. I have to go see Isabella."

"Why? What's wrong?" Thane said in alarm.

"Henry Navarro somehow managed to slip past the guard stationed outside his hospital room and escaped from the secure ward. He's gone on the run."

Thane jumped to his feet. "What? They let him get away? What about Isabella's safety? Henry will come after her. You know he will."

"I'm taking care of it. I'll put a guard around her twenty-four/seven."

"What good will that do? We need to come up with a better plan than that," Thane pointed out.

"I'm all ears."

Thane began to pace. "Normally I'd say a defensive position is the answer but in this case we need to go on the offense."

"I know you don't mean a stakeout. That's what brought Henry here in the first place," River said, helping Luke out of his booster seat. "I'm sure you wouldn't want to put anyone else at risk that way."

With those words, something inside Thane moved. The scales tipped all the way in Isabella's favor. She'd pulled off an incredible feat. Why hadn't he been able to see that and be more supportive? The realization hit him then that Henry Navarro had to be dealt with once and for all. If the man was allowed to remain free, Henry would never stop coming after the woman he thought was his wife.

During the rest of his shift Thane went through the motions at work, considering his change of heart. He went over everything in his head again, like keeping track of an inventory list. He slid what he knew into columns of pros and cons. But in the end it was what he felt in his heart that eclipsed everything else. Maybe it had taken something like this to admit he'd fallen all the way in love.

Later, there was Jonah's homework to check, bath time to deal with, and story time before bed. Once that was all done he was too tired to think anymore.

Thane turned out the lights and plopped down on the couch in the dark. He didn't seem to be able to muster the energy to do anything else. What a mess, he decided as he let his head fall back on the cushions. At some point, he drifted off to sleep.

Soon, it was as if he'd landed in a dream that kept fading in and out. All he could see in his mind was a man standing in the shadows holding a knife watching Isabella from a distance.

The angle changed and he was able to zero in on her face. She looked so defenseless, so ill-prepared to take on an armed attacker. Looks, though, could be deceiving. Even in this version he knew she could handle herself. She'd already proven she could.

As the fantasy played out, Thane called to her. When Isabella turned to look at him, it was the intruder who sent him a wry smile and took advantage of the distraction to go on the attack. Henry brought the knife up and then down. Thane started running, doing his best to get to her in time. But no matter how fast he ran it wasn't fast enough. Through a haze he saw Henry hit his mark again and then again, more and more determined with each slice of the blade to end Isabella's life. Thane watched as blood turned the sheets bright red, watched as the pool grew larger and larger until…

Fischer walked into the dark living room, spotted Thane tossing and turning in his sleep. He went over to the sofa, jostled an arm, trying to roust him awake. "Hey, Thane, what are you doing in here? Go to bed," Fisch directed. "You look awful."

Thane bolted upright, almost knocking Fischer off his feet.

"Whoa, it's just me. You're really letting this whole thing get to you."

Rubbing his eyes, Thane gave Fischer a look of disgust. "I was dreaming that Henry came after Isabella again. It was like being a witness to murder this time. Like before, he carried a knife…" Thane held out both hands as if measuring. "About this long."

"You were dreaming, buddy. Go to bed. Put on some music or watch sports highlights. Do something to get your mind off all this."

"Weren't you listening to Brent earlier? Henry's on the lam. And now… I'm beginning to feel really stupid about the way I reacted. On some level I can see why she felt the need to do what she did."

"That's crazy, man. What about how she put Jonah in jeopardy? What about her lying to you?"

Thane eyed the man he'd known for a decade. "I appreciate your loyalty, I really do, but I realize I'm in love with her."

"All the more reason to let it run its course."

Thane furrowed his brow. "What's wrong with you? Didn't you hear what I said? Aren't you listening to me?"

"Yeah, I heard you, loud and clear, for the past three days. So excuse me if I'm not used to seeing Thane Delacourt going all-in over a woman, okay?"

"She's a good person."

"So just ignore the fact that she claimed to be someone entirely different all this time? See, I don't get doing that, don't see how you're able to do that either."

Not wanting a discussion about it, Thane reassured his friend, "Look, I'm okay now. You go on to bed. I'll sort this thing out on my own."

Fischer shook his head and grumbled, "You've changed since you've been here."

"Is that such a bad thing?"

"The jury's still out," Fischer mumbled, heading off down the hall to the guest room.

Tormented and confused, Thane tried to get his mind on something else so he picked up the remote, turned on the TV. Something was seriously wrong with him if he couldn't focus on ESPN.

He pushed off the sofa, went over and turned the lights back on. His eyes immediately wandered to the familiar man sitting in the chair in the corner of the living room.

Put off at the sight of Scott, Thane sighed. "Not you. Not tonight. What are you doing in my house? Go away." Before the apparition could speak, Thane added, "No doubt finding a way to bug me. Whose side are you taking in all this?"

Not waiting for an answer Thane slogged into the kitchen to get a glass of milk, keeping up a steady stream of chatter as he went. "By the way, thanks for pointing me in the right direction so I could find Izzy. Helluva sight though when she came bursting out of that house with blood all over her. I don't mind telling you the blood splatter got to me. I didn't know whether to hug her or wring her neck right there on the spot."

"Doesn't really matter, does it? You broke up with her. I wouldn't worry too much about it if I were you."

"Taking my side in all this? Somehow that surprises me. Reverse psychology? From a ghost? Priceless," Thane uttered, gulping down the milk straight from the carton.

"Henry is still a very real threat. Did you ever once consider what it was like for Isabella to have to deal with someone that crazy on a day-to-day basis, to do it for years, how much courage it took over the past thirty-six months to put herself in a position to try to stop a man like Henry?"

"What do you want me to say?" Thane insisted. "It took guts and nerve to do what she did to come out on top. But Henry's out now and where does that leave all that she risked getting him, all the lies she told to do it? What if this Henry goes after her again at a time she's in my house with my boy? What about that?"

"She's proved to me she can take care of herself and your boy. I might point out that just because you're angry with her does that equate to abandoning her entirely when she needs help the most? In case you haven't figured this out by now, we take care of our own in this town. And keep something else in mind. No matter how upset you are at her, it doesn't change the fact that Henry is still out there."

"Yeah, I know."

"Then do something about it."

"I'm working on it."

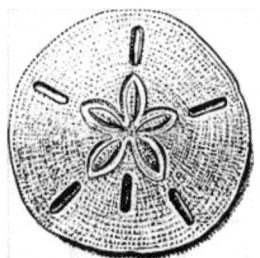

Chapter Twenty-Nine

The next day Isabella got up and rode her bike to work despite having the headache from hell. She hadn't slept well for days and it showed on her face. The bags under her eyes were a tribute to the restless nights she'd endured and all the tears she'd shed.

As she pedaled down Ocean Street near the same spot where Henry had snatched her, she went on alert for anything out of the norm. But nothing seemed amiss, not today. As the water shimmered in the bay to her right, she took in the beautiful crisp day. Along her route, towering oak and sycamore released their leaves in a signal that fall had given way to cooler temperatures.

She waved to a group of children walking to school and thought of Jonah, wondered how long the wound would take to heal. She reminded herself she'd been hurt before and she'd come out on top. She'd do it again this time getting over Thane Delacourt, no matter how long it took for her heart to stop the ache. Hadn't she proved over the last three years she didn't need a man dictating how and what she should do?

She spotted Drake Boedecker, who did his best not to look obvious trailing after her. Drake had taken over the day shift after Brent had spent last night parked near the woods determined to keep an eye on her while she slept.

Grateful for the protection, she realized she needed to be vigilant on her own.

She also realized something else. No matter what happened with Henry, she would make this town her home for good. No one was running her off.

After all, she and Thane might be kaput, but despite their breakup, Isabella knew deep down she'd found the place where she wanted to spend the rest of her life. This little town had been a good fit for her. Where else could she find people who cared about what happened to her after living here for such a short time? She also knew Brent was just doing his job, sitting out at her house on guard duty. But she also knew others cared. A long list of people—Jordan, Hayden, Keegan, Kinsey, Julianne, Bree, and Drea—had called to ask if she needed anything. They were all concerned for her well-being. Every one of them had offered her a safe place to stay in spite of the jeopardy her being there might put them in. With that kind of sentiment foremost on her mind, she steered to the curb in front of the museum, parked her bike, and headed inside to start her day.

"How's it going, boss," Izzy said by way of cheery greeting.

"Never mind me, how'd you sleep? Any better?"

"With your hubby babysitting from that forest of trees, how could I not sleep like a rock?"

River tilted her head, studied Isabella. "You may put up a brave front to everyone else but I know it's unnerving having Navarro on the loose."

"Well. Yeah. But what can I do? What can Brent do?"

"His presence must have paid off because you seem…I don't know…more chipper today than you have been."

"That's because I've seen the light. I'm fed up with moping over some lamebrain who doesn't appreciate me. Don't get me wrong, I'm still in love with said lamebrain, my heart's still broken, but I won't live my life mired down in regret for something I thought was a good idea."

"Plus, you kicked Henry's ass before they allowed him to escape."

"Maybe it takes having a psycho ex to get it."

" Could be. Maybe it takes membership in the narcissistic ex club."

"Not to mention, I already wasted too many years of my life trying to please one of those egotistical, self-important beasts to make that same mistake again. If Thane can't see that I'm a terrific person then I shouldn't squander another minute boohooing over him."

"Atta girl."

"I do miss Jonah though."

River told her about the scene at Longboard Pizza where the boy had wanted her to read him a story. "I believe he mentioned a baby dragon."

At the reminder, Isabella's shoulders slumped. "*My Father's Dragon*. I picked it up at Hayden's bookstore because my mom read that book to me when I was in first grade."

"Then maybe you should come over to my house tonight, read it to Jonah when you tuck him into bed," Thane suggested from the doorway. "I followed you to work. I need to talk to you."

River cleared her throat. "I think I need to get something out of the storage room." With that, she disappeared into the back leaving the two of them alone.

"Jonah misses you. I miss you. But if you come over tonight, plan to stay."

Isabella's breath hitched. The knot in her stomach relaxed. "I missed all those silly funny faces you do that make Jonah and me crack up."

He ambled toward her, reached out to touch her cheek, ran a finger down her jaw to her long elegant neck. "I feel empty without you. I haven't been able to sleep a wink in four days."

"That makes two of us."

"I'm sorry for acting like such an ass about this whole thing."

"I'm sorry for lying to you without letting you in on the secret I was keeping. It was wrong. I should have handled it better. I never meant to hurt…"

He held up a finger across her lips to shush her, slid his arm around her waist. Tilting his head, he touched his lips to hers, felt her comply, give way to the rush before they both fell into the kiss.

"For now, I'll let you get back to work. Where's Jazz?"

"I left her at home with her chew toys. I planned to go back for lunch and check on her."

"If you give me the keys to your house, I'll go pick her up. I'd like you to stay with me until this whole thing with Henry blows over."

"After escaping from the hospital, Henry probably ran to Mexico or the nearest boat dock and caught a ride back to Spain."

"Probably. If that's the case then you should humor me and stay at my place."

She shook her head. "I don't think so. I don't want to put you or Jonah in jeopardy. I'm fine. Really I am."

"Okay, then tonight I'll come to you."

Isabella spent the rest of the day wondering if her conversation with Thane had been real. No argument that he'd certainly done an about-face. But was it a true indication of the way he felt now?

When she arrived home, there'd been a shift change. Instead of Drake, Brent had taken up his position from last night and stationed himself near the trees again. She sent him a wave, headed inside where Jazz greeted her with tail wagging and a lick on the face.

"Aren't you a good girl," Isabella said rubbing the puppy's ears. "And look, no accidents, or should I check every nook and cranny? Nope, not gonna do that. Let's take you for a potty break instead."

She and Jazz circled the lighthouse twice, the dog exploring every shrub and blade of grass. They walked as far out to the cliffs as possible, sat near the edge and listened to the waves crashing like the roar of thunder below on the rocks. The sound of it soothed her as she stayed put to watch the sun go down over the glimmering water in the bay.

Returning to the house, she fed the dog, reheated the vegetable chowder she'd made the night before and sat down to enjoy her soup.

There were dishes to clean up, clothes to sort and laundry to get started. She did all of it while waiting for Thane to make his appearance. But by nine-thirty, when he failed to show up, she headed to bed, sad that he hadn't come to her like he promised.

At the bottom of the hill, Henry Navarro paused to look up at the lighthouse on the cliffs. Like a beacon it drew him to his Isabella. He'd show her once and for all that disobedience simply wasn't permitted.

For the past thirty-plus hours Henry had been taking refuge onboard one of the sailboats in the harbor. He'd stolen bottles of water stacked behind the restaurant on Ocean Street and found food scraps to eat inside the trash cans near the pub. Earlier, he'd broken into a house across from the wharf, taken what food he could stuff into his pockets, along with a nine-inch butcher knife.

Now that his belly was full he needed to find the best way into Sea Glass Cottage. He didn't understand how she could still be alive. How could she have survived the beating he'd given her that night? Days ago he'd had her in his grasp again and she'd fought back.

That was not the Isabella he'd known since childhood. That Isabella would do everything he asked her to do. This one had fought him. She'd taken his knife and stabbed him. Tonight, he would make her pay for that. He'd be certain to finish the job this time. After all, third time had to be the charm, he decided to himself, as he snuck around to the front of the house. Stupid woman didn't even have the sense to put in a decent security system, he thought, as he picked the lock without much effort at all.

He stood inside the entryway, caught his shadowy reflection on the wall mirror over the hall table. The blade of the knife he held in his hand shone like a silver symbol of hope glinting back at him. He crept past the living room and headed down the hallway, checking out each room.

When he opened Isabella's bedroom door, there was a slight hesitation, or maybe confusion. His eyes darted to the lump under the cover. There was movement from the corner that made him turn.

Thane sat near the French doors in the dark. He'd watched the man's lengthy approach, held back as long as he could. But once he spotted the knife in Henry's hand, he rose out of the chair, reached to turn on the lamp on the nightstand. Light flooded the room.

In the glare, Thane studied the psychopath who'd killed Isabella Rialto, the man who'd kidnapped Izzy.

"Who the hell are you?" Henry demanded.

"I'm your worst fucking nightmare, Navarro," Thane stated. "Now drop the knife."

"No. No, I want to see Isabella. I'm here for Isabella."

"I'm aware of why you're here."

Izzy came out of the bathroom, stood in the doorway. That brief moment of distraction was all it took for Thane to charge, rushing Henry and knocking him to the floor. Pinning the man's arm back, Thane twisted his arm so tightly that the smaller man let go of the blade.

Thane brought Henry upright and set him on his feet. "Face it. You've been set up, Navarro. I hope you like solitary confinement because that's what they do to prisoners like you who've already tried to escape. They put them in a windowless box. Say goodbye to freedom. I doubt you'll ever see your beloved Spain again."

Brent entered the room from the hallway his weapon at the ready. "Maybe Navarro prefers cold weather because I see a Canadian prison in his immediate future."

Confused, Henry rubbed his forehead. "I don't understand. I must have the wrong house. Where's my Isabella?"

"I'm right here, Henry," Izzy said. "Ever since you broke out of the hospital ward yesterday, we've all been waiting for you to show up. Thanks for not disappointing us."

Henry turned to stare, squinted at her appearance. "You've changed Isabella. Your coloring is different. Your hair, it's much lighter than it used to be. What have you done to your hair?"

When he took a step toward Izzy, Thane squeezed the back of his neck while Brent slapped a pair of cuffs on Henry's wrists.

"Henry Navarro, you're under arrest for the kidnapping and murder of Isabella Rialto."

"Don't be absurd, she's standing right there. How is it possible for a dead woman to divorce me? You're all insane. If she's dead then who the hell divorced me?" Henry yelled, as Brent tried to get him to push him out of the room. "They'll never make it stick. I know people," Henry muttered.

As Brent brought Henry out of the room, Logan stood in the hallway, leaning up against the wall. Logan watched as Henry got closer and grew more agitated until he went ballistic at the sight of him.

"What the hell is going on here, Donnelly? I didn't kill anyone. Isabella divorced me. She's alive!"

Logan smiled. "Hello, Henry. How's it going? I wanted you to know it was me who paid the solicitor in London to put together the phony paperwork...for show. Chatswick went through the motions, made it look like the divorce was a typical, legal transaction. And it worked. But look what happened? You just had to be an asshole, didn't you? For Chatswick's efforts, the man got his house burned to the ground. Not that you give a shit, but Chatswick managed to get his family out before he lost his wife and kids. By the way, London police issued a warrant for your arrest, too. I doubt you'll ever set foot again in the UK though, or in your beloved Spain either. You can forget about Tangiers or Istanbul or getting another stamp in your passport. I hope you have a lot of pictures stored in your head because you won't be seeing the light of day for the rest of your life. You're facing a murder rap in Alberta. You remember that, don't you? If I have any say in the matter you'll pay for what you did to Javier, too."

"But…but…I don't understand. Isabella's right there, plain as day. Look at her. Look at her, Donnelly. How could you not know she's alive? My wife is alive. You're all making a terrible mistake."

"You don't think there's a chance that he'll get away with an insanity plea, do you?" Thane wanted to know from Logan.

"There's always the chance a judge will see things differently than we do. Henry can deny his wife is dead as many times as he wants, but we all know his denial has no basis in fact."

"Exactly. Isabella Rialto is buried in a small cemetery outside Calgary, Alberta. Logan and I were there along with a small group of women from the shelter."

Thane squeezed Izzy's fingers, kissed the palm of her hand. "I admit I wasn't fully convinced he'd fall for it."

"Same here, but people have stalkers all the time that manage to find a way into houses even with a gate out front. If given enough rope Henry was bound to hang himself eventually. We're lucky he showed up so soon after he escaped though. He did us a favor not dragging it out."

Thane turned to Logan. "Which means…"

"I'm on it. I'll call Brent to make sure Henry's put on suicide watch. Look, I gotta get back to Kinsey. I've been in the doghouse for almost a week. I keep trying to foster a little goodwill."

"I just want to say, this plan of yours," Thane looked at Izzy, took her hand. "Both of yours, it was a stroke of genius. I don't think I would've had the patience or the fortitude to stick it out." He turned to Logan and admitted, "Hiring the lawyer in London to make it look as though there was a real divorce was a brilliant touch."

Logan pointed to Isabella. "It was her idea. Look, I'll talk to both of you tomorrow. Get some sleep. You both deserve it."

Thane watched Logan leave and asked, "So this was all you?"

She grinned. "Not everything. But you should probably know all of it. Starting with this, the guy who filed the divorce papers is the same man who filed what's known as a deed poll in the Royal Courts of Justice to get my name changed. Officially. It cost something like a hundred pounds to do it."

"That's how you were able to get a California driver's license."

"First, there was a passport, then a driver's license in New York State. As long as I didn't intend to deceive or defraud anyone, and I wasn't trying to hide from anyone, it was all legal."

"There was no intent to do that. You and Logan *wanted* Henry to find you."

"Before I go on, before I tell you everything, I need to know what made you change your mind about me and show up at the museum this morning."

"Because I came to the realization last night that I don't care what your name is. I don't care if it's Isabella Rialto or Marisa Lattimer. I fell in love with the person *you* are. You were right about that. Besides, I freely admit it was a huge rush, punching that guy's face and watching Brent snap the cuffs on that asshole."

Isabella smiled, ran a hand down his jaw. "We won't let it become a habit though."

"What if I wanted it to become a habit? This might be bad timing on my part, but I'd like to point out how your eyes lit up at the idea of Julianne having her wedding here at the lighthouse. We could make it two, you know."

"What are you saying?"

"I'm asking you to be my wife, become Isabella Delacourt, a mother to Jonah, and any other little Delacourts that should happen to come along."

She threw her arms around his neck. "Yes. The answer is yes. I'll do all of that. Would you be willing to move into Sea Glass Cottage though? Logan's agreed to sell it to me."

He narrowed his eyes. "You have that kind of money?"

She smiled broadly. "It's a long story."

"All of a sudden I've taken a liking to your stories. Logan said something to me a few days ago that I found interesting. He said I might want to ask you who funded the three-year plan. I thought it was Logan. Now, I'm beginning to think differently."

"Initially, he did. But down the road I had to start contributing to my own upkeep. My parents died in a plane crash about six months after I married Garth. They'd set up a trust fund for me that was so airtight Garth couldn't touch the money. But he wouldn't let me have it either."

"How did he do that exactly?"

"Easy. If I put the money in one of our joint accounts, he'd immediately pull it out and transfer it to one of his own, one I didn't have access to. So it didn't take long for me to put a stop to that. Whenever I opened an account of my own and put the cash into that, he'd hound me, subject me to verbal and physical abuse until I closed the account and handed the balance over to him. So the safest path to take was to quit taking any money out of the trust at all. To Garth, I made up a story that the trust was tied up in a string of legal issues. Then later, that the money was gone, taken up by legal fees. Fortunately the trustee backed up my version."

"Good thing. What your ex did was so very wrong on so many levels."

"I know. But there is an upside. Since Garth could never sink his greedy paws into my trust, you aren't the only one in this relationship who's financially independent. I'd like to reopen the movie theater next to Longboard Pizza, put up the old marquee we found at Cleef's place. We could even name the lobby in his memory since Henry took Cleef's life."

"You have big plans, woman."

"I had days alone to contemplate my future in this town. You know the 22-footer the guys are working on at Tradewinds Boatyard?"

"Sure, everyone in town keeps wondering who this mysterious guy is…" He looked down into her green eyes and recognition lit. "It's you?"

"Yep, it belongs to me. I'd like to take you and Jonah out in it when it's done."

"Jonah would love that, guaranteed. I'm curious. Who owns the estate back on Long Island in Oyster Bay?"

She cracked a grin. "It's amazing how much money is in the Vidalgo Trust."

"Changing your name didn't affect your inheritance?"

"I told you my parents created this airtight trust. They hated Garth because they knew he was mean and abusive. One of the things they had the lawyers write in was that they wanted me out of the marriage, no matter what, no matter the circumstances, no matter how I had to do it. If it took changing my name to get away, if it took hiding under an assumed name to escape, then I should leave the marriage by any means necessary."

"Your parents sound like savvy, smart people."

"They were the best. They would have loved you, especially knowing what a great father you are with Jonah."

"I'm beginning to appreciate how intricately woven this plan was in order to work."

"I had to rely on Logan after Isabella died because I knew Garth would hunt me down. My trust would no doubt give me away within hours. So the lawyer worked with Logan to funnel funds to me as needed."

"As Isabella Rialto?"

"It was my legal name in the UK and the endowments were directed into an account the trustee opened for me there. But then I really didn't need that much once I moved into the house on Oyster Bay. I had a place to live, food to eat. The only thing I didn't have were friends. There were times I felt so alone."

"Those days are behind you now. Plus, you had to be on guard twenty-four/seven."

"That took its toll."

"No more of that. From now on, I'll make sure Henry is locked up so tight he'll never see the light of day again. I'll make sure Garth will never find you either. "

"We both will. Together."

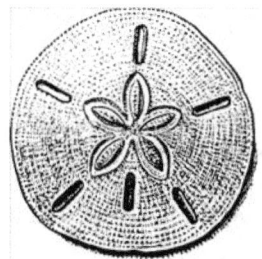

Epilogue

On the last day of December the weather stayed crisp and clear for the wedding between Isabella and Thane. The bottom floor of the lighthouse was lit up in festive lights for the reception. Isabella's friends had seen to that. They'd rallied the troops to help decorate and set things up on short notice.

Isabella stood before the mirror in her bedroom and turned to study her image. Wearing the dress Emma Colter had designed for her, if she did say so herself, the seamstress had done some of her best embroidery work on the strapless silk and satin gown. The beaded sweetheart bodice flowed from a narrow waistline into a layered sweeping train that made her look like a combination of stylish Grace Kelly and Audrey Hepburn classy.

She'd hired Abby Pointer to style her hair into a regal pulled back, curls-down-to-her-shoulder look.

"I hope you don't mind that I chose the lighthouse for the ceremony instead of Promise Cove," Isabella told Jordan as she helped her with her veil.

"Of course not. That would mean I'd be upset at Ryder and Julianne, who did the same thing, which is ridiculous. All you have to do is take a look out the window and see what a gorgeous backdrop the lighthouse makes. No one could argue with standing between Sea Glass Cottage and the massive tower to say your vows."

"I know. It's just that I thought it would be fitting to hold it here because I consider the town mine right along with this beautiful place. After everything that's happened to me I feel so fortunate. Thane and I talked about it. He feels the same way I do about Pelican Pointe. We want Jonah to grow up here."

Fluffing Isabella's train Jordan turned to check out the look. "The co-op idea has taken off. I hope you're prepared to organize all the volunteers who want to be a part of getting that up and going because the list is growing."

"I can't wait to get started. On the other hand, Thane's excited about reopening the old movie theater. It'll be months before that renovation starts though."

River came in about that time. "Did you get a load of Jonah in his little tux? That kid's adorable."

"In my opinion, Thane making him best man was brilliant. It makes him feel so much more a part of the ceremony." Fussing with the headdress, Jordan adjusted it without messing up the hairdo.

"Which reminds me, I want to thank both of you for helping Fischer watch him while we take some alone time for a honeymoon."

River patted her growing stomach. "You've already done that several hundred times over. Besides, I'm not a taskmaster who would stand in the way of love."

Isabella stared at her boss. "You may not want to hear this but pregnancy suits you."

"I know. It must be the hormones. That's why I think you two should take longer than four days. Four days is nothing."

"Listen to her," Jordan added. "The kids don't start back to school for another week. I remember how fast ours blew by. And with kids, as soon as you get back, it's hit the ground running. When you get back, trust me, you'll wish you were still sailing."

"I don't want to be away from Jonah that long though."

Jordan and River spurted out in laughter. But it was Jordan who warned, "Well, that will certainly change and when it does don't think less of yourself as a mother. Remember that."

As if he'd heard his name, Jonah burst through the door, skidded to a stop in front of Isabella. "Wow! You look…beautiful."

She did a little curtsy. "Thank you. So do you. What are you doing in here anyway? I thought part of your job was to keep your dad from getting too nervous."

"It is, but…Dad says I can call you 'mom' as soon as the wedding's over."

Isabella looked over at the little boy she already considered her son. She sent him a wide smile. Every time Jonah mentioned calling her that now she wanted to melt. "Come here. Give your 'mom' a kiss. And you can start calling me 'mom' from this point forward. How does that sound?"

"Sweet!"

For the first time she realized he held something in his hand. "What's that you have there?"

The boy waved it in front of her as if he'd just remembered carrying it in. Now, it moved back and forth. "I forgot. The mailman told me to give you this. He said it was real important."

"The mailman?"

Eyeing the paper addressed to her, Isabella noted its worn look. "Maybe it's from someone back in New York who decided to send their good wishes the old-fashioned way instead of via email."

"Maybe," Jonah uttered. "But the mailman was freaking out about it."

Alarm rose. It curdled in her throat. "Why?"

Jonah shrugged. "I don't know. He said he found it in his mailbag shoved down between the pockets. He said it had been there a really, really, long time."

Isabella's brow furrowed as she took the envelope. She did her best to calm her trembling hands. After all, Henry could still get a letter out from jail. But it wasn't from Henry. The return address showed an APO for Scott Phillips.

She glanced over at her friends before turning the envelope over, noted the postmark, dated December 31, 2004. "What is this? A joke?"

"See? That's what the postman thought it was too. It really freaked him out," Jonah told her.

Flanked by the two women, Isabella ripped through the seal and unfolded the letter. "Oh my God. It really is from Scott."

Jordan's lips bowed up. "He's famous for his letters and getting the last word in. I love that man."

River shook her head. "The last one of those I saw was addressed to Luke. I'll say one thing for him, Scott's consistent."

Tears formed in Isabella's eyes blurring the words. "I don't understand. How could he write this when he was in Iraq? That's impossible."

"What is it?" Jonah asked. "Is it bad?"

"No. No. Nothing like that, honey. These are happy tears even though my makeup's running," Isabella said fanning her face.

"If anyone could bring a tear to the eye, it's Scott. The question is how exactly did he lick the stamp?"

Isabella snickered at Jordan's joke and reread Scott's words.

There are times when a person has to start over. There's no other way. It's nothing to be ashamed of. View it as an opportunity. It's never too late to get a fresh start in a new place with new people. Your idea to help feed the town is a stroke of genius. Don't let anything or anyone detract from pulling the town together to get it done. You already know that during times when people are the most difficult try to practice patience. Because unless you walk in someone else's shoes you don't really know what kind of journey they've had.

Remember that love is not a shallow tide pool, but rather an ocean of waves and storms. Together if you paddle in the same direction, you'll be able to get through both.

Take care of my town, Marisa / Isabella or whatever you choose to call yourself. A name is meaningless if you don't use what you have to make an impact. Make an impact. Be the mother Jonah's never had. Be the partner in life Thane needs. And above all help others to achieve their greatness.

Love, Scott

Dear Reader:

If you enjoyed *Sea Glass Cottage*, please take the time to leave a review.
A review shows others how you feel about my work.
By recommending it to your friends and family it helps spread the word.
If you have the time, please let me know via Facebook or my website.
I'd love to hear from you!

For a complete list of my other books visit my website.
www.vickiemckeehan.com

Want to connect with me to leave a comment?
Go to Facebook
www.facebook.com/VickieMcKeehan

Don't miss these other exciting titles by bestselling author

Vickie McKeehan

The Pelican Pointe Series
PROMISE COVE
HIDDEN MOON BAY
DANCING TIDES
LIGHTHOUSE REEF
STARLIGHT DUNES
LAST CHANCE HARBOR
SEA GLASS COTTAGE
LAVENDER BEACH
SANDCASTLES UNDER THE CHRISTMAS MOON
BENEATH WINTER SAND
KEEPING CAPE SUMMER (2018)

The Evil Secrets Trilogy
JUST EVIL Book One
DEEPER EVIL Book Two
ENDING EVIL Book Three
EVIL SECRETS TRILOGY BOXED SET

The Skye Cree Novels
THE BONES OF OTHERS
THE BONES WILL TELL
THE BOX OF BONES
HIS GARDEN OF BONES
TRUTH IN THE BONES
SEA OF BONES (2018)

The Indigo Brothers Trilogy
INDIGO FIRE
INDIGO HEAT
INDIGO JUSTICE
INDIGO BROTHERS TRILOGY BOXED SET

Coyote Wells Mysteries
MYSTIC FALLS
SHADOW CANYON
SPIRIT LAKE (2018)

ABOUT THE AUTHOR

Vickie McKeehan's novels have consistently appeared on Amazon's Top 100 lists in Contemporary Romance, Romantic Suspense and Mystery / Thriller. She writes what she loves to read—heartwarming romance laced with suspense, heart-pounding thrillers, and riveting mysteries. Vickie loves to write about compelling and down-to-earth characters in settings that stay with her readers long after they've finished her books. She makes her home in Southern California.

Find Vickie online at
https://www.facebook.com/VickieMcKeehan
http://www.vickiemckeehan.com/
https://vickiemckeehan.wordpress.com